Radiant Dawn

by Cody Goodfellow

Radiant Dawn

Cover art by Scott Riggs

ISBN 0-9704000-0-4

Coming in 2001 - Radiant Dawn II

For more information about this author or to order this and other great works of speculative and weird fiction, please contact:

Perilous Press, LLC
PO Box 51181
Seattle, WA 98115
www.perilouspress.com

SAN 253-3987

First Edition

0 9 8 7 6 5 4 3 2 1

Prologue

January 16, 1991.

Somewhere in the Tigris River Valley, Southern Iraq.

When it was all over, the eight of them waited in four spiderholes on the lip of the canyon, eight hundred yards away from and two hundred feet above the ruins of the objective. Chief Warrant Officer Nedick motioned to stand down, so they talked, like men in holes who have communicated only with hand gestures for fourteen sleepless, marching hours. Like men filling up smoky black air and desperate hours until a helicopter comes to exfiltrate them back to Bedrock in Riyadh, a helicopter now ninety-seven minutes overdue. They didn't talk about the mission.

"—blow your brains out at the top of the waterfall and the rocks in your pockets'll make you sink and nobody can ever say for sure…"

"—No, you dumb fucking hick, you can't just use cheap American beer to marinate bratwurst, or it's just gonna taste like hot dogs…"

"—and that dog, you know, that collie that's the mascot for Texas A&M? Jesus, but that's gotta be the most pampered fucking animal on the planet. Sirloin and eggs three times a day, and brushings, and even his own fucking car, for Chrissakes."

"Georgie, I do believe you want to be that dog."

Sgt. Storch liked sharing a hole with Sgt. Tuetagoloa, the SAW gunner. The Samoan's bulk would've crowded a hole twice as wide as this one and his stomach growled louder than bombs, but at least he didn't need to babble to feel safe. Still, when he looked at Storch, he seemed to be mentally covering him in a pineapple glaze and stuffing an apple in his mouth. All racial stereotypes aside, Tue's stare made Storch very uneasy.

1

Storch watched the guttering flames in the crater at the bottom of the canyon through the slitted screen of their hideout, licking his finger every once in a while to test the winds for a shift that would send the green-black clouds trickling out of the bunker their way.

Fourteen hours ago, they were dropped in the marshy hill-country of the Tigris river valley by an MH-60 Pave Low helicopter, and tabbed across twenty miles of bombed farmland to this site. From the get-go, it'd seemed like a goat-rope, a pure bullshit mission: a single bunker in the middle of nowhere nestled in an elbow of a box canyon that sacrificed all defensibility in favor of a dubious invisibility, isolated from military support where most chemical weapons compounds were right under the noses of an airfield or a Republican Guard barracks.

Arriving eight hours ago, they scouted the air defenses, two heavy recoilless guns and a SAM launcher, and took them out. Radioing in the air strike was a bust; the entire area for a two-mile radius was under an anomalous blanket of magnetic disturbance that blocked out even synthetic aperture radar, which could pick up an RC dune buggy on a bad day in Mexico City. Taking it on faith that the mission was still on, they'd painted the compound with laser pointers and waited. In less than ten minutes, they'd heard the planes, three F-111Fs diverted from a sortie on nearby Ad Diwaniyah, flying low enough they could probably hear Tue's stomach, and seen the laser-guided GBU-27 bombs gliding down the canyon to the target like they were on wires.

For his part, Storch was fucking glad they weren't going to have to get any closer. They goofed on the fireworks display and enjoyed an extra helping of their three-day rations, and some French field meals that Wachowiak traded for, and some whiskey-sweetened pemmican that Stauffer's wife made. At the time, they didn't think they'd be needing them. The Pave Low would be whispering in overhead any minute, and they were stoned on being alive and untouchable on the eve of the Mother of All Battles.

They were just starting to chew over the possibility that the helicopter wasn't coming when a man-mountain silhouette crested a craggy rockpile on the next hill, no more than eighty yards away. Sgt. Storch was the first to make it out against the smoky night sky. "Chief, I make a single, armed man at five o'clock, about eighty yards off!" he stage-whispered. Because no one seemed to be able to pronounce Nedick's name in haste, he was always simply Chief in the field. Nobody in the squad would go on record as saying they liked the man, but they trusted him with their lives more readily than they would their fathers or their gods. He motioned for silence, gestured for his men to be alert and to prepare to fall out if they were made.

Preston made a pile of their two hundred pound Alice packs and primed a block of C4 explosive on top of them, with a one-minute fuse ready to be set if they had to move to a new defensive perimeter. The rest of the squad turned and peered at the shape of a very big man atop the rocks, making no effort to conceal himself. He held a rifle across his shoulder and carried some sort of big case on the other. "Holy shit," Stauffer breathed.

"What do you see? What?"

"I think he's one of ours."

The big shadow stooped to heft something up alongside him. A rotund silhouette easily three times his size dangled from his arm. A third clambered up onto the rocks with what looked like a fifty-five gallon oil drum strapped to his back. The first one looked around for a moment, as if he was hiking in the Grand Canyon and sizing up a good spot for a midnight picnic, and then they were swallowed up again by the darkness as they made their way down the canyon wall, cutting a straight path towards the bunker.

"Two M16s on one of them, another has a Barrett sniper…third one looks like a flamethrower, or somethin'…" Preston mumbled as he scanned them. "All of 'em're carrying some kinda steel drums, like oil barrels with handles…They're wearing GI boots and flak jackets, all ripped up like they've been through the shit and back…No MOPP gear, no masks…one of 'em's wearing a helmet, says…'Spike Team TEX' on it…the other two're wearin' berets…black, maybe green…"

"Means shit," Wachowiak growled. "Saddam wears a fucking beret. Half the shit they have they bought from us. I say they're Republican Guard and we frag 'em."

"No…that's not right…" Stauffer said.

Storch tried to read details in the dwindling forms and kept his gun leveled. Tue set the SAW on its bipod pointed at the men. "This smells like bullshit," he said.

"What the fuck're they doing? That place is full of fucking gas," Stauffer said.

"They seem to know what they're doing," Chief grumbled. "Their mission is to get melted inside, that's their lookout." Resentment colored his tone, and Storch knew he was too busy wondering who'd gone over his head to even want the intruders dead just now. Wondering why anyone would knowingly walk into certain death—unless there wasn't any gas, and the reason they were here wasn't at all what they'd been told.

"They looked like mercs," Stauffer said. "We're supposed to be the only Americans this far east. If they were Special Forces, we'd have heard about it, right?"

"Maybe they're SAS, or the fuckin' Australians. Shit, maybe they're Delta," Wachowiak said. "Fuckin' spooks."

"What?" Stauffer scoffed. "Those guys looked older than our dads! And that one guy was like two Tues. They're mercs, and they're probably working for the Iranians."

"How do you figure that?"

"Who else would want to go in there? They were at war with the Iraqis for eight years, and you know Saddam gassed 'em. They want his secret recipe, or something."

"Russians," Tue growled. "Russians been supplyin' 'em for years, lot more'n us. They sold 'em something, they don't want it dug up by the UN."

Storch yawned and rubbed his eyes. "Maybe they are working for us, like Wachowiak said. Maybe it's for our own chemical warfare program."

"Then why weren't we briefed, Sergeant?" Chief barked.

"Because we're not supposed to be here, sir. Our ride's overdue. Shit, maybe they called for us to be left out here to assist and just forgot to tell us about it, but I don't think so."

"What are you suggesting, Sergeant? That they could be a threat?"

"Sir, they didn't trust us to know about it beforehand, so whatever they're here to do isn't just about cleaning up. They're here to get something. And if they didn't trust us before, d'you think they'll trust us to keep our mouths shut after we see it?"

"Zane, we're not grunts. We are Green Berets."

"And what the hell are they?"

"Spike Team Texas," Preston mused. "Didn't they call Green Beret raiding squads Spike Teams in Vietnam?"

"Do any of you still have them?" Chief snapped.

Wachowiak answered. "They're just outside the ruin now, sir. They're—oh shit, they're going inside! They don't have MOPP suits or anything! They're fucked!"

"Then they're not our problem anymore," Chief grumbled, and bit into an apple. The subject was as dead as the three interlopers were, by now.

They waited, rediscussing the best way to grill bratwurst and overpampered college mascots for fifteen minutes, nobody mentioning the men who'd just appeared out of the desert and vanished into a ruined chemical weapons plant and certain death.

Storch was prepared not to say anything about it when he got back, and knew the others would do the same. More than anything else, the importance of image had been driven into their heads from the day they set out from Fort Campbell in Kentucky. When this war went public the following morning, it would be the most watched television event in the world, perhaps in history. Special Forces units had been forced to fight harder to get into this war than they ever would in it, against the prejudices of the Joint Chiefs and the CINC and Stormin' Norman himself; against the media, who wanted only things people could watch over dinner in their wars; against Pentagon spin doctors who thought elite strike teams tarnished the cherished American myth of the citizen soldier, trading his briefcase or his pitchfork for a rifle in times of trouble abroad. The Green Berets had struggled for something they hadn't been allowed to earn since they'd lost it in the unholy Brobdingnagian clusterfuck of Vietnam: the admiration of the American people. It didn't matter that this mission would, officially, never have happened. Hinky ghost stories about phantom A-teams slipping into their theater and stealing their thunder would not be welcomed, if they were taken seriously at all.

They were still talking desperately about nothing when the entire canyon seemed to rise a few inches on a titanic bubble of force, then fall back into place. A tremendous, dull throbbing stirred the sand beneath their feet, subsided. Rockslides poured down the walls of the canyon. Fresh gouts of heavy, half-liquid smoke gushed out of the split facade of the bunker. Storch braced himself against the wall of the hole as Tue trained his SAW platoon gun on the ruin below.

"What the fuck was that?" several of them, all at once.

"Unexploded ordnance, maybe a power source of some kind," Chief said, his voice tight. "CIA and USAMRID both said everything inside gets cooked. The air itself was on fire, in there."

"What if it's a reactor? What if there's fucking plutonium down there?" Wachowiak demanded.

"You got some place to go?" Storch snapped. "Tie down your suit, get your atropine kit ready and shut the fuck up."

"Omigod," Stauffer gasped. "Pres, Donny, look at the front of the compound. I think I got movement."

Wachowiak tilted his goggles back down over his eyes. "What, I got movement too, Ted. It's called fire. It's whiting out your goggles."

"No, look through it, there's something—"

Storch heard the first shots, rolling over the hills at their backs on the chill wind. Three single, tentative cracks, dry and flat, like sheets of sandstone clapping together, but close enough to leave no doubt who the targets were. Storch clearly saw pebbles leap within arm's reach of his hole.

"We're compromised! Abdul's at six o'clock!" Before the words were all out of his mouth, the rest of the squad was turned to face the shots, rifles at the ready, Stauffer's sighting forgotten. Stauffer, Wachowiak and Preston cranked up the gain on their goggles, their faces cadaverous in the green witch-glow from the displays. Tue dragged the cover of their hide back and shouldered the SAW, while Gagliardo knelt down at Chief's feet to try the radio again, scanning through all bands several times a second. "St. Bernard, this is Pit Bull One Three, we're taking fire from an unknown opposing force, requesting exfil soonest—" He got only sandstorms of static.

"My ass, it's Abdul," Wachowiak grumbled. "Dunebilly dirt-farmer going after jackrabbits with a musket, maybe."

"These hills're crawling with Shiite resistance groups, shithead," Stauffer hissed back. "Kill you for your food and boots."

Chief signed for silence. The breeze dropped off, drawing a curtain of lunar quiet. Even in the dark of the new moon, the stars cast almost enough light to read by. The lone tumble of boulders where they'd seen the strangers offered the only cover within range for an antique rifle. Storch trained his gun on it, breathing shallow through his nose, ticking off each rocky silhouette and daring it to move. Hillpeople wouldn't tangle with them even if they did spot them, and Shiites hated Saddam more than they did, and would probably beg for food rather than try to take it. For a change, Wachowiak was probably right.

"Chief? Dale, man, look at this."

Storch turned back to find that everyone was staring down at the burning bunker again, and when Storch looked with them he could understand why they had forgotten the shots.

The three strangers were coming out of the ruin, as calmly as if they were strolling back from the latrine. The ghastly particolored flames washed them in livid colors as they walked out of the most deadly place on earth.

Green smoke streamed off them like the fumes from burning plastic. Their hair and headgear was on fire, weird tongues of greenish flame dancing around their skulls like Blackbeard's pitch-soaked braids. One of them stopped and waved once, pointed something right at them.

"He's flashing us with an infrared pointer," Stauffer said. "He's saying 'Howdy'."

Two more shots sounded from behind them just then. One struck Preston's and Chappelle's screen; the other made the back of Chief's head into a drive-thru. Gagliardo stood up from the radio to face his holemate and squad leader and sat back down too hard to get up again soon. Stauffer barked "Jesusfuckinchrist" as the ghoulish green image of Chief's brains on the half-shell swam into focus, ducked down and proceeded to empty the magazine of his MP-5 up the canyon. They all joined in, laying down a perfect three hundred sixty degree fan of automatic fire for four seconds, then ducked for incoming, straining to hear past the deafening echoes of their own shots.

The silence dragged on, nobody acknowledging Stauffer's "Nedick's dead. Storch is the one." Storch, wanting so badly to see something, alive or dead, couldn't open his mouth to reply, wasn't asked to. That control had slipped out of their hands so fast, that they'd just seen men walk in and out of a burning chemical weapons bunker, that they'd lost Chief Warrant Officer Dale W. Nedick to fucking sheepherders, sent his brain spinning.

Storch barked out orders by rote. "Preston! Watch the canyon for those three interlopers. Shoot on sight! Wachowiak and Stauffer, watch those rocks!"

"Nothing, nothing down there," Preston whispered. Twiddling the gain knob on his goggles, he turned round and round. At Chief's feet, Gagliardo continued his unanswered prayer into the phone, "St. Bernard, this is Pit Bull One-Three, repeating, we are compromised, surrounded and squad leader is down, requesting exfil soonest, over."

Storch was the first to notice the wind changing. "Suit up and shoot up!" he shouted, and pulled his own atropine kit out and injected the anti-nerve gas serum into his right thigh, watched the others do the same. He wrestled his way into his MOPP poncho, struggling against Tue to get it on without putting down his gun. The big Samoan already wore his heavy rubber chemical suit, but didn't move to put on the hood until Storch yanked on it. Steeped in the new-plastic-hospital-vomit stench of the hood, Storch couldn't imagine how gas could smell much worse.

Something deep within the chemical lab exploded again. The shockwave was almost a visible wall in the sand, cracking like a whip underneath them, shaking them to their knees in their holes.

Storch fought not to get trampled as Tuetagoloa scrambled out of the hole, held down the trigger of his gun and started spinning. He didn't see the advancing cloud of black-green vapor that oozed up the canyon walls until it was at his feet. The chemical plant was a cauldron of superheated toxic gases, and it was boiling over. The heavier than air fumes slid among the rocks like serpents. In seconds, they would fill in the holes, and in a few seconds more, eat through their suits. Tue's body jolted with three shots to his chest, but a shout from behind the boulders answered his sacrifice. A robed silhouette collapsed atop the rocks, and another went down trying to pull him back out of sight. A volley of rifle fire finally knocked down the burly gunner, who dropped and was immediately swallowed by the green fog.

Stauffer climbed out of his hole next, even as the vapors poured in. The legs of his suit dripped a trail of molten plastic. The Bedouins shot him down two steps ahead of the tide. The others froze, all their training suspended for a moment as they stopped thinking how to survive and took up choosing how to die.

"Evacuate the hide! Fall out and take that fucking rock, gentlemen!" Storch did his best imitation of the Chief, punctuated it with a grenade from the M203 launcher mounted under his rifle. The grenade skipped off the top of the rock, soared up in a lazy arc and dropped on top of the remaining Bedouins just as the fuse burnt up. The dull crump, the sharp screams awakened them to who they were.

A bullet, or a piece of shrapnel from his own grenade ripped through his right hand. He ducked down and examined it for a full second, waiting for the pain to come. He was still watching it, could still almost feel his thumb there, when the green fog spilled into his spiderhole. Hands knotted in his plastic hood and hauled him out of the hole.

They were climbing out of the holes, but too late, the fog closed over them, and their suits were sloughing off of them and their skins burned, and the tendrils of gas worked their way into their sinuses, and they were holding their breath...

And the wind whipped the green gas to ribbons and scattered it away from them, scoured their wounds with pure, stinging sand. The wash of a helicopter just above their heads, voices in their ears, and sleep, and Sgt. Storch was already beginning to forget what really happened...

~ 1 ~

July 4, 1999.

It rained on the Fourth of July in Death Valley. Great black clouds tore themselves apart in the livid blue noon sky, punishing curtains of gunmetal rain that the Bad Mood Guy swore would be full of frogs and octopi.

"Is it over?" the Bad Mood Guy woke up and wanted to know. His shrill voice vibrated the weatherbeaten porch beneath their feet. "Did it happen?"

"No. We're still here. Go back to sleep," Storch told him.

"Fucking gyp."

"Moody's got a point. Nostradamus said the world's going to end today," Ely Buggs said. He quoted, "'The year 1999, seven months. From the sky will come a great King of Terror—

—To bring back to life the great King of the Mongols, before and after Mars to reign by good Luck,'" Hiram Hansen finished. "Bullshit. He only said it would start to end. Anyway, Nostradamus was just a courtier-spy for the Merovingian dynasty—"

"Hugenot," interrupted Bad Mood Guy.

"—and all his prophecies were either coded reports on the royal family's private business, or attempts to influence same. Edgar Cayce said we've got a good five hundred years yet. And he was an American."

"Cayce predicted in his sleep. He was dreaming. Nostradamus predicted wide awake. Stared into the sun. He saw the day coming. Nostradamus and five bucks says it goes down on the Fourth."

Zane Ezekiel Storch moved to swat a fly dancing a tarantella on his scalp, gave up. It would drown in sweat soon, anyway. "Both full of shit. Don't want to hear any more apocalyptic bullshit on my porch."

"Two kinds of people 'round here these days, young Zane: them as're afraid the world's gonna end and them as're afraid it won't," Hansen said. "This ain't no place for an honest man with his head on straight anymore." The coroner/taxidermist/librarian fumbled out his tobacco pouch, a tanned baby gila monster with a zipper in its belly, dumped out a pinch of his rust-red blend. Rolled a cheroot.

"Tellin' ya, if it was gonna happen, it should've by now. Fucking gyp," the Bad Mood Guy growled from under the porch. The Bad Mood Guy had sacrificed two hundred dollars and his satellite dish to the Field Marshal's Armageddon Betting Pool—and eaten two sheets of acid to forget about it.

They sat on the porch of Sgt. Storch's Quartermaster Supply, watching the old man they called Pop Sickle as he weighed and pinched at foil pouches of freeze-dried astronaut ice cream on aisle three like they were cantaloupes. Pop Sickle never talked, and Storch nurtured a supernatural dread of what he might say if he ever did. An albino giant with a beluga whale's torso and pipestem limbs, Pop Sickle had horrible weeping lesions and gigantic bruises on nearly every exposed inch of moonstone skin. Circulation so bad you could hear whatever he used for blood sloshing inside when he moved. He was hairless but for a tumbleweed goatee of fiber-optic polar bear hair. He wore a spelunker's helmet, ski goggles and a nylon and rubber spring wetsuit, but even on a hundred and six degree high summer day like today, he didn't—or couldn't—sweat. But even so, Pop Sickle lived up to his name. He melted.

"Shit, Hi. It ain't just here," Ely picked up the lost conversational thread. "The artificial threshold we've set up in the Millennium is nothing more than an appointed time for us to clean out our collective unconscious. Millennial psychosis is a timed anxiety release, throughout history. The problem is, the nuts who really expected the big one to come down get really fucked up when they're denied the cathartic vindication of their psychoses. Case in point the Bad Mood Guy down there."

Storch knew who Ely Buggs was really talking about, but he let it lie. Pissed about Harley Pettigrew, his store manager, two hours AWOL; pissed at his cashier running down his old man. Pilgrims came to Thermopylae in the heart of Death Valley to burn their insanity away, or gave it free rein to thrive in a boundless wilderness of blank canvases on which to paint their fantastic, paranoid mindscapes. In one way or another, they were all pilgrims.

Ely Buggs, smiling, always smiling into the sun, smiling and waving, cooking up apocalyptic prophecies, posing for satellite photos, wants to believe he's blowing some National Reconnaissance Office spotter's mind. Ely was obsessive-compulsively driven to kick people in the brains. He had been much sought-after as a computer programmer, but collected SSI because he couldn't pass someone who wasn't looking where they were going without assaulting them. Always said that when people surrender their personal safety to a painted crosswalk or the defensive driving of others, it is incumbent on their fellows to shock them back to their senses. He hitchhiked into town one morning eight months ago, and immediately signed on. To Storch's one question job interview: "Why are you here?" Ely Buggs answered, "To get away from the powerlines. They play hell with your DNA." The first and only time he jumped on his boss, Storch broke three of his fingers and his wrist with one twist of his bad hand. He apologized, got a field splint from aisle five and went back to work. Buggs was a good cashier.

"Judas git home, he's doing it again!"

Pop Sickle doffed his helmet and commenced to scratching at his bald pate. The wound flaked and slobbered clear plasma tears into his helmet. The albino's scalp glittered like the bowels of a geode, adorned with crystalline keloid scars; his bare skull shining through the bloodless sores. He swam in flooded uranium mines, reservoirs tainted with mercury and illegally dumped DDT. He glowed in the dark, made the geiger counters go batshit on aisle nine. He paid cash.

Storch cocked an ear, heard an engine, civilian RV wheels chewing gravel. The RV hove into view and came to rest in front of his store, a gargantuan refrigerated biosphere on wheels. With it, an ambitious tourist could colonize Venus. The cabin door popped open with an audible hiss and a middle-aged couple climbed out. Banana Republic togs, urban cowboy boots, no sunburns. The man had a video camera on his shoulder. Tourists. Plastic in high impulse-buy gear.

"Buggs, behind the counter. Hi, don't you scare 'em off, or you can start paying rent for that bench. And go wash yourself, you're making everything stink like fucking formaldehyde." Storch felt the headache coming on.

Buggs behind the counter, Storch eyeing the tourists as they ogled the wares. City-slicker types video-sightseeing, insurance against Deliverance-style yokels, snaps from the fringe for the folks back home. They poked around the surplus goods, Storch thankful he took down his father's exhibit of SS regalia, wishing Harley was here to handle these idiots so he could get back to work. The Army taught him to obey orders and like it, but not to look like he enjoyed sucking up. The tourists, conspicuously not bargaining or asking questions, not trying on doughboy helmets or gas masks: just swiveling, scoping through the camera for the folks at home. Sidling up to him, needling the local yokel suddenly the main attraction. He recoiled from the greedy camera in his face.

"So, are you folks survivalists?"

"Everybody's a survivalist, mister. We just cater to those who take their survival seriously." His father's words, sounding stupid from his mouth. "Death Valley is a harsh place. You may or may not've noticed, in your RV, out there. It takes a lot to stay alive here. We sell most of it."

"There a lot of militia groups around here?"

Question hinky from a tourist. Storch smelled fuzz. "None that I know of. We get a lot of hermits. People who just want to be left alone."

"Death Valley is the last refuge of the true individualist," Buggs chimed in.

The camera homed in on Pop Sickle as he approached the checkout. The old mutant jumped back like a bushman afraid the infernal device would steal his soul.

"Mister, I'm gonna have to ask you to turn that thing off."

The tourist-wife stepped in front of the camera, did a bizarre little wave. "I think we've seen everything we came to see. Mother?" Too late, Storch spotted the kinky wire jacked into the camera running up the tourist's polo shirtsleeve, the plastic dong sticking out of the back of the camera. Antenna?

The doors blasted open, black Kevlar-suited berserkers stormed Sgt. Storch's Quartermaster Supply. "Down, get down!" guns in faces, jackboots on ribs.

The end of Zane Storch's world had come.

Storch and Buggs grabbed for sky, but Pop Sickle let out an eerie bleat and made for the back door. Phut Phut Phut: three shots in the old morlock deflating him like a boiler bag half-full of rancid clam sauce. An armed and armored stormtrooper braced Storch like an invitation to dance, all his hand-to-hand training jamming common sense, he can take the guy and feed him his rifle, but eight more like him? And the tourists have automatics, and Buggs down behind the register to appease the fucker on the counter, Storch's last glimpse of his cashier a bloody gash from a rifle barrel on his forehead.

Where the hell is Harley? Did he know this was going down? Was he an informant? Informant on what? Harley and Hiram talked his dad down out of the hills before I got here, hated the government like poison, and anyway, what would there be to inform on? Storch didn't even sell half the shit you could buy at any gun show, let alone anything the ATF would want. He never did business with militia or cult groups, and knew of nobody in the area who was making or selling drugs. Did they just come for Pop Sickle? Storch saw the crumpled body for the first time, a trickle of something like scorched motor oil reaching out from the corpse to where he lay. He jerked up, came back down hard under a jackboot in his ear.

"Stay down! Close your eyes!"

From behind the counter: "So, are we gonna be on the teevee?" The countertop-commando jumping down on Buggs with both feet. Screams, silence.

"Are you Sergeant First Class Zane Ezekiel Storch, retired, acting proprietor of this establishment?" Mr. Tourist leaning down in his face. Cold, freezer-burn breath.

"You've gotta know I am. Let me up. I'm not gonna hurt anybody." Boot off his head, sitting up, rubbing his temples. Ten guns and a camera still in his face, Mrs. Tourist zooming in on his government-issue welts. "Who the hell are you people? You got a warrant to serve?"

"They're from Majestic, Zane! They know Pop Sickle's a saucer-man." Buggs begging to be kicked again. The commando obliged.

"Stop kicking him, goddamit!" The abuse stopped.

"Will you cooperate?" Mr. Tourist playing Good Cop.

"You ATF?" Storch asked.

"We'll ask the questions. Where is Harley Pettigrew, your stock manager?"

"You oughta know," Storch muttered.

"Elaborate." Mrs. Tourist leaned into his face so he could see his defeated image in stereo in her enormous sunglasses.

"You know who we are, you scoped out our place. You bust in, kill one of my customers and beat the shit out of my cashier inside of sixty clicks, and no due process. We're law-abiding, tax-paying citizens, and I'm a fucking vet! You tell me where my manager is, and what the fuck you're doing here!"

Mr. Tourist waved off the stormtroopers: "Search." Six of them fanned out, stomping down the aisles and sweeping his inventory off the shelves. "Mr. Storch, you can help things along by showing us where the cache is."

"What, the safe? This is a stick-up?"

"No, the weapons cache."

"I don't know what the fuck you're talking about."

"Don't lie, Mr. Storch."

Mrs. Tourist, watching him through the camera, seeing more than was there. "He's telling the truth. So far as he knows." A polygraph-camera?

"Did Harley Pettigrew have the run of the store after hours?"

"Of course he does. He closes five nights a week! But he wouldn't hide anything from me."

From the back: "Jackpot."

Hands hoisted Storch to his feet, guns in his back herded him to the corner where Hiram Hansen did his taxidermy. Rearing prairie dogs, striking rattlesnakes, rampant gila monsters. In Hi's loving hands, the gentlest of Nature's creatures looked rabid, which led many to speculate on whether they were really dead when Hi stuffed them. Formaldehyde made Storch go into convulsions, so Hansen used a special preparation of herbs from a mail-order catalog that claimed to be the same process used on the Pharaohs.

A big section of the floor pried out to reveal a beam-reinforced hole, four feet deep, dug out of the sand beneath. Filled to the brim with gray shrink-wrapped bricks, propane tanks with BABY MILK PLANT and something in Arabic stenciled on them, and guns, guns, guns: Heckler-Koches, Enfields with grenade-launchers, Barrett sniper-rifles, Uzis, Cobrays, Kalashnikovs, AKMs, Spas auto-shotguns. Ammunition: NATO 7.62, 9mm, AK tracer, armor-piercing and anti-personnel rounds, shotgun shells, grenades. A black-market armory under his dad's store, under his nose.

"Assault weapons and ordnance stolen from an ATF impound armory in Idaho; high explosives from Hong Kong and Libya; VX gas from Iraq. Can you account for any of this, Mr. Storch?"

The phone rang, splitting the silence like a fat man's pants. Storch looked at Mr. Tourist.

Storch's handler gripped his neck and steered him into his office. "Answer it. Just be yourself."

Storch picked up the phone at his desk. "Sgt. Storch's Quartermaster Supply Store. Harley?"

"Zane. Zane, I'm sorry, partner."

"Where did all that shit come from, Harley? Who are these fucking guys? They shot Pop Sickle in cold blood and beat the shit out of Buggs, and there's a Jesusfuckingchrist huge stash of terrorist ordnance under the store. Why didn't you come in to work today?"

"Zane, I didn't mean for you to get involved. I just had to do something. The future of our race is at stake. I just couldn't just sit by, while those Radiant Dawn freaks pissed in our genepool. Shit, they're listening, ain't they? Well, now hear this, you pricks. Zane didn't know a fucking thing about the weapons and shit under his store. I take sole responsibility."

"Harley, who were you holding that shit for?"

"Don't try to do their job for them, boy. I don't expect you to understand, but I'm sorry I let you down, and I'm sorry I let your father down, and...shit, I'm just sorry about the whole fucking thing." A fat pause, then, "Zane, some people are going to try to contact you soon. Don't..."

"Don't what, Harley?"

"I'm sorry, Zane." BLAM. The gunshot peaking out the phone so Storch barely noticed the second shot before the line went dead.

Mr. Tourist standing in the doorway. "We believe you, son."

Outside, two hours later. Storch and Buggs back on the porch, holding ice to their battered heads. At least there were no TV cameras to immortalize their disgrace.

Mr. Tourist debriefed the Sheriff's Deputy, who seemed eager to cooperate. He'd been not nearly so solicitous with Storch, who gathered they'd told him nothing, because the deputy gave out even less to him. Sheriff Twombley himself would've come and might've made a difference, the Deputy allowed, but he was laid up with a case of hemorrhoids, and wouldn't get off the cushioned seat behind his desk in Furnace Creek. An ambulance had come and gone with Pop Sickle's body. Hansen's library truck was gone.

Buggs munched a sandwich and Storch smoked his first cigarette in eight years. It fed fresh fuel to his migraine, but it steadied his nerves.

"Did you know that soon all American beef-cattle will be living on a diet consisting almost entirely of their own manure?"

"Buggs, shut up. I don't want to hear any more of your bullshit Earth Day schemes today. That's the most fucking disgusting one yet."

"No, really, boss, it's a good thing, because as the human population rises, it consumes and converts more and more of the earth's organic resources into people. Cattle eat a lot of grass, and we eat a lot of cattle. So, if we close the system by feeding cows their own nutrient-enriched shit, we'd stabilize population growth and save the remaining natural biomass from being turned into more people. Think of the possibilities if we just eliminated the middleman and ate our own shit? We owe it to future generations to adapt to the idea. You want a bite of my sandwich?"

"I'm going home. Buggs, take the rest of the year off."

From under the porch, the Bad Mood Guy snarled, "I told you the world was going to end today."

~ 2 ~

It was the kind of day that makes one glad to be working in the ER. Death had seemingly taken the Fourth of July off, at least in Bishop, and one could almost feel content that something, for the moment, was right in the world. With dusk, however, would come the fireworks, and the earnest, patriotic consumption of alcohol. Four staffers were due to come on duty in about an hour, and if the peace kept up until then, Stella Orozco would be able to go home before the casualty parade got started.

Stella sipped from a steaming mug of herbal tea at the reception desk and watched the sunset through the smoked glass of the outer doors. Rosalinde and Terry, the other nurse and orderly on duty, were playing cribbage in the breakroom. Ruth Fisher and Jean Velazquez, the other two nurses, and Dr. Balsam, the attending physician, were taking their dinner break in the cafeteria. Dr. Quon, the intern, had gone up to Radiology with a scared eight-year old who'd broken his elbow falling out of a tree.

Stella herself had handled only two injuries this afternoon, one an epileptic, autistic boy who'd bitten his tongue during a seizure, and a teenaged girl who'd managed to lose a condom in her uterus. Despite the boy's writhing and the girl's panicking, she'd sent them both off in under an hour.

All of the carts had been stocked, the instrument pans sterilized and dried; all the soiled sheets were bagged for either the laundry or the incinerator; all the duty rosters had been made out and approved. Like a college town diner awaiting the end of a homecoming game, the ER was only taking a breather in anticipation of the non-stop chaos that was sure to begin with the first shadow of dusk.

In the lazy, air-conditioned silence, Stella's mind reached out to previously unnoticed minutiae to keep itself busy. She wrinkled her nose at the fetid, rotten-foot odor that hung in the air. Someone had been eating Fritos. The powerful antiseptics used in the hospital subdued even the reek of charred flesh, but mutated the smell of any fatty fried snack into a palpable cloud reminiscent of gangrene. A Muzak rendition of Nirvana's "Come As You Are" spewed from the speaker above her head. Every so often, the nasal squawk of the intercom summoned someone she'd never heard of to somewhere she'd never had cause to go, but nothing was going on in the ER.

Stella Orozco's features were what men called "exotic," and women called "striking," when they wanted to say "weird" and "intimidating." From her father she'd inherited the bronze skin and ebony hair common to Mexican mestizos, but her face was a gift from her Indian mother, with angular brow and cheekbones, deepset black eyes, an aquiline nose and an almost too-wide, generously lipped mouth that scarcely moved even when it spoke, which wasn't often. Her shortness, her fragile slimness could do nothing to contradict that face, those eyes that were forever saying, *Leave me alone with my secrets, or I might just tell you one.*

At twenty-nine, Stella had been an LPN for only three years, having taken community college courses for four years to get certified. Her age and temperament led her coworkers to think Stella had drifted into nursing the same way other young women of poor prospects might end up in retail or clerical work, and she offered them nothing that made them think otherwise. But Stella's path to her present life had been a struggle up out of depths none of the other staff could imagine, and she wanted no one's pity.

Her parents were migrants from lower Mexico who began crossing the border to work the fields of Central California in 1970. They scrambled over fences and through sewers to get into the U.S. every harvest season; toiled for twelve to fourteen hours a day for a few dollars every week, inhaling pesticides like DDT, malathion, parathion and experimental compounds the USDA would never hear of; lived in shanties with no electricity or running water for five months out of the year, and snuck back over the border like thieves, their only crime a season of backbreaking labor for pennies.

Stella's mother was already three months' pregnant with her that first season, and they stayed in California long enough for her to be born a U.S. citizen. They still migrated back to Mexico for the next couple of years before legitimately applying for citizenship themselves and settling in the dusty farm town of Modesto. By the time she was eight, Stella's father was doing landscaping and construction work and owned a truck, and her mother stayed home and devoted herself to spoiling her only daughter rotten. Stella's mother was so generous and radiant with love for her that Stella never noticed how sick she was. She died just before Stella turned twelve; her father started drinking in earnest and abandoned her less than a year later, most likely returning to Mexico.

Cycled through a route of wildly variant foster homes, Stella forgot that parents were for loving, and learned to view them as models to be observed, obeyed and evaded. She quickly picked up which responses earned her her privacy, her meals, and minimal emotional support, and learned to spot which ones simply couldn't be reasoned with, and how to keep them from hurting her. From them, she had learned that an education and a calling were what separated the former from the latter types, and she threw herself into getting both.

She worked long and hard, and got further than statistics predicted for one so poor, and so late in learning English, but not nearly so far as she'd dreamed. For all that her quick, cautious mind ran circles round most others who'd never had to work as hard, the language would always be a strange tool on her tongue, with appendages she could not grasp, and textures that eluded her palate. Fortunately, Stella recognized this early on, with the characteristic talent for accepting hard, ugly reality that comes naturally for those who have never been able to afford self-pity. Taking stock of her marketable natural talents, Stella discovered that she enjoyed caring for people, was excited by science, and (perhaps a scar of her years in the fields, an untouchable whom even transients never willingly saw) needed invisibility. She decided to become a nurse.

She'd worked odd jobs to pay her way through college while interning as a candy-striper in the hospital, then moved in as a nurse. Now, she felt secure and safely detached, and wanted nothing more from life. She'd reflected deeply and meaningfully, and seen that she would do all right if things stayed this way forever, with or without a man or a winning lottery ticket or a best friend.

The only thing wrong now was that she had liver cancer, and about six months to live.

She hadn't told anyone at the hospital about this, either.

"Heads up, Stella." The voice made her jump and scald her thumb on the tea. She turned, biting her lip to avoid embarrassing herself further by voicing her pain.

Nurse Fisher, a red-headed anvil in pink surgical scrubs, crept up behind her, a mug of coffee in one hand and a cinnamon roll on a saucer in the other. For such a large, loud woman, Nurse Fisher glided through the ER like a hologram. The nurses and orderlies squeaked furiously on the heavily waxed tile floors, while the heavier oxfords of the doctors and the boots of the police and EMTs sounded like the Budweiser Clydesdales in a gymnasium. But damnable Nurse Fisher was always slipping up on her, surprising her, throwing her off guard.

"Brought you this," Fisher parked the cinnamon roll in front of her. Stella eyed it dubiously.

"Thank you. How much do I owe you?" Stella started to reach for her wallet. Ruth's hand intercepted hers, her red, rough skin hot on Stella's wrist.

"Don't sweat it, sweetie. You'll get me back, sometime. Oh, I almost forgot. Life Flight chopper went out to near Big Pine just a minute ago. Coming back in about thirty. You might want to get Trauma One warmed up."

"How many? What happened?"

"You know, same old story: boy meets train, boy loses train, limbs and a whole lot of blood. I'm gonna go get Doc Balsam and Quon."

Stella hurried to Trauma One and busied herself with unpacking the surgical tools and laying out bedding. She hesitated a moment, then went into the trauma storage closet and pulled out a vinyl bodybag, folded it and laid it neatly on the counter. Then she went back to her tea and waited, fingers drumming on the desk. A Muzak rendition of "Folsom Prison Blues." She waited for Terry and Rosalinde to wind up their game and wondered what kind of pervert picked the songs for hospital music tapes.

When it came just minutes after sunset, they were waiting on the rooftop. Stella, Terry, Ruth and Dr. Balsam stood on the lip of the heliport deck, tracking the noisy speck on the horizon, looking like pallbearers in search of a coffin. The Life Flight helicopter grew larger by the second and in less than a minute, it hovered overhead, wheeling round to come down on the deck even as the two EMTs inside threw open the loading door and climbed down. Something about their movements sent a signal that all four emergency personnel read clearly; there was no reason to hurry. Stella wished she'd been bold enough to bring the bag up on the deck with her. Lately, it had become much harder to look the dead in the eyes.

The EMTs trundled their gurney off the chopper and kicked the legs out, then steered it towards them, heads bowed under the ferocious wash of the propeller-blades. Stella caught only a glimpse of the shape between them. She made out an ice chest resting on the foot of the gurney, and a flash of blood-flecked fleshtones at the other end. Whatever they were bringing back was in pieces, but it was also alive.

"John Doe, condition's stable!" the first paramedic shouted. "Bleeding's stopped, pressure's a hundred over sixty, no sign of shock-trauma, he's doped up real good, and we got most of him in the box. You're gonna love this one!"

The emergency team flanked the gurney as it barged through the doors into the corridor. Dr. Balsam, the short, owlish senior attending physician, stepped up onto the crossbars of the gurney like running-boards and rode as they pushed, rechecking the victim's vitals. The doors closed, enfolding them in a quiet they split wide open with their footfalls. Stella looked down at the patient and just kept looking, because there was nothing else to do.

The patient was a Caucasian male, mid-forties, with receding gingerbread hair and whitening eyebrows, dressed in a black tracksuit with a white sunburst logo on the breast. His eyes were closed, his mouth hanging slightly ajar beneath an oxygen mask, as if he'd simply nodded off. Stella knew he wouldn't be nearly as composed when he woke up.

The patient's right leg was severed less than four inches below the crotch, and not neatly, either. Clearly, the wheel of a freight train had crushed the leg. The same had happened to the left hand, an inch or so above the wrist. A tourniquet had been applied at the hip joint and elbow; below, gory streamers of skin, muscles and crushed veins and arteries hung from the stump.

By all rights, the patient should've bled to death within five minutes of the accident. It'd been over forty minutes since the Life Flight chopper had taken off. Even if some extraordinarily gifted Boy Scout master with a Nobel Prize in First Aid had tied off the man's injuries in time to stop the bleeding, he would've sunk into a coma. By the steady pulse Stella heard on the stethoscope, this man appeared to be sleeping comfortably. His blood pressure argued that he hadn't lost any blood, either.

Stella palpated the flesh of the leg to prove the effectiveness of the tourniquet, and withdrew her hand with a hiss of disgust.

The insides of the leg looked like a cross-section of a lamprey from the depths of Lake Erie. A riotous garden of bulbous black and pink tumors blossomed from the muscle, the veins, even the flattened stub of bone. Like toadstools sprouting from the circuit boards of a computer, they stood out as a violation of the orderly functionality of the anatomy, a transgression every bit as awful as the injury itself.

Stella sucked in air as she saw the same monstrous growths blooming inside herself.

"Stella? Stella? Are you with us, dear?" Ruth Fisher chiseled her out of her fugue. They were getting on the elevator now. Terry hit the button, and they descended, cramped uncomfortably over the dismembered man.

Dr. Balsam was asking the EMT questions in a quavery voice. "How long ago did this happen?"

"We took the call fifty minutes ago, anonymous tip from a payphone. The caller said it'd just happened, he found him lying on the southbound track of the Southern Pacific line. We radioed the depots here, in Mojave and in Lone Pine, to get a lead on the train."

"Just the short of it, please," Dr. Balsam said. "When did it happen?"

"That's the thing," the paramedic shot back. "There was no train this afternoon. That track's barely used anymore. The last bunch of them to come through went at three forty-five this morning. They're looking it over now."

"Did you tourniquet him?"

"Yeah. But he wasn't bleeding when we got there. He was clotted."

"Did you give him blood?"

"Hell no."

Balsam pinched the soft belly of the man's left biceps. Blood seeped back into the capillaries as soon as his finger released the skin. "This man has lost maybe a pint of blood- from losing an arm and a leg to a train. Was there much blood at the scene?"

"Yeah, everywhere." The EMT hesitated, then his brow furrowed. "You know, if this guy was chopped up, you know, somewhere else, and dumped there…"

"That's something for the police to decide. I presume one was on the scene?"

"Yeah. Detective Foley. He'll probably be waiting downstairs."

"Have any of you looked inside him?" Stella heard herself asking. She bit her lip. She'd followed their words with her eyes turned to the wall, but she couldn't stop her mind from racing ahead of the conversation, ahead of the afterimage of those cancers in the man on the gurney.

"What? Oh, you mean those…the tumors. We figured that was why he must've been lying on train tracks at four in the morning."

"Sweet Jesus," Balsam whispered through his droopy mustache as he pressed down on the wrist and the polyps lolled out like a cluster of makeshift tongues. "Have you gone over him with a Geiger counter?"

The elevator doors yawned open and Terry hauled the gurney out. It rocketed across the corridor, but suddenly nobody was in a hurry to follow it.

As expected, the ER began to fill up after dusk, and Stella was pressed to stretch the night shift. The nameless patient waited in a cul-de-sac outside Trauma One. They'd verified that his condition was stable, and assessed the condition of the recovered limb. Only the leg was in the ice chest, far too badly mangled for reattachment. The police were unable to discover either his identity or the time of his injury, let alone the final disposition of the severed hand. Detective Foley took a short statement from Stella and the other personnel who'd treated him, shrugged, and left. Without a relative to worry or an insurance company to pay for him, the John Doe was forgotten.

Stella sneaked away from her other patients whenever she could to check on him. Once when she adjusted the glucose IV mounted to the railing of his bed, the patient seemed to come awake and whispered something. She recoiled from the bubbling plea that escaped his lips, then saw his eyes were open, and focused on her.

She marveled at the way they seemed to shift in color from green to a steely gray, and the way his complexion flushed and paled, as if roiling clouds of blood and melanin churned beneath his skin. Most of all, she wondered at the expression on his face. Over the course of her life, Stella had ample opportunity to study the faces of suffering: of horror at an unexpected catastrophe coming home to rip apart lives; of despair at the capricious appetite of disease; of drugged oblivion; of lifelong fear. Here, in this man who had lost his limbs to a machine, whose remaining limbs were riddled with cancer, there was only awe, and some glimpse of a wonder that made Stella lean closer to hear.

"The...moon ladder..." he murmured. "Moon-ladder..."

"What can you remember about what happened?" Stella whispered.

His eyes rolled, tracking something so wonderful it had taken him away from the hospital, from his broken, dying body. "So...beautiful...the Radiant Dawn...I want...to go home now."

"And you will, Stephen, you will. Pardon me, Nurse." A leather-gloved hand politely separated her from the bed, and a man in a heavy woolen overcoat rolled it down the corridor, towards the exit. Stella looked up, her head swimming.

After a moment, she focused on Dr. Balsam, looking more owlish and bemused than ever. Stu Balsam was on his twentieth hour at the ER. He was the only physician Stella'd ever heard of who had to be chased out of the hospital, and she'd never seen him back down from a fight. Now he looked whipped, ready to accede to anything that would empty a bed.

The man beside him was Balsam's opposite in every way: tall, aquiline, not crushed by age so much as sharpened by it, with a regal mantle of white hair and gray eyes that speedily took stock of Stella, then flicked back to Balsam. The doctor withered under his scrutiny like a waxwork under a hydrogen laser, and Stella sensed that whatever was going on had already been settled.

"This is Dr. Keogh, of the Radiant Dawn Hospice Village," Dr. Balsam said, trying badly to look as if he'd heard of it before.

"They're taking him away," Stella managed.

"Stephen is very, very ill," Dr. Keogh said. "If his condition is stabilized, we would like to return him to the hospice to make his remaining time as pleasant as possible."

Clearly, Dr. Balsam wasn't even going to ask any questions. "What was he doing out on the train tracks?" Stella asked.

"Stella, please, don't bother the man," Dr. Balsam said, but Dr. Keogh made an expansive gesture and drew a breath, as if gathering his wits to deliver tragic personal news.

"Stephen has terminal cancer in almost every major organ in his body, including his brain. His brain tumor triggers seizures, in which he may sleepwalk. Somehow, he walked out of the Hospice Village last night, and must've stumbled on the train tracks. His treatment included the implant of a time-release sedative drip, as well as a coagulant. These two factors probably saved his life, for I'm told his wounds had closed, and he'd lost very little blood. Remarkable, that." Keogh started down the corridor after the bed, then stopped. "One more thing. I'd like to have any blood or tissue samples you might have taken from Stephen. Also, a copy of your report, Doctor. And yours, ma'am."

"Yes, of course, Dr. Keogh." Balsam turned away, flagged down Terry, barked, "Get down to the lab and bring up all the samples from the John Doe."

"The blood...and the reports?" Stella whispered in his ear. "That's ridiculous, Doctor. The tumors stopped the bleeding!"

"Yes, everything," he grumbled, looking eager to wash his hands of the whole mess.

"Right away, boss," Terry said, and sped away.

"Stella, I think you'd better get back to work. There are still patients we can help here." Balsam rubbed his hands together in an exaggerated that's-that gesture and turned away. Stella started to leave, but she felt Keogh's eyes on her, and froze. Turning to meet his gaze, Stella wanted to cover herself up, because those eyes made her feel not only visible, but naked, vivisected, laid bare down to her bones, down to her liver. His gunmetal eyes seemed to melt for a moment, and Stella gasped, because he could see it, she could see in his eyes that he knew she was terminal.

"Have courage, senorita. This, too, shall pass." He spoke to her in a voice like a gentle rain of oil. Stella drew in a stabbing breath at the touch of his gloved hand on her abdomen. He turned away then, and disappeared down the corridor that Terry had taken a moment before.

As she moved back to the nurses' station, she chanced a look back and saw two men in paramedic's uniforms loading the patient Keogh'd called Stephen into an ambulance. The man in the overcoat stripped the sheets from the bed Stephen had lain in, and bundled them into a plastic bag, which he stowed on the ambulance before slamming the doors. He leaned against the ambulance and looked around idly. His eyes pinned her down, and Stella scurried away, feeling the same chastened fear she'd seen in Balsam's eyes.

At the station, Nurse Fisher presided over the rows of chairs in the waiting room, over a cattle call of minor and major injuries, of knots of distraught families and friends wringing their hands and wondering why they let Uncle Jed drink all that whiskey and drive home from Pioneer Days in Mammoth, or why they gave little Cousin Jenny all those bottle rockets to play with. Nurse Fisher did triage effortlessly, sending the night nurses off with the more serious cases, dictating the proper procedure for filling out forms, deflecting unreasonable panic, and keeping an atmosphere of wry humor afloat in what looked like a war zone. The cinnamon roll she'd brought for Stella still sat parked at the desk beside her cold tea, its icing scabbed over.

"Stella, why don't you try to weed out the kooks and the drunks for me, there's a good girl," Fisher said, then, "Excuse me, that's a courtesy phone, it won't dial out. Use the payphone by the restrooms, thanks."

Still shaken, Stella waded into the crowd of holiday casualties. Hands grasped at her smock, pleading voices wheedled at her for news of loved ones, for a doctor's attention, for drugs. Half these people didn't need medical attention at all, they just needed to go home and sleep it off. She passed out reassurances and moved on, trying to get back into her job.

A hand clutched at her smock and tugged when she tried to move away. Stella tried to pull free, but the hand wouldn't let go. A voice that cut through all the others asked, "Is the man from the train going to be alright?" Stella looked down.

The owner of the clutching hand was blasted almost purple by a lifetime of hard sun and harder alcohol; a livid nebula of nuked capillaries spread across his sunken face. A white beard tinged with the sickly yellow of a polar bear pelt in the zoo fringed a sinkhole of a mouth, radiating a visible haze of booze-breath and advanced tooth decay. The eyes, bloodshot and swimming in tears, bored into her own. "Is he going to live?"

"What do you know about him?" Stella breathed.

"I'm the one who called," the old hermit wheezed. "I'm the one who found him."

Stella led the old man to the cafeteria and bought him a cup of coffee and watched him stir sugar and Cremora into it until he could eat it with a fork. The man stared fixedly at his beverage, seemingly unwilling to acknowledge her. So used to listening to others who couldn't seem to stop talking, she couldn't frame the words to get the old man started.

After a few more minutes, Stella dared ask, "There was a detective here looking into the accident. You spoke to him?"

"Not gonna talk to no cops," the hermit bristled.

"Well, you sure came a long way for a cup of coffee."

"I just come to make sure he's alright."

"Well, he's not alright. The people who took him away say he's dying of cancer, and they can't reattach the leg, couldn't find the hand."

The old man swallowed hard, slurped the coffee, and went back to staring into the blank formica expanse of table between them. Damn this old drunk white man, too gutless to open his mouth, too frightened of something to leave. Was he to blame for the accident?

"There something you want to ask me, mister...?"

"Napier, name's Napier. Seth. Live hard by the tracks south of Lone Pine. I just wanted to make sure he was gonna live. I called the ambulance, like I was supposed to..."

"You called as soon as you found him, right after it happened."

"Yup." The man was almost completely out of the habit of talking, let alone lying.

"You didn't call until just before sunset, Mister Napier. He was run over by a train coming from Lone Pine at three-thirty this morning. If he was run over by a train..." She honestly didn't know she was going to say this last. What the hell was she trying to do, play detective? Was this man supposed to throw his coffee in her face and run, a psycho-killer unmasked by Stella Orozco, terminally ill LPN detective? She wanted to leave, wanted this man not to know what she was asking about, but she could tell from the way his face fell, as if the table was no longer blank, but a dreadful window, that he knew.

"You won't tell the cops?" Napier asked.

"No."

"I don't want to talk to no cops," he growled, and then the words started to come out all in a rush. Like so many wounded or distraught people in hospitals, Napier saw her as a confessor. "I didn't do nothin wrong, ma'am, an' I'll swear to that on a stack of Bibles. If I didn't call right away, it's only 'cause the man was a goner anyway, an' I didn't want to tangle with no cops. I figgered if I just kept to myself 'til the railroad folks came back for him, I could say I was on a bender, an' slept through it. Shit, wouldn't be far from the truth, at that." He sipped at the coffee again. "Can I smoke in here?" he asked.

"No, but there's a stairwell down the hall." She got up, led him to it, and stood as far from him as she could while he lit up. She could see the gibbous moon rising over the town's main drag through a narrow slit in the concrete walls, could hear the blaring of horns, the sporadic popping of firecrackers and, she knew, a few real guns, from outside.

For a long time, Napier only stared at the guttering cherry of the cigarette, and Stella began to think he'd unloaded his peace, and wanted her gone. "You want to know how he's still alive. That's why you're here."

"I don't s'pose you know, either, do you?"

"No, Mr. Napier, I don't suppose we do."

~ 3 ~

Like the Spartans whose fateful stand against the Persians gave the town its name, the proud citizens of Thermopylae would gladly kill or die for their independence. Some wag who spoke for the rest of the town nailed a sign to the "official" one on the Interstate.

Thermopylae
Elev. –10 ft. Pop. 63
REDS, FEDS & DEADHEADS KEEP ON DRIVING

They would fight any invader, foreign or domestic, who threatened their hermitage, and it was only because no pair of men among them could agree on the color of sand, let alone mobilize against a common foe, that the town had not presented a genuine threat and been wiped out long ago. The only way the Field Marshal was able to collect anything like a tax for public improvements was with the Apocalypse Pool, a standing kitty of pooled bets on the date and manner of the End. If you weren't waiting for Armageddon in the form of wrathful angels or the ATF, you had no business in Thermopylae. Few of its citizens slept for more than a few minutes at a time, and all of them had something much more substantial than a baseball bat by their beds.

Despite their steely-eyed vigilance, the raid on Sgt. Storch's Quartermaster Supply Store had caught the town in mid-siesta, sleeping off the excesses of the Millennial Fourth, and word of the raid sent the entire town into the hills, with their houses in tow.

Aside from Storch's store, there wasn't a single structure in Thermopylae that couldn't be towed away or knocked flat and buried inside of an hour. The library was a converted ice cream truck; the post office was a Volkswagen Thing, and Town Hall was the cargo hold of the Field Marshal's half-track. Only one permanent relic of Thermopylae would remain on the Day of Wrath. Someone had laid out a winding grid of cul-de-sac traps for an insane tract-housing scheme that never materialized. Like the mysterious designs on the Nazca Plain in Peru, they codified some inscrutable invitation to visitors from space. Buggs preached that the Nazca lines were the work of a mysterious race predateding the Incas, and were beacons for aliens to pick them up before the Conquistadors came.

As if Buggs's stupid theory was true after all, the entire town of Thermopylae was gone. Sgt. Storch's Quartermaster Supply stood alone on the plain, the hub of a wheel of tire tracks radiating out to every point on the compass. Storch couldn't bear to sit on the porch anymore, so he went home.

Storch had run Sgt. Storch's Quartermaster Supply for his father, who'd been in an asylum in Norwalk since 1992.

Zane Ezekiel Storch was named for his father's penchant for paperback westerns and his mother's fervor for the Bible. He was raised an army brat, Sgt. Major Dad stationed at Taegu, South Korea; Schweinfurt, West Germany; Ft. Hamilton, Brooklyn. When he was sixteen, Zane caught his mom in bed with a Captain. She packed her bags and was gone before Dad got home. Dad flipped out, got religion, got born again hard, got Section Eighted, ditched Zane, fled to Death Valley to live in a borax mine, eating surplus Air Raid shelter biscuits and writing the New Dead Sea Scrolls on toilet paper. Storch boarded with his grandparents until he was old enough to enlist in '83. Made it through Airborne, Rangers, made Sergeant, joined Special Forces. Combat duty in Desert Storm, seven confirmed kills, maimed in action, awarded the Silver Star and Purple Heart.

But within a few weeks of his return home, Storch began to get sick. Little by little, he lost things and forgot he'd had them: fluency in Arabic, German and a little French, field operations training, recollection of faces. Chemical fumes—gasoline, solvents, even hairspray—made his blood pressure and histamine levels skyrocket, scrambled his brain so his words came out wrong. Because he was an injured vet they kept it off paper, but they told each other it was a nervous breakdown.

Discharged for medical reasons only officially connected to his wound, he came to Death Valley at his father's summons. The old man had wrestled his demons and come down from the mountain to put his life savings into a survivalist's general store in the middle of the desert. With no other prospects, and too ill to live in the city, Storch thought of getting right with the new, saner dad and then moving to Needles or Bishop, becoming a deputy sheriff. He bought his dad a TV and a satellite dish. That night they watched the '92 Presidential Debates.

Dad got born all over again. Dad looked at the screen and saw the Unholy Trinity: Bush, Clinton, Perot the abominable Anti-Father, Anti-Son and Unholy Ghost of the Apocalypse. He knew that the public was merely being asked to choose the form of its destruction, and that unless they either voted for all three or abstained from voting altogether, the world would begin to end on Election Day. He stole his son's truck and the next time Storch saw him was on TV, a week later, when he tried to drive the truck into the hall where the second debate was being held. That the truck was full of barrels of holy water and Eucharist wafers only made the media less sympathetic to his case. At least if he was only trying to kill the candidates, they would've understood. Character witnesses who attested that his dad apologized to God whenever he stepped on a bug only helped thicken the padding on his cell. Dad looked to be a lifer, and Storch, up until this afternoon, did too.

Storch lay on the bed in his trailer, mowing his head with an electric razor, pounding distilled water with lemon juice and watching CNN, Reno, Los Angeles, San Francisco local news. Nothing about the raid. He felt like doing a whole lot of pushups, running to Mexico or blowing something up. He'd frozen up in the raid; now his body jolted with impulses hours too late. He looked at the bottle in his four-fingered right hand and wished to God he could stomach even the odor of hard alcohol.

What kind of war was being fought in this country, that the government could keep it from the news media? If the Oklahoma bombing and bank robberies perpetrated by white-supremacist groups were so extensively covered and caused such a furor, wouldn't the government want to make sure the public saw that they gave as good as they got?

Militia groups. More than anything else, they were the cause of Storch's leaving the army; them and the gas-sickness. Nearly half the regular soldiers he served with belonged to one or another of several cabals of frustrated racist patriots, whose agendas parted ways with the U.S. Constitution the moment they got their hands on guns. It became next to impossible to try to give orders to people who were in different armies, and who'd just as soon kill their black comrades or their CO as an enemy.

He couldn't figure Harley Pettigrew for the militia type. Harley couldn't cooperate with anybody, and the militias hated individualists as much as they hated ethnic federal employees. His final talk about racial purity didn't jibe with a widower thrice married, to a Filipino, a Vietnamese and a Mexican.

His phone rang. He picked it up but heard only a constant dial tone. Ringing again, the receiver still in his hand, and for a moment Storch thought, this is it, this is how you start to lose it, and then he pinpointed the sound. It was coming from his closet.

Storch slowly sucked in a deep breath, held it, and produced a serrated survival knife from beneath his pillow, speed-crept up beside the closed door. Third ring, not like his at all, cellular. Whoever's in there, he's too stupid to live, he told himself. He coiled up inside himself, playing the scenario in his mind so that when it happened, he'd be watching a familiar old movie.

He seized the knob and yanked it back and in a single motion stepped into the closet with the knife out-thrust, and slashed a fearsome pile of dirty laundry twice before it registered. He stepped back and spun to meet a possible attack from behind, but he was still alone. A tiny cell phone lay on the top shelf of the closet, between his detergent and a box of signal flares. Warily, still looking over his shoulder, he picked it up, looking it over, finally decided there were simpler ways to blow him up, and pressed the SPEAK button. Waiting for the caller to speak, he exhaled. No doubt even this phone was being monitored, he'd volunteer nothing.

"Sergeant Zane E. Storch?" The voice warbled like a badly tuned shortwave signal, or an anonymous witness on a talk show. Digitally scrambled, pitch shifted.

"This is."

"This is the Mission speaking. You've been awakened. Do you wish to go back to sleep?"

"I'm wide awake, thank you. Who the fuck is this, really?"

"We have not contacted you before to protect you from violent reprisals such as the one you experienced today."

"So you're the people who fucked me out of my livelihood. I don't know you, I've never heard your voice, and I couldn't care less about your cause. Please leave me alone."

"Don't hang up, Sgt. Storch. This is a secured line. You have nothing to lose by listening to what we have to say."

"You're the people who were going to buy those weapons from Harley."

"What has happened to Serapion?"

"Who? Is that a code name for Harley?"

"Yes. What is his status?"

"He's dead. Lucky you."

"No money was to change hands. Brother Serapion acted out of true patriotism, expecting no reward in this world. Did you see him killed?"

"No, I heard it on the phone. He shot himself over this whole thing. You assholes have a lot to answer for."

"How many times did he shoot himself?"

"What the hell kind of question is that to ask?" Two shots. Harley could miss the sky with a shotgun when he was sober, which he seldom was in the morning. "You think he was killed?"

"They always shoot twice."

"Who shoots twice?"

"The race-traitors' secret police."

"You mean the federal government? They'd be happy to lock up Harley for a hundred years if he was giving weapons away to Nazis, but they wouldn't execute him. You motherfuckers better hope I never find you."

"Oh, we hope you do find us. Harley was waiting for the right time to approach you about our cause."

"My grandfather died at Normandy. I fucking hate Nazis. And you're giving me a headache. You're so hot to meet, why don't you tell me where you live, shithead?" Let the compartmentalized Kevlar killers sort it out, the crackpot bug-scrambler story smelled like bullshit. He hoped this was going down on tape somewhere.

"You hold us responsible."

"You're fucking-A right I do. And you're gonna pay. I've got about ninety days off to kill before the feds give me back my store, and I'm gonna spend 'em hunting you pencil-neck Nazis down."

"Whether or not he took his own life, Serapion acted in accordance with the highest principles of our mission, and his name will be remembered always among the patriots of our struggle. As for your store: go there now."

The line went dead. Storch breathed deep for awhile, watching his hand lay down the phone, willing it not to smash it. When he knew he wasn't going to break something, he got his keys and his coat and his 9mm automatic and jumped in his truck.

He drove back to Thermopylae, even though he could see the pillar of smoke from a mile away. The payphone across the street was ringing, and he went to answer it.

"If you think we're Nazis, you're mistaken. And if you believe you were raided by the feds, you're almost too stupid to bother with. Are you stupid, Sgt. Storch?"

His head throbbed like he was sweating blood. "No, I can be pretty goddamn clever when I put my mind to it."

"Good. You have to want to know. You have to want to come to us for the right reasons and know who the real enemy is. Go to exit 137 on the northbound I-395, near the Convict Lake junction. Look in the faultline."

"What'll I find there?"

"If you want to hurt the ones who hurt you and yours, go there and hold onto what you find there until we contact you again. And be quick about it. There's going to be an earthquake tomorrow."

He drove there that night, after parking his trailer in a box canyon and covering it in camo tarps. He'd seen enough of his life go up in flames, today. The desert rolled by like a Hanna-Barbara backdrop, features repeating, recycling distance, protracting the hours into infinite spaces Storch filled with questions.

He'd been used by someone, by terrorists fighting a secret war against the government within the United States. A war so radical and so far underground that the rest of the country was kept in the dark. Now, on only their say-so, he was setting himself up again by going out to the middle of nowhere to dig up something. He tried to tell himself it wasn't as crazy as his father's delusion about the Unholy Trinity, couldn't.

More than anything else, Storch would come to wonder why he didn't just call the police that night. He wanted to believe the raid wasn't by his own government, that his friend Harley Pettigrew wasn't a terrorist, that he hadn't killed himself.

And, craziest of all, he found he wanted to believe his father had been right. With only the moon following him, Storch drove to Owens Valley.

He reached the Convict Lake rest stop shortly after midnight. He cruised the parking lot, empty but for a station wagon filled to the windows with dirty laundry and trash. An old woman in a matted frightwig slept against the wheel in a foxhole she'd burrowed out of the scraps of her life. A bumper sticker epitaph: I CRAPPED OUT AT THE SHOWBOAT CASINO-HOTEL, LAS VEGAS.

The restrooms were murkily lit by flickering fluorescents filled with dead and dying moths and flies, casting spastic, fluttering wing and leg shadows on the slimy walls. All the toilets were blocked with a heady primordial stew that looked to be on the verge of birthing a whole new ecosystem. His gorge rising in his throat, Storch reconned the place thoroughly, then wandered out into the desert behind the visitor's center.

He would have missed the faultline if not for the plaque. Peering into the moonlit sands, he made it out, like a zipper in the earth, running to the San Francisco Bay to the north and Riverside to the south. He walked along the faultline, kicking rocks into it and beginning to feel stupid. Then he saw it: a lily blooming out of the fault, a perfect flower basking in the lunar glow. It was a girls' hand.

He went back to his truck and got a shovel.

~ 4 ~

People often observed that Special Agent Martin Cundieffe bore an uncanny resemblance to the nerdy, bespectacled character actor Wally Cox, if Wally Cox had gone bald before age twenty-five. He looked like the kind of guy who never gets laid, who has no friends excepting other geeks on the Internet, and who still lives with his parents. All of which was true, and all of which made Cundieffe the kind of FBI agent Hoover would've been proud to have in his service. Cundieffe never tired of being treated like a naive weakling, because he never tired of being underestimated. It opened doors that stayed closed to those who looked like they knew what they were doing. Opening doors, learning secrets, made Martin Cundieffe tingle. It was all he knew or needed of physical pleasure.

Right now, as he was passing through the third of five checkpoints in the nearly deserted corridors of the Federal Building in Los Angeles, on his way to an emergency briefing with officers of the Navy at five in the morning, he felt an especially strong tingle that zapped through his mind, undiminished by the hour, let alone by his section chief's order that he sit in on the meeting, and do nothing else. Deputy Assistant Director Wyler, head of the counterterrorism section, at least did not underestimate Martin. Lane Hunt, the special agent in charge of the LA field office's counterterrorism squad, was in Riverside, following up on a bank robbery by Aryan militiamen, but Wyler had asked for him, Martin Cundieffe, the unit's resident bookworm.

In the half-hour since he'd received the call to go in, he'd compiled a file of all recent suspected anti-government activity in the western United States, cross-referenced by military service, as per Wyler's instructions. It wasn't as complete or as updated as Martin would've liked—he'd simply printed out the thirty-six dossiers he'd had activity on in the last six months—but it would more than suffice for scaring the Navy brass out of their shorts, if that was what they wanted.

Cundieffe reached the fourth checkpoint and presented his photobadge. A guard in dress blues took it, scanned it through a reader and held it up to his face like a bar bouncer. Cundieffe obligingly smiled the lopsided, squinty grin that matched the photo and was rewarded with a wave-through.

Although he'd never had occasion to deal directly with the Navy himself, Cundieffe could read sailors as well as he could anyone else, which was extremely well, indeed. These checkpoints were more cobbled together than his report; this sudden case of paranoia, on top of the emergency meeting itself, painted a picture of a fat old man waking in the night on his soft mattress in his big bed in his sprawling mansion, convulsing with terror at finding its veil of security penetrated—and something missing. Cundieffe had a good idea of what he'd be hearing this morning by the time he reached the fifth checkpoint, where he presented the sealed envelope delivered by special courier four minutes after the call. The secrecy agreement within it was more Byzantine by half than anything he'd seen before, and the ink on it smeared under his hand. He'd found five glaring typos just glancing at it.

When he saw who else was waiting at the door to the briefing room, it snapped into place. Ted Atherton, the Assistant Deputy Director of Investigations leaned against the door frame, sharing a whispered joke with Wyler. Behind them stood an irritable-looking man whose ID tag marked him as CIA. A craggy older man with a silver beard and a black military uniform regarded him with biblical contempt, and scowled blackly at Cundieffe's hapless grin. Cundieffe fell in behind this last man after wordlessly passing a copy of his report to his boss. One by one, they passed the Marine at the door.

He was even more stunned by who wasn't here. Over two-thirds of the seats in the briefing room were empty. The Special Agent in Charge of LA was absent, likewise his assistant, likewise anybody else Cundieffe recognized from the field office. Each of the players present sat alone, sans the inevitable delegation that accreted around them. Dark suits meshed with the murky shadows, pale faces and winking insignia floated like a banquet of ghosts, feasting on secrets.

Cundieffe took a seat beside Wyler, who slid the report back to him and nodded gravely. "Marty," he whispered, "have you ever heard of a criminal investigation being run by the victim?"

"Excuse me, sir? No—I haven't."

"You have now."

The last few filed in and took their places at the two long tables spanning the conference room, and the Marine shut the door. There were only six civilians to the military's nine. Rear Admiral Wayne Meinsen leaned on the podium, his wattled jaw propped on one hand.

"What you're about to hear has been passed on to the Joint Chiefs and Pentagon Intelligence only an hour ago, gentlemen. The SAC of this field office has been briefed, and is en route to Washington to sit in on the executive conference with the FBI director. The President hasn't been notified yet, and, God willing, he'll never have to tell the people about it, because we're going to fix it.

"Four hours ago, a security breach occurred at our China Lake Weapons Station. Due to the, ah, unorthodox nature of the incident and the limited intelligence gathered so far, this briefing will be more rumor control than anything else. Here are the facts, such as they are.

"At oh-one hundred hours exactly, station radar picked up a MH-60 Seahawk helicopter on approach. The pilot correctly identified itself to security at the storage quadrant of the station, and proceeded to instruct for an impromptu inspection. The duty officer logged the request, as well as the order that the senior CO not be notified. Five minutes later, he logged a visual on *two* helicopters on final approach: a Black Hawk and another that he identified only as 'Russian'. That is his last entry. Shortly thereafter, the security measures and monitors and the entire staff of the station were incapacitated by a weapon of undetermined nature. For the next hour, we have only deductive intelligence about what went on inside."

Chatter boiled up among the officers, hardened career military and intelligence men all. Cundieffe kept his mouth shut, but his mind was spinning several feet above his poker-faced skull. Hostile invasion of a domestic military base. It exceeded the most audacious scheme ever cooked up by the militia-prone braggarts he monitored.

Wyler surprised him by interrupting the already aggravated Admiral. "No corroborative visual fix on the helicopters. No security video. And they used your own codes to get in."

Oliver Froud, Naval Intelligence, cut the Admiral off, this time. "The second helicopter did not register on radar at all, and neither of them showed up when they took off. We haven't determined the cause of that. No active satellites were over the base during the occupation, and nothing showed up on the shots taken just after we knew something was wrong. All internal security measures were disabled in the security center, and incoming security checks were intercepted. All the tapes were bulk-erased. The clearance codes used to approach the base were previously thought to be uncompromised."

More mumbling. Cundieffe caught the smile behind his boss's hand. "No casualties, either?" Wyler asked. "I thought softkill technology—"

"Please, please, hold your questions. No, there were no direct casualties. As near as we can tell, the base was saturated with some kind of electromagnetic field which disabled the entire garrison of eighty men, and all electronic equipment in a two square mile area. All of them experienced seizures and unconsciousness, but no other ill effects. One man fell down a flight of stairs and broke his leg. Another man bit off his tongue. The first response team on the scene swept the area for chemical and bioweapons agents, and came up clean."

Nervous laughter all around. This was thrilling. The Navy, a Delta Force Commander, even the CIA were scared. The harder they were, the more disturbed they looked, he noted; the act violated their most deeply cherished rules of engagement. Whoever the thieves were, they played by a totally different field manual. Cundieffe thought of the peculiar custom of the Plains Indians, called *counting coup*. Bands of warriors would steal into forts and mark their white enemies' heads with charcoal or paint, to show them how safe they really were. He doubted the Admiral would appreciate the anthropological precedent, however, and so kept it to himself.

Captain Roger Stenson, Naval Intelligence: "As far as our best intel goes, softkill option weapons don't exist. The Pentagon's research on all nonlethal projects was shelved in '94. Our friends at JSOC—" a nod to the black-uniformed officer "—have made use of subsonics and chemical incapacitants, but nothing like an EMP wave ever got past the testing stages. The KGB and GRU only did minimal research on those projects under the Soviets, with the same results. France, Germany, Japan and South Korea are all still trying it, but, again, they can't induce a seizure in a single subject in a lab, let alone an entire base. There are about fourteen private corporations around the world pursuing EMP weapons technology as a sideline, but they're years away from anything remotely like what the Admiral has described."

"I think the Admiral's here to report a flying saucer," said Willis Kopko, the NSA rep. More laughter.

The Admiral flushed so red Cundieffe expected him to spit blood. "Please, would you shut the hell up until I've finished the goddamned briefing? Thank you. Now, a sentry from the north gate and one on the flight control tower made their routine check-ins every thirty minutes during that time, and received the proper countercodes until oh-three hundred. They were on a tape. At oh-two hundred five hours, a civilian outside the base saw two helicopters flying low over the desert, headed east. They were inside for only an hour, and when they left, they were loaded down."

"Shithouse mouse, it's an inside job," said Sibley, the CIA rep. "They've got your fucking codes, back to front."

"At oh-three ten," Meinsen went on, "the security hut personnel had come to and phoned in the breach. We scrambled helicopters and alerted NRO, who snapped these KH-11 satellite prints of the area."

He stood back as the lights dimmed, and a projection of a satellite photograph came up on the wall. Cundieffe studied it for a few moments, feeling as if he was looking at one of those Magic Eye stereogram prints that his mother seemed to think he enjoyed. A blocky spiderweb lay tacked out on the desert, bedizened with dewy spots of luminescence that indicated vehicles and other large heat sources. This was China Lake. Around it, the desert spread like the rumpled sheets of a vast bed. With digital enhancement, Cundieffe knew, the Admiral could zoom in to examine cacti and Joshua trees and shotgunned beer cans until Y2K day, but he wouldn't find any helicopters. The stormy, purple knot his face had become told all in the room that he was well aware of this. He nodded toward the military end of the room, though Cundieffe hadn't seen anyone move to address the group. "Yes, Mort?"

Lt. Col. Mort Greenaway of Delta Force cracked his knuckles over his report and fixed Meinsen with his fierce gaze. Cundieffe could see in those eyes that he'd already been braced by the Admiral, and was plenty peeved about something. Cundieffe could almost read the tight-beam message that leapt from the Admiral, could easily enough read it.

Mort, did your Delta assholes pull some kind of psycho wargame maneuver on one of my bases?

And the equally naked broadcast from Greenaway, who'd just tumbled on to why he, and not a SEAL Team Commander, was here: *Admiral, has one of your elite units gone rogue?*

When he finally spoke, the Lieutenant Colonel's fingers twisted and tugged at his beard. "A Black Hawk has a range of three hundred eighty miles. Unless they can refuel in the air. Can you at least say with any conviction that they're still in the desert?"

"No other radar stations picked up anything but fixed-wing aircraft in the region. We've set our eyes on all the roads in and out of the area, and have patrols checking all freight vehicles passing through. I think it's safe to assume they've gone to ground somewhere in the Mojave."

"Shit, that narrows it down," Sibley hissed. "You only read one helicopter, when two were visually confirmed. If they can't be reliably tracked on radar, you may as well start looking in Mexico."

Wyler threw his hands up. "We've all been sitting here shitting biscuits listening to this, and wondering why we're here at five in the morning when the President hasn't even been told yet. What the fuck did they take, Wayne?" Cundieffe's ears burned to hear such language from his own supervisor's lips.

"Just four tons of twenty-five year old napalm in fifty-five gallon storage barrels. Just enough Vietnam-era incindergel to torch a small city."

This time, there was no mumbling. A few pens clattered on tables, more than a few indrawn breaths, but in between, Cundieffe could hear sweat breaking out of pores. A crisp plastic snap resounded in the silence, and Cundieffe looked over to see Lt. Col. Greenaway's hand was black with ink from his broken pen. He made no move to clean himself, staring into Meinsen, his fist drizzling fat droplets of ink all over the desk.

Atherton drummed his bony mortician's fingers on the thin report in front of him. "That just doesn't make any goddamned sense, Admiral. A tight operation like you described, and they just took napalm? What the hell would terrorists with effective softkill technology want with something as crude as napalm? They may as well have stolen a catapult."

"Shows what you fucking idiots know," Lt. Col. Greenaway said, his voice receding down a tunnel that led back to Vietnam. "Four fucking tons of nape, my God." Most of the uniforms present today had served in Nam, and it loomed over them like a shadow whenever talk turned to mass troop commitments and limited wars for political goals. Now it had followed them home. Right now, it was taking a bite out of the Lieutenant Colonel. Cundieffe took copious notes.

"It's bullshit," Atherton said.

Cundieffe tapped Wyler on the shoulder, scribbled on his yellow legal pad. "NOT TERRORISTS! VIGILANTES!" Wyler's eyes stalled on the note, and he leaned in close to Cundieffe. "What the hell?"

"Sir—"

"I think my assistant has something to offer," Wyler said. Cundieffe knew he was meant to see his boss's smile, this time.

"Well, it's just—"

"Go ahead, then."

"—Thinking out loud, really—"

"Out with it, young man!"

Cundieffe sucked in a deep breath of the room's stuffy, recycled air, and shuffled his files. "Well, in my, ah, experience, anybody who takes up arms against the government usually expects to have to take lives. If they don't, they're not terrorists. These, um, intruders of yours went to great lengths to do exactly the opposite: they didn't harm anyone, when they could've massacred the whole base and taken everything. In their hands, then, the napalm is useless as a lever of extortion, because we know they won't hurt people."

"That's what I'm thinking," Sibley replied. "They won't hurt sailors because they're armed forces themselves, or vets. But that hardly dismisses them as a threat."

"Hate crime," Atherton, buffing his glasses on his tie. "Tomorrow, they'll melt down Chinatown, or Watts, or the Fairfax District."

"Hell, why not the fucking White House?" Greenaway shot back, grinning.

"Maybe it isn't even for them," said Roger Stenson, the Defense Intelligence Agency civilian liaison. "They could sell it to another group who isn't so squeamish."

"Again, I don't think so, sir." Cundieffe was running now. Wyler's hand seized his wrist like a parent trying to steer a toddler away from a bear-trap. Wyler didn't fret that he'd get hurt; he just wanted the bait for himself. "You see, if they were planning to drop the napalm on a politically or racially motivated target, or even to sell it, secrecy would be paramount. They have to know this'll provoke as large a counterterrorist operation as can be managed in secret, and they have to know they'll never get to keep it for long, let alone deliver it on a target. Napalm has to be dropped from a plane or a helicopter, and there are dozens of ways to kill lots of people that are infinitely more efficient than napalm."

"We're aware of that, son," Meinsen said. "Are you still just thinking out loud, or do you have a point?"

"I think I—what I'm getting at, sir, is just this: that the theft may be more for your benefit than theirs. Maybe it's their way of trying to tell you they're going to do something, to challenge us. This reads more like vigilantism than terrorism." Blank stares from all but Lt. Col. Greenaway, who seemed to be trying to melt him with his gaze. Cundieffe could almost feel it working. "Admiral, have you ever heard of counting coup?" Oh nuts, where'd that come from?

"Mr. Peepers is all done, who's next?" Sibley said, and got a few muffled laughs.

Stenson was still looking at Cundieffe as he spoke. "Maybe he's got something, Wayne. The foremost goal of a comprehensive strategic terrorist plan is to destabilize the military, and alienate the government from the citizenry. You're going to have a hell of a time explaining door-to-door searches of an ever-expanding portion of California. It sounds stupid, I know, but look at the Unabomber."

Cundieffe sucked in another deep breath. He had to make one more run for it. "Captain Stenson's partially right, sir, but it's more than that."

"You're done, son—"

"Wayne, for God's sake, you don't have any more ideas. Let him talk." Cundieffe's hair practically stood on end. Two shocks in as many minutes. Captain Stenson was the one speaking up for him.

Silence. "Sure, they wanted us to know about the napalm, which almost invalidates it for anything but sale abroad, and anybody with the time and resources these people have could probably make it themselves. But they took it out into the desert, and they took much too much to move easily or quickly with it. A search for it in the desert could be passed off as an extended counterterrorist exercise, and they've got to know that.

"And the whole softkill strategy makes a racist militia seem unlikely. Not impossible, mind you, but typically, anyone who's worked up enough to even contemplate genocide will kill anyone who stands between them and their chosen enemies. Militant bigots generally believe the government's a tool of the Zionist conspiracy. They're fanatical about it; so anyone who isn't one of them is a dupe or an active agent of oppression. They deserve to die."

As he paused for breath, the room erupted in conflicting voices, and Cundieffe had to shout to start up again. Remarkably, the room fell silent. "Moreover, no militia group we know of is as connected or as disciplined as it would take to pull this kind of thing off. The two largest groups in the southwest have both had their backs broken in the last year. The leaders of the Bear Flag Brotherhood are serving in Leavenworth for bank robbery, and the two leaders and only real hardcore members of the Aryan Crusade are in jail in Nevada for trying to synthesize botulinum—"

"Bring it home, Marty," Wyler whispered.

"I guess what it comes down to is, their need for the napalm is the loose thread. They're sophisticated and they don't want, nor do they have to kill. They've calculated this. They're good enough they could probably manufacture their own napalm, given enough time. So we need to look at something recent that would necessitate a napalm strike very soon, something that would be worth alerting the military, something they'd still feel confident they could destroy, and that we, after the fact, might even approve of."

"But what?" Sibley shot back, reaching into his breast pocket and taking out a pager. "We're supposed to relax and wait for them to drop napalm on a target—" His thought died and he was looking at the pager confusedly, like it was printing Chinese. "Excuse me," he muttered, and pocketed the pager, but made no move to get up. Cundieffe lost the thread of the argument, couldn't stop staring at Sibley, but the CIA man was far from noticing.

"Trying to get a theory to stick here's like nailing Jell-O to a tree, so long as you avoid the obvious," Atherton said. "We're looking at disenfranchised kooks with connections inside the military. Hell, you probably have the right people already on the base. Ask them."

"Those men are being questioned," the Admiral shot back coldly. "But how dare you suppose I'd kick up this much of a stink if my own men were responsible! Do you think I'm that stupid, or just that the Navy's as corrupted as the Army?"

"Hey, fuck you, Meinsen—" Brigadier General Arthur Cross started, but Lt. Col. Greenaway cut them all off.

"Roadblocks have been set up at all the weighing stations, and we're drafting a plan to sweep the desert in every direction for fifty miles by lunchtime. Seal Team One is on standby at North Island, and can be on-site in an hour on a moment's notice. As soon as the President and the Joint Chiefs wake up to this, I'll have three units of my own men on site. The mission is well in hand."

Atherton practically exploded. "What is this mickeymouse shit? Delta Commandos operating on U.S. soil? This is your idea of containment? The fact that he's here—" pointing a spear-finger at Greenaway "—and not Seal Six, says that, one, you don't trust your own men, and two, you're eager to dump this on another branch's turf, while keeping it inside the Pentagon. FBI tactical teams are more than adequate."

Despite the yawn that preceded it, Rear Admiral Meinsen's retort was all adamant resolve. "It hasn't been approved yet, but in light of the deep dark shithole we're in here, I'm confident the President will allow it. We want this over with fast, Carl. I've been advised that Delta's at a higher state of readiness than Six for this kind of thing, at this time."

Wyler took up the argument, his voice calmer than he looked. "Wayne, the FBI is capable of running down the perpetrators far more discreetly, with far less chance of civilian casualties, than any SpecWar force. This is our own goddamned country, and you've got to know it's going to be handed to us by the President. We have all the intel, we have the experts…"

"And you'll share them with Mort's boys. Until sunrise, it's my ass, my crime, my rules. I want four-eyes here and anyone else you can spare from your counterterrorism squad here in LA to be on tap for the duration."

"I've got forty here. I can free up half of them right away, more as soon as their unit chief gets back into town this morning." As he spoke, Wyler passed a note to Atherton, who nodded and added to it. Inclining his head ever so slightly, Cundieffe caught most of it around Wyler's screening hand. WAYNE'S ASS = OUR MESS headed what Wyler'd written in a microscopic scrawl, while Atherton's response ended with GIVE HIM MORE ROPE.

"Share, Atherton?" Rear Admiral Meinsen growled.

Atherton shrugged. "On the off-chance that a foreign power is involved, I'd like to bring in a team of my people to put out feelers. Also, I'd like to brief the inspector in charge of international liaison, and our legat in Mexico City, and prepare something for the INS, in case they cross the border." Meinsen and several others scowling, he added, "I think the crime's proximity to the border merits at least that much."

"Fine, fine," Meinsen answered, "as soon as the President weighs in, you can do what you want. But not yet. I know how fast rumors spread in that sewing circle of yours."

"Anything else we can get for you, Admiral?" Wyler's facetious tone was lost on Meinsen.

"I want an exhaustive dossier on everyone with a grudge and a military background and one or more friends with same, prioritized by region and service. I want a fucking Bible, Carl. How long will that take?"

"It's already done, sir," Cundieffe said, looking sidewise at an approving Wyler. "I can broaden the field, but the most likely candidates are all in this file." The Marine from the door swept by and scooped it up.

"And in return," Wyler spoke up, "I'd like an FBI forensics team to have full access to China Lake, immediately."

"Outstanding. Send 'em on out. Be glad to have 'em. Ted, Carl, I'll get back with you at oh-eight hundred." He hiked a thumb at the door. "Screw."

Wyler and Atherton confabbed for a few minutes in the corridor while Cundieffe watched. Atherton sped off to find a phone as Wyler approached his junior agent. "What do you think happened here, sir?" Cundieffe asked.

"I think all they wanted us for was exactly what they're taking, and they wouldn't let us in if we didn't have it. They want to turn this into a military conflict before the President is even briefed."

"I don't think we're in at all, sir. I think the real meeting's just getting started, and we're getting sent to the little kid's table while the grown-ups carve the turkey. Whatever the outcome, I sincerely doubt that we'll know what it was, unless the FBI is their target."

Wyler nodded and laid a hand on Cundieffe's shoulder. "That's not going to happen, Martin. The President's going to give them some token authority on this because it was their screw-up, but it's our case. While they're playing wargames out in the desert, you're going to come in the back door and identify the perpetrators. They want to treat this like a war on domestic soil, but on paper, it's a simple theft of federal property. You're going to name them, and the FBI's going to bring them in."

"But sir, I just keep track of these people. I never—"

"Don't worry, Martin, you're not going out door-to-door. Hunt'll be coordinating our efforts in the field. I'm going to get you a selective temp Top Secret clearance."

"The softkill weapons project." Cundieffe's eyes went wide. He had to resist saying Gee whiz or Jiminy, the kind of thing that made Lane Hunt laugh, but would probably stun pottymouth Wyler into puzzled silence.

"Exactly. The people who did this deed have access to weapons that don't exist. That should narrow the search considerably, for anyone who's smart enough, and likes to read."

"I'm your bookworm, sir."

Wyler nodded, *Yes I know*, turned smartly and headed for the elevator.

Cundieffe felt so wound up he could spin in circles. He felt like whistling. A major breach of military security, and he'd been one of the first to hear about it. He was there! His father had worked car thefts and audited telephone taps his whole career, and look at him. He couldn't wait to tell Mom. He went looking for a phone.

He turned down the next bend in the corridor, where he thought there was a phone booth he could use, and saw Sibley standing there, just Sibley alone, whispering into a cellular phone. His lips moving so fast he seemed to be stuttering, his face contorting like he was having a seizure. Cundieffe caught only a snippet: "Now? You tell us now? What kind of a relationship do you expect to build on a fuckup like that?" and Sibley saw him and threw him a look that seized his motor controls and propelled him back down the corridor and out of earshot.

Cundieffe stopped and leaned against the wall. His heart hammering, his breath in short, sharp bursts. He took off his glasses and cleaned them on his handkerchief. Secrets within secrets. It was like he'd stumbled through an enchanted wardrobe and into his wildest dreams.

~ 5 ~

"Hi? Hi, it's Zane! Come down and let me in, you mean old bastard!" There was no door to Hiram Hansen's cave, but anyone who truly knew him knew better than to barge in uninvited. Hansen had forgotten more about booby-traps than Storch would ever know. He waited at the mouth of the mine, casting nervous glances at his truck. Best he get his cargo into the cave before sunrise, and the rosy fingers of another scorching summer day were reaching even now into the box canyon.

The location of Hansen's cave itself was a closely guarded secret, known only to a few in Thermopylae. The hills within the square mile around his home were swiss-cheesed with twenty-nine other abandoned borax mines, with nearly a hundred entrances. Hansen parked his truck in another canyon a mile away, and threaded a labyrinth to reach his subterranean home.

He heard footsteps crunching gravel for several minutes before Hansen skulked out into the light. Wearing only thongs and a wrestling singlet, Hansen gave Storch unpleasant flashes of Pop Sickle. Hiram Hansen was not what you'd call a fat man, but only because it didn't do him justice. He had an enormous, bloated sac for a torso, with a belly like a flaccid tongue and pendulous teats that sometimes wept blue-gray milk. His knurled limbs resembled prostheses sculpted of sinewy leather, as if they detached and partook of some dreadfully strenuous labor while Hansen slept. He was like some aborted prototype for a vehicle for boneless alien monstrosities to infiltrate humanity. A breeze from deep inside the mountain washed over him, smelling of mold and his herbal taxidermy formula.

"So pleased to see you, son. Always welcome, always welcome." He scanned Storch with a metal detector and patted down his chest and armpits. Hansen was in an unnaturally good mood. Strange as he was, Hansen succumbed to the common human inclination to derive giddy joy from other people's trouble. He usually met visitors with tear gas. Storch had built up an immunity to tear gas in the army, and it bothered him about as much as a good-sized blob of wasabi. Why he felt like crying now was quite beyond him.

"What seems to be the trouble? I would've thought you'd be in Mexicali by now."

"Something came up. I found something I want you to take a look at."

"Well, I'd be delighted. Do you have it on you?"

"It's out in my truck. Come on, I want to get her inside before the sun gets up."

"I'm liking this more and more, Zane."

Hansen led Storch through the mines to a spot within fifty feet of his truck, wheeling a hospital gurney down tunnels preternaturally free of gravel. Hansen was a medical doctor, sort of. Studied the books himself, picked up wetwork experience wherever he could pose as a doctor. Kept moving around the country, one step ahead of a labcoated AMA death squad, to hear him tell it. For practicality's sake, Hansen turned to M.E. work and taxidermy, and found his life's true pursuit. The dead didn't piss him off nearly as much as the living. Storch was too much a man of the world not to suspect Hansen's penchant for rooting around in dead things, but he knew the world was probably a lot better off that way. He radiated an amoral zeal for the mysteries beneath the skin that could just as easily have made him a killer of killers.

They climbed out into blinding sunlight from a narrow crevice in the sheer rock wall of the box canyon, not ten feet from his truck. With all his training at spotting ambushes and troop tunnels, he never would have noticed the cave. Hansen smiled wickedly at Storch as if to say, for this one secret pried out of him, there were a hundred more he would never reveal.

The razor edge of dawn crept over the cab of the truck like the line of a phosphorus fuse, licking at the fluttering nylon dropcloth wrapped round the bundle. He was restless looking at it, still more unsure whether Hansen wasn't the worst possible person with whom to entrust his secret. He'd gone out there hoping to find closure, the last piece in the puzzle of what had happened in his store yesterday. Instead, he'd found a hitherto unimaginable piece to a whole other puzzle, or a larger conundrum of which the ruin of his life was only one remote corner.

Storch climbed into the bed and gingerly hefted one end of the bundle as Hansen eased the other end onto the tailgate, then down onto the gurney. As he strapped her down, he sighed and studied Storch's evasive stance. "I think I'm entitled to ask you a very stupid question, Zane."

"Go ahead."

"Was this girl a friend of yours?"

"I didn't know her. I found her—it—like this. Somebody called me on the phone, told me where to go. Swear." The sun edged closer to the gurney, eager to burn what lay on it. Storch couldn't face Hansen, couldn't look at the gurney, so he faced the rising sun.

Radiant Dawn

The white glare behind his eyelids only heightened the sense that he was being interrogated.

"You went to the dumping site on the say-so of 'somebody on the phone'?"

"They knew Harley. They were the people he was running guns for."

"And it didn't occur to you that somebody on the phone might be framing you for a murder charge so they can extort more guns out of you? For all you know, it was something like that tied Harley to them in the first place."

"No, Hiram. He believed in what they were doing. They said this was what they're trying to stop. If you're gonna help me, I'll tell you what I know, but let's for Chrissakes get her out of the sun."

They wheeled the gurney back underground, down a dizzying sequence of branching shafts; many blasted out of the raw, living rock, still others crumbling tunnels through damp sand carpeted with bizarre gardens of crystals and pulpy white fungi. After one hairpin turn, Storch heard ghostly strains of music wafting on a powered breeze. They passed through a beaded curtain and into Hiram Hansen's secret domain. A vaguely circular grotto, thirty feet in diameter, supported by ancient wooden beams and lit by green and mauve paper lanterns, the cave was divided by black rubber privacy curtains into something like a hospital ward. Only two of the cubicles were given over to living space; the rest was jammed with avalanches of painstakingly sorted, efficiently catalogued, totally useless, extravagantly weird shit. Four other tunnels opened onto the room at the bottom of a labyrinth: entrances, getaways, probably all booby-trapped. Hansen was nothing if not cautious.

The tropical lounge treacle of Martin Denny's "Quiet Village" was piped in through drive-in speakers mounted around the walls. Storch was glad that it was at least an instrumental. He couldn't abide lyrics; anything with comprehensible, rhyming words poisoned his mind, careening round and round and drowning his train of thought until he had to break something to purge it.

Hansen hefted the bundle onto an examination table, tugged on a pair of heavy rubber gloves and reached for a pair of shears. Storch found himself crowding the foot of the table.

"Are you sure you want to see this?" Hansen asked.

"I—um, I didn't really—I mean I tried not to look before. It was dark, and I was in a hurry."

"You want this to become personal, is that it?"

"No, I just have to know."

"As you wish," he said, and cut away the layers of filthy drop cloth over the face. He peeled it back like the skin of a rotten banana, and for once, his face betrayed more shock than Storch's.

It was a dead girl, Caucasian, aged about sixteen. Her face was intact, and strikingly undecayed, but the frozen expression of agony on that face spoiled its innocence more than a year in a grave would have. Hansen backed away from the table, his face hooded in shadow.

"What is it?" Storch asked.

"Bless my soul, she's one of my girls," Hansen said.

"What do you mean? What did you have to do with this?" Hansen turned and ducked through the curtains, lumbering off into the labyrinth of his collections. Storch looked at the girl again.

One of my girls

And he remembered that Hiram Hansen was a very good taxidermist.

Hansen grabbed him from behind, spun him around, almost before Storch could palm the scalpel he'd instinctively snatched from the tool tray. "Here, look at this!" He dropped a huge cardboard box full of flattened milk cartons on the foot of the examination table. They appeared to be alphabetized, but not by dairy, for there was no rhyme or reason to the color scheme. Hansen flipped through the carton file excitedly, like a Playboy collector who thinks he just spotted Miss October '75 in church. "I knew I had her somewhere, Zane. I never forget a face. Here!"

He waved a cracking, yellowed carton under Storch's nose. A small girl's portrait sandwiched between coupons for Knott's Berry Farm and a headline—HAVE YOU SEEN ME?

Sidra Marie Sperling

DOB: 04–01–82

Last Seen: 12–23–90 at Inyokern rest stop along Hwy 395

If you have any information about Sidra's whereabouts, please call (408) 555–6797. $2000 REWARD OFFERED.

Storch shivered, his muscles snapping taut like sails in a chill wind. The rest stop. How was that for closure? "Why do you keep these, Hiram?"

"Now, don't look at me that way. I never harmed a little child in my whole life. When they started putting these pictures on milk cartons, it just wrung my heart to look at them. And I thought to myself, what if one of those little children were to cross my path months after I'd finished my milk or it went rancid, and me not able to remember their face? So, I just started keeping 'em. Never spotted one, though. Now all you can get are the clear plastic jugs, so—"

"So this girl was kidnapped nine years ago, and she's been alive ever since?"

"Why don't you go into the waiting room while I look over the rest of it. And don't touch anything!"

Storch sat in Hansen's waiting room, idling away three hours with *Popular Mechanics* back issues promising technological wonders both ridiculous and banal ("Commuter Ultralites: Antidote To Gas Crunch?", "Build Your Own Microwave Oven," "'Star Wars' Space Platforms Put Heat Back In Cold War"); weird old pornography where the models' pudenda were airbrushed out, as sexy as your sister's Barbie dolls; a portfolio of "Tijuana Bibles", bootleg porno funny pages from the thirties, featuring Little Orphan Annie repaying Daddy Warbucks's generosity with a blowjob, Popeye's spinach-trick enlarging his organ so it split Olive Oyl in half. A yellowed sketchbook with page after page of the same fever-dream sketch, an elephantine humanoid with an octopus for a head, all dated between February and March, 1925, all splattered with the same childish nonsense word: "Dali."

Bored, he tried not to think about what Hansen was doing to the body of the girl. Only what a doctor would do. What wouldn't a doctor do, if he enjoyed it? He knew far too little about how Hansen took his pleasures to want to speculate. He had to believe Hansen was a doctor, after a fashion, and bound by an oath, if only one administered to himself.

He got up during the second round of "Quiet Village", when Hansen's tinkering behind the curtain was drowned out by the nasal whine of a radial saw. He skulked around the far curtain and fumbled for its edge in the dim, volcanic lantern-light. The saw ripped on. Storch had to find something to take him away from the sound of the saw, and the things he saw when he heard it. He stepped through the gap in the curtain and drew it shut behind him. The thick rubber muffled the sound adequately for him to look around him.

Rocks of various lusterless shades and textures lay in piles or propped against wooden sawhorses, some pebble-sized, others larger than Hansen himself. Not rocks, he saw as his eyes adjusted to the dimness: fossils. The light glinted on sheens of iridescent color and ribbed contours of petrified flesh inscribed in the rocks. The largest, Storch saw, looked like nothing so much as a gigantic sea cucumber.

"What the hell are you doing in here?" Hansen's rubber-sheathed nails bit into his shoulder, dragged him back through the curtain and into the waiting room. "Don't you ever touch anything if I tell you not to!"

"I'm gonna go somewhere. How much longer you gonna be?"

"A few hours, I think. I lose track of time when I get into a good one. She's full of mysteries."

"This isn't a fucking game, Hiram. This is a fucking war. At some point, we may have to turn her over for evidence. You can't carve your initials into her, or—whatever you're thinking of doing. Just find out what happened to her, okay? I'll be back."

Hansen smiled. "If you pick up a tail, don't come back. We won't be here."

~ 6 ~

When the light of dawn fell on Highway 395, Stella Orozco was on it, her mustard yellow '78 Honda Civic hatchback whining like a mad hornet stinging itself to death as she floored it down southbound blacktop. She knew her beeper was going off on her dresser at home, summoning her to help with the cuts and bruises from the minor tremor this morning. She knew she'd be reprimanded, maybe suspended, unless she had a damned good reason for lighting out of town while she was on call. She knew she wouldn't tell them anything. She didn't know just what she was looking for out here, or what she'd do if and when she found it. Any more than she knew why she was wearing her best suit, the one she'd worn only twice since she interviewed for her current job. Or why she'd brought a binder with a recently updated resume and her biopsy results.

For as long as she could remember, a sizable part of Stella's consciousness had thrown off all other duties to doggedly, ruthlessly fend off all harm, real or suspected. Whether you'd choose to see it as a freak of nature or nurture, or a guardian angel with a stalker's persistence and the key to her neurochemical medicine chest, Stella had survived her life so far because she listened whenever that inscrutable inner voice whispered *danger,* and told her what to do. She knew her survival organ, her paranoid angel, had told her to go to the hospice village *now,* to wear her best tweed skirt and blazer in the middle of the summer, and to be ready to fight for her life. She knew it would tell her what to do when she got there.

Where were you when I was inhaling DDT, guardian angel?

Her survival voice had been keeping radio silence in the week since she'd found out her liver and lymph glands were inoperably malignant, and she'd begun to wonder if it hadn't deserted her, as if keeping Stella Orozco alive wasn't a lost cause, now. She'd been unable to bring herself to review the treatment regimen brochures Dr. Tranh had given her in Fresno, where she'd gone to get the tests done. Stella had always thought of the survival voice as the part of herself that was always watching out for her because no one else would or could. When the voice went dead, Stella was cast adrift in a way she hadn't experienced since her mother died and her father abandoned her.

Last night, she lay in bed unable to sleep for seeing the rampaging tumors in Stephen's severed limbs, pulsating among his blood vessels, staunching the bleeding that should've killed him; the benevolent divinity in his eyes as he said, "the moon-ladder," over and over like a prayer; the evangelical glint in the eyes of Dr. Keogh as he touched her cancer in a way that made her wonder if it wasn't already healed.

Her voice stirred then. It told her to come, and she slept in peace. And in the morning, she'd come.

Less than twenty miles south of Bishop, the dense coniferous curtain of the Inyo National Forest abruptly fell away, succumbing to the sere plains of the high desert. This part of the state was like a jigsaw puzzle of clashing terrains, rudely hammered into place by a petulant, capricious god. As this morning's earth tremor demonstrated, the pieces didn't always rest easy alongside each other. Seismologists predicted that nearby Mammoth Mountain was long overdue to blow its top a la St. Helens and cover the whole state in ash.

From the day she arrived here to interview for the ER position, Stella had found it irresistible. The contrasts shocked her senses out of the utterly tamed flatness of the central valley that'd dominated her childhood. To the northwest stood Mt. Whitney, the tallest mountain in the lower forty-eight states. Only one hundred miles south by southeast lay the Death Valley Basin, the lowest point in North America. Bishop lay within a few hours' drive of Yosemite, arguably the most beautiful natural vista in the country, and Manzanar, an abandoned W.W.II internment camp, reminder of one of the ugliest pages in recent American history.

As the highway slipped into the Owens Valley, the sandscape became a tossing sea of brown waves and dust devils—the arid summer winds swept the topsoil into towering chimerical forms that warred on the plain. With the lion's share of the Owens River diverted to water lawns and feed flashy fountains in Los Angeles, the valley was being stripped to the bone. It was a damned strange place to locate a hospice, so remote from loved ones and so stark a scene to contemplate in the last months of a cruelly abbreviated life.

She urgently needed to use a restroom and freshen up before she got there, but the only rest stop between Bishop and the hospice village seemed to have collapsed in the tremor. She blew past the brickpile and the CalTrans and sheriff's trucks parked around it, clamped her legs together and prayed she'd be able to pee into her travel mug without wetting her skirt.

When the exit came it was suddenly, simply there, and she had to slam on her balding brakes and heel the sketchy little Honda to the right in what almost amounted to a u-turn. She slammed on the brakes again as the road gave way to loose gravel. The tiny car fishtailed to and fro down the turnoff and skidded to a stop just short of a formidable steel gate. A steel fence ran out from it for about a quarter mile in either direction, enclosing the desert up to the boulder-crowned hills a half-mile to the east. They enclosed the desert up to the boulder-crowned hills beyond, a half-mile to the west. Stella saw no sign of any village, or any other kind of manmade edifice, for that matter. Was it in the hills? Was it underground?

"Please state your business," said a voice from a box mounted on a post alongside her window.

Yes, there was an earthquake—and I have cancer—can I use your restroom?

"Um," she said. She'd thrown herself into this situation on faith that the next thing to come out of her mouth would get her in something besides trouble, would maybe save her life. She opened it, blanked her mind, and it came to her.

"I'm from the Inyo County Hospital, I'm here for the follow-up outpatient consult on Mr. Stephen...s—"

A moment passed. The wind whipped handfuls of powdery fine dust into her car; she wiped dust-caked lipstick from her mouth, taking her hand off the stick shift, which popped out of neutral and the car stalled with an ugly ratcheting noise that didn't exactly bode well for a quick getaway. Why was she thinking like this?

"Please, come in," a familiar voice sounded in her ear. The gate swung wide, soundless on oiled hinges. Stella struggled with the clutch to get her car started. On the fifth try it caught, and she drove inside, inches before the gate that closed her in.

The dusty, pitted road that approached the hospice community confirmed her fears even as it made her angry enough to keep going. Clearly, this was some kind of fly-by-night operation designed to part the dying from their wealth and dignity, and the only capital outlay she could see went into keeping them in and the curious out. Why else locate in such a desolate, remote spot as the high desert? Why else have security fences and medical conservatorships and men on motorcycles dogging visitors?

She watched the cape of gray dust running parallel to hers, about a hundred yards on her right. There was nothing else to see here, only the road and the fields of sun-baked alluvial silt and the occasional rock. While it was next to impossible to track a car in a place like this without being seen, she doubted subterfuge was their intention. *Keep moving*, the message of the motorcycle said, *and know we see you*. She wondered how many motorcycles might be cruising around out here when she tried to leave.

Tried to leave? Chica, you're losing your mind.

Rage filled her, that people could and would do this, would sink to this souped-up holistic grave robbery. That they'd lured her out here to ask them to take everything she had, too. She almost forgot about what she'd seen, and why she had to learn more. Her life seemed to have an understanding with her, that it threw her something to get worked into a fury over whenever she started to feel low and desperate. Almost.

Stella's car nosed over a ridge and stalled. Rather than try to start it again, she got out and looked at the view.

A bowl-shaped valley enfolded the fifty-odd buildings of the Radiant Dawn Hospice. Two broad, concentric circular avenues encircled a boxy three-story central building that must be the medical center. The houses were attractive tract spilt-levels built according to one of three styles out of adobe brick and redwood timbers. A long second glance was required to recognize that they were prefabs, probably brought out here on trucks. Each was fronted by a hurtfully green lawn and lovingly tended flowerbed. A recreation center beside the medical compound featured an Olympic swimming pool and a field, presumably for some intramural sports. She saw a few people in black uniform track suits—*like Stephen's*—wandering here and there, and others tooling about in golf carts. She saw no cars, and no garages. A few broken windows were the only visible damage from the tremor. She looked around her, but saw no sign of the motorcyclist.

She'd seen plenty of private residential developments before. Like any other fancy place in California, they needed landscaping done, and like rich folks everywhere, they were cheap. But for the hospice, the desert simply did not exist. It stopped at the rim of the valley, and was denied entry, yet there was no sign of laborers, or even a sprinkler system. There was something about the sight of the Radiant Dawn community that gave off an effortless aura of hope, of health... of home.

A golf cart struggled up the hill toward her, its overtaxed electric motor whining loudly in the still desert morning air. Stella fought the perverse impulse to jump back in the car, was surprised to feel her legs buckling under her, halfway starting to do it. She gathered herself and waved in an exaggerated fashion, put on a big fake smile. Two men rode in the cart, a driver in a track suit, and an older man in a charcoal suit and white labcoat, with silver hair fluttering like cold fire round his skull, and black wraparound sunglasses of the kind vampires might favor, because they covered almost half his face.

As the cart approached and coasted to a stop, she recognized him as none other than Dr. Keogh from the night before. Either he'd been more impressed with her than he let on last night or he was charged with all the hospice's unpleasant tasks: retrieving strays, driving off pests…Still, he'd known, he'd reached out and touched the very spot where she had begun to die inside, and he'd as much as promised her—what?

He climbed out and shook her hand, smiling broadly. Although it was clearly meant to ingratiate, his grin had her half–scared and thinking about the car again, now it was too late.

"Ms. Orozco, I didn't expect to see you so soon. I hope everything is as it should be?"

"No, no, sir, everything's fine—I mean, if Stephen's—"

"Passed away in the night as a result of his injuries, I'm sorry to say. It's moving that you should come all this way for a patient. Your kind of sympathy is a rare commodity in the current climate of the medical community."

"Thank you." *God*, was she blushing?

"But you didn't come all the way out here just to inquire about Stephen, did you?"

Stella was forced to look away from the sudden sharpness in Dr. Keogh's voice. Watching the horizon didn't take away the chilling penetration, the feeling of being opened up. When she opened her mouth to speak a moment later, she hesitated, certain he'd already seen through her. "No, Dr., actually, to tell you the truth, I was surprised and intrigued to hear there was a hospice community up here. As a nurse in a small town, one rarely gets to make a difference. And I thought that, in such a remote area, you must have some difficulty keeping trained medical professionals on-call. I wanted to—"

"You'd like a tour of our community, Ms. Orozco?" He cut her off quite politely, but without quite leaving enough inflection for the statement to qualify as a question.

"Yes. Yes, I'd like that very much."

He stepped back toward the golf cart, then stopped her from returning to her car.

"Leave that here. It'll be safe. Leave the keys with us." She must've stared, because he added, "We try to expose our residents to as little pollution as possible."

"Of course," she said, feeling stupid. "But I have to get something out of my car. Would you—"

"Not at all," he said, and her keys weren't in her hand anymore, and he opened the car door and removed her purse and binder and presented them to her. Leaving the car unlocked, he took her arm and seated her on the cart. With no more speed but considerably less noise, they returned to Radiant Dawn.

"Why haven't I heard of this place before, Dr. Keogh?" Stella asked, instantly regretting it. *Curb your suspicion, chica, at least for now.*

Keogh's expression, however, showed no ire. His eyes, hidden behind those black glass cages, might've been twinkling with pride as he said, "I'm surprised you haven't, really. After all, we've been covered in all the major papers, though we've tried to keep the media and the general public at arm's length from our work here. It would be a grave injustice to our residents to place a higher priority on publicity than on our work with them."

"And how are the pa—residents selected? Not everybody could afford something like this…" What's wrong with you today?

Again, she failed to get a rise out of him, wondered why she couldn't stop trying. "At first, I admit, money was a factor, but we've become self-sufficient, and now operate, as much as possible, on a need-blind basis. We have a crisis intervention hotline which handles all manner of personal traumas, providing referrals to counselors, doctors, and so on. But we take a special interest in those with cancer, because no one else can tell them how to live with it, let alone why it happened to them. Those who need us most, who have nowhere else to turn, will eventually find their way here."

They cruised down the main avenue, and Stella heard nothing but the breeze and the dragonfly hum of the electric cart. Residents standing outside their houses or waiting at the intersections smiled and waved, and Dr. Keogh waved back. The residents were of all ages and races, dressed in identical light cotton tracksuits. Stella saw workers now, but they wore the same outfit, and were clearly residents themselves.

"So this place is a commune," Stella said, turning to face Dr. Keogh. His mind seemed a million miles away, and he looked at her for a long moment before he seemed to gather himself. He felt it too, the same sense of belonging that washed everything else away. Only her mistrust had spared her.

When he focused on her, however, his gaze was as penetrating as before. "We strive to create a sense of community here, Ms. Orozco, a society with its collective eye on the goal of surviving. By taking responsibility for every aspect of their survival, from maintenance to growing their own food, they come to renew their appreciation for life itself."

Great. Every hospital could save a bundle if they could convince their patients that they'd mend faster by cleaning out their own bedpans. "But your policy doesn't extend to medical staff? You have trained medical people here?"

Keogh laughed. "Of course, aside from myself, we have five other doctors, ten nurses, an anesthesiologist, an oncologist and a radiologist. All of them are also patients. Well, here we are."

The cart pulled into a cart-sized space in front of the medical center. Stella noticed an RV and an ambulance beside the door—the same one they'd picked up Stephen in. A bulky cable ran from the wall of the medical center to a port on the side of the van. "I think you'll be impressed with our facilities, Ms. Orozco. Our emergency room is especially noteworthy." He held open the door for her and followed her in. A gust of refrigerated air blew past her as she stepped in. Over her shoulder, Dr. Keogh said, "Pressurized, you understand, to minimize airborne infection. Now, as a medical professional yourself, what do you think of this?"

She stepped into the room, and all doubts about the integrity of Radiant Dawn crumbled away. Whatever they were, they weren't just peddling snakeoil.

The emergency room boasted three trauma stations and an on-site radiology station. Peering in the window of what she thought was an odd closet, she saw a baby MRI apparatus. She'd never seen a model half that small before. There were a dozen beds, lining the L-shaped room. All empty.

At the crook of the bent room, a middle-aged woman in a track suit sat at the nurses' station. Four computer workstations alternated patient charts and video feeds from different parts of the building. A massive wall monitor behind her displayed a schematic of the hospice community, with red dots moving across it. One by one, the nurse highlighted a different dot and clicked on it. A health chart that appeared to be monitoring in real time sprang up. Satisfied, she closed it and moved on to the next.

"Our patients regain the world by getting out of their beds, but they receive more attentive care than any health enterprise in the world could provide relative to our costs."

"How do you track—I mean, how do you monitor them?"

"A computer chip in their ID bracelets monitors their functions and location for us." He looked at her and saw her next question gathering, cut it off. "Stephen had the misfortune to have misplaced his."

She watched the board as he talked. She counted eighty-five residents on it. "Not a lot of people for such a big place," she said, trying not to sound like she was angling. What was she angling for?

"The residents we have take up all our time. We do much more than merely care for them. We do quite a bit of research, as well. That's what occupies the upper floors. We're looking for a cure, but in the meantime, we try to teach our residents to live with their cancer."

"So nothing like what happened to Stephen has ever happened before," she said, more sharply than she intended.

"Oh, no. Stephen had other issues which contributed to what happened. We deeply regret it, but there's nothing one can do for another who has simply renounced the life force."

"Is his body going to be sent on to his relatives?"

"He had none, I'm afraid. We're going to bury him here in Radiant Dawn. The state recently granted us license to inter remains here. It may seem paradoxical, but we find it helps to maintain the network of mutual support we've built here, to allow the dead to continue to provide comfort for those still engaged in the struggle."

After talking to Dr. Keogh last night, she'd reviewed the morgue records, and by computer, those of Lone Pine and Independence. In the thirteen months they'd been in operation, they'd had twelve deaths, all of cancer. The bodies were delivered to the hospital in Lone Pine, which was a smaller facility and took a more parochial view of autopsies and such. Which explained why she'd never heard of them. But now they were burying them here. Why now?

The moon ladder

Stella suddenly felt that same wind she'd felt before at her back, and she turned to see Dr. Keogh was holding the door open for her. "Well, I hope you've learned all you hoped to learn from us. I've got to return to visiting with my residents, so, if you don't mind…"

She hurried through the door and retrieved her notebook from the cart. Dr. Keogh approached her. Plunged back into the blasting high desert heat, she was breathless, her lungs seared, and her mind bleached clean of lies.

"Dr. Keogh, I think you should know the real reason that I came to see you," she stammered. "I'm a fully trained, registered nurse with five years' experience in trauma medicine. I also have cancer—of the liver. The doctors have said it's inoperable and I have a year, maybe less, to live. I saw how advanced Stephen's cancer was, and how strong his body was even in the cancer's metastasized state. I'd like to come here. I don't want to die."

Dr. Keogh gently took her in her arms, stopping her from pulling out her resume or her charts from the hospital in Fresno. He held her for a long time, waiting for she knew not what. And then she was sobbing, and she knew this was it. She hadn't cried in front of anyone for as long as she could remember, perhaps not since her mother died. And now here she was with her puffy-eyed face buried in the shoulder of a strange doctor, bawling her heart out for a life lost before she even knew what to do with it. He held her and let her cry, drew the pain out of her like venom, and let her cry some more, until she felt nothing but the peace Radiant Dawn had given her when she'd first seen it. Dr. Keogh let her go and looked into her eyes, and she could almost see her sorrow swimming around behind them. "I'm sorry, my dear, but it's quite impossible right now."

Slapping her would've elicited less shock. "What? You won't…take me?" She sniffled and choked up in the middle of talking, hated herself for her weakness. The cleansed, open space he'd made inside her filled with hurt and red, red anger.

"We can't admit anyone once the residents have embarked upon their journey into the life force. There's no catching up, Stella. These people have transcended their illness, made themselves as one with it."

Her tears came again, but this time they were hot, stinging. Her hands ached to slap and scratch them. She made them hold each other back and scratch each other as she yelled at him. "How the fuck can you say that to me? How can you tell me I can't have what they have? What kind of heartless chingalo are you, to tell me I have to die, when these people can go on raking your leaves and making your beds? We Mexicans can pick a mean head of lettuce, you gringo bastard—"

His implacable calm wasn't even dented. "Please understand, Ms. Orozco, that we regret this more than you can understand right now. We wish it could be otherwise, but this process can't be revised. We all serve the life force, in our way."

"But as far as you're concerned, the brown people of the world can serve as fertilizer, eh?" An undercurrent of livid self-hatred rolled back on her as she slipped deeper into race-baiting. Never shamed of her heritage, she'd never invoked it for anything. Stella Orozco was a race of one, and it made her sick to hear her own voice using her Hispanic blood as a weapon.

"No, Stella, no. Listen to me," he said and he was closer to her than she would have allowed, just now, if she'd noticed him coming. His hands were on her arms again, but not restraining. She felt comforted, and she fought it. She lost. "Where there is life, there is change. Where life fights change, it breaks through...as cancer. But if your will to live is strong, you'll see the next Radiant Dawn. This is only the first such hospice. There will be others. And you will go among them. We will teach you to live with your illness, which is the life force. We will help you to become one with it, and live."

He let her go again, and steered her toward the cart. As the driver backed it out, Dr. Keogh waved to her once and went inside. As oblivious to the driver now as he apparently was to her, Stella cried some more.

She was still crying when they topped the ridge beside her car and she made out the shapes of residents at work on the dusty field. They were digging irrigation ditches, laying the groundwork for turning the desert into a farm. She wiped her eyes and climbed into the car. She stopped and stood up again and craned her neck, looking at one of the fieldworkers. His ginger hair and lanky build. She'd never seen him upright, but that same perverse voice that'd urged her to flee told her she was looking at Stephen. Standing on his two legs in a field. Holding a shovel in his two hands. He was talking to someone with their back turned. She shielded her eyes against the glare and the airborne dust and strove to see just a bit more clearly, but the dust was caking her face, miring in her tears. Then the man he was talking to turned and faced her and he seemed to see her very clearly indeed. It was Dr. Keogh. He waved once more to her and watched her as she dove back into the car, started the engine and sped away.

She couldn't stop crying until she got home. After a long bath, she realized that despite what Keogh'd told her, despite what she'd thought she'd seen, she was beginning to hope, and that nothing else mattered.

~ 7 ~

Storch drove out to the place where he knew they hid. The place that immediately leapt to mind when Hansen had told him she'd been missing nine years. He didn't know why he hadn't thought of it before.

The skin traders.

A year before, they'd come into his store. They smelled like organized crime. Three men, two bodyguards flanking an out-of-work Greek lounge emcee in a powder-blue Dacron suit that seemed to squirt sweat from strategic gutters when he walked or waved his arms. Which he did constantly, as if he were freezing to death in the hundred and three degree heat. His shopping list reinforced Storch's suspicion that they were penny-ante crooks on the lam—sleeping bags, lanterns, shotgun shells, and such—but a few unusual items, like bolts of canvas, camcorder batteries, pepper spray and handcuffs led him to believe they were going into the rough-trade porn business. They had four moving vans that came and went at odd hours from a mining hut two miles north of Thermopylae.

Storch minded his own business and took their money, until about four months ago. The emcee was trying to hustle Hansen into procuring Thiopental for them in industrial volumes, and Hansen must have complained to the Field Marshal, who chased them out of town. Storch visualized the two or three underage girls he'd spotted in the van that tore out of his parking lot inches ahead of the Field Marshal's half-track. They'd never stopped in town again, but the vans kept coming and going.

The mysterious combatants whose secret war had trampled his life whirled about in his mind. He couldn't figure out which side was which. The feds—if they were feds—had raided the weapons cache that Harley was sitting on for someone involved in a race war, but had shown little or no interest in him. If he were under surveillance, they'd surely have stopped him by now. They'd have Hiram, and they'd have the girl. The girl…

What did the body of a girl kept alive for nine years, then unceremoniously dumped into the San Andreas Fault, have to do with a militia group? The skin traders were strictly business, however depraved. Why did the militia want so desperately for him to dig up a body and hide it? Why not call the police, or the media? People far less clever than Storch had concocted less far-fetched schemes to frame someone for murder. It had to be something they wanted *him* to see, to provoke him to take action. Harley's last words swam into his thoughts, that incomplete sentence that at the time had told him only that he wasn't alone in his room, and probably not holding his own gun to his temple.

Zane, some people will try to contact you soon. Don't…

Don't what? Don't believe them? Don't lead the feds, real or fake, to them? Don't do anything? DON'T—

Don't mess with Texas

Thinking made what he was about to do seem more absurd by the moment, and it was like throwing burning sticks into the cave of the Headache. For all that he had already lost, for all that he believed in, Storch stopped thinking.

He drove up a service road that paralleled the gravel track to the mining hut. A quick glance told him the hut was a losing proposition: two sentries in desert camo milled around out front. Storch counted eight ATVs and two pickups out front. All the real action was downstairs, anyway. He drove another half-mile up the service road before he found what he was looking for. A ventilation shaft, ten feet in diameter, bored into the sandstone beside the road. Chain link fencing stretched across the mouth of the vertical shaft, a rusted sign warning that the shaft was CONDEMNED BY ORDER OF THE U.S. GEOLOGICAL SURVEY. He looked around again. The road was rutted with knobby ATV tracks; they patrolled up here regularly.

He'd seen men in combat who sought their own deaths in action, and seen in them a cowardice that other idiots mistook for fearlessness. Had he already snapped?

He climbed back into his truck, drove it back out and two miles up the highway, pulling over at the beginning of a nature trail. He climbed out, filled a knapsack with his MP5, four extra clips, a modified Beretta, a hooded flashlight, a compass and a canteen, and began jogging. The awesome heat fired his blood like clay, burning all flexibility out of him. Any outcome short of victory or death would shatter him.

Twelve minutes later, he belly-crawled across the road and up the rampart of tailings around the shaft. With a tool off his belt, he snipped out a semicircle of fence and lowered himself into the hole. He shined a light down below. Sand and rocks and soda cans, fifty feet below his feet. He dropped a fist-sized rock, waited. It hit the bottom with a raspy thud, but the ground around it rippled, an oily motion, like waves in taut fabric.

Storch took out a compressor gun and fitted a piton into the barrel. The walls of the shaft were conglomerate, a peanut brittle of well-worn igneous rocks suspended in adobe and sand. Granite boulders littered the tailings below the shaft, in plain sight from the road. He drove the piton into one of these, hoping that the meth-crazed mob soldier who pulled patrol duty would be too busy trying to run over jackrabbits to notice the cable dangling from the rock into the shaft.

He lowered himself into the shaft, rappelling off the walls, sending showers of pebbles and larger rocks ahead of him. His feet scraped the bottom, dimpling matte black canvas. He shifted his weight to hang head down on the rope and drew his knife, listening. He heard water spraying from sprinklers. Beneath the dust of the shaft, he smelled a palpable musk of mold, sweat, shit and sinsemilla. He slashed the canvas and paid out another foot of rope through his clenched fist. An evil purple glow bled through the hole.

Storch descended into a Martian jungle. Hydroponic troughs lined the floor; ten-foot marijuana plants filled the tunnel as far as the eye could see in either direction. Each was laden with clumps of livid ultraviolet buds the size of coconuts. Their pungent funk curdled his brainwaves, so strong it became a noise, a fuzzed-out sub-bass under lilting sitars. He inserted his nose plugs, slipped on a surgical mask.

The stifling air was pregnant with mist, a sea of quicksilver mirrors in which Storch could almost see pointillist reflections of himself, stalking himself amidst black and violet phantoms. He rubbed gobs of resinous sleep from his eyes. Mist-irrigation hoses snaked along the canvas-lined tunnel walls, and fluorescent grow-lamps and space heaters made the mine a subterranean sauna. Storch dropped to the ground on a narrow path that divided the crops in half, listening. Beneath the white hiss of the sprayers, he could hear, no, feel, music, a throbbing bass pulse that shook motes of dust from the tunnel walls. His compass verified that it was coming from the direction of the hut. There was a junction of three shafts about five hundred yards ahead, where the generators were located. Storch hugged the right-side wall, wading through the pot plants. The music continued to wax louder, covering the sound of his passage. He moved as quickly as he could while scanning for tripwires, mines or cameras. He saw none. Apparently, the sweaty emcee trusted his remote location and perimeter security to deter intruders.

He sidled through two bushes and ran into a barricade of translucent heavy plastic, stretched taut across the mouth of the shaft. Storch dropped back and knelt between the five-gallon plastic tubs in which the plants grew and peered out. At the intersection of four or five shafts, the slavers had erected a little studio, complete with a glassed-in dubbing booth, three tripod-mounted camcorders and a satin-sheeted bed large enough to have its own zip code. They were indeed in the porn business, but not the kind Storch, or any sane, healthy human being, could watch for pleasure.

Chains and leather straps dangled from a wrought-iron cage that enclosed the bedroom set, and from them hung a girl, limp, hooded. There was no one else in sight. Storch sliced the plastic with his combat knife and stepped into the studio. The air was cold and gelid with air conditioning. He could already feel the migraine building in his head.

A rack beside the cage was stocked with whips, riding crops, cattle-prods, a soldering iron, an acetylene torch, and something Storch had seen once in the museum of torture inside the Medieval Times theme restaurant in Anaheim. It was called the Pear, and it was designed for extracting confessions from wanton women. It looked like a lemon juicer made of steel, with a handgrip and an artichoke-shaped knob sticking out of it. When the inquisitor squeezed the grip, the knob opened up like a cruel flower, its edges honed to wicked sharpness. Storch couldn't eat his microwaved Medeival banquet meal for thinking that some member of the same species as him could conceive of such a thing for the express purpose of mutilating wombs.

Storch crossed the studio and took the girl's pulse. She was alive, but drugged into a stupor. He yanked off her hood. She was pretty, and probably not even fifteen. A rubber ballgag was stuffed in her mouth. Gingerly, he pried it loose, squeezed her earlobe to wake her and whispered in her other ear.

"Hey, miss, hey, don't make a sound. I'm gonna get you out of here. Hey, can you hear me, miss?"

The girl's head lolled back, her cheeks flushing with the pressure on her ear. Her eyes fluttered, opened and looked at him, a girl who should have been in junior high school regarded him with that same stoned, disgusted look that whores gave him when he turned them down. "Jimmy, are we on? Is this the show?" She started giggling, and Storch, backing away towards the slit in the plastic, began to think, *this is stupid, this was*

the very beaucoup fucking stupidest thing he could be doing right now.
He'd never been on a mission alone before, never went in without locking
himself away with the team and the mission plans, without rehearsing
them so when it happened he was just watching his body running through
it. He was here for a girl he'd found in a ditch, who just might have some
connection to why men posing as feds burned down his store, and now the
girl was screaming for somebody or something called crank, and a Latino
man in a mesh tanktop and Speedos with a Glock 9 stuffed in them entered
the cave, a bag of corn chips in one hand and an Ithaca pump shotgun in
the other.

Storch ducked through the slit just as the man looked around. "How
the fuck did you get your hood off?" he screamed at her. Coked to the
gills, he was likely to shoot anything that confused or challenged him the
way a couch potato changes a channel when Jeopardy stumps him.
"Who's here with you? Is somebody fucking here with you?" He prowled
the room, passing the slit twice without noticing. Storch, smothering in
sinsemilla stench, held his breath and waited to see how many more of
them there were.

"Some fag, Leon. I'm broken, daddy. Fix me." Twirling on her
restraints, the girl trying to coax more drugs out of Leon and see where
he'd gotten to at the same time. Her glazed, light-blinded eyes passed over
the rent in the plastic without registering surprise, passion, life.

Leon set down the shotgun and pulled her to him by the rope binding
her ankles together. His hands slid up her nubile young body with a loan
shark's eye for value, came to rest cradling her head. Tender caresses
made her swoon, dangling in his arms.

"You want a rush, baby? There's all kinds..." Gripping her ears
fiercely, he shook her head like a master bartender mixing a really good
martini, the way the Shah's SAVAK secret police were trained to torture
their prisoners without marks. The girl whimpered as her brain rattled
against the walls of her skull, then went horribly silent. Leon let go and
stepped back, genuinely enjoying her suffering as only one who has never
known any other way of touching a woman can. "Just remember, baby,
only the first one is free."

The sprinklers came on full-blast behind and above Storch, who
hunched over his rifle. The wet white noise muted his involuntary cough
of disgust. On top of everything else he was forcing himself to ignore, the
sight was simply too much. If he could've held it in, he might've heard the
rustling of the plants behind him even over the splattering water. The first
blow from the baseball bat drove his head down into his shoulders; his
teeth clicked together through the tip of his tongue. The second scooped

him through the slit and out onto the cavern floor, where his legs carried him across the studio to crash into a wheeled toolcaddy. His brain soared on, out of the park, and into the dark.

Leon hogtied Storch and sat on his shoulders, grinding his face into the gravel floor as he came awake. Scattered screws and bolts from the toolcaddy cut into his cheek. Still reeling from the bat blows, he wrenched his head free and, stretching out his tongue, scooped a three inch screw into his mouth. Leon raised one knee and brought it down hard between his shoulder blades. Storch coughed, almost swallowed the screw. Leon's arm came around with a pair of adjustable pliers and clamped the bridge of his nose. The pain of the ridged steel biting into his skin was scorched away layer by layer as the slaver cranked it down, vising the join of nasal and frontal bones. The pain was so intense he could hear the ocean in his skull, could feel his forehead catch fire. He made the ocean louder until the pain became manageable. *Shit*, Storch thought to himself. *Leon here reads one book in his whole life, and it turns out to be the CIA Manual of Interrogation Protocols.* "Torture away, asshole," he hissed through gritted teeth. "I just hope you don't have a batch of crack in the oven, 'cos we're gonna be here all night."

"Fucking big balls! Turn over so we can get a good look at you, big-balls." Still gripping the pliers, he knelt hard on Storch's right arm, bending it in a direction it wasn't meant to go, so he rolled over. Leon sat on his midriff. his arms immediately began to fall asleep.

The man who'd apparently sucker-whacked Storch spoke up. "Just kill him now, dude. He's probably a fucking pig."

Leon's face leaned in to his, and Storch gagged on his breath, a melange of corn chips, vaginal mucus, unfiltered Camels and rampant tooth decay. "Shut up, Keith. He's just some survivalist shithead. He's pretty ugly, but I think we can use him. Hey, jarhead, you ever been in a snuff video?"

Storch spat the screw like a watermelon seed into Leon's right eye. The eye popped with a wet sucking sound, like the float bladders on a piece of kelp. His face split open in a scream as he jolted back, allowing Storch to sit up and drive his forehead into Leon's nose at an upward angle. Storch made cartilage buckle and slide up the sinuses into yielding brain matter. Leon sat down hard, eyes wide open, one russet brown, the other a flathead notch in steel. His last breath gushed out, and he flopped over.

Storch humped out from under the corpse, wrangled the automatic free of the Speedos and pointed it at Keith, a fat guy in a jungle camo poncho. Keith halfheartedly brandished the bat he'd used to brain Storch, staring at his dead friend until Storch shouted at him.

"Hey! Untie me!"

"Fuck you!" Keith, backing away, turned to run. The gun barked in Storch's hand, kicking Keith's right leg out from under him and toppling him into the wall. Keith goggled at his own half-severed leg, lost, so Storch had to shout again.

"Asshole! Untie me!"

"How'd—you—?"

"I was aiming at your spine. Untie me!"

"You're one of those guys, right?"

"What guys?"

"The guys—who—robbed China Lake last night. We know lots of—Navy guys."

"China Lake Naval Weapons Station? What're you talking about?"

Keith's eyes were glazing over, already going into shock. Slowly, painfully, Storch wormed his way across the studio to the toolcaddy. Kicking it over, he fumbled around among the tools until he found a hacksaw and went to work on his bonds.

The girl vomited on herself, came to with a gurgled, "Leon? Leon, where's my fix, you faggot?"

Storch's bad hand clasped over her mouth, his bloodied lips pressed to her ear. "Don't scream. I can get you out, but you have to try to help me. How many more are there?" Teeth clamped down on the meat of his palm was her only answer. Her hungry eyes told him where her loyalties lay.

"If I get you your fix, will you cooperate?"

Vigorously, she nodded.

"Where is it?" He tracked her eyes over to the glassed-in editing booth. Storch started to let her go, gripped her head harder to drive home how quickly he could snap her neck. "How many more?" He let go.

Her voice was a low stage-whisper, her eyes eager to please now they spoke the same language. "Just the guys outside, and they can't get in unless you buzz them in from down here. My name's Gina, what's yours?" She looked around. "Omigod, what'd you do to—"

"Leon's dead, Gina, and Keith's in shock, going on dead," he answered as he retrieved his MP5 and sidled over to the booth. "Nobody's going to hurt you any more." Inside, towering racks of dubbing decks blinked like miniature skyscrapers in a bottled Toho Tokyo set. At the end of one aisle, Storch spotted an editing console. A thick whoosh of chilled air pushed past him when he opened the door; the booth was pressurized to keep out dust. Tinny shrieks and moans pealed out over the massed hum of the decks. "I'll just be getting your works, and we'll go out the way I came in. How long have you been here?" he asked, but the door swung shut, cutting off her reply. The booth was soundproofed, as well.

Storch crept up the aisle, training his gun on the oversized office chair parked before the console. A half-moon of bald pate peered over the top of the chair; the editor, so engrossed in the bloodletting on the screen that he never noticed the killing on the other side of the glass. "Hey, Leon, look at this smash cut I got in from the prodding sequence to the double-dong—"

Storch strafed the chair. The bald head shuddered and sank out of sight. One of the monitors exploded. There were six others. Gina was on all of them, and she was dancing. She slam-danced with another girl who was hanging in the rig she was in now. Both were naked, and Gina was jabbing the captive with a cattle prod. The camera slamzoomed into her eyes, sparkling with a gleam of ecstasy that was only half narcotic-driven. When the camera zoomed out again, the hostage was covered in gleaming oil, and her legs were suspended akimbo by more chains. Gina knelt before her with the cattle prod in one hand and the Pear in the other. Storch couldn't figure out how to shut it off, so he shot at it until the last red light stopped blinking.

He pushed open the door and Gina's screams filled the cavern. Her shrill voice scraped sand off the ceiling. "Mr. Otis! Mr. Laliotitis! Somebody! There's a fucking psycho down here! He killed Leon and Keith and he's gonna kidnap me!" She shut up when he stuck the gun in her navel. "When he catches you, Mr. Laliotitis is going to fuck you with a chainsaw, you jarhead faggot. He's going to make you love it. Then he's gonna give you to me."

Storch felt like throwing up, like something deep inside him was spoiled and festering. "You like it here, don't you?"

"It grows on you. No, like, don't get me wrong, it's, like—but—you get used to it."

"Then stay here." He stuffed the ballgag back in her mouth and hooded her again. She didn't hear him when he passed her and ducked through the plastic, she was screaming so loud, and her sinuses were too congested to smell the smoke from the editing booth, so she didn't know about the fire until she felt it.

~ 8 ~

Deputy Kenny Landis liked the cowboy life. He liked heat. He liked guns. He liked lazy days around the office, shooting the shit with Sheriff Twombley and Sammy Asaro, the other deputy. He liked the jumbo burritos Mr. Montoya had his nephew bring by, free of charge, every day. Even on a hundred and eight degree scorcher like this, nothing beat a good spicy carne asada burrito slathered in guacamole and *chile verde* sauce. He liked cruising around the desert, helping people with flats and busted radiators, the way they beamed at him like he was an angel of the Lord, and sometimes tried to tip him. He liked the relaxed pace; there were few felonies, just local folks blowing off steam and tourists getting stupid doing things they couldn't get away with in the city, and thought they could here. He liked life in Furnace Creek. And life in Furnace Creek seemed to have no beef with him. Least it hadn't until yesterday; since then, life in Furnace Creek had begun to seem a lot like police work.

First, there was the raid. Sheriff Twombley didn't have much contact with or use for the FBI, which he took to calling either the Keystone Kowards or the Federal Barbecue Idiots after the mishandled Waco siege. The nearest resident office was in Victorville, and they didn't get out to Death Valley too often. Twombley honestly believed he just hated outsiders trying to pave over his citizenry with their intrusive and irrelevant federal law, but Deputy Landis knew him well enough to understand he just liked being the biggest fish in the pond, even if it was a dried-up sandpit like Furnace Creek.

In Landis's time on the force, there'd been exactly one fugitive who'd aroused the federal beast, a note-passing bank robber who crossed the state line after a one-man crimewave in Las Vegas. The man knocked over six check-cashing places in two days, unarmed.

He crossed the state line and holed up in the Furnace Creek Castle Motel, seemingly oblivious to the implications of interstate flight.

The Victorville and Las Vegas offices had each sent out a team, and they'd used up reams of paper and miles of tape, and tied up the phones for hours, waiting for the fugitive to fall asleep. The Sheriff had been happy to oblige while they were around, but cussed up a blue streak as soon as they took their man away. Fags and Hooverite cowards, every last one of them, Twombley grumbled. The Sheriff was a certified master marksman, and could have taken the chiseler out at a thousand yards, right on the state line, but the FBI stepped in and smothered him in G-men in his sleep.

So it was no mystery why the tactical raid on Sgt. Storch Quartermaster Supply the morning before had stuck in the Sheriff's craw. At least the FBI had the minimal courtesy to tell them beforehand what they were going to do. These assholes had simply stormed into Thermopylae right after breakfast and seized a bunch of contraband weapons, shooting that poor mutant fella whose legal name nobody seemed to know, and scattering the town—well, squatters, really, but decent people, on the whole—to the four winds, but arresting nobody.

What's more, they ordered—yup, ordered—Sheriff Twombley to keep mum about the whole thing, and under no circumstances put anything on paper, for twenty-four hours. Said Storch's gang were just bait, the big fish were due in to pick up their gear sometime during the night. The way the Sheriff had looked when they released him—yup, that's what they called it—from the interview in his own office—all milk-white under his leathery eternal sunburn, and with his mouth hanging open like he'd been punched in the stomach or just awakened from sleepwalking—that had Landis worried, but by the time the their stink was out of the air, Jim Twombley was back in form.

The Sheriff stayed in his office with the door closed all the rest of the morning, cussing the paint off the walls. He respected authority, Landis heard him say more than once, clear as a bell through two adobe walls, but he didn't have to hunker down and suck its dick.

They hadn't even caught their breath from that one when Asaro fielded a call from the manager of the trailer park in Death Valley Junction, saying he'd heard shots from one of the trailers, and wanted they should come check it out. The resident in question was one Harley Pettigrew, the—small world, this—assistant manager of Sgt. Storch's Quartermaster Supply. Sammy was the first one brave enough to go in, even though no shots had been fired since the first two, almost two whole hours before. As you might expect, Pettigrew was tipped over in a rocking chair with a gun in his hand and his brains in the next county.

Him still being too burnt up to talk civilly, Sheriff Twombley had Landis go and call the feds up at the cell number they'd left to report it. They surprised yet again by saying they'd be satisfied to take a look at the Sheriff's report on the incident after the fact, as they were busy observing the survivalist store.

Apparently, they were busy jerking each other off or praying to their Almighty Hoover when it burned down, the Sheriff would say. When Steve Goines, the local Park Ranger, reported the fire, they sent in the volunteer brigade, but the whole place was flattened, and nobody in sight to explain it to them. Minutes later, the Sheriff got a phone call telling them the situation was under control, and to proceed under his previous instructions. *Hunker down, Jim, suck that dick.*

This morning had gotten off a little less eventfully than the one before, but not by much. Kenny Landis had been awakened not by the shrill beeping of his cheap alarm clock but by a rumble deep within the earth, like a subterranean freight train trying to force its way to the surface, and a pummeling rain of Louis L'Amour paperbacks from the shelves above his head. Landis had leapt out of bed and braced himself in the doorway of his trailer, feeling like an idiot, because the tremor'd subsided right then and there, and then his alarm went off, as if he might've slept through the quake. The radio called it a minor tremor epicentered in the Owens Valley, some seventy miles away. No fatalities, no major injuries even, just a lot of folks dumped out of bed with a few minutes lost sleep and their refrigerators' contents all shook up and busted. A religious man might take to believing these were the last days, indeed, if a streak like this kept up.

Now, Landis and Asaro sat in the front office at their respective desks, looking at each other every once in awhile and listening to Sheriff Twombley winding into another cursing fit in his office. The twenty-four hours the federal agents had demanded were just about up, and the Sheriff was trying to decide whom to call first.

Landis had ten bucks said Twombley was going to call the FBI, work his way up the chain of command, burning the ears off everyone from the Barstow office to the Director. Asaro reckoned he'd call the press first, either the *Los Angeles Times* or the *Las Vegas Journal*, to make sure the whole affair didn't get buried under a government gag order. But so far, he hadn't called anybody, just sat there at his desk swearing his head off, like he couldn't do anything else. Landis picked up enough of the Sheriff's ranting to understand that he didn't want to go off half-cocked and end up looking the fool, because all he had was the feds' say-so that any crimes had been committed, and said feds hadn't kicked down with enough information to make a plausible dimestore yarn, let alone an account of conspiracy.

"Side bet," Landis said in a stage whisper. "Sheriff's gonna come out and tell us to clear outta here in a few minutes. Side-side bet, he calls us 'goldbrickin' bastards' at least once."

"Not takin' that bet, Kenny," Asaro answered, and stood up, adjusting his Sam Browne belt with his thumbs to let his belly settle. "'Bout time one of us hit the road, anyway. Rate this place's been tearing itself apart, there's bound to be something brewing somewhere we ought to be on top of." He picked up his hat and checked his gun. Landis took special notice of that, because he hadn't seen Sammy do that but one or two times before, when there was clear and present trouble around the corner. Sheriff Twombley was a certified high-power rifle marksman and a bully pulpitbanger for the NRA, but both deputies held the unspoken opinion that guns were dangerous, and once they entered the picture things went downhill fast so far as control was concerned.

"What're you fixin' to do, Sammy?" Landis asked.

Asaro strolled round to the door and put his hand against it. When he turned back to look at Landis, all the native playfulness was drained out of his face. "Sheriff's chewing his own ass off about this thing. I'm going out to Thermopylae to see if there's still G-men around."

"Maybe I oughta go with you, then. Maybe we all oughta go," nodding toward Twombley's door.

Asaro shook his head. He didn't have to say what he thought of bringing Twombley back out there. The Sheriff was spooked, and they didn't want to put him in the position where he'd come away again looking like he did yesterday. "Just gonna look, is all. I'll call you if they're still there." He started to push open the door, then stopped. "Wait a little bit before you tell Jim, won't you?"

"Sure, buddy. Stay out of trouble, alright?" Landis stashed his book, *The End Of The Drive*, where Twombley wouldn't notice it if he came out.

"You try to stay awake, now, y'hear?" Asaro smiled and waved and walked out.

Landis heard Asaro's cruiser pull out of the front parking lot with a crunch and spray of gravel. Landis went over and turned up the radio. He'd wait four, no, six songs and then he'd go in and tell Sheriff Twombley about Asaro. He picked up a Las Vegas western station, KOWW, all Cowboy Classics. The lazy, ghostly strains of "Driftin' Along With The Tumblin' Tumbleweeds" ambled out of the speakers. Truth to tell, while Deputy Landis liked the lifestyle, he actually hated cowboy shit, hated L'Amour and Zane Gray and *Shane* and all that bygone redneck crap. His tastes ran more to Grisham and classic rock, but the Sheriff wouldn't tolerate any "lawyer" books or "hippie" music, and Landis was bright enough to sacrifice his own tastes to understand which way the boss would jump.

Landis did feel a mite sleepy. He was just going back to his desk, thinking about a catnap, when he saw a truck come up the main drag in one hell of a hurry. He recognized it from the morning before, when they'd been standing around on the sidelines in Thermopylae, although he'd seen it countless times before. Big black Ford F-350 with a rollbar with shielded hi-beam lights on it, belonged to Zane Storch, acting owner of Sgt. Storch's Quartermaster Supply and son of the original Sgt. Storch, who was weaving baskets in Stockton or Mendocino, or somewhere. The man the G-men said was not to be arrested, although his store was chockful of guns and explosives.

The truck braked hard and skidded a bit as it came off the road and stopped in the gravel just out front. The door opened and a big man climbed out and approached the door.

"Well, I'll be," Landis murmured. "I think we're fixin' to find out what's going on around here, at last. Hey, Sheriff, come out here!" he yelled.

"What is it? I'm busy, goddamit! Why don't you get out on the road, you goldbricking bastards?"

"Sheriff! Get out here! It's Storch! He's here!"

The Sheriff threw open his door and charged out into the front office. He'd been waxing his mustache, and was only halfway through. One end curled up into a spiral that would've shamed Salvador Dali, while the other still dangled limply down past his jawline: half Wyatt Earp, half Fu Manchu. Twombley wasn't a vain man, but he had a thing about his grandiose handlebar mustache, which Landis, in his early days on the job, thought looked like the Sheriff's nose had trapped and half-inhaled a great big gray bat. "Been tryin' to get the FBI office in LA for most of an hour. Goddammed long-distance lines're all out—Shit, it is him."

Twombley joined Landis at the front desk, the two of them looking less like law enforcement and more like the manager and bellhop of a really, really lonely motel, about to get their first customer in a long time.

Storch was dressed up in that brown desert camo gear that everybody wore in Desert Storm, the kind the soldiers called chocolate-chip suits, and he carried a duffel bag slung over one shoulder. He reached for the door and stepped in and just stood there, not saying anything, not moving, just looking at them like they knew well enough what this was all about.

"Mornin', Mr. Storch," Sheriff Twombley said, tweedling the limp end of his mustache, his tone a little hesitant for Landis's taste. He didn't exactly worship the Sheriff or anything, but he certainly didn't like to hear his boss and the head lawman in Death Valley go all quavery in the presence of this man, who may be the key or the cause of all their troubles. Landis's hands couldn't seem to decide where they wanted to go.

They'd all known this fella for years, seen him pass through town, pick up supplies—hell, they'd bought things from him themselves more than a few times. He had a reputation as a hermit, a bit twitchy because of Gulf War Syndrome, which may or may not have been a real illness, but he was a decorated soldier who'd fought in the Gulf War, for chrissakes, he wasn't a troublemaker, and he sure wasn't some militia nut. But he still said nothing, just stood there.

"You come to tell us what the hell's been going on, Storch?" Twombley said, his voice striking sparks now. "We sure are hungry for some answers…"

Storch's grim expression gave way to a smile and his eyes rolled in an *Oh, have I got a story to tell you* gesture. And that's when Storch's duffel bag fell away and they were looking down the barrel of a Heckler-Koch MP5 assault rifle. Landis recognized it from *Soldier Of Fortune* as the weapon of choice of special forces groups the world over, because of its light, short design, ideal for close quarters wetwork. A real nice gun, Landis thought, his eyes glued to it, real nice, but why Storch'd be showing to them like this—

"Didn't I tell you what would happen if you tried to call?" Storch asked, and Landis thought his voice sounded wrong; not strange in and of itself, but not Storch's voice, either.

Sheriff Twombley reacted as if the words were dry ice down his back. "You're not—naw, you're not—"

The Sheriff was going for his own gun, but certified master marksman though he was, he couldn't reach it from where he was standing. It hung on the back of his chair in his office, because the belt chafed him. His trembling, empty hand came back up and covered his heart and just hung there, and Landis watched as the gun pinned the hand to his chest, watched as it drilled his boss full of more holes than the Panamint Range had in it. Jim Twombley took flight, moving faster in death than he ever had in his life, slamming into Landis's desk and sprawling across it.

Landis himself was still just watching, still just looking at the fancy German assault rifle, because this couldn't be real, he was still asleep beneath a shelf of neatly alphabetized Louis L'Amour paperbacks, and any minute that damnable alarm clock was going to awaken him into a world where Sheriff Jim Twombley was alive and unperforated, a world without earthquakes and fires and hinky suicides and shadowy federal conspiracies and crazed, homicidal veterans. He hoped so, he hoped so with all his might, because he could see the gun looking him in the eye now, see the starburst muzzle-flash like a little Big Bang, a flashy period at the end of his incomplete life sentence, could see the bullets emerging from it like hornets, on their very short trip to his heart.

Deputy Kenny Landis closed his eyes. He didn't wake up.

~ 9 ~

Driving back to Hansen's, Storch saw something that somehow freaked him out more than anything else that had happened that day. He was doing ninety, riding the tidal surges of the road like a ship at sea, the humps of tarmac merging with rolling waves of quicksilver fata morgana. Every so often he rose to a crest on the highway and glimpsed another truck, an RV or a semi coming towards him before he slipped into a trough. At the next crest, the stranger was a little larger, then still larger until it roared past.

Storch must have been running out of sync with the truck that was coming from the direction of Furnace Creek, because he didn't see it until he was charging down to meet it at the bottom of a trough and it filled his windshield, riding the center line at over one twenty. It was a black Ford F-350 just like his, and for a split second, he thought he was driving into a mirage, a trick of the heat haze making a mirror of an updraft under the punishing midday Death Valley sun.

Then its horn sounded, and Storch heeled the truck over into a controlled skid that went awry when he saw what looked like himself driving the other Ford. His truck slid off the road and bit into the washboard sand of the shoulder. The truck juddered and jolted but stayed more or less parallel to the road. His hands fought for control as he risked another look over his shoulder at the shrinking truck's license plate. It was his.

He stood on the brakes and jumped back onto the road, started to whip the truck around in a one-eighty. He was just crossing the center line when a police cruiser crested the hump above him fast enough to catch air off of it. Sparks flew off its chassis as it touched down one hundred feet away and bore down on him. His gas foot seemed to be stuck, the truck seeming to coast into the path of the oncoming cruiser as if that was the whole plan. The deputy's jaw dropped as he took in the twin trucks, one speeding away, one heeled across the highway in his path. Storch jammed his foot down on the gas and bolted across the road onto the opposite shoulder and into a stand of yucca bushes as the police cruiser flew past, then a Highway Patrol car, then another, then two more.

Faces turned to look at the towering pillar of dust that enveloped Storch's truck. For all they knew, he was a dust devil, and they went on after his...doppelganger? He gave Furnace Creek a wide berth on the way back to Hansen's.

Storch found no one waiting to welcome him back when he returned to Hansen's mineshaft. An iron gate covered the mouth of the cave, all heavy bars and reinforced pistons. Knowing he could blow it up if it came to that was no comfort. Hansen had some sort of change of heart, either because of the corpse or because of something that happened during his absence, something involving the very high profile flight of a fugitive matching his description from Furnace Creek. The day hadn't yet gotten so weird that Storch doubted that he was who his driver's license said he was, but he knew he'd have his work cut out for him trying to convince anyone else. He knew he had only Hansen's natural paranoia working in his favor. When he thought about it, he couldn't think of anything Hansen wouldn't be likely to believe.

A crackling voice from just inside the cave relieved him of the fear.

"You've been busy."

"I'm having the weirdest day of my life back-to-back with the second weirdest, Hiram. Don't test me."

"Twombley was a yellow-bellied old tool, but he wasn't an especially bad man."

"What? What the fuck are you talking about? What am I supposed to've done now?"

"You really want to know?"

"Just spill it."

"I was listening to the radio. The news says you went postal and killed Pop Sickle and burned down your own store, then shot Sheriff Twombley and Kenny Landis in Furnace Creek, then fled."

"They catch me?"

"Nope. You lost them just short of the state line, near Funeral. Area police, highway patrol and the FBI are putting together the biggest manhunt in the state since Andrew Cunannan."

"Nothing about the raid on my store. Nothing about the feds."

"It was all you, Zane. You're a fugitive nobody wants taken alive."

"What did the news say about China Lake?"

"What, the Naval Weapons dump? Not a thing. Why d'you ask?"

"Nothing, I guess. You gonna let me in, or what?"

A buzz of electricity so faint that Storch hadn't noticed it until it cut out, and a bolt shot with a clack that echoed down the mineshaft. The gate swung open.

Storch followed the blinking lights to Hansen's lounge/waiting room and collapsed on a sprung couch in the center of the cavern. Hansen sat at a bar of lacquered bamboo and white leather, sipping a mint julep. Storch hunched over and clamped his hands over his head so tightly he thought he could hear the sutures of his skull grinding against each other.

"You didn't kill the Sheriff."

"Nope."

"You didn't kill anybody."

"I didn't say that. I just said I didn't go to Furnace Creek, and I sure as shit didn't kill Jim Twombley."

"They were pretty sure about it."

"I just saw somebody in a truck just like mine leaving Furnace Creek on the 395 with state troopers in hot pursuit."

"Then it seems to me you're in a world of shit, Lee Harvey."

"Why in hell would anybody take so much trouble to frame me for this? Why don't they just kill me?"

"Same reason somebody burned your store, I suppose. Get you running. Maybe see where you run to."

"That's so fucking stupid."

"There's more."

"There's always more. What?"

"There was an earthquake out towards Convict Lake just before dawn. Your faultline yawned and ate a big chunk of your rest stop. Place you found the girl isn't there, anymore. Scared yet?"

Storch sat looking off into space until his eyes began to burn because he hadn't blinked. "It's not so much being wanted, or having no life left that scares me. What gets me is that I still can't accept any of this shit, because it means I'm trapped in my dad's fucked up vision of the world. I'm going insane, Hiram. I'm losing my fucking mind, just like my dad."

"You're not losing anything that's worth holding on to. Your expectations that one day will be like the next, and that you can skate by doing the bare minimum to stay afloat. You've been in a war. Shit, you've fought in secret wars, the ones nobody will ever know even happened. You know how fast the terrain changes."

"But the war made sense." He thought about the Headache. What he could remember about the war, he didn't like to think about. He didn't want to talk about the war anymore.

"This is a war, too. And the only reason you haven't seen it on the TV, or heard about it from Harley or me before now is that it's too important for the world to know about. Only those who are fit for the struggle can take up the cause, and they have to find out in their own way."

"Maybe my father might not have been such a nut after all." The statement was half a question, Storch letting out a whiff of the uncertainty he'd buried so deep so long ago he didn't know the sound of his own voice when he heard it.

"Zane, the world isn't what you thought it was yesterday, but your father was still crazier than a shithouse rat."

Almost an hour passed in silence, Storch poured into a mildewy beanbag, trying to map out the alien terrain of his new life, Hansen puttering around him, dusting and reordering. Storch looked around the cavern without seeing, not wanting to close his eyes, because he was starting to see the faces of the people he killed this morning—sociopathic scumbags killed in self-defense, but still they haunted him.

How many people have you killed in your life, Zane?

Seven confirmed kills in the Gulf War, eighteen in other black ops that the world would never know about. None of those men—soldiers defending their homelands and families—had ever troubled his sleep. Why did he still hear Gina shrieking at him when he closed his eyes?

But like, you get used to it—

Because he hadn't taken a life in nearly a decade, and because all those other deaths were on Uncle Sam's head, not his. Sgt. Storch had had *plausible deniability*, he was *only following orders*. Right or wrong, those four dead skin traders were *his* kills, killed by what amounted to one part restlessness and two parts stupid dumb luck. He was not an instrument of Hammurabi's Code or the great karmic cycle or any of that, he was a spooked, terrified man whose world was falling apart. The only difference between him and any other man who snapped when his world fell apart was he could efficiently execute people. Storch found himself watching Hansen for far too long before he snapped to and asked, "What about the girl?"

"The girl?" His fatuous smile was wormy with sincerity.

"You know? Sidra Sperling? The dead girl?" What the hell, was he trying to pretend Storch was insane in hopes he'd forget, and he'd be able to keep her?

"Ah yes, yes. I've never seen anything quite like it. Turns out my earlier diagnosis was somewhat premature, yes."

"Premature how? You mean she wasn't tortured, or she's not the girl from the milk carton?"

"Oh, there's no doubt in my mind about that. But she wasn't raped, no, no, no. Opened up, certainly, but not tortured."

"What's the difference?"

"She died in childbirth, is what it looks like. Her pelvis was wrenched outwards, her cervix and vaginal canal were obliterated, her lower vertebral disks were pulverized, and the perineum was surgically incised from the vagina to the rectum, even her floating ribs were broken off. Her blood was inundated with hormones, but there was no trace of any of the common sedatives. Someone cut the bottom out of her to accommodate a birth, Zane, and the fetus was of such prodigious size that it took her life, if the procedure itself didn't." He cast an awestruck gaze at the privacy curtain encircling the examination table. "How proud she must have been."

"What do you know about Radiant Dawn? Hiram?"

The hermit snapped out of his reverie and turned a quizzical face on Storch. This time, at least, his puzzlement seemed genuine. "What?"

"Harley said something about a group called Radiant Dawn. That's who he said they were fighting against."

"Who was fighting against?"

"I don't know. I don't know anything."

"Try to sleep."

Storch nodded feebly. The aching of his limbs and the leaden fatigue in his head would no longer be ignored. He looked around for something resembling a guest room. Hansen got up and fetched a kerosene lantern from a hook in the wall, and led him through a curtain of hanging beads, down a lightless, unadorned cavern. Thirty feet from the curtain, Storch made out the shape of a deluxe camper shell on an old Chevy pickup. Beyond it, stretching into the darkness, was a line of vehicles of every description, parked nose to bumper as if waiting to pass through a tollbooth: pacing down the line, Storch saw a Nash Rambler, a Chevy minivan, a '62 Chrysler Imperial, a tow truck, an AMC Pacer, an ancient police cruiser from Pahrump Nevada, a Mexican Highway Patrol car peppered with buckshot holes, a Honda Odyssey minidunebuggy, and a world war two surplus amphibious "duck" truck before Hansen called him back. The back door of the camper was open, and Hansen was unrolling a sleeping bag on the fold-out bed in the kitchenette. "You'd be more comfortable here than anywhere else I have…I keep odd hours."

"Where'd you get all these?"

"I got a few at police auctions, but most of them I just found abandoned, in perfect working order, out in the middle of the desert. Some get killed by drifters, and I take those, but they're nothing special. But alot of other times, people leave them there with a suicide note, claiming they're going out to shoot themselves where nobody'll ever find them, or throw themselves into a mine shaft. More than half of them, they slip onto a Greyhound at a rest stop or hitch a ride on a semi, and start over again. The Golden Gate Bridge is the most popular spot, but Death Valley would run a close second if not for people like me. Collectors. People say the American dream is to own a house or a business, or whatever, they're wrong, or they're deluding themselves. The American dream is and always has been to shed your old life and start a new one somewhere else. Go to sleep, Zane."

~ 10 ~

As a child, Martin Cundieffe's secret vices were two and he spoke of them only in prayers. The first was people watching, which wasn't a vice in any sense except for its intensity. He was a snoop, nosy, a buttinski; but where other children earned reproofs for asking too many questions, Cundieffe merely stared, making mental notes in his earnest, childish fashion, on every observable aspect of human behavior. He might've picked up this habit in imitation of his father—who'd served under Hoover as SAC of the Washington, D.C. listening post in the Old Post Office Building, in the days when every kid wanted to grow up to be Ephraim Zimbalist, Jr.—if his father had spent any time with his boy. Cundieffe was a firm believer in nature over nurture, and apologized to God every night with the caveat that snooping and secret-lust ran in his blood, and he hoped it was okay, if it made him a better agent.

His second vice was that he liked to stir up anthills. He never intentionally killed a single ant, goodness no, he meant them no harm. But he would lose himself for hours in the backyard, watching them tirelessly repair the methodical damage he wreaked upon them with a tiny twig or a little water. The way the nest came to life to undo chaos filled him with a sublime sense of nature's master plan, of individuals and societies as machines for preserving order, that saw him through his difficult and lonely childhood, and made him the agent he was today. It'd been widely acknowledged throughout the Bureau that he was a very good agent indeed—better than his father, in fact. When Mother passed on and no longer needed him, he'd been told, he'd be welcome at Headquarters or at the Academy in Quantico.

Thus it was that Cundieffe hadn't been able to go home after the briefing, indeed hadn't been able to so much as sit still since he'd left Assistant Director Wyler. He did his work at an optimum efficiency even as the rest of the field office churned and buzzed like a breached ant nest, wrangling with the rapidly snowballing crisis in the desert.

Lane Hunt had come back from Riverside as soon as he completed his stakeout and jumped on the case with both feet, but his attitude, Cundieffe had to conclude, wasn't nearly as sunny or can-do as his own. As he'd gone over the summary Wyler'd left for him before jetting back to Washington, he'd chugged piping hot coffee and chanted "Fuck" over and over again, as if he were venting off the steam building up between his ears. Cundieffe tried to keep his poise; even with his rather limited experience in the field, he'd heard foul language often enough, but it rankled him to hear such a word out of the mouth of another FBI man. His father, who never drank coffee even at home because Hoover thought it bad form for his men to ingest any sort of drug, never once used that word, Cundieffe knew.

When he was done reading and blaspheming, SA Hunt had looked at Cundieffe with that patronizing expression he knew of old, from school days. The strong, not-too-bright boy looks that way at the class bookworm who's going to do his homework for him if he doesn't want to get stuffed into a locker. Cundieffe knew Hunt was a good agent who carried his weight, but he also knew his own use to the Domestic Counterterrorism Section began and ended with research and more research, and that was what he was going to do.

He'd reviewed and collated his files all day long, while the rest of the office milled around, spreading rumors, waiting like fans of a secret sports team, awaiting the outcome of a championship match that would never be televised: The FBI vs. the Navy in the White House.

More than a few times, Cundieffe had solved a case from his desk, telephoning Hunt and the others with the answer like a bright child with a Junior Jumble solution, while they were still out chasing themselves in the field. He simply dumped out all the data he could lay hands on from the region in question: dossiers on the relevant parties, police and news reports, applications for firearms and explosives, local newspapers. Taken as a whole, they were a junkpile of tangents and random trivia, but each piece, observed keenly and without prejudice, could point the way to the next and betray the hand of its author.

First, Cundieffe reviewed police reports and sundry other data from the Mojave area. Military materials would be a few hours coming, as clearances were obtained and turf wars waged. It had been a busy week, just counting the items forwarded to the resident agency office in

Victorville. Four telephoned complaints were filed, all anonymously, about a raid by "agents of the New World Order" on the unincorporated town of Thermopylae, near Furnace Creek in Death Valley. All of the accounts varied in detail and would be consigned to the kook file, but Cundieffe smelled something significant in them that all the other hands the reports had passed through had not. The squatter community of Thermopylae had been referenced in Cundieffe's database time and again as a possible temporary haven for disgruntled anti-government misanthropes, and had been observed a few times as closely as the FBI dared in years past, but without conclusive results. In Cundieffe's estimation, the people of Thermopylae were fellow travelers and inveterate Internet ranters, but hardly a threat to anyone but themselves. The reports might be a prank or mass hysteria, and had been judged as such by the agent in Victorville who took the reports, because no such action had been undertaken by any government agency. But look again. They coincided in a few details: that one unidentified man was shot in the back while attempting to flee, and that a cache of weapons was seized, but no arrests made. Shortly thereafter, the embattled store burned to the ground, cause unknown. Beyond that, the stories all digressed into individual hysteria, and couldn't agree on which government agency had staged the alleged raid. A follow-up check by the Victorville agent with the Furnace Creek Sheriff's office had turned up nothing, because no one had answered the phone. Another report on Cundieffe's desk posited a logical reason for this: an earth tremor localized in the Inyokern area of the Owens Valley had caused some structural damage in Furnace Creek, and they were probably out putting things back together.

Cundieffe leaned back in his chair and laced his hands behind his heavy head. Lane was probably already at China Lake with a forensics team by now. The evidence turned over to them by the Navy wasn't terribly promising; the audio tape which contained the coded security transmissions that'd granted the thieves access to the base, and a tiny pool of chewing tobacco juice on the landing deck where the rogue helicopters had landed. Hunt had control issues, and was prone to fly off the handle when he felt he wasn't getting full cooperation, or when his investigations butted heads with other agencies. Even if AD Wyler toughed out the turf war with the Navy, Cundieffe thought, Hunt probably wouldn't be able to hold onto the case after today. He hoped he would be kept on himself, at least long enough for Wyler to give him that security clearance. New files to read, new mysteries to plumb.

His phone trilled, the blinking light above the section's intra-agency line. Cundieffe looked around the office, saw no one else reaching for it. He picked it up. "Counterterrorism, Special Agent Cundieffe here."

"Agent Munoz in Victorville, here. Lane Hunt around?"

"No, Special Agent Hunt is on assignment. Can I relay a message?"

"I'd like to talk to him myself, if you can locate him for me. We've got a situation in Furnace Creek, and I think his expertise may come in handy. Understand he's got a hell of a database on militia activities."

Furnace Creek? *Hunt's* database? Cundieffe felt two or three almost irresistible urges to use foul language hit him at once. "Actually, I'm the primary agent in charge of our background database. If there's some checking you require—"

"We've had a double homicide. Local named Zane Storch burned down his place of business and shot up the Sheriff and a deputy a few hours ago. He's a fugitive. Probably a solo nut, but after interviewing a few people in town, we decided to give you a call."

Cundieffe printed out the name Munoz'd given him at the top of his yellow legal pad in block capitals. "Any reason you think we could help?" he asked.

"Well, to hear them tell it, Storch is a paramilitary nut—ran a survivalist supply store in a squatter community called Thermopylae—"

Cundieffe sucked in air through his teeth, felt a mild cold sting in his left lower rear molar. A cavity, maybe. "I've heard of it."

"And he was a Green Beret some years back, got sick in Desert Storm. Not all there, people said. Anyway, Storch pulled up in his truck, went in and shot the two of them cold. The other deputy was on his way out, but saw Storch leaving the office and came in after him. He notified the Highway Patrol and the Sheriff's in Darwin, and pursued him. They lost him on dirt roads just short of the Nevada line, and have asked us to cooperate in his capture. Just thought you could tell us if the guy had any past associations with militia groups in the area, you know, people who might be hiding him."

Cundieffe tapped his pen on the paper, making circles within circles around Storch's name. "Tell you what, Agent Munoz," he said, "I'll do a search in just a few minutes, and we'll get something faxed over to you in about a quarter hour. Sound good?"

"Sure. Probably nothing, but you have to cover all the bases, you know?"

"Right, right. I'll give you a call just before I send anything I have over to you."

Cundieffe hung up with one hand and riffled through his Rol-A-Dex with the other. Suddenly, he felt in his mind that he did have all the pieces he needed, now. In his gut, however, he began to wonder how many puzzles he was really trying to put together.

He pulled out the new card for the direct line to Wyler's office at headquarters. He didn't expect the Assistant Director to be in, and he wasn't disappointed. Wyler's machine was succinct, if a little unprofessional. "Gimme the bad news," it said, and beeped.

"Chief, this is Special Agent Martin Cundieffe, from Los Angeles? You'll recall we spoke this morning about—" *Bring it home, Marty.* "Well, I think I have a related case that could provide us with a break in the China Lake affair."

A plastic clatter and a hoot of feedback, then a voice said, "Agent Cundieffe? Don't hang up."

"Yes, sir, I'm still here. I've got—"

"This is Deputy Assistant Director Warden. Agent Cundieffe, Assistant Director Wyler's still in conference, but he left me a message to forward to you."

"I'm listening, sir."

"The LA field office is off the investigation. Your people are about to get the call, in ten, maybe fifteen minutes. Lane Hunt's team is already packing up."

His chest tightened and he forgot to breathe. His assignment. His clearance. His rapport with Assistant Director Wyler. Gone. "I don't understand, sir. Why are they taking this away from us?"

"The Navy pushed its suit with the President, and he's listening to them. This is to be treated as a military affair, at least until the contraband is located. The FBI has been explicitly tasked to offer support and intelligence only, to issue from headquarters. Is that clear?"

The chill in Cundieffe's molar seemed to eat its way out of his mouth and engulf his whole head. As a Special Agent of the FBI, Martin Cundieffe thrived on the warm glow of unearthing truth, of unraveling conspiracies and flushing liars. Lies made him cringe. Lies hurt. He'd never thought he'd have to sit and listen while a fellow FBI agent, let alone a superior, lied to him. His jaw clenched, the cold sparking blue pain-telegrams down his spine. Through the pain and his cold, cold anger, he kept seeing Sibley the CIA man stuttering into his cell phone, and knew the case had ceased to be theirs, his, in any meaningful fashion then.

"Clear, sir."

"Assistant Director Wyler would like a detailed report of all your actions on the matter up until now forwarded to this office as soon as possible. And he said one more thing."

"What was that...sir?"

"'Keep doing your homework,' is what he said. That's all. Do you have any more questions?" His voice was strained, wrung-out, no more answers.

"No, sir. Thank you for telling me. I'll commence on that report immediately."

"Good." Warden rang off. Cundieffe set down the phone and scanned the office. Everyone still running around, dancing like headless chickens in the minutes before they realize they're dead. *Strike that last,* he thought. *That's no way to think about your coworkers.*

The Navy had come to them, spilled the bizarre details of their appalling failure on them, and now the Navy was taking it away to handle on its own. The clumsiness of it all made it seem almost too stupid to be entertained. Clearly, the Navy didn't want or even understand the case, if there was a case to begin with. *Either Rear Admiral Meinsen misstepped when he brought us in, or they let us in only to get access to our database right away, and figured they could keep us quiet.* Would Rear Admiral Meinsen get a paddling for his indiscretion? Would there be any visible outcome at all?

The possibility that it'd been a military exercise all along loomed large in Cundieffe's view. *They didn't tell us because we were part of the test. They kept Rear Admiral Meinsen out of the loop to see how he'd dump it in our laps, and how we'd react. That was the most plausible explanation; that would be the official story if this ever got out.*

And Martin Cundieffe, who'd never been able to walk away from an unfinished puzzle or an unrepaired anthill, placed a call to the Military Records division of the National Archives.

~ 11 ~

The message light on Stella Orozco's answering machine was blinking when she came in from work. A full shift riding along in the ambulance, covering for a paramedic who'd broken his ankle grass skiing; three calls and endless hours fending off the driver—but three hours passed before she took notice. After showering, fixing herself dinner—a tossed salad with fresh tomatoes from her pocket garden, salmon and steamed rice—she cleaned her apartment and read for an hour in the bath. So long as she was doing something, living in her hands and head and not her heart, she wouldn't cry. There would be time enough to cry when she could no longer work.

At ten o'clock she went round the apartment, switching off lights, prepping the coffee maker, and double-checking her alarm, when the blinking light registered. She realized then that she'd noticed it when she came in, and tuned it out. Often enough, it was an especially pushy automated telemarketer, or a too-distant relative from Mexico looking for a place to stay, or Thor the ambulance driver, who was only two years her junior, yet wore full dentures, because his motormouth had so annoyed someone once they'd kicked all the teeth out of it; Thor who supposed that if he got drunk, took his dentures out and whispered sweet lovetalk into her answering machine enough times, she'd make his Penthouse Forum fantasies come true. Work would've paged her. She listened to the first few seconds, then stopped it, her finger on the ERASE button, when the strange, stammering voice she heard sank in.

"—one that called in about that fella, you know, uh, the one from the accident. We talked about it some, you 'member, and you seemed real honest, like, and like maybe a fella could trust you. If'n that's true, well…I found somethin' the hospital's gonna want, but I ain't about to call 'em again, you understand. I, uh…found somethin' the fella lost. I got…somethin' what belonged on him. This is stupid, I gotta…My number's, um…just star-six-nine me, and…um…Call me, if'n I can still trust you, and if you can 'member my name. Thank you, ma'am, I hope I haven't been a bother." This last part sounded muffled, as if the man were slamming down the phone in mid-sentence. He was guilt-ridden and fearful, yet he'd called her. Because he'd found something he couldn't throw away or turn in to the police.

Somethin' what belonged on *him*

But she'd seen him there, intact, whole—and possibly standing.

Seth Napier, the name came back.

She didn't call Napier. She called directory assistance and, using the ambulance creds, got his address. Then she called Wenda, the ambulance despatcher, and promised to cover a weekend shift if she'd look up the address of where Stephen was picked up. There was no proper address, just a rough description, but it was less than a quarter mile from Napier's house, or at least his postal box. Whatever he'd found, or thought he'd found, he'd sounded as if he'd changed his mind about telling her midway through his message. A nagging doubt about the hermit, and the whole improbability of it all, told her to bring her gun.

She was dressed and in her car in five minutes.

It took almost an hour to find the place. It was halfway to Big Pine, at an unmarked turnoff from the highway that simply wandered off into the woods behind a Bigg Piney gas station. Stella drove slowly for fear of missing it, homeward-bound tourists blasting past her, leaning on their horns. When she found it, she saw she needn't have bothered.

After the drive through the pre-moonrise blackness, under the naked starlight, radiant dust that illuminated only itself, the gas station was an alien eyesore. Steeped in a grotesque orange sodium glow that seemed to be some kind of nature repellent, a gigantic Winnebago and a Sentra full of sleeping college students draining its petroleum teats, the gas station made her wonder for perhaps the first time in her life how animals perceived human structures. The Winnebago lumbered away as she pulled into the lot.

Stella walked in to ask for directions, noticing on the way the pay phone and the row of battered mailboxes at the edge of the lot. The walls behind the counter were crowded from floor to ceiling with mounted deer heads, a forest of accusing antlers and incurious glass eyes. It took a moment to discern the cashier's mulish face peering over the counter. He knelt on the floor before the safe, which stood open. His hand went behind the cashbox and brought a revolver into view.

"I'm not a deer," Stella said.

"Yeah," he said, still gripping the gun, breathing hard. Cranked up on meth. LESTER, said his nametag. "Ought not sneak up on a man like that."

"I'm looking for Seth Napier? He lives on an old logging road near here, by the railroad tracks?"

Lester appeared to think about it a bit, or maybe he was just thinking about the gun some more. Finally, he came back and smiled much too much. "Yeah, hobo kind of guy, always buys Red Man by the box, last friday of every month." He stood and came around the counter. "He's in trouble, right?"

Stella stood her ground, dropping her arm and twirling her purse behind her back. It was only a simple, teardrop-shaped canvas sack with her pocketbook and pager, and a few bottles of prescription medications and ibuprofen, but she'd thrown in her .22 revolver and two speed-loaders for heft. "Is his house back there? Behind your station, in the woods?"

"Yeah," Lester said, looking at the gun as if he could hear it speaking. "In the woods. 'Bout a half-mile. Bunch of other cabins and trailers and shit back there, but he's the only one left."

Stella backing towards the door now. "Thanks a lot, Lester. Thanks a whole bunch, okay?" Turning away from his too-wide smile only when she got outside, running back to her car, getting in, loading the gun.

The road was dirt, of course, and hadn't been graded in decades. Knurled pine roots fanned out across the road like ribs, rocking the car on its rusty toy suspension, Nature's own speed bumps. Should she be watching out for booby traps? Beyond the range of her headlights pine trees loomed to either side of the road, pine trees and velvet blackness. Clearly, it'd been a long time since this road had been used for logging, if ever. She came to a fork after three tenths of a mile, and went right. The road immediately began to veer left, presumably arcing around to rejoin the driveway as the left fork. The pine trees parted and she saw two trailers, a silver Airstream and a fiberglass Chinook. Both had been crushed by a fallen tree. Some of the tree's limbs had been sawn off for firewood, and the trailers had both been ransacked, but she saw no sign of life. This could've happened years ago.

Cruising on, she saw a clapboard cabin with no ceiling, the front door standing open and a pea green Datsun pickup truck up on blocks in the living room. Beyond that, another motor home, in relatively good shape, the windows boarded up the door studded with four deadbolts—on the outside. As her car drew near, the trailer started rocking back and forth, roaring and snarling, rabid and starving. The trailer was an alarm, stuffed to bursting with dogs in a feeding frenzy. Stella noticed a chain running from the bottom of the kennel, trailing off into the woods. Nestled in the darkness into which it disappeared, she saw the pale will-o-wisp glow of a Bug Zapper lamp. She pulled her car as close as she could to the cabin, which stood off thirty feet from the clearing behind a screen of pine and willow trees, an old blue Chevy pickup out front. Watching the throbbing motorkennel, she slowly climbed out of the car, leaving the door hanging wide open, and began to walk towards the sunken porch of Seth Napier's cabin with one hand in her purse.

As horrible as the dogs' racket had been before, it was magnified now the car engine was off and her back was turned to it. It prickled her skin. It was hot. She had to tell herself it wasn't dog breath.

Halfway to the porch, the chain jerked taut.

She saw now that it ran up to a boarded window beside the front door. She saw a sliver of yellow light through the crack, saw a shadow pass across the light as the chain snapped again. Behind her, she heard the click of a lock, and the dogs were suddenly much, much louder.

She sprinted across the yard, gaining the porch in a few seconds. "Mr. Napier?" She screamed, trying to catch her breath as cramps knived her fluttering lungs. "It's me! Nurse Orozco, from the hospital! You called me! I'm outside! Please let me in! Call off your dogs!"

Her gun caught on something in her purse and wouldn't come free. She spun on her heel and saw the first dog, a misshapen gutter-mutt of pit bull-rottweilerish extraction, only twenty feet away and closing fast, with three more a few paces behind it. The dog's eyes were cloudy, rolled back in its knobby, hairless head, its muzzle bedizened with bloody foam.

Stella fired over their heads, and her purse exploded. The lead dog reared back as if to close with her on its hind legs, then recoiled, yipping in shocked pain as pills, spare change and fragments of Stella's beeper and a tumbling .22 slug rained down on it. The others crashed into it and tore at its flanks before it could hit the ground.

Stella turned and lunged for the door, noticing as she did the three Kwikset locks bored into the heavy pinewood door. *Oh shit*, she thought, *oh Jesus, I want to die of cancer…*

Die running, she thought, and seized the knob.

The doorknob turned in her hand and she fell through the doorway, into the light. She collapsed on a rug so filthy that plumes of dust shot up around her. Her first breath was mostly dog hair, and she gagged as her throat slammed shut. She kicked out at the door and heard it slam behind her, careening dog bodies pounding into it from outside.

When she caught her breath, she checked her gun and followed the chain across the living room, through a kitchenette, down a short hall, and into the back bedroom. There was no light here, and the light switch did nothing when she flicked at it. Still, she knew he was here. Breathing, regular, deeper than Carlsbad Caverns, smelling wet and meaty and—like death and new life.

"Mr. Napier?" Stella whispered, pointing the gun at the breathing, reaching around for the door behind her that opened on the closet, reaching into it, fumbling around, she found a string, and pulled it.

And the light came on.

Seth Napier lay sprawled across a bed, naked, half-covered by a woolen Army surplus blanket. His exposed flesh glistened, gelatinous, translucent, rumpled and bulging like an oversized wetsuit the color and texture of clotted rubber cement, or smegma. Napier's skin and probably most of the subcutaneous tissue beneath seemed to have spontaneously necrotized. The chain was wrapped several times around one wrist, cutting deep into it, and still twitched spasmodically on the floor.

Even as she watched, his face became almost unrecognizable. As his mouth worked, his features seemed to sag, sliding around on his head as if trying to rearrange themselves, or escape. Stella gasped and backed away, and Napier, his filmy eyes bulging out of tunnels of slime, reared up on the bed. The blanket fell away, and she saw it.

Embedded in the center of Napier's chest was a human hand, black and engorged with nearly luminous black-red blood. Like a piece of fruit suspended in Jell-O, it had almost sunken completely into Napier, and tendrils of violet radiated out from it like the first shoots of a virulent weed. The hand pulsated like a second heart, sending tremors shivering through Napier's dissolving body. He regarded Stella impassively for a moment, trembling, and started to climb off the bed.

Stella drew the gun and pointed it at him, the shredded remains of her purse still clinging to the barrel. "Stay back, Mr. Napier. I'm going to call for an ambulance." *Don't breathe*, she told herself. *Whatever it is, it's highly infectious. Whatever it is…*

Napier's eyes regarded her as if he were sinking into himself, succumbing to an inexorable pull that was dragging him so deep into his body he'd never see out of his own eyes again.

His sad, sick old eyes studied her, as if to engulf her image and take her with him wherever he was going. And then Seth Napier's eyes seemed to fill with smoke. And when they cleared, they were not brown anymore, but green.

And Seth Napier's face slid off.

Tearing like the skin of a rotting fruit bursting with the gases of its own corruption, the gray jelly split open along the lines of Napier's jaw, splattering on the dirty tile floor in sizzling chunks. Cloudy pus spewed out of the opening, perversely reminding Stella of a pregnant mother's water breaking at the beginning of labor. Underneath, clean white flesh peered out, shiny and elastic like the new skin beneath a scab. Napier's hands came up and tugged at the clinging shreds and ripped them away. Stella backed against the far wall, still holding her breath, the gun shaking as she made out the new face beneath the one Napier tore off.

It was Stephen.

His benevolent, blissful grin took her in, approved. He settled back onto the bed and folded his arms across his chest, as if he'd arrived from a very long journey and wanted to rest a spell. The outer shell of rotting flesh slid away even faster, melting, pooling in the folds of the sheets. Stella could not scream, could not run, because the only conclusion that made sense froze her to the spot.

Stephen's cancer infected Seth Napier. Remade him…into another Stephen. Perhaps it had already infected her.

Then Stephen's face contorted and his back arched like a galvanic current was going through him. His eyes, when they opened again, were the same color they'd turned in the hospital, steely gray.

"The Moon-Ladder," Stephen murmured.

Outside, the sounds of the dogs barking gave way to a thunderous chorus of gunfire. Automatic weapons bratted, turning the barks to agonized whines and howls.

Stella dropped to the ground and belly-crawled towards the front window, peered out through the hairline crack out into the yard. There were at least a dozen men in the yard, standing up from the beds of two monster pickup trucks, spraying the attack dogs with assault rifles. In moments, every one lay dead, most cut in half.

Then they climbed down. Several of them shouldered ungainly metal tanks in shoulder-harnesses, ignited cobalt flames off the metal hoses that came off the bottoms of them. Then they turned and fanned out to surround the cabin.

Stella lay down against the baseboards and reloaded her gun. What are you doing? You're going to die here unless you surrender. These people want Napier, not you. Give yourself up.

And die like a dog. No way.

Stella looked around, studying the warped hardwood floor for signs of a trapdoor leading to a crawlspace. She yanked on a filthy throw rug in the middle of the room. One leg of a recliner held it tacked down. She leaned back and put her whole weight into pulling it free. The recliner tipped over backwards with a resounding crash, knocking over a TV tray littered with empty whiskey bottles.

Under the throwrug, she made out a rectangle of raised boards.

In the bedroom, she heard rustling, followed by the whining creak of old nails pried free from boards. Flashlight beams stabbed through the cracks of a rear window. Two boards were ripped away, and her face was washed in blinding white light. Frantically, she scrambled over to the trapdoor and clawed at it. There was no visible handle, she couldn't make out a recess or a handhold or anything to lift it up. Another board was ripped away from the window, and she saw a black-gloved hand reach in and grab at the next one, working it free.

Stella brought the gun up. "Stop where you are, I have a gun—" she said, unconvinced herself by her quavering tone, "—I'll shoot." Will you?

A rifle barrel peeked in through the crack and sprayed the room. The sound was deafening. Stella leapt sideways, taking shelter behind the overturned recliner. She raised the gun over the chair and fired twice in the general direction of the window.

"Ow! Goddamit!" Someone shouted. "Gas!"

From behind her, a whoomp and a crash, and something burst through the front window-boards and clattered to the floor beside her.

Stella held her breath, pinching her nose shut and lying low. Clouds enveloped her, folding over her and taking her away from the awful place in which she'd just been getting used to the idea that she was going to die. It wasn't just tear gas either, oh no, Stella knew the distinctive flavor of teargas from the baddest of the bad old days down on the farm. Sure her eyes streamed like they were melting, and her stomach wrung itself out on the spot, hot salmon vomit splattering her knees and her trail boots, but she was also fading away and the sensation of her body was fast becoming a vicious rumor she'd rather not have heard about, and she was falling fast into sleep, or into death, and didn't care which.

Don't let this happen.

Like it matters, whether it happens now or in six months. Least this'll be quick. But still she held her breath, still she told herself, *I'm supposed to die of cancer—*

Her head was too heavy to keep off the floor, so she just let it go, followed it down. Down to the floor and she dropped like dead weight, and a floorboard cracked beneath her, it was rotted and her hand went right through the crack and waved in empty space. The crawlspace under the cabin.

Stella watched her body drag itself over the hole and press her face against it. The dank, moldy air of the crawlspace woke her up instantly.

Furiously, she pistoned her fists against the surrounding boards. She couldn't see, but she felt the pulpy chips against her arms and shoulders as she broke through both boards. She lunged into the gap, and with barely enough time to throw out an arm, she hit the dirt beneath the cabin so hard it knocked the wind back out of her. But she was out. Her arm was numb from the elbow down and she tasted blood from something she'd bitten through in her mouth, but she was out. *Thank you, God, I'm going to die of cancer after all*, she thought and tried to laugh.

After she gave up on that, she let sounds come in, and blinked the tears from her eyes. The first thing she noticed was the sound of a waterfall, it was roaring all around the cabin.

The crawlspace was open and empty, as far as she could tell. A few lines of lesser blackness from missing siding boards crisscrossed the dirt, but the light from the side directly before her was almost hurtful. It came from the truck parked out front. She peered out through a crack in the porch just beside the stairs, and saw she was only half-right.

The roaring was not water or wind, but fire. A man with a flamethrower stood in the front yard, hosing down the front of the house with flaming gasoline. The man wore a gasmask and dark brown combat fatigues, but Stella couldn't make out anything like a badge or other insignia of authority. They knew somehow about Stephen and Seth Napier, or why else just burn the house down, without even searching it? She wasn't part of this, she hadn't touched anything, but she was there, and they hadn't seemed too interested in checking for innocent bystanders. They were treating this like an epidemic, and if it was, then she knew, as any nurse would, that she'd probably been infected. *Then I'll turn myself in at the fucking hospital*, she thought.

Stella got up on all fours and crabwalked backwards towards the rear of the house. Even as she backed away, the porch collapsed with a cheery puff of flame. The fire spread through the rotten, termite-riddled wood in seconds, and the crawlspace began to fill with smoke. Her right hand stomped in something that was once a cat or an opossum and skidded through it so she lay down in it. She rolled over and retched bile and dog hair. Through her tears, she saw too-bright firelight through the slats on both faces of the house, and spreading. They were circling around it.

She scrambled the rest of the way across the crawlspace in three bounds and seized two slats, yanked as hard as she could and they came loose with a whining protest of rusty nails. She threw herself into the crack, her head sticking out into the clear, clean night, the darkness and safety of the woods just beyond her arm's reach. She wrenched her body sideways, the jagged corners of the neighboring slats tearing at her back and breasts. She dug her feet into the moldy dirt and kicked and the slats snapped and she spilled out onto a carpet of pine needles and fresh forest air that was only beginning to reek of burning. She staggered to her feet and took a step towards the forest, one step, and she was pinned to the spot by cold white flashlight beams and the roiling orange glow of idling flamethrowers. There were four men, two on each flank, and the flashlights were taped to the barrels of stubby submachine guns.

Stella threw herself down on her knees and laced her hands over her head. "I surrender, goddamit I didn't touch a fucking thing in there don't you dare fucking burn me you Nazi *puto* motherfuckers I'm not dying like this—"

The soldiers closed in on her with their weapons leveled. "Bravo Charlie, Bravo one-three," one of them said in flat headset monotone, "have possible second subject, please advise." No one spoke for a moment, then the same man said, "roger that," and he shouldered his own rifle, painted a laser dot on her forehead.

Stella threw her arms wide to show them she was unarmed, but that only seemed to make them more nervous. One of the flamethrowers splashed hot death across the forest floor just inches short of her, and she leapt back. Her face seared and eyebrows turned to ash. Incredibly, no one else fired just then. They seemed to be trying to do it, but they couldn't quite bring themselves to shoot, like they were waiting for her to give them a reason. Like they were maybe a little bit afraid of *her*.

She was about to cry now, and that made her angry, and wasn't that stupid? After all this, getting mad because she was going to cry in front of all these macho asshole soldiers who were about to cremate her?

"Lock me up," she growled, "Quarantine me for a year if you want to, but don't shoot me. I'm not infected. Is this an airborne virus?"

The soldier with the headset exchanged looks with the others, shrugged and asked "How long were you inside?"

"A few minutes. I saw—" *you didn't see a goddamned thing!* "—a man on the bed inside, and I—and then you showed up."

They didn't seem any less likely to kill her, but they were at least listening to her. She tried to keep talking, tried not to scream. "I am asking you. Not to kill me. I'm a trauma nurse. I work in the ER up in Bishop. I know about infectious disease. We took in a man two summers back who came down with bubonic plague from a squirrel bite up at Twin Lakes. He recovered in three days on antibiotics. If I'm sick, I want to be quarantined, but I don't want to die out here in the woods because of something I don't even fucking understand! Will somebody please fucking talk to me?!"

"Stand down!" someone shouted, and a fifth soldier stepped into the circle. He was black, as dark a man as Stella'd ever seen, and bigger than any of the others. His gait and the forceful way his hands grabbed and subdued the air made any signs of rank he might've chosen to wear seem unnecessary. "The lady said she'd go into quarantine, Lonny. I ordered you to contain. Contain and collect."

Lonny, the soldier with the headset, raised his gun to port arms. "*You* were ordered not to risk men, *Major.*"

"I don't know about you, but I'm sick as shit of killing the wrong people," the Major said, and turned and walked back towards the truck.

Another soldier grumbled at the retreating commander. "Not like we could've killed her if we had to, with the shit gear we got. If she's—"

"I'm not infected with anything, goddamit!" Stella shouted.

"We'll see about that, ma'am," the Major called out over his shoulder. "Secure her, bagged and tagged, and keep up the perimeter. The primary's still in there."

The roof caved in. A hail of brilliant sparks danced up into the night sky. Over the roaring of the blaze, Stella heard screaming. From inside.

The house had been burning for several minutes. The crawlspace was working like a carburetor, sucking the night air in under the house so the whole structure collapsed moments later. The soldiers fell back, widening the circle to enclose the whole back half of the cabin. "Bravo one-two, Bravo-Charlie, get your shit together, he's coming out!"

The soldiers were all pointing their guns at the fire, now. She drew herself into a crouch. Their eyes off her, waiting for something to come out. She could get away.

Seth Napier/Stephen burst through the toppled back wall of the cabin, wreathed in flames and flailing limbs that no longer seemed to have any bones in them. He hit the ground hard and flopped like a freshly caught catfish, a burning worm hurling itself blindly eight feet into the air. The flamethrowers converged on him, spewing gas until the burning was too bright to look at, until the man inside was lost to view. Stella huddled in a ball on the ground, any thought of running away far beyond her.

"Looks like we got two warm ones," the Major said. And Stella looked up. And saw two soldiers in full chemical warfare suits lifting the charred remains off the blackened ground. Stephen's head rolled back on a neck that was carbonized jerky and charcoal bone—and he smiled at her. Lips made of ashes, working—

This too shall pass.

A hand from behind her held something soft and cold and wet over her face, and she was allowed to forget.

~ 12 ~

Zane Storch only remembered two dreams from his whole adult life, and those only because he'd had them several hundred times each. Whether it was because of the gas or out of some craving for regimentation, he'd never quite lost the habit of sleeping the way he'd been trained in Rangers: controlled catnaps whenever time and enemy action allowed, seldom more than two hours, and the slightest noise jolted him into full awareness. It was for this reason as much as any other that he'd lived in Death Valley, where anything that made enough noise to wake up a soldier was probably worth waking up for.

The first was his sex dream, which was more or less the same dream he'd had since his first nocturnal emission at age eleven, and which had become the only outlet for sexual desire that Storch wanted or needed since he'd come home from the war. The contents of his sex dreams are none of your business.

The other dream was a lot stranger, although its purpose as a psychological outlet was every bit as self-evident as the first. He had first begun having it during the war, although he could not remember its details until long after.

He dreamed of the Rocky Horror Hostage Show.

When Saddam invaded Kuwait and took hostages from among the diplomatic contingent in that tiny country, they didn't just disappear into a cellar somewhere. Always hands-on and never camera-shy, Saddam wanted the world to see his hostages as his personal guests. So he set them up in a studio audience and wandered through the aisles, pressing the flesh, like some sort of Oprah-fied Hitler. It looked some kind of surreal gameshow, a totalitarian hybrid of *Let's Make A Deal* and *You Bet Your Life* with contestants competing for release or quick death at the hands of an off-camera executioner, and it had exactly the effect Saddam should've known it would. It drove American and European military personnel out of their minds with rage, as if the Butcher of Baghdad was copping a feel off their own wives and daughters, and motivated previously neutral or even antiwar television viewers the world over to believe that if Saddam wasn't evil, he was certainly rabid and needed putting down.

Storch dreamt of the Rocky Horror Hostage Show, as some clever Army pundit dubbed it, but with a difference. The show was American, with a slick gameshow host and a bevy of heavily armed chicks in Solid Gold Dancer outfits for guards. The audience were Iraqis: starved, shell-shocked Republican Guardsmen with makeshift splints and bandages over awful, suppurating wounds; Kurdish peasants with the frozen faces of porcelain dolls from exposure to VX gas; veiled, robed women with arrow-slits in their veils from which flowed torrential stream of tears; the Shiite Bedouins who'd overrun Storch's squad's position in the Tigris valley. The host moved through the audience, asking them questions in English, yet almost too fast for Storch to understand; questions about American pop trivia, questions about the war, questions about their dictator's personal life, questions that provoked only blank stares and spurts of incomprehensible Arabic. When a question wasn't answered correctly, a deafening fanfare sounded and a dancer pressed a pistol to the contestant's temple and executed him or her.

Then something happened that never happened in the dream before, and Storch bolted into full wakefulness.

There was an explosion. The Hostage Show set vanished in a white blast that resolved into TV snow. Storch opened his eyes. He could still hear the snow, but now it had become the sustained, deafening roar of rocks tumbling. Storch rolled out of bed and scrambled to the camper door, peered out the window. Clouds of dust rolled past, gravel rained down from the roof. A cave-in. But he had heard a bomb. Had he dreamt it? He wanted to wait until he could see what he was diving into, but the cave-in might cut off any route to the surface, if it hadn't already. Then there was Hansen. And Sidra Sperling.

Storch rummaged through the drawers of the camper's kitchenette until he found a flashlight and a couple of dishcloths. He wrapped one over his nose and mouth, and folded the other up in his hip pocket in case Hansen needed it. A boulder slammed into the roof of the camper, rocking it on its shocks and making a dent visible from inside. Storch jumped out and ran down the tunnel, down the length of the ghostly fake-suicide traffic jam, to the mouth of Hansen's hermitage. Even running, he could feel the vibrations of the cave-in radiating outward through the earth. The wooden supports groaned, and here and there snapped like old bones in a vise. He supposed an aftershock was possible, but the ramifications of that were too paranoid, even on a day like today. Wherever Sidra Sperling's remains went, so went seismic havoc. Buggs would've loved it.

Storch stopped at the head of the tunnel, because the entrance to Hansen's grotto was now a dead end, an almost vertical wall of boulders, as if the ceiling of Hansen's cave had given in.

Or it had been blown up.

A timber directly above Storch's head cracked in half, and he heard the awful, determined grinding of huge rocks slipping out of place. He turned and sprinted back up the cave, two steps ahead of the second cave-in. His heart did its level best to leap out ahead of him, while his mind just spun in circles. He threw himself down in the berm of soft gravel at the mouth of the cave, coughing and choking on the dust that had worked its way under his makeshift gasmask. The stars were a dense powder spilled across the maddeningly big sky, the moon a gibbous lump blooming on the horizon. He rolled over on his back and stared at them, motionless.

That someone might've come for Sidra Sperling and destroyed the cave, as somebody destroyed his store, made the most sense. It was just turning out to be that kind of week. But then again, what kind of outfit would go to all the trouble to find the place, and then not search it thoroughly enough to find him?

Assuming such badasses existed, they'd probably have been crushed by the cave-in, which, like as not, was probably the result of a Hiram Hansen booby trap. Hansen wasn't one to let things get that far, though, unless he wanted them that way.

And what Hansen wanted most was to be left alone. The chill Storch felt was only half because of the wind.

Here Storch had shown up on Hansen's doorstep with a corpse, a rather remarkably weird corpse with a history, and Storch had involved Hansen in something no normal, sane person would want any part of. No, it was the simplest explanation. Hiram Hansen, who kept records of disappeared girls and obsessed about counterfeit suicides, had packed up his most irreplaceable treasures—and Sidra Sperling?—and lit out for the territories. Mexico, most likely. It was beginning to seem like the thing to do.

Whatever was going on here, Hansen's disappearance had severed his last connection to it. To his old life, such as it was. He lay there for a long time, letting the silence of the desert fill him up with blankness, until a voice swam up out of it.

"Good fucking riddance," he said out loud. He got up and stretched, picked his way back into the mine. The camper hadn't been crushed, and he got his clothes, a sleeping bag, some canned food and a warm bottle of Perrier out of the fridge. By the camper's registration stickers, he guessed the bottle had been sitting in there for fourteen years, and he normally hated mineral water. None of which made it feel any worse than heavenly when it washed the thick layer of grit down his throat. He grabbed two more bottles. It was going to take a while to find his truck.

The sun was not yet up, the wind roaring through the cab of his truck still bracingly chill, when he climbed up out of a narrow ravine and swung onto the highway, headed south. The desert outside, stripped of its associations of refuge and filial obligation, was endless rotting walls of ash, glowing mellowly in the predawn murk. He let himself shout wordless anger into the wind until his throat was hoarse and his head was clear. A more or less straight two hundred and forty miles of highway lay between him and the border. The red line down the dry hindquarters of the state unfolded in his mind's eye, becoming an exploded diagram of the journey, with likely spots (Greyhound depot in Johannesburg, Ryder truck rental in Red Mountain) to switch vehicles and gather provisions highlighted and running subroutines (disguises? Hostages?) to trump the towering obstacles that turned the open road into a gauntlet. He felt ready.

He was less than ten miles from Hansen's when a black van edged up behind him, flashing its lights to pass. He waved it on. The road ahead was a hypnotic straight line, undulating in subtle waves like a zipper in the sand. The van came alongside Storch's truck but didn't pass. His gut began to throb, as if with gas. His muscles began to ache, the humming vibration of the road penetrating him, like those ribbed contours on some turnpikes designed to awaken nodding late-night drivers. His ears ached the way they did whenever he dove too deep in a swimming pool. He looked left at the van, still pacing him. Suddenly the throb in his bowels became mailed fists wringing him out. He lunged forward into the steering wheel, starring the windshield with his forehead. He thrashed across the cab, if he could only get away from the van, get out of the truck, even at seventy-five miles an hour, he'd be okay if only he could get away from the sound that was coming from the van, that was crushing him to a pulp...

His truck leapt off the road and sailed a very long way before hitting a rock big enough to stop it. The only sound was the sizzling of steam pouring out of the ruptured radiator. The van pulled alongside him before his engine stalled, but not before he was asleep.

~ 13 ~

SPECIAL MEMORANDUM
FOR: Special Asst. Dir. Wendell Wyler,
Counterterrorism Section, FBI HQ, Washington D.C.
FROM: SA Martin Cundieffe,
Counterterrorism Section, Los Angeles Field Office
RE: Sgt. Zane E. Storch

I hope this is what you meant by "doing my homework." If you're already familiar with the Storch fugitive case (C99-22727A), please disregard this memo, but if not, I feel it merits your attention because it 1) is a case we are sanctioned to work, and 2) may be highly pertinent to our discussion of 5 July. If #2 invalidates #1, again, please disregard this memo, but please let me know ASAP so I don't get myself or anyone else into hot water.

This case came across my desk within hours of our meeting, and immediately struck me as highly relevant because of the suspect's background as well as the geographical significance. I won't bore you with the details, but if I may make so bold as to proffer an unsolicited analysis, I feel it incumbent upon me to forward my thoughts on this matter to you, in light of your warmly regarded trust in me on 5 July.

Sgt. Zane Ezekiel Storch served in the 5th Special Forces Group during the Gulf War. All records of his service are DOD-classified, but interviews with Furnace Creek-area residents indicate he suffered from symptoms corresponding to GWS (i.e., fatigue, aphasia, extreme chemical sensitivity), though they maintain he appeared to be in excellent physical condition, excepting a hand injury sustained in the war. His father, George Gorman Storch, a former Army Sergeant Major discharged by Section Eight, is currently a patient at Norwalk State Mental Institution, a manic with religiously oriented delusions, and potentially violent. The younger Storch would seem, then, to suffer from a psychosomatic disorder, rather than the allegedly physical suite of complaints common among Gulf War veterans, which is congruent with his questionable mental state. Storch appears to be the classic "lone nut" of whom acts such as these are sadly typical, but for a number of circumstantial factors which the agent in charge of the case fails to interpret adequately in his initial report (see Document #1, attached).

1) Thermopylae, the squatter community where Storch lived and operated his business, literally vanished on 4 July, shortly after Sgt. Storch allegedly shot one of his customers and burned down his own store. A number of anonymous and grossly contradictory tips coincide in their insistence that a government raid on Storch's place of business was staged by an unspecified agency at noon on 4 July, which precipitated the fire. One could, as the case agent has done, simply discard the tips, or one could take them at face value and begin calling round to ATF and DEA, and so on. (I have. No one has so much as surveilled Thermopylae in six months; the last contact, a DEA agent working undercover to pinpoint a supposed industrial-scale marijuana farm in the area, was made by the residents and rather savagely harassed, but came away convinced of their innocence). Or one could speculate that a militia organization affiliated with Storch posed as government agents to seize a cache of weapons in Storch's possession, either with or without Sgt. Storch's cooperation, and that his response was either a psychotic reaction to the ripoff or a preplanned bugout. If the Sheriff and his deputy were the sole witnesses to this transaction, the most likely scenario is the latter, masquerading as the former.

2) Storch was the employer of one Harley John Pettigrew (NCIC #4557439857; see Document #2, attached), a convicted illegal firearms dealer with associates in both militant anti-government and organized crime circles. Pettigrew was found dead in his motor home in Death Valley Junction at 2 PM on 4 July, an apparent suicide. A cordless phone in his hand, when auto-redialed, contacted Storch's business line.

3) Of the Special Forces A-Team in which Sgt. Storch served, three were KIA in the Gulf War; the other five received medical discharges and re-entered the private sector. Two have never collected veteran's benefits: they have no employment, financial or criminal records, and have not applied for passports. They have seemingly dropped off the face of the earth.

While it is all too common for elite veterans such as these to hire out as mercenaries abroad, it is also not unheard of for such men, feeling as they might to have been betrayed by their government, to go underground among militia organizations, which are unfailingly solicitous of disenfranchised military veterans. Such men would be extremely capable of posing as government agents and raiding a weapons cache. They would, given the unusual modus operandi described to us on 5 July, have little or no difficulty performing that action themselves. Pursuant to this assumption, it would follow that Storch would return to Furnace Creek to terminate the only remaining witnesses to the raid, and himself go underground. In all likelihood, his flight and disappearance near the Nevada border was a ruse, to imply interstate flight and draw attention away from the other matter on which we were briefed. His abrupt disappearance suggests that he didn't fly as far as area authorities feared, but also suggests that he may have outlived his usefulness to those unknown parties who would seem to have raided his store.

No examination of the declassified portion of Sgt. Storch's records indicate a violent anti-government extremist (see Document #3, attached); aside from Pettigrew, his associates are not known felons, let alone threats to national security. This exception on the basis of character, however, only underscores the point. Storch, as described by the witnesses in Furnace Creek, had always been an upstanding and honest citizen. This would not be at all contradictory with the event of 5 July: soft on rank-and-file military personnel, with imminent and extreme threat potential for civil government.

I hope I have not bored or abused your sensibilities with my rather haphazard analysis, but I feel there is a crying need for this case to be addressed in light of the larger issues presented on 5 July. If this matter is already under investigation by another agency in connection with that matter, or if I'm simply overstepping my duty by pressing it, I do humbly apologize. But I feel that a great injustice would be done, both to the Bureau and to the American people, if it were overlooked. I eagerly await any reaction you might have, even if it's to tell me to stick my head back in the sand.

Sincerely Yours,
SA Martin Cundieffe

~ 14 ~

The pain in Stella Orozco's head pushed down on her for a shapeless eternity before it reminded her she was alive. She pushed this realization into a box and sat on the lid while she tried to negotiate with her ache, coax it into its own little box so she could get to unpacking the other. The pain churned between her ears like the sound of a chainsaw, sputtering and growling for long stretches, then firing up for a prolonged staccato attack on her temporal lobes, hitting sporadic peaks as it snarled on some critical synapse when she was trying to use it. The agony it caused her stopped her from even feeling the rest of her body, let alone surveying her surroundings, but Stella was an old hand at putting things into boxes: fears, disappointments, even her own imminent mortality. *That's all it is*, she told herself, *a big loud noise, but it's outside you. Put it outside.*

She made a plain, sturdy house with shuttered windows, walked inside and shut the door. Outside, the pain hurled itself at the door, at the walls, but they held, and slowly, slowly, the pain grew fainter. Now she could feel cold. Numbness in her toes. Hard, smooth surface against her side. Her left arm crumpled under her, mellow needles of oxygen deprivation percolating in her hand. Pain worrying at her walls, blunted but still blinding. She'd been drugged; a mild overdose of chloroform or ether would account for the ripping headache. Judging by the way her arm and bladder felt, she'd been lying here for several hours. Drugged—by the men who came to that old hermit's trailer, the old man who found Stephen, the one who...

Before the questions could run away with her, she put it all in another box and shut it up tight. The walls around her faded in and out of her mind's eye as the pain started to get in.

She made another door and crossed the room to it, closed it behind her, this one thicker still than the last, now she could begin to focus. The pain was just a wasp's angry buzzing. She could feel its undiminished force thrumming through her house, but she made things in the room to soothe her, familiar furnishings, soft violin music playing, a low fire glowing on the hearth. She camouflaged herself in creature comforts, and slowly, slowly, the buzzing faded to a sensation she could deal with. She discovered with relief that, if she held her head very still, she could move.

She slowly drew her legs up against her belly, then slid them out in front of her. Less than a foot away, they dangled out over empty space. She levered herself onto one buttock, bracing herself with her right arm, and stretched her legs out to touch the floor with her bare feet. Chill poured concrete floor under her toes. She clamped her jaw tight and lifted herself off the ledge, winced as blood gushed into her left arm and it burst into flame. Her house buckled around her, whining steely migraine-claws shredding the walls of her crackerjack shelter. The arm felt like a parasite in her hand, a dead thing that had attached itself to her and was filling her with its venom. She stood up in one swift motion. Tears started from her eyes, and for a split second she could *see* her headache inside her, and it was a tumor shaped like an atomic mushroom cloud, and it was still rising, rising, and she could *feel* how it hated her, how it wanted her to die. Stella fell back on the ledge, hunkered down in the animal guts of her brain's basest functions and mended her walls.

Slowly, over what might have been hours, the pain fell back, from a nuclear firestorm to a four-alarm blaze, to a chainsaw, to a gardener with a pesky leaf blower. Her right hand pumped her left until the last of the needles were worked out. When she could move it again, she rubbed her eyes, and found they were gummed shut with tears and sleep. They burned, but they worked.

She sat on a bare wooden bunk in a dimly lit cell, concrete walls stained with a sulfurous yellow glaze. A thick steel door with a small, double-paned window of steel-reinforced Plexiglas. A round steel air circulator was mounted in the ceiling, and an intercom speaker beside the door.

She was in a quarantine cell, a more spartan version of the one she'd seen on a tour of a hospital in Fresno. *But this is not a hospital.*

By the feeble light falling through the window, she could see that she wore a mint-green hospital johnny, with no stenciled hospital markings or manufacturer's tags anywhere on it. They'd left her undergarments, but they'd taken the bobby-pins out of her hair. She didn't wear jewelry, but as she looked at her hands, she noticed they'd cut her nails down to the quick, her toenails, too. An IV tube dangled from the crook of her left arm, terminated in a socket in the wall. Pumping her full of fluids, maybe vitamins, probably sedatives. *This is a killing jar. These people take no chances. They expect me to try to escape, to try to hurt them. But they put me in a smock. And I'm not dead.*

So?

So if you don't fuck it up, you might live through this.

She held herself very still and heard violin music, willing herself to get up and go to the intercom. Her head bobbed on her neck like a half-empty helium balloon, weak from hunger, she could still feel the pain rolling around in her skull like a wrecking—no, a *pin*ball, a little BB, getting smaller all the time…

She was halfway to standing up when a shadow flitted over her. A silhouette at the window, all eyes. Glint of reflected light off a bald skull, contours of a broad, chiseled jaw, corded neck. One of the soldiers. She held up one open hand, to let them know she was awake, pointed feebly at the intercom. The soldier stepped away from the window. Stella leapt to her feet and half ran, half fell across the cell to the intercom. Her right thumb stabbed the send button, and she screamed, "Hey, *pindejo,* come talk to me!"

Through the window, she could see the soldier standing in a room lit by hanging bare bulbs, the walls and ceiling lost in shadows. He stood next to a bulky, androgynous woman who held a clipboard and regarded Stella with an utterly neutral gaze. They both wore fatigues with the kind of chocolate-chip camouflage pattern the Army wore in Desert Storm, with no insignia. They had the same severe, white-walled haircut. If they could hear her, they didn't seem inclined to respond.

"Hey, where am I?" *We could tell you, but we'd have to kill you,* she thought. "What's going on? Where's a doctor? Can you hear me?"

They just stood there watching her, like she was a stray dog barking as they put her to sleep. Her pain was coming back for her, let in by her shouting. She clenched every muscle of her body against it as it carpet-bombed her brain. The window swam in and out of focus, the soldier and the mannish woman with the clipboard disappeared, then another soldier ran past with a rifle, and she thought she heard noises that might've been shots, then she swooned, and the wall slammed into her forehead, and the floor kicked her ass.

She knew some time had passed since her collapse because her eyes were gummed shut, and her bladder and stomach protested their respective fullness and emptiness with dire urgency. Still, her head felt better. She could see without the curtain of free-floating animosity for the world that only serious headaches can evoke, and her dizziness had given way to a keen lucidity. She figured they'd pumped her full of stimulants in preparation for something. An interrogation. Good. It was high time these assholes explained themselves.

Stella went to the window. The bare bulbs still glowed, but she had to strain to the left to see anyone. A soldier sat on an examination table with his back to her. Over his shoulder, Stella could make out a silvery, crewcut head—the bulldyke with the clipboard—doing something to the soldier's chest. His shirt was off, and it looked as if the woman was stitching him up. He jerked more than once, and Stella saw the woman's mouth working as she ordered him to sit still. Stella learned to read the lips of whispering foster parents, social workers and bullies before she learned to speak English herself. *Be a man*, the dyky woman snapped at him.

Presently, the soldier stood and buttoned his shirt, but not before Stella saw the puckered furrows running from his clavicle down to his navel, and the rows of Y-shaped nylon staples holding the wounds together. With a downcast look, he reached out and placed his hand on the woman's shoulder, mouthing the word *Sorry* over and over again. She shook it off as if it were a parrot that'd just shit on her, and pointed forcefully towards Stella's cell. *Quarantine*, she was saying, and she reached for an intercom mounted in the wall beside the corridor door, presumably to call an armed escort. The soldier picked up his ruined tunic and stalked towards Stella. She ducked away from the window, saw the doctor follow the guard past her window and out of sight. Stella guessed the soldier was being locked in a quarantine cell just like hers. "And leave the goddamned staples alone!" the woman shouted loud enough for Stella to hear.

The woman—presumably the medic for this militia, or whatever they were—could've passed for a man, if not for the broad, flattened swell of her bosom and chubby, button-nosed features, which put Stella in mind of Mrs. Claus in the old Rankin-Bass stop-motion Christmas specials. She'd always suspected Santa Claus was a white supremacist, but this woman was nobody's wife. Stella's hand went to her gaping mouth as the doctor removed her own shirt and stood with her back to a full-length mirror on the wall opposite Stella's cell. Her breasts were mashed down by a sweat-streaked sports bra. Her broad, fishbelly-white back was well-muscled underneath a stubborn sheath of hereditary flab, the tone of one who'd struggled for years against the genetic programming for obesity.

A deep gash grooved her right shoulder, scant inches from the delicate plumbing in her throat. Instantly, Stella recognized the wound type and understood what had happened after she'd fainted. In the panic she'd observed before, someone or something had badly gouged the soldier, who'd accidentally grazed the doctor as he tried to shoot it. What it was that attacked them, Stella could well guess. Seth Napier, or whatever he'd become. They had him here, maybe in the next cell. The idea sparked a moment of pure panic as the implications tumbled together into some sort of prognosis. They were waiting for her to change, too. And for all that she felt better than she had in a long time, who was to say what would happen in twenty-four hours? Would the soldiers have to be called to put her down, too?

She went to the intercom and jabbed the button. "You going to stitch that up yourself?"

The doctor looked her way, reached for her fatigue blouse and threw it over herself before she approached and pressed her send button. "How long have you been awake?"

"If you let me out of here long enough to use the restroom, I'll stitch that up for you. I'm an ER nurse. And I'm human."

The woman only stared at her for a moment, then went to a utility drawer and fetched a chrome tool that resembled a staple gun. Returning to the mirror, she applied the surgical stapler to the gunshot wound and slammed a staple into one end of it, wincing a bit but gritting her teeth and proceeding down the length of the injury, ten staples in all. It wasn't as tightly clamped as it should've been, but she looked at Stella defiantly as she returned the stapler to its drawer. Here was a woman who fought her own inner inferiority with every action, thwarting real or imagined rivals was the sole source of her tenuous self-esteem. Stella understood her instantly.

She adjusted her tone to something calculated to open her jailer up. "We never had anything like that at the ER in Bishop. Is it Army-issue?"

The doctor shrugged her blouse back on and buttoned it up with her back to Stella.

"Listen, I'm not going anywhere, so I'd appreciate it if somebody could tell me why I'm in this box."

When the doctor turned back, her face was carefully composed to flat neutrality. She switched on the intercom outside Stella's cell and, taking a deep breath, began firing off questions. "You visited the Radiant Dawn Hospice Community. Why?"

Stella suppressed the urge to answer back with her own questions. She'd told no one about the visit, so they had the place, had her, under surveillance. Her greatest fear was of others holding her life in their own hands. She knew only a patient's meek, forthright demeanor would earn her any points here, but she wasn't prepared to give them any more control over her than they already had. "One of their residents was brought into the ER. He was hit by a train. They came and took him back. I was just following up. What was wrong with him?"

"Why did Seth Napier contact you instead of the police?" Stella gathered from the line of questioning that they'd seen her at Radiant Dawn, followed her, tapped her phone, and sent out their commando teams to collect Napier and her. Because they'd had contact with Stephen, who ran away from Radiant Dawn...

The doctor tapped on the glass. "You still awake? Answer the question."

"I spoke to him at the hospital. He trusted me. This is about Radiant Dawn, isn't it? They're doing something to people."

Silently, the doctor nodded once.

"You're with the government, right? Army? CIA? That's what this place is, isn't it? A secret government installation out in the desert, to keep people from finding out what they're doing there?"

The doctor heaved a mighty sigh and closed in on Stella, looking, really looking, at her for the first time. Stella tried to appear to lay herself bare for inspection, felt her defenses pushing her face into the fierce scowl with which it always met the scrutiny of strangers, especially strangers in authority. Perhaps that was exactly what the doctor was looking for in her, because she let slip half a smile. "We're not with the government, and we're not trying to protect Radiant Dawn. You went to Radiant Dawn to apply for treatment."

It wasn't a question, and there was no denying it. Anyone who could tap her phones and spirit her away to a hermetically sealed hole in the earth could easily have ferreted out the news of her cancer. She nodded. "They turned me away. I don't want to die, doctor. I don't want to die from cancer, and I sure as hell don't want to die here."

"Your quarantine will last twenty-four hours. If you show no sign of infection—"

"You'll let me go?" The sneer in her voice would've shut up a lesser woman. The doctor didn't flinch.

"When this is over."

"You can't just keep me here! You're not the goddamn government! It got out earlier, right? You were exposed to it too, you and that jarhead. Why aren't you in a can?"

"I'm not going anywhere." The doctor pointed to the outer door. It was like a bank vault or a hatch on a submarine, set into a massive collar of steel, with double-paned, wire-reinforced glass in a porthole, through which Stella could just glimpse another hatch just like the first. An airlock. This sick bay was designed to deal with contagious diseases. To deal with…this.

"My name's Stella. Stella Orozco, but I guess you found that out when you tapped my phone."

The doctor released a chuckle, as pained by it as if she'd farted. "Delores Mrachek. We're going to be here together for awhile, but I'm not very good company, I'm afraid." Mrachek turned and busied herself with a stack of files on a countertop. She began laying them out as if she were playing solitaire, noting the color-coded tabs on the edge of each before laying it down.

On the well-founded principle that few people are too busy or introverted to argue, Stella pressed. "So, what is this gang you're in? Are you a militia? Paramilitary Nazis? KKK? What?"

Mrachek didn't look up from her busy work as she answered. "We are an army, a very small one, fighting a very big war."

"Against a cancer treatment hospice. Against terminally ill people."

"They aren't people anymore. You saw that much."

"Whatever they are, they aren't dying of cancer anymore."

"No. They don't *have* cancer anymore."

Stella gave a barking laugh as she thought now that she understood. "Is that all this is, then? Two tribes of crazy white assholes fighting over the cure for cancer?"

Mrachek did look up now, a dogmatic fire in her eyes. "No, dear, we're fighting to cure the world of *them*. They've ceased to have cancer. They've *become* cancer."

Her hand went up to forestall any further questions. "Now if we're going to be together for twenty-four hours, we shouldn't exhaust the only conversation we're liable to have in the first hour, should we?" And she got up and shut off the intercom, then returned to her files.

Stella shouted at her for awhile, indifferent that the intercom was off; just trying to be heard gave her anger somewhere to go besides back into her head, where she'd kept it in check for far too long.

About an hour after she'd yelled herself hoarse, Mrachek came back over. Stella went to the intercom, thinking she was going to reopen the lines of communication, but she merely fiddled with something beside the door, and Stella suddenly felt very cold and dizzy. In the time it took for her to realize what she'd done, it was too late to rip out the IV, the cell was spinning, and she staggered into the only stable axis, the barren anchor of her cot, and flopped onto it. Her anger spilled out of her even as her bladder let loose, but she was already asleep.

~ 15 ~

SPECIAL MEMORANDUM
FOR: Special Asst. Dir. Wendell Wyler,
Counterterrorism Section, FBI HQ, Washington D.C.
FROM: SA Martin Cundieffe,
Counterterrorism Section, Los Angeles Field Office
RE: Softkill Technology

Attached please find the requested comprehensive list of private contractors with softkill weapons development programs (File Document OC171-08A). I have separated domestic from foreign corporations, as well as those with electromagnetic antipersonnel programs. As I perused them, I was disturbed by the large number of contracts with foreign powers of a totalitarian or otherwise ideologically oppressive nature. While a foreign power would have little motive for an act such as China Lake, it would be well within the bailiwick of an extremist group, perhaps with foreign or radical third party domestic financial backing, which might have purchased the technology from a corporation, perhaps even an American one. With SA Hunt's approval still pending due to his disposition in the field, I took the liberty of assigning twelve division and main force Bureau personnel to further investigate the research and financial records of the domestic, and a short list of the most suspect foreign, corporations.

For myself, I endeavored to learn as much as I could about the Pentagon's own softkill programs (see Special Memo #3, re: Theories, intramilitary terrorism), both current and defunct. Upon reviewing the rather sparse Pentagon webpage on the subject (see attached Document Packet #1), I concluded that little more than lip service is being paid to the matter currently, with appropriations for the office providing for only theoretical models of potential softkill projects. (The mostly civilian staff of the division staunchly endorse the term "nonlethal", despite its countermilitary appeal. Small wonder they're broke.) Upon cross-referencing the Pentagon's contractors with domestic corporations with foreign contracts, I found several possible instances of abuse of federal contracts. (For instance, a quick-hardening "riot control foam" compound, synthesized with Pentagon funding by the Syndecon Corporation of Cincinnati, Ohio, 9/94, but never implemented or tested, was offered to the South Korean military and the Japanese Self-Defense Force. Syndecon has yet to notify either the Pentagon or the Federal Trade Commission, and has taken steps to obfuscate their attempts to market the government-owned compound.)

However, no ultrasonic or magnetic projects have passed the preliminary research stage. Several companies (see attached document #2, Short List of Ultrasonic, Infrasonic & Electromagnetic Anti-Personnel Technology Manufacturers) make somewhat effective infrasonic disabling devices which incapacitate by low frequency, high amplitude sonic bombardment. This induces extreme physical discomfort and high probability of incontinence, but seldom induces unconsciousness. While local and federal police forces have yet to secure funds to purchase such weapons, countries such as Taiwan and Peru have used them effectively in riot control and resolution of hostage situations.

I spoke briefly this morning with a civilian consulting supervisor of the Pentagon Nonlethal Defense Projects Office, a Richard Tuttle, who is also a committee chairman for the International Strategic Nonproliferation Center, a privately funded research group and lobby for softkill conflict resolution (see attached document #3, Tuttle's background file, and Document #4, Radical Leftist Environmental Groups). Mr. Tuttle was tolerably cooperative after certain facts about his background status were established, and he provided me with an insider's overview of the state of softkill technology. (All of Mr. Tuttle's information was independently verified by a surreptitious entry into the ISNC's local area network database.)

Mr. Tuttle and others of his ilk are bullish on the substitution of nonlethal weapons in warfare, but are suspicious and fearful that they could become powerful tools for civil control in the hands of an unscrupulous law enforcement agency. He told me that very few top-notch scientists are involved in softkill research at present, but that there was a mini-boom in the program in 1983. Under the lavish patronage of the Reagan administration, a relatively large-scale directed energy softkill research project was conducted under the aegis of the Defense Advanced Research Projects Agency at Lawrence Livermore Laboratories, by a handful of the best scientists in the field, many of whom had worked the atomic weapons programs and become "ethically burned out" (Tuttle's words). According to Tuttle, the White House asked for a weapon for civil control in the event of worst-case scenarios with regard to the escalating homeless population. After less than a year, however, the team was diverted to an SDI project on which no records are available, or believed to exist. By 1985, at least three members of the research team had died under sudden and unforeseen circumstances which should have aroused far more suspicion among local and federal authorities than they did. (See attached Documents #5, #6 and #7, Death Certificates and Police Reports for the Deaths of Dr. Cornelius Darwin Armitage and Dr. Calvin Wittrock, and DoD records for Maj. Delores Mrachek.) Armitage was atomized in an explosion and fire at his home. A defective tank of pure hydrogen was blamed, but no lawsuit or finding of fault was brought to bear on the manufacturer. Wittrock was abducted and executed in Bogota, Colombia, allegedly by narcoguerrilas. Allegedly, his mutilated head and hands were delivered via post to the US consulate there. (Strangely, it never even made the news.) Dr. Mrachek died of an unidentified viral infection while on medical relief mission in the Sudan. Her remains were cremated there in direct contravention of US and United Nations policy. Tuttle went so far as to infer that the deaths were "awfully convenient for the Administration", a suggestion odious in the extreme, but highly provocative (see Conclusions, below).

The contacts and codes with which you graciously provided me expedited the fulfillment of my FOIA request on the DARPA documents pertaining to the scientists working on this "shadow project" (again, Tuttle's words), but I was able to glean very little from them, as they consisted of a small sheaf of unnumbered printouts, with all but a dozen or fewer words blacked out on each. From this skeletal record, I was able to construct the following:

1) A small team of scientists, primarily physicists from Lawrence Livermore Laboratories, but including a group of biologists conscripted from projects at NIH and USAMRID, was assembled for a DARPA directed energy weapons project, code named RADIANT, in September of 1983. Authority over the project is blacked out, but the chain of oversight is distressingly short, and probably included only the DARPA Appropriations Committee and the Joint Chiefs. One wonders if the President was aware of the project at all.

2) Only a few names of RADIANT researchers are disclosed: Dr. Cornelius Darwin Armitage, and Dr. Calvin Wittrock, both attached to Livermore Labs, both of whom retained security clearances from Los Alamos and Alamagordo Research Facilities, and Major Delores

Mrachek, MD, a cellular biologist from USAMRID. All three are deceased. Armitage had headed the last six projects on which he worked for the government, but was attached to RADIANT in a "consultative capacity." I was unable to identify just who was in charge of RADIANT, but presume that it would have included reps from NASA and the National Reconnaissance Office.

3) Funding for the project was appropriated from the SDI budget; though the amount is undisclosed, it was somewhere in the low seven-figure range (a paltry sum for a Reagan-era defense research grant, let alone one under the high-profile SDI aegis), and provided for an "independent research facility" at an undisclosed location. The goals of the project, though almost universally blacked out, hint at an extremely short-term expectation of result: funding was acquired on a one-time basis, and the facility is specifically designated a "temporary" installation, though whether this is an appeal to economy or plausible deniability remains unclear.

4) Liaisons with the Office of Naval Intelligence, Joint Special Operations Command and the 5th US Naval Fleet Command are stipulated, from which one may infer that provisions were made for testing RADIANT overseas.

5) RADIANT was discontinued in April of 1984, with the vague statement that the project had "failed to yield repeatable results," but had opened "promising avenues for further research under different auspices." Just what they actually tried to achieve, and what became of the project, is beyond our reach at this time.

CONCLUSIONS:

That Doctors Armitage, Wittrock and Mrachek all died within twelve months of the completion of Project RADIANT is suspicious indeed, but in itself lends little to recommend it as a corollary to the present investigation. However, building upon hypothetical scenarios extrapolated from the China Lake incident, one may proffer the following inductions:

1) The China Lake incident was perpetrated by military professionals working with highly advanced energy-based weapons technology, who took steps to take no human lives, but did steal a huge amount of a destructive incendiary. It follows that, if they are indeed bent on unleashing the napalm, it will most likely be upon a strategic target, and not a population center. They have adequately demonstrated both their power over, and respect for, human life.

2) Armitage and Wittrock were involved in nonlethal weapons research when they were pulled onto RADIANT, and not as principals. Dr. Mrachek was a medical doctor, and nothing in her public record shows

anything less than a passionate dedication to the preservation of human life. What little record of RADIANT still exists does NOT indicate that it was a softkill project. RADIANT was the last project any of them worked on for the government: after its murky conclusion, Armitage retired, Wittrock vanished into the private sector, and Mrachek resigned her commission and went to Africa.

3) I realize this is even more far-fetched than an assassination conspiracy theory, but it must, I believe, be considered, as no one other scenario addresses both the implicit motive and modus operandi of China Lake. What if one or more of them is still alive?

My department has reviewed thousands of documents and hundreds of dossiers, and found no one alive with the expertise and resources to devise a working electromagnetic antipersonnel device of China Lake magnitude. If Dr. Armitage was the leading authority on the effects of radiation on living tissue, and a specialist in nonlethal solutions to armed conflict, he may have been the only person capable of designing a device such as was used at China Lake, and if he's been living underground for fourteen years, he will have had ample time to build ties with a militia group composed of fellow scientific and military veterans, and continue his research. Moreover, his work on RADIANT may have triggered his move underground, and may be the impetus for the current activity. Why now? The RADIANT papers' conclusion that "further research under different auspices" may take place in the future looms large in my mind.

Taken *in toto*, the facts suggest a disturbing scenario, wherein the military arm of this investigation must be considered tainted by conflict of interest: it would be in their best interest to see the "terrorist" threat neutralized without oversight from either the Department Of Justice or the American people. If the Bureau is to remain true to its core mandate, I do not see how it can without securing sole authority over the investigation, and, in fact, opening a new and separate investigation on the Pentagon's possible culpability in the possibly deliberate mishandling of this case.

I must apologize for not having more scenarios to present, but the chain of evidence leads me in this direction each time I take it up. We know entirely too little about RADIANT, and I must urge that more pressure be brought to bear on the DoD to disclose the unblacked files if we are to put this line of reasoning to rest once and for all. In humblest dedication, I remain

Sincerely Yours,

SA Martin Cundieffe

~ 16 ~

He awoke in a world of cold and darkness, on a floor of vibrating rust. He was blindfolded, his hands were cuffed behind his back, and his legs bound with heavy plastic restraints. Their tingling soreness told him he'd been out for at least an hour. A band of surgical tape held a cotton swab in place on the inside of his right elbow, but he didn't feel drugged. They'd taken his blood? He lay still, feigning sleep as he drank in the sensations of his prison.

The floor throbbed with the regular pulsation of a semi on an interstate, and the way it rocked told him he was probably in a storage container on a flatbed trailer. The cold was not refrigeration, though he could feel an icy draft against his ankles; it was the dead of night, so he'd been out for the entire day.

He was not alone. Feet shuffled beside his face, whispers threaded through the gray diesel rumble. He jerked away from a boot that prodded his shoulder. A voice, commanding, with a high Southern drawl, boomed in the small box.

"We know you're awake, son. We want some answers."

Storch suddenly felt a wave of recognition. He knew the game they were playing. Robin Sage. Every Green Beret knew it, for it was the core of Special Forces training. Robin Sage was an extended war game that separated the rank and file, order-following soldier from the commando by demanding that they think for themselves. Trainees were dropped off into Pineland, an embattled nation that was really North and South Carolina, which was striving for independence from the tyranny of Opforland. Storch's four-man squad had to meet with and negotiate a relationship with guerrilla leaders in the region, civilian locals who played the role of terrorists with fierce gusto. In initial contacts, they became willing hostages, enduring the guerrilla's muscle-flexing and interrogation tactics to show they could be trusted. Long, bumpy rides in trunks, guns in his face, sudden mock field executions, hours lying hogtied on cold floors just like this one. These people weren't real terrorists, they were playacting from the same script on which he'd been trained. Storch felt he knew what to expect, and wrapped himself up in it, to shelter from the creeping certainty he still had no idea what he'd gotten into.

"Look alive, soldier!" The booted foot stomped the floor just before Storch's face so the floor thrummed, shocking him back into the present. A ramrod-stiff backbone of pure commanding officer behind that voice. And some residue of an accent that sounded familiar.

"I'm awake, sir. What do you want to know?"

"Where's the body?"

"Your guess is as good as mine, *sir*," he replied, pouring all the acid he had into the last word. "It was in as safe a place as I could find."

"Oh, I doubt that very fucking much, Sergeant. I find it hard to believe you possess the wherewithal to tuck your dick in your shorts without a note pinned to your sleeve. You were a mistake, Sergeant, and you will never know how much your fuckups have cost us. If Harley hadn't been killed because of a breach of security in your store, he could have done it, and it would've been done right. And another thing, what the fuck were you doing, killing all those cops?"

"I didn't kill Twombley. I wasn't even in Furnace Creek yesterday morning. I saw a pickup that looked like mine and had my license plates on it coming back from there yesterday morning, and if there's anything you can tell me about that, or about what went down at China Lake, I'd sure as hell like to know about it."

A moment's hesitation, indrawn breath louder than the wind whipping at the sides of the cargo container. "You're full of shit, Sergeant."

Another voice cut him off. "We had nothing to do with framing you for any murder. If you were framed, it was to drive you to us."

"By who? Why would I come to you? Why would they think I'd come to you assholes?"

"That's what we'd like to know, dickweed," the commander snapped back.

Storch listened for the others in the container with them, wondered if he was supposed to take this man's abusive bullshit or try to kill him to show his worth. It amazed him how quickly the unacceptable decisions awakened as instinct again. He decided to see how far he could push with words. "Sir, what rank are you, and in what Army do you serve? Because I never enlisted in it."

"We're all in this war, boy."

"You hid ordnance in my store. Without my knowledge. You involved my friend in some bullshit crusade that killed him, or drove him to kill himself. You caused the Federal government—or whoever—to raid my store, which somebody burned down, and scattered my town. You ordered me out to take a lost little girl's dead body and hide it for you, making me an accessory to murder. You—or somebody else, I don't give a shit who— killed Sheriff Twombley and framed me for it, so now I'm a wanted copkiller. Then the body disappears, along with another one of my friends. You want me to go along under your good word that I'm hurting the people who hurt me? I don't even know who the fuck you are!"

The commander took a big deep breath, so deep Storch thought he could hear the walls buckle. Behind it there was whispering. That was where the real power was, he knew.

The shouting that should have come blew out in a big sigh, and Storch thought he could see the man's breath as a cloud of brighter blackness. "We are the Mission, the army of *homo sapiens*, Sergeant Storch. We are a militia of human beings fighting a holy war against eugenic terrorists. Our cause is survival of the fittest, and we are every bit as fanatical about our cause as any towelhead suicide bomber you ever saw on CNN."

A woman's voice, older, military but well-educated: "You've proven your loyalty to the United States in combat, but where do your loyalties lie as a human being?"

"I don't know what the hell you're talking about." Turning in the dark towards the voice, his senses so keyed up he could hear their breathing through the drone of the truck, could smell sweat on their bodies. Four men, one woman. They were wearing nightvision goggles. Thankfully, they only smelled of nondeodorant soap, sand and machine oil. The woman was menstruating.

"Do you believe that the human race, such as it is, should remain at the pinnacle of the evolutionary ladder?" someone demanded. Storch thought of superior specimens like Leon and Gina and tried not to laugh, not to scream at them as the solemn voice went on. "Do you believe that eugenics and genetic engineering are a crime against the natural order, demanding extreme force to prevent their application to the human genome?"

What was this, a loyalty oath? "Yeah, I believe God created Adam and Eve in his image, and they ate of the fruit of the Tree of Knowledge of Good and Evil, and were cast out of Eden into a world of shit, and it's been all downhill ever since." Two of the men chuckled behind their fists. Storch had never uttered so much as a word of prayer since his parents divorced, but his father's faith had come rushing in along with the willingness to kill. God, he was even *crazier* than his father. "But I didn't come here to join up. I just want to know who they are, and where."

"You're a god-fearing man," the commander replied, "so understand it like this: they are the ultimate abomination, for they sin against nature as well as God. They are a foe before which governments, commandments and creeds are nothing but sticks and stones in the paws of dumb animals. They are the Test which humankind must pass to prove its right to exist."

The woman chimed in. "They have taken great steps to drive you to join us. You weren't followed, but you're being watched. If they have not contacted you already, then know that they will, and that they will tempt you to betray us, and your kind, in the coming war. Look inside yourself, Zane Ezekiel Storch, and ask yourself what side you will take in that war."

Then there were hands on him again, and a rag pressed to his clamped mouth, and sleep.

When he woke up, he was still in the cargo container. The truck had stopped moving and he was alone. A remote square of pale daylight stabbed at his eyes from one wall, and he realized they'd unbound him. What was this, another test?

Storch sat up and hugged himself. He couldn't hold his head up, let it settle against his knees. He hadn't asked for this, for any of it. All he'd wanted since he came home from the war was to be left alone, to grow old in peace, a latter-day Cincinnatus. In the last eight years, he'd managed to strike some sort of deal with his past and with his illness, and he'd been able to become almost normal. The others, the few men from his squad that he'd kept in touch with for awhile after they got back, had all retreated into bitterness and paranoia, hating their own government as they'd once hated its enemies. But he'd gotten it together as well as he knew how and gone on with his life. He didn't want to kill anymore, didn't want to think in terms of "US" versus "THEM." He wanted to be free, and didn't harbor any illusions about what the word meant or about how hard it was to keep. Now, in the span of three days, he was a prisoner again—of somebody else's war, and not any kind of conventional, *sane* war, either. Both sides in this conflict seemed to be competing to drive him insane, to pry him away from everything that made sense in his life, to reduce him again to a soldier, a headful of hardwired fight or flight instincts. They wouldn't let him fly, they wouldn't explain it to him, wouldn't let him decide. He wanted to fight, now, yes indeed. But he wanted answers, to see for himself what was what, and what the fight was over, before he cast in his lot on either side. And perhaps they'd all regret that they'd ever decided to disturb Sergeant Zane Ezekiel Storch from his sleep of self-exile, because he'd fight them all.

The blackness of the cargo container was merely darkness again, the absence of light, not a void fraught with phantom inquisitors. He could get out of a box.

Kneeling, he tugged at the heel of his left boot. The false bottom of the heel came away in his hand and he pulled out a spool of monofilament wire. It looked like metallic angling line, or silvery dental floss, but Storch handled it gingerly, taking care not to touch it as he unspooled it and stretched it between his fists. As a garrote, the wire could cleanly saw the head off a victim, but its primary purpose was as a saw. He'd ordered the boots from *Soldier Of Fortune* magazine because of their sturdiness and comfort, and never in five years had he opened the heels to use the special tools inside. Now he blessed the earlier, edgier incarnation of himself that'd seen the necessity of carrying hidden weapons in his shoes.

Sidling up to the tiny crack of sunlight in the wall, he pressed himself against it and tried to peer out. Nothing more definite than a wall of unvaried grayness outside, but no movement, either. After feeling up and down the slot of the door, he looped the cutting wire around the first of the three bolts that held him prisoner. Each was as thick as his index and middle fingers together, but the wire worked through them like a stick of dry mesquite. The minutes flowed by unnoticed, Storch living in his hands and in his ears, hearing nothing but the muted whine of the wire worrying away at the steel, and the next, and the last. Suddenly, finally, the wire popped free, and the door settled on its hinges with a resounding groan, drifted open. Storch put away the monofilament wire and leaned cautiously out.

The cargo container was apparently parked in a field of trailers, because another exactly like it was next to it, parked so close that the door clanged against it when it swung open. The light was deep blue, the last gasp of night before the dawn of another brutal midsummer day. A sputtering breeze carried dust, diesel and the growl of idling semis. A truckstop, somewhere in the Central Valley.

Storch climbed down from the container, bracing himself against the edge of the flatbed trailer it rested on, lowering himself as steadily as he could to keep from crying out. His shoulder muscles complained, but he willed himself to ignore them. His feet found the tarmac and he pushed the cargo door to. Within minutes, he could be on another truck, bound for anywhere but here.

"Freeze!" a stage-whisper from just over his shoulder. Storch whipped around and saw a man in black fatigues racing down the narrow alleyway between the trailers, holding something out in front of him that looked like an electric shaver. Storch backed up a step. The sentry wasn't a regular trucker or a security guard, he knew. The three-quarter profile stance he adopted as he charged Storch was almost exactly the tactic he himself would have chosen, if their roles were reversed. Storch crouched at the last minute and stepped inside the outstretched hand, bent it over his shoulder and started to pivot, intending to break the arm as he threw the man against the cargo container.

But the man was turning in his grip, the arm twisting so it bent over him. A knee came up between his legs from behind and slammed into his groin even as the razor-thing—taser-thing, he corrected himself—jabbed him in the neck. Hot blue sparks flashed in his brain and he felt his legs buckle, his control over them becoming as tenuous as a long-distance telephone connection with a demilitarized zone. His hands spasmed, but Storch held onto the arm, threw his nerveless weight against the sentry, slamming him hard against the cargo container. The taser broke contact with his skin and his body, shaky though it was, was suddenly his again. He swept the sentry's feet out from under him and twisted the arm back around his neck, drove the crackling mouth of the taser into the sentry's face once, twice, then pressed it against him until his closed-mouth screams subsided and he smelled hair and skin burning. His own hands tingled as the current jumped from the man's sweat-slick skin into his. He heard a startled gasp and the wriggling body behind him went limp, draped across him like a wet bearskin rug.

Storch staggered under the dead weight, caught himself against one wall and shrugged the man off. He slumped to the ground beside the body, froze and listened. There was no change in the faint, utterly mundane noises from outside the trailer-maze. He looked at the man for a long while, considering killing him. A twist of the neck, and the man would never trouble anyone again. But Storch noticed the Walther PPK holstered at his side; it was mounted with a short silencer. He could've put a bullet into Storch without arousing any attention from the outside world, but he'd tried to subdue him, instead. The thought of killing a soldier in his sleep made him shivery, nauseous.

Methodically, he searched the sentry's pockets. No big surprise—the sentry carried no ID, not even a wallet. He took the gun and stuck it into the waistband of his pants, snugging the silencered barrel into the small of his back. He found a cell phone—dead, unresponsive when he thumbed the SEND button—shorted out from the taser jolt. A card with a list of numbers was glued to the back of the phone. Storch peeled it off and slipped it into his pocket, returned the phone, and rolled the body into his cargo-cell, arranged the door so it looked secure. The light was already turning from blue to grayish gold as the sun began to fight its way above the horizon. Storch had a long way to go, but where?

Answers. He had to find somebody who could tell him who was fighting who, and why. Somebody on the right side of the law, somebody who would listen to him.

He ran down the line of trailers, ears pricked for more sentries, but he heard nothing. He found his way out of the maze so suddenly that he was still running when he came out into the open. He stood at one end of a vast parking lot filled with semis, most idle, but some dozing noisily with their running lights on. A diesel fueling station stood fifty yards away; sleepy-looking men in flannel shirts and greasy jeans stood at the pumps, not noticing him. In the center of the lot sprawled a vast and brilliantly lit truckstop, the Mojave Outpost. He checked himself over—he looked like another trucker, dirtier and more freaked-out looking than most, but not so much as to attract undue attention. Head-checking both ways, he crossed the tarmac, looking for a way to get to San Jose.

~ 17 ~

Stella cleaned the instruments they brought back from the trailer, then sat aside to watch Mrachek process the blood sample. She never looked at Stella as she worked over the slides she laid out on the countertop. A lesser judge of character might've mistaken it for trust, but Stella had worked under enough doctors to see the contempt it represented. As a nurse, she was just another tool, a little more autonomous than the others, which represented more of a drawback than an asset. Stella had come to admire a few of them, but never liked any. She was beginning to dislike Delores Mrachek a great deal. To have fallen down a rabbit hole into a twilight world, the hostage of a terrorist faction, and still be taken for granted, dismissed as an instrument just like at her day-job, galled her almost as much as the quarantine.

Since she'd gotten out of quarantine, she'd been treated pretty decently, for a hostage. She'd been assigned a slightly bigger cell opposite the sick bay, and she'd been allowed to come and go as she pleased. Not that there was any chance of escape, or manpower to spare to watch her. The corridor she called home branched off into a maze of sturdy, identical concrete halls, staircases and ladderways that had the deep chill and sepulchral staleness of underground. She doubted she could find the door that led to the surface, let alone pose enough of a threat to be allowed to leave. They seemed to be willing to grant her as many privileges as she earned by being an invisible guest, and Dr. Mrachek had begrudgingly told her she'd appreciate her help in the sick bay. There was quite a bit of trauma work to be done, she'd said, but Stella couldn't be sure if she meant regularly, or in the immediate future.

They seemed to be a group of less than thirty men and women. Most of them were obviously soldiers. They didn't leer or try to flirt with her. They merely noticed her. The rest of the cabal seemed to be scientists, though they wore the same fatigues as the others; they were always rushing around carrying files or walking blind with VR goggles and datagloves on. All were in their late forties to early sixties, and reminded her of Dominican monks: silent, somber, lost in contemplation of some grim truth they hoped to keep secret from the outer world. They made her nervous, and she avoided them. For them, she was invisible.

When she'd been asked to accompany Mrachek on a "field trip," she'd been giddy, and hard-pressed not to blow her cool as she accepted. To get outside into the fresh air again, to see the world outside this bunker. Even if escape *was* impossible, she knew she'd never get a better chance.

She should've known better. When she'd helped Mrachek and two soldiers load the gear for the trip, they'd filed into a huge underground vault with a steel plank ceiling that looked removable. Four green, windowless vans and two familiar pickup trucks were parked along the side, but the lion's share of space was taken up by two helicopters with their rotors removed: both heavy military choppers. They sat on a massive lift rack that could, presumably raise them up to the convertible roof for liftoff. A squad of soldiers worked in pits beneath both the helicopters, assembling outsized racks that would probably hold missiles. She'd climbed into the back of a van and squatted on the shag-carpeted floor in a circle with four mute soldiers in civilian clothes. They'd passed around chocolate glazed donuts and a thermos of coffee, but Stella hadn't taken much. The way they wolfed them down, as if they might not get to eat again anytime soon, made her loath to deprive them, whether it was out of real danger, or bad manners born of habit. The van started and lurched into a steep, twisting ascent, like they were going up a spiral ramp in a parking garage. Sunlight flared through the tinted front windshield, but she felt afraid to stand and try to look out, for fear of the silent men around her.

A few times they whispered in each other's ears, but for the most part, they seemed perfectly at ease with the silent treatment, as if they wouldn't have said much more if she'd been absent.

They'd ridden in the van for an hour, then stopped in the midst of a huge maze of semi trailers in what Stella guessed must be a truckstop, probably in the Mojave Desert from the arid heat and the stinging blue sky. The soldiers fanned out to stand watch while the driver opened one of the cargo containers and nosed the van into it. He opened the back doors and offered Stella a fresh thermos of coffee and a package of chocolate doughnettes. He nodded at her thanks and went to work.

She watched Mrachek climb out of the other van with some other scientists. They all followed an armed escort into one of the trailers, then, a few minutes later, Mrachek came out and approached Stella, helped herself to the last doughnette. Without a word, she led Stella to another trailer, where a soldier held the cutout door open for them and shone a flashlight in after them to light their way. Mrachek turned sideways and edged past stacked wooden crates with HECHO EN MEXICO stenciled on them to what looked like the blind front end of the trailer, then pulled on a steel panel to reveal a ten-key pad. Too fast for Stella to read the code, Mrachek tapped it in and the wall beside her slid back in upon itself, revealing a darkened doorway. Mrachek stepped through and hit some buttons that sent fluorescent lights spluttering to life. Stella crept into the hidden space, expecting to find a smuggler's hole filled with armaments, or something. What she found instead was a miniature laboratory, the size of a kitchenette, no wider than the breadth of the trailer, but Stella saw most of the equipment she'd noticed in the sickbay reproduced here. There was a rudimentary trauma station and surgery, and an incubator in an isolation booth. Like the sickbay, the lab was designed specifically for the bizarre war Mrachek claimed her weird militia was fighting. Who funded these people? Against her nature, she'd been impressed into silence.

She'd held her feelings in check for an hour, watching Mrachek, trying to learn what they were up to without giving herself away. Mrachek prepped five slides with blood samples, and, after depositing three in a glassine in the freezer, donned a clear plastic faceshield and heavy gloves. She turned and squeezed past Stella to get to a locked cabinet. With one of the keys on the ring around her neck, she unlocked it and selected an unmarked green glass bottle. Stella recognized the test. Over the course of their awkward quarantine together, Mrachek had performed the same test on their own blood samples every hour on the hour. Stella never saw or heard anything of the soldier who got scratched, and never asked.

Stella had never taken her eyes off Mrachek's broad, square back as she stood and took a silent step towards the outer door, but she never saw the doctor's hand go for the strange gun she held in her hand as she turned. Some sort of dart cartridge rested in a transparent sheath where a barrel should be. "This has enough pharmaceutical curare in it to kill you before you feel the prick."

"I was just stretching my legs."

"We're leaving in a little while. Going back."

"I...just wanted to see the sun again before we went back."

That can be arranged once we return to base. I'm going to need your help running this batch of slides through in a few minutes."

"Is he one of us?" Mrachek raised an eyebrow at this. "I mean, is he human?"

Mrachek thought for a moment. She was not a woman who needed someone to talk at. But Stella was clearly not going anywhere, and had helped process the tests, had earned some answers. She was smart enough not to let it come to a fight. "He seems to be uncontaminated, but that isn't the issue." She started to turn away, and Stella reached out to touch her. Mrachek recoiled as if there was still some doubt about Stella's own biological status.

"He's a sick, emotionally damaged Gulf War veteran who may or may not have committed mass murder in the last twenty-four hours. We were forced to entrust him with a very special task which we lacked the manpower to complete ourselves, and he bungled it. If not for poor Mr. Napier, we might've been up shit creek without a paddle."

"You mean you still have the remains?"

"Oh, he's still very much alive," Mrachek said, shaking her head. Stella had no words. "We couldn't kill him."

"After what it did in your own fucking base, and what it could do? Burn it with napalm, if you have to."

Mrachek smiled humorlessly at this. "No, I mean, we haven't been *able* to kill him. That's what we're going to try to do when we get back. We're going to kill him again and again until we get it right. You want to help?"

"Don't have anything else to do, do I?" She looked at the charts on the table again.

When Mrachek had left the trailer to get the blood, Stella'd messed with the closed circuit TV system. Flipping through the dozen-odd cameras they had, she'd seen that they were at a truck stop somewhere in the Mojave desert, maybe Death Valley. There were no other vehicles parked near them, only row upon row of semi trailers parked at the edge of the lot. Dawn was coming, the sunrise an impressive sight even on the grainy color monitor. It felt like the first she'd seen in years.

Then she'd switched to a channel that carried a handheld camera feed. The cameraman followed Mrachek and an armed guard into a cargo container resting on a flatbed freight trailer. The camera had a light on it, so she'd clearly seen the man lying bound on the floor, his limbs secured behind his back in a position that in itself looked like a form of torture. She'd watched as Mrachek had extracted blood from the large, rawboned body, as the guard had complained over and over that they ought to have a flamethrower with this guy, human or not. She'd seen his head, hairless and sunburnt, and when they rolled him over, his face, carved down to sinew and unlovely, proto-Neanderthal bones, and clenched tightly, even in drugged sleep. His mouth worked, bit off the first three swabs Mrachek tried to get between his thin, chapped lips. The guard, in thick, clumsy rubber gloves, had to pry the man's jaw open to get a swab in. Even in sleep. Something about his instinctual defiance appealed to her and would not go away, despite what she heard about him later. This man was someone she'd only ever see on a TV, so it was safe to think about him.

"Are you going to kill him, too?" Stella asked, touching the charts.

"That isn't for me to decide," Mrachek answered, unperturbed. "But then," she said, "I think killing him would be granting him his secret, fondest wish."

One of the monitors blinked on just as Stella was thinking about turning it on. She flinched. The big, dark black man was on the screen, the Major. He was looking at a point just off-screen, the monitor that was showing him the sickbay trailer. He nodded towards Stella, then looked towards Mrachek.

"He's gone," Stella said.

~ 18 ~

Martin Cundieffe had never hungered for power, at least not power for its own sake. Any privilege exceeding the efficient execution of an agent's duty was something akin to hard drugs, not to be considered, lest one be swept away to destruction. He had never even "roast-beefed" a civilian, never flashed his badge to demand preferential treatment. Indeed, his childhood camping trips were stamped with memories of tales his father told over the fire, of vainglorious agents who abused their positions and were toppled by the dreaded Office of Professional Responsibility. The mere notion made him shudder.

Now he shuddered as the symptoms of a new relationship to power began to take hold.

After the giddy thrill of the midnight damage control meeting had been rudely snatched away, he'd settled back into routine, overseeing the minutiae of the section office's daily operations in Lane Hunt's absence, cautiously making inquiries into the China Lake incident and visiting with his mother. There'd been no further contact with Assistant Director Wyler, and only Hunt's increasingly frustrated lack-of-progress reports to process, and the entire situation had been on the verge of being filed in the drawer where Cundieffe kept things he did not officially Need To Know. This was a cardinal phrase in the Cundieffe household, one which Cundieffe had grown up honoring as much as any bright, curious son of a purebred FBI family could. He would never breathe a word of it to anyone, excepting maybe his mother, who still held her oath as a Federal employee as a lifelong sacred trust.

Then, at quarter past seven, not ten minutes after he'd arrived at his desk, came the call from Assistant Director Wyler. He was on a plane, bound for Washington. In light of the Death Valley developments, the FBI was back on the case, if only in a "cooperative" role, and the team was being called back out to Mojave. Would Martin be so good as to meet him at LAX to discuss the "ramifications of China Lake?" A car would pick him up outside the Federal Building and bring him to the airport to pick up the Assistant Director for a brief meeting over lunch. Cundieffe looked around to see if anyone was watching him, leaned back and spun in his chair until the physical dizziness canceled out the mental.

The driver had called at ten forty-five, and held open the door of a discreet black sedan with nearly opaque rear windows. The car had pulled out onto Wilshire and immediately onto the 405 South, where the traffic was moderately backed-up due to highway expansion. Invited to help himself to the minibar, Cundieffe had poured himself a tonic water and watched the endless construction slip past. The relevant files on his laptop were all committed to memory. He'd spent the entire morning composing his briefing, and felt confident that no question of detail or alternate point of view would catch him off guard. Certainly, one's career couldn't help but benefit from such a meeting, but Cundieffe refused to let vanity or ambition color his presentation. He would be a transparent screen for the Assistant Director's understanding of the China Lake incident, or at least the incident as the FBI had been allowed to pursue it—which would be the delicate thesis statement. Beyond that, his recommendation, in a Need To Know envelope of his own, contingent on the Assistant Director's visible and explicit approval of his brief on the case-in-progress. Yes, the Assistant Director would come to feel he'd done the case—and, by extension, the Bureau—a great service by coming to SA Martin Cundieffe.

After fifty-five minutes, the car slipped into the two-tiered traffic loop that fed LAX its human cargo, and the driver hugged the empty inside lane, whipping round the loop and back into the return lane. After the twelfth circuit, Cundieffe leaned forward and tapped on the partition, also tinted, between driver and passenger. "At what time is Assistant Director expected to make his arrival?" he asked. The driver turned and glanced at him for a moment, and Cundieffe thought he saw him shrug.

They circled the terminals eighteen more times before the driver got paged to come to the American Airlines arrivals gate and park. The driver rammed through the logjam of cabs and shuttlevans and SUV's to swoop into an open space in the taxi loading zone. A pair of Somali drivers approached him shouting loudly, but the driver sent them away by tapping the placard on his dashboard. Cundieffe whistled. The human hurricane of the busiest airport on the west coast roared over them like a river around an invisible rock. They sat there for another half an hour unmolested, somewhere in the middle of which Cundieffe guiltily took another tonic water. When Cundieffe spotted Assistant Director Wyler coming out of the terminal with a single briefcase and an overnight bag, the driver instructed him to sit tight and keep his door shut and his window up. He climbed out and met Wyler, took his bag, opened the rear passenger-side door for him, stowed the bag, got behind the wheel and skinned back into the inner lane again, in less time than it took Cundieffe to stammer out a greeting. Wyler nodded blandly and reached for the minibar.

Assistant Director Wyler looked as if he hadn't slept since the fifth of July meeting. On top of his briefcase, he expertly mixed a gin and tonic and quartered a lemon, plopped a segment in. He returned the lemon remnant, then fumbled around inside the minibar for a moment, then hit the intercom button. "Herb, where's all the goddamned tonic water?"

Cundieffe began to stammer out an apology, but Wyler cut him off with a dismissing wave and dug out a can of 7Up. "So," Wyler began after a steadying gulp of his drink, "I agree with your new assessment of the incident, one hundred percent. Top work, Cundieffe. And almost secure. Speaking of which, I have no secrecy document for you to sign. That should tell how you strictly confidential this conversation is. No one hears about it, Cundieffe, not even your immediate superiors. Not even your mother."

Cundieffe nodded, swallowed hard and looked down at his laptop. The only copies were on this computer, and the hard copy he'd printed up at the office. He'd only been connected to the system for a few minutes, to print it, and he'd erased the file's path from the system completely—or so he'd thought. The Assistant Director must've uploaded the file off the system during that time and read it on the plane. "I'm—honored to have had the opportunity—"

"The Bureau is being frozen out of the investigation by the military, because the militia is composed of, led by and/or includes, former or current military personnel, and not just grunts. This group is a brain-trust. Take a look at this, when you get the chance." He passed Cundieffe a Zip disk with a printed serial number on it. "Then erase it. Then burn it. Ah, this looks like a good spot. Herb, let's have lunch."

The car had pulled into short-term parking in the high-rise structure inside the traffic loop of the airport. Herb steered them into a shadowy alcove at the bottom of the structure, where the ramp leveled off before dead-ending at a cage filled with janitors' supplies. "I've got a connecting flight in half an hour, so we'll have to make do," Wyler said. "Hope you don't mind."

Herb slid back the partition and passed through two brown paper bags and some napkins, then climbed out, wandered up to the top of the ramp, and disappeared. Cundieffe tried to hide his disappointment until he opened his sack and a familiar aroma tickled his nostrils. Only one woman made egg salad sandwiches that smelled like this. Wyler must've been watching him, because he explained, "Everyone at the office says you never have anything else, when they see you eat." Wyler bit into his own sandwich, said, "Boy, this takes me back. Your mother uses a touch too much lemon pepper for my taste, but don't ever tell her I said so."

Cundieffe mopped his brow with his napkin, noticed only just in time that it'd come apart and left shreds of sodden paper pasted to his eyebrows. What was there left to say? "Sir, then, if you agree with the summation of facts, then, would it be presumptuous to inquire as to your—the, ah, the Bureau's assessment of my, um, my recommendations, which I suppose were, ah, also, ah, perused?"

"It's a bold course of action, well in touch with your astute evaluation of the probable forces in play, Martin. It's a tribute to your skills that you'd have to go up several levels of authority in the Bureau to see what a stupid idea it really is. No, refusing to cooperate with the military arm of the search would gain us nothing from them but a turf war, and it would backfire on us when this became public. It'd be a bigger plate of shit than the ATF served us when they lost control of Waco." Cundieffe winced at the unsavory language more than the humiliating and tragic memory. "And threatening to go public first would hardly alleviate our culpability in the public eye, even if nothing ever comes of the weapons theft. You may think that, but it's already too late in the game to try to look like boy scouts. We've cooperated with a sweeping regional search in the course of which we've conducted countless surveillances and searches without due process. We'll look like jackbooted idiots."

Properly dressed-down, Cundieffe stared at his hands feeding him the sandwich his mom made for him. He wondered if she put a note in his bag, hoped not. How would that look? He'd been an idiot to presume to propose Bureau policy on an issue of such staggering delicacy and magnitude. He hoped none of this would end up in his file. "I won't make the same mistake again, sir," he said.

"Oh God, Cundieffe, pull yourself together. As you observed yourself, you are not in possession of the full facts. And the Agent-In-Charge on the ground is an idiot. That's why I'm replacing him."

Cundieffe's head whipped around, nearly tearing a muscle. "What?" He massaged his neck, asked, "You mean Special Agent Hunt, sir? He's been head of the Section for four years, and has an exemplary internal report—"

"Hunt's a doorbuster, and always will be. You do most of his paperwork, feed him nearly all of his intel, most of which he doesn't even follow up on. Case in point the current debacle, with its possible connection to the murders in Death Valley."

"I'm sure Agent Hunt is pursuing the search with all due diligence, but if you have someone else to bring in, wouldn't that slow everything down even more, as he was brought up to speed?"

"You're already up to speed," Wyler said, finishing his sandwich and his drink and mixing another.

"Me? What? Sir, there're so many more experienced agents with counterterrorism backgrounds, who've logged more time in the field, let alone commanded a task force…" He ran out of breath and words at the same time, took a deep breath, and—nothing.

Wyler let him dangle for a moment longer, then patted his shoulder and sipped his drink. "You're the only agent in the Bureau whom I completely trust who has any inkling of the true significance of this incident, Agent Cundieffe. You hit the nail on the head at the meeting when you deduced that the terrorist group were military insiders with access to advanced softkill technology, and you pursued that course to the limits of your security clearance. I think you can find them, but Hunt could do that, if he thought more deeply. More than simple policework is called for, here."

Assistant Director Wyler leaned close to Cundieffe, close enough to envelope him in his mantle of booze-breath, close enough to give Cundieffe a split-second spasm of homosexual panic. It was those dirty, nasty stories about Hoover that no agent could completely put out of his mind. *What if he—No.* Such thoughts were unworthy of the Assistant Director, of himself, of the Bureau. *Pull yourself together.*

"The technology used to disable those sailors has been in use for over a decade. The disk I've given you proves that. It was used against the U.S. military and the contras on several occasions in Central America. You were half-right in your assessment of probable suspects. We are relatively certain that the group we're looking for includes former DARPA scientists, as well as defected Army and Navy personnel. The military wants to cover this up because of the black eye it'd give the Navy, and we don't want napalm dropped on Federal property, but the real pearl here is the softkill weaponry, and that's why the DOD's keeping us at arm's length. It's far in advance of anything they've developed, and they want it. With that kind of power, the military could justify expansion of peacekeeping operations abroad to create a de facto American empire, and renew their bid for a domestic policing mission in the major cities, which is the only reason they give a damn about the War On Drugs. It would be the greatest step towards fascism since the HUAC hearings, Martin." He said this with a straight face, so Cundieffe had to assume Wyler honestly believed the FBI was wrong to persecute known Communist subversives. He wondered at the man's politics, but he held his tongue.

"Now think of the possibilities for the Bureau, Cundieffe. Think of what we could accomplish if that kind of technology came under the auspices of the Department of Justice, of law enforcement, instead of military might." He didn't need to spell them out, and they both lapsed into a moment of silent visualization as the implications cascaded over them—bank robberies would become inconceivable, hostage crises and armed standoffs could be ended swiftly and decisively with zero casualties. No more Ruby Ridges, no more Wacos, no more Patty Hearsts. All through the gift of a new technology that could simply be seized by the right agency. Sure, there were thorny ethical questions to be worked over, but the light of the Greater Good shot them all full of holes. "Think of how much better the Bureau could serve the American people, Cundieffe," Wyler was still talking, leading Cundieffe out of his fugue and back to the present, with all its stupefying revelations and new responsibilities.

His skin felt tight, as if he were about to burst out of it and float away. He clenched his hands round his kneecaps until the discomfort brought him back to himself, and he said, "It would be an honor to serve in this capacity, sir. How soon can the transfer be affected?"

"Hunt can't be pulled out of the field by regular channels, so there'll be an emergency OPR review convened on some charges which will keep him suspended for the next ninety days, at least. A blot on his record, but a temporary one. You'll be posited as his interim replacement, but you're the man I want to see this through to its ultimate conclusion. Give it two days. During which time I'd like to see more information on this Storch character. I'd like him nailed down as either a co-conspirator or coincidence. If he worked with them, he's probably dead now, whether or not his actions in Furnace Creek were sanctioned. But I'd like to know. Can you put that together in forty-eight hours, Cundieffe?"

"If I don't sleep, sir."

"Good. Don't." As if summoned by silent alarm, Herb climbed back into the car and steered them out of the structure. The car bellied up to the curb and Herb got out and held the door for Wyler, who'd said nothing and done nothing but sip his drink. He shook Cundieffe's hand, said, "We're all counting on you, son," and merged into the torrent of bodies rushing into the terminal. Herb returned to the driver's seat and headed back for the freeway. "Back to the office?" Herb asked.

"What? Ah, yes, please," Cundieffe managed. He had a lot on his mind, he'd probably collect his things and go home to review the disk— and weigh everything else Wyler had dumped on him.

"Here," Herb said, handing something through the pass-through. It was another brown paper bag. "Your mother packed you a second sandwich."

Shame-faced, Cundieffe thanked him and took the bag. Inside was another egg salad sandwich, into which Cundieffe tucked with renewed gusto, and a note. Looking out for Herb's prying eyes in the rearview mirror, he sneaked a peek at it.

Martin,

Sounds important! Your father and I always knew you'd rise to the top of the Bureau, but not on an empty stomach. Here's a little extra treat to celebrate your whatever-it-is!

XOXOXOXO,

Mom

Wrapped up in the note, inside a tightly sealed envelope of wax paper, were two oatmeal cookies. Cundieffe ate them, and began to feel better.

~ 19 ~

He wasn't prepared for the city.

The constant roaring of cars, voices shouting at nobody, the stench of burning, of consumption. The day was hot, not nearly so bad as Death Valley, but muggy. The heat supercharged the motes of industrial dust and moisture in the air. He had no choice but to breathe it in, felt in congealing in his blood, oozing out of his pores with the consistency of glue. The sky pressed down on San Jose like a tarpaulin stretched taut under the weight of megatons of rain that would never wash the filthy ground. He felt it against his neck, smelled the reek of ozone and knew in his bones from one step to the next that he would be struck by lightning.

Storch had never liked cities: growing up on army bases, cities, by comparison, were like zoos with no bars. Too squeamish to fight real wars, civilians nevertheless killed each other, and themselves, in a myriad of sick, cowardly ways. Cities were unsafe, teeming with weak, unscrupulous people, the Army taught him, and everything he saw with his own eyes only endorsed their view. It wasn't as much of a stretch, then, for Storch to embrace the Special Forces take on civilians. They felt about them as white blood cells must feel about fatty tissue. Although they defended them and their way of life, albeit in a very roundabout way, they were disgusted by them, and secretly longed for a purging that would make the body of the nation a leaner, more efficient machine.

He stopped at the first payphone he saw with an intact phonebook and looked up Sperling. There were two in the county, one in Sunnyvale: Donald Sperling. He thought it strange to find the name there, despite his having looked for it. Most parents who'd lost children stayed put for the first few years, as if the missing had merely wandered, and would one day come home to them. Once hope melted away and the police stopped calling with leads, the memories caught up with them and they cleared out.

He called the number. It rang seven times before someone picked up. A hollow voice, nominally male, croaked, "Hello?"

"Mr. Sperling? Mr. Donald Sperling?"

"Yes? Who is this?"

"You don't know me, sir, but I need to know you. I've come a long way—"

"What's this about?"

"I don't know how else to tell you this, sir, so—I've found your daughter."

"My daughter? But…that's impossible…Who is this?"

"Mr. Sperling, does the name Radiant Dawn mean anything to you?"

The line went dead.

Storch walked into the Sunnyvale Public Library and had to stop, had to grab at his temples and tell himself he hadn't walked into a giant beehive. Everywhere, beneath every hushed sound, the sinister buzzing of fluorescent lights, like the all-pervading, susurrant voice of the library's secret custodians. Like a tuning fork, it set up a resonance in the fillings in his teeth, like his mouth was full of hornets. His eyes took several moments to adjust to the darkness; in the meantime, all he could see was a sickly sea-green murk out of which flashing shapes swam, like the emerging details of an overexposed Polaroid.

Storch stopped just short of the security portal, ignoring a woman who ran into his back as he considered the automatic still concealed in his waistband. It took a moment before he recognized that the portal wasn't a metal detector at all, only a screening device for detecting the foil security strips in the library books. By then, everyone at the circulation desk was staring at him, and he moved as quickly as he could across to the periodicals room. He found a computer in a shadowy alcove and set about trying to get some answers.

The computer offered a keyword search feature for local and national newspapers. First, he tried 'Radiant Dawn.' Three hits, one each from the *San Jose Mercury News*, the *Fresno Bee*, and the *Sacramento Bee*. All three articles were more or less the same sort of fluffy human-interest story that leads the local news section on a Sunday morning. He read only the first few paragraphs of each.

RADIANT DAWN HOSPICE OUTREACH SERVICE OFFERS RAY OF HOPE FOR TERMINAL CANCER PATIENTS

Georgette Kassel, 13, loves to paint with watercolors. Her bright, cheery renderings of the flower garden outside her window cover every inch of wall-space in her room at the secluded Radiant Dawn Hospice Village, near Convict Lake. As she puts the finishing touches to her latest creation, she tells me that the sunflowers are her favorites.

Georgette has had a harder row to hoe in life than most. Already an orphan and a ward of the state, she understands that she has less than three months to live. She has an especially aggressive brain tumor known as a Grade IV glioblastoma multiforme, which has spread through most of the tissue of her cerebrum. Radiation and chemotherapy have failed to stem the cancer's growth, and surgery was never an option. A massive regimen of medications keep her seizures under control, but doctors have written off Georgette, and hope only to sustain her quality of life for the time she has left. But Georgette smiles as she signs her sunflower picture and hangs it up to dry. "I still have hope," she says, in her soft, shy voice. "The counselors here have told me that with every new sunrise, there's the chance that something wonderful will happen."

Storch scratched at the irritable stubble on his scalp. It had to be a coincidence. There was nothing in the fluff pieces that smacked of child abduction or genetic terrorism. Still, something nagged at him. If only they'd turn down those lights.

He tried a search on Sidra Sperling. Twelve hits, the first few stories carried on UPI, the rest merely regional as interest and hope dwindled. He called up the listing for the first article, from Christmas Day, 1990, two days after the girl was taken.

LOCAL GIRL MISSING, FEARED ABDUCTED

Donald Sperling, 38, and his wife, Marie, 36, were en route to visit Donald's parents in Southern California, for the Christmas holiday when they pulled in to the Inyokern rest stop along Highway 395. What happened then shattered their plans, their Christmas, and their family.

"She just went in to wash her hands," Sperling said through tears at an Inyo County Sheriff's Dept. press conference last night. "We didn't turn our backs on her for but a moment, while Marie was getting drinks and I checked the map. We never saw her come out."

Inyo County's Sheriff Mavoli has formed a joint task force with the Kern County Sheriff and has asked for the FBI's help in picking up the trail of the missing girl...

Storch rubbed his hands over his skull, cupped his ears. A few moments away from the lights, and it came to him. He ordered another search of Radiant Dawn, this time going back to the time of the kidnapping. Nothing new. He tried again, this time going back to the time of the girl's birth, the only other milestone he had. One hit, from December 12, 1981.

UTOPIAN DESERT COMMUNE FOUND ABANDONED
This morning, Sheriff's Deputies led reporters through the clapboard ghost town that lies in the nameless, bowl-shaped valley a mile east of the 395, and two miles south of Convict Lake. With windows knocked out, doors hanging ajar and tumbleweeds piling up against the exterior walls, it resembles most ghost towns of the Old West, but with a chilling difference. Only a few months ago, deputies say, this was a living, breathing community, albeit one you'd be hard-pressed to find on any map, and one where visitors were never welcome.
Very little is known about the apparently defunct "New Age" commune that called itself Radiant Dawn...

The same fucking name. In the same fucking place.
A connection between the things he'd read nattered at him like the noise of the fluorescents, but he couldn't make out what it was trying to tell him for all the buzzing. Unable to stand it anymore, he lurched up and ran out.

As he wandered the city, first on foot, and then on a bus, Storch tried to put together what he'd read. Maybe it was stupid, trying to get a handle on some secret organization fighting a covert war in California by reading old newspapers, but something about both groups irritated him, made him do something he hadn't been able to do properly since the war. It made him think deeply.
Neither of the two organizations seemed to tie in to the abduction. One was a utopian hippie dream almost twenty years dead, the other a charitable organization for cheering up the doomed. But Donald Sperling, who still lived in the same house from which his daughter was taken and in which his wife had died, had bolted at the mention of the name.
He found it passing strange that a bunch of weirdos living out in the desert should've been able to keep such a low profile until they disappeared. True, a commune was hardly cause for alarm in California in the 1970's, but Jim Jones' Peoples' Temple and the Manson Family were still raw wounds in the mass psyche back then, and a large group in the

middle of nowhere under the leadership of a fringe religious guru should've attracted more attention. That they broke up four or five months before the girl's birth, that she was snatched from a rest stop that was practically their front door, compounded his certainty that this was the link. Indeed, it was the only thing that tied Sidra Sperling to Radiant Dawn. That and the say-so of a star-chamber of paramilitary lunatics. What had he fallen into, and when would he hit bottom?

~ 20 ~

Lt. Col. Mort Greenaway hated civilians. He hated SCUD hunts even more. His immediate future looked to be chockfilled with both.

Never one to command from the rear, Greenaway had spent most of the last three days riding shotgun in a small, unarmed Navy TH-57 Sea Ranger helicopter, tracing the ever-expanding perimeter of their search field, watching the chopper's shadow sliding over a million different varieties of godforsaken wasteland, shepherding each of the motley assortment of search teams the Navy and FBI had mustered.

To say they were a mixed bag was putting it mildly. The FBI agents he'd been sent, under a dickbrain named Hunt, were in charge of bracing the locals, coordinating with local law enforcement to perform house-to-house interviews and surveillance. Fourteen teams of Navy SEALS swept the ground, from Joshua Tree National Monument to the Owens Valley. Greenaway was fast becoming disgusted with their lack of initiative. Their reports came more and more frequently and offered less and less in the way of useful data. They were freaked out, sent on a search when they were told only that it was not a drill, and placed under a strange commander. Like hunting dogs tracking a scentless fox for a new master, they were chasing their tails, especially after the accident.

On the first day of the search, a SEAL team in the Panamint Range had come across an abandoned borax mineshaft out of which a copious amount of smoke was pouring. The medic in the group had provoked the ribbing of his comrades when he identified the scent of marijuana in the smoke. Greenaway thought it sounded wrong, but ordered them into the mine before the park rangers or the local law enforcement took over. Four went in, and almost immediately tripped an explosive charge which collapsed the whole shaft, killing three of them. The rest of the SEALs took a negative shine to him thereafter, blaming him, rather than themselves, for exposing the team's ineptitude. Several near-fatal friendly fire exchanges had further enlivened the search into an exercise in logistical clusterfucking that would be studied by scholars of covert ops for generations to come. In another day, he hoped, his own people would be totally mobilized and could step into the main search, and things would go more smoothly.

Greenaway hunted Scud missiles in Kuwait and western Iraq, and had come up empty, unless the hundred-odd wooden decoys they destroyed counted. The British SAS had run circles around them, picking off four launchers in their sector. No matter how well-schooled at taking down actors and mannequins, Delta Force was still a relatively green outfit, with only the Desert One debacle in Iran to their credit, while the SAS had been honed on countless anti-terrorist assignments, from Ireland to Hong Kong. Greenaway had earned his reputation for taking advice from nobody and paid for it in assault charges, but if he never seemed to learn, he could adapt. The lessons were not lost on him, and within a year, he had thoroughly drilled his teams to sweep hostile territory and isolate offensive forces, no matter how small or how well dug in. He had made zealots of his men, martyrs to the code of SpecWar. Greenaway silently hoped that the SEALs would continue fumbling and shooting at each other until he could replace them. His men wouldn't stand out; half of them would recon the entire eastern half of the state undercover as bikers, truckers, traveling salesmen, even wetbacks. His people would root out the group. It was a strange feeling not to be looking forward to that event. Now that Greenaway had been told who they probably were, he was more confident that he could find them, but the thought of actually neutralizing them almost reminded him of what it felt like to be afraid.

Because he wasn't looking for terrorists.

When the early morning meeting on the fifth of July had gotten out, Lt. Col. Greenaway had found himself invited to join the meeting's inner circle for a "corollary briefing" with the CIA, DIA, NSA and Rear Admiral Meinsen. Sibley, the CIA rep, looking freshly terrorized, took the floor and laid out an amended shortlist of suspects. Greenaway was familiar with more than a few of the names, and for once, he'd been stunned to silence rather than bored. There followed a lot of explaining, after which Greenaway took his leave with a Zip disk filled with photographs and scanned documents requiring a Top Secret clearance to review.

Now, Sibley sat opposite him on the bench seats usually occupied by pilot trainees on this outdated old helicopter, sniping animatedly at one of his colleagues into a cell phone. Greenaway eyed Sibley's geek junior partner, clattering away on a laptop, and his own lieutenant, watching a small convoy of Navy trucks thread a condemned two-lane highway below. He tapped the lieutenant, who passed him a folded Geology Survey map on which he'd been marking their position.

They were on the outskirts of Baker, a wide spot on the road to Las Vegas. The trucks were bound for an abandoned industrial park that a spotter plane had found to be occupied by a large group of people. Guards with small arms had been observed outside. Greenaway had seen the thermo shots the spotter chopper had taken last night, and had no interest in setting down. The groupings of the bodies inside the rusted out warehouses had been huddled together for warmth. They were illegal Mexican immigrants who'd paid the wrong people to get them across the border. Greenaway rubbed his temples, tugged at his beard until brittle red and silver hairs came out in his hands. In a week of searching the hottest, most desolate place in North America, they'd only succeeded in rooting out drug kitchens, smugglers, and well-armed hermits who'd been scattered from their squat-town by a crazed Gulf War vet who'd shot up the local law and set fire to a store. Greenaway had been out of the world entirely too long, but decided now that he'd missed absolutely nothing.

Sibley was tapping his knee. Touching him. The urge to seize him by the lapels of his double-breasted blazer and heave him out into the noonday sun was overwhelming. The pleasure of the fantasy would have to do, for now.

"There's a junkyard about two klicks south of our present position that merits a quick look, we think," Sibley said, his tone defensive in anticipation of another argument. The morning's sweep had amounted to a lively exchange of ideas on search methodologies, which had accomplished nothing, but put a lot of mileage on Greenaway's flying-lesson fantasy. Every trailer park, every burned-out gas station, every solitary derelict propane tank in the middle of an empty lot became a bone of contention, and here was Sibley with yet another, throwing around the royal *we* like Queen fucking Victoria and putting his sweat-slimed little pink rat-paw on *his knee*. At least Hunt wasn't here. He would've tried to bring a newscrew along.

"What, are there a couple of helicopters parked out front?" Greenaway asked. "How many military reconnaissance missions have you overseen in the field, *Mr.* Sibley?"

"How many Scud launchers did you and your teams find in Desert Storm, Lieutenant Colonel?"

Greenaway just stared, then, while Sibley studied something fascinating on the empty desert floor, he switched on his headset and ordered the pilot to turn south and find the CIA's precious fucking junkyard.

As it turned out, Sibley's junkyard had once served as the town drive-in, and the huge screen of whitewashed sheet metal still loomed over the lot like a shuttered window into another world, the cars stacked before it seemingly having gone to rot and rust waiting for it to open again. The marquee rose up out of a mound of tumbleweeds outside the yard. On one side, in faded red paint, LIBERTY SALVAGE YARD. On the other, the last drive-in features: RED DAWN and MOTE HELL, and a message: GOD LESS ERICA. *Amen*, Greenaway said in his heart.

The Sea Ranger swept over the junkyard at about a hundred feet, banking so Greenaway could survey the interior at a glance. A cinder-block bunker, which once housed the projection booth and the snack bar, still stood in the center, and he spotted two Hispanic males in ragged flannel coats and jeans picking through the wreckage. They looked up and backed out of the blasting wash from the props, but didn't bolt.

"Looks promising, Mr. Sibley," Greenaway said with syrupy contempt. "What's up your ass about this place?"

Sibley looked absurdly proud of himself as he answered, "Going over Agent Cundieffe's files on activity in the region—"

Cundieffe. The junior G-man behavioral scientist. The little paper-pushing eunuch had bothered Greenaway more than made any logical sense, not least because every speculation he'd offered at the meeting had dovetailed neatly with what the spook subcommittee had briefed him on later.

"Remarkably exhaustive," Sibley went on. "Cundieffe's quite the overachiever. He covers reported incidents the local cops never even followed up on. About four years ago trucks came and went out of this yard at odd hours, and passersby thought they saw aircraft landing. The Baker sheriff investigated, staked the place out for two weeks, but never found anything. It was dismissed as a onetime illegal immigrant smuggling operation, and no further reports were ever filed. I think maybe your men should comb the area, check for underground bunkers, that sort of thing." He smiled, then turned the page. "Moving along, there's an old railyard just over the Cal-Neva border—"

Greenaway raised the pilot. "Set down anywhere."

Sibley went white. "What? We're not prepared for—"

"Three SEALs died reconning a hole in the ground on my watch. You want to call searches? Fine. Do this one."

The helicopter set down just outside the front gate, throwing up a sandstorm into which Greenaway and his lieutenant leapt readily, but Sibley had to be dragged.

"This isn't how it's done, Lieutenant Colonel. We're putting ourselves at risk—"

"Then you're beginning to see how much confidence I have in you and your tip sheet," Greenaway shouted back, and made for the gate. The four Delta operatives sitting in the back row of seats sprang out and took up a perimeter around the chopper.

A sun-bleached plastic sign hung from the chain-link fence of the gate, TRESPASSERS WILL BE EATEN, but there was no sign of dogs, and the pair of Mexicans who met them at the gate seemed none too eager to talk, let alone devour them. Greenaway ordered his lieutenant to take the patrol group and walk the yard, with both eyes on the ground, and shouted at Sibley's lackey to do the same. The milquetoast little creep looked at Sibley for a countermand, but Sibley was wary of pushing Greenaway any further. The group of them went off at right angles, eyes glued to the oil-spattered sand, while Greenaway and Sibley rushed to brace the Mexicans. The pair of them stood looking sheepish

"*Buenos dias, amigos,*" Sibley stammered in Yale Spanish, "*Donde esta el jefe?*"

"Shut up, shithead," Greenaway hissed in Sibley's ear. He turned to the workers and said, in unaccented peasant Spanish, "*The United States needs your help today, gentlemen. The United States helps its friends, yes?*"

The Mexicans looked at each other, then back at Greenaway. "*You looking for smugglers?*" one of them asked at last. "*This is a clean place. No drugs here.*" Greenaway pegged a noticeable Salvadoran accent in the man's mumbled response.

"*You are from El Salvador, yes?*" the man nodded. "*Came here to get away from the troubles, yes?*" The man nodded again. "*Then you know how the US Army feels about guerrillas. That's what we're looking for today. Guerrillas.*"

"*Salvadoran guerrillas?*" the man asked, then smiled. "*No, no, no. We love this country. America number one!*"

"*Yes indeed,*" Greenaway answered, smiling. "*My stupid colleague here,*" he pointed at Sibley, who'd retreated back into his cell phone, "*thinks there's an ammunition dump here, or close by. Many big barrels of bad chemicals, maybe stored in a cave or a truck trailer, maybe buried in the sand. Have you seen anything like that around here?"*

The man shook his head emphatically, but the other one whispered in his ear, eyes fearfully glued to Greenaway all the while. The speaker shook his head and moved his hands in a suppressing gesture. Greenaway reached into his breast map pocket, fished out two green cards and held them up before the astonished wetbacks.

"Do you gentlemen really love this country? I can arrange it so you don't have to hide anymore. You can apply for citizenship. Legally. I just want to know what you know. The United States takes good care of its friends, but friendship has to be earned, yes?"

The men conferred a bit longer, then the speaker said, *"We were told not to say,"* he said, eyes downcast.

"Where you're from, you should know better than anyone else how the United States treats its enemies." He held the cards out, certified and processed by the INS for just such an eventuality. The other operatives empowered to hand them out called them Get Into America Free Cards.

"Men in trucks come," he said, *"they come and they put barrels into the ground."* He waved his hands around to take in the whole of the junkyard.

For a single, glittering instant, Lt. Col. Greenaway felt as he had the last time he'd seen combat, a tiny engagement in Lebanon that'd made no papers and which all nations involved had agreed to keep secret. His hands became a hundred hands, his brain subdivided into a thousand chambers, each parsing a step in his survival and the enemy's demise. It took fierce self-discipline not to give in to that illusion of omnipotence, to do everything at once and leave it to someone else to apologize. Greenaway hadn't risen to the rank he held, the highest an officer could reach while attached to Delta Force, which he dearly loved, for want of self-discipline. The enemy was *here.*

"Where are they now?" Both of them shook their heads like they were covered in hornets. *"When were they here last?"*

"They come every month, sometimes twice. Maceo and me, we let them in and then we go down the road to the gas station until they go away."

Sibley's clammy hand on Greenaway's shoulder. He fought the urge to seize it, twist it off and beat its owner dead with it. "A word, Colonel?"

Greenaway took a very deep breath and turned on the CIA man.

"I've just got off the phone with a congressional aide," Sibley said. He looked sicker than usual. "This place is off-limits."

Greenaway took hold of Sibley's shoulder now, bore down on it and drove the man halfway to his knees under the force of his full weight as he leaned into the man's sweaty pink raisin of an ear and hissed, "It's *here*, fuckhead. It's *HERE*."

Sibley staggered out from under the Colonel and backed away a few more paces, stumbled over the gutted chassis of a Datsun hatchback. He smiled. "There's nothing here, Lieutenant Colonel, nothing we're looking for. The aide works for the Representative for this district. About ten years ago, when said Congressman was the state assemblyman for this hellhole, he began taking a series of sizable donations in return for letting a waste disposal company—"

Greenaway looked at the ground beneath his feet, at the oily sheen on the gravel. "Shit," he said. "We're standing on a toxic waste dump?"

Sibley nodded. "Those trucks. Up until about four years ago, they were filling an open pit with barrels of PCBs. The company stopped paying him, but they own him down to his soul, so they still dump here. I suggest we exfil out of here posthaste."

Greenaway turned and walked away to cover the doubt spreading across his face like ink in a clear pool. Sibley was as hot to get them out as he'd been to get them in, and this sudden revelation of toxic waste… Despite its legendary hubris, the CIA did know everything, just too late to use it effectively, and this smacked of classic CIA infobackup. But Greenaway had seen too many notes passed in secret, too many radical about-faces, in the last week not to wonder.

He barked his LT over and ordered him to pull the search team out, but only after collecting samples of sand from each quadrant of the yard. "Do it smoothly, without Sibley or his freak on a leash seeing." The LT snapped a salute and went to make it so. Greenaway met Sibley and the Salvadorans at the gate. Sibley was shifting from foot to foot as if the toxic soil was eating through the soles of his burnished wingtip shoes. Greenaway ignored him and buttonholed the two laborers, handed them the green cards. They looked them over in wonder, eyes twinkling. *"Welcome to the United States, gentlemen. Always remember who your friends are. And get a real job. This place'll make you ill."* They nodded, practically bowed, but Greenaway was already getting back on the helicopter. Watching his men slipping on board and the ground dropping away beneath them, he put on his headset, and almost immediately it chirped in his ear.

"Greenaway. Speak"

"Special Agent Hunt, here," the voice warbled through waves of distortion and whipping wind at the other end. "We've recovered a pickup truck from the bottom of an arroyo out in—" muffled, "Where are we?" then back in Greenaway's ear, "—two miles north of SR 190, three and a quarter miles west of Darwin, in Death Valley. It was driven in, then buried. We would've missed it, but for the flare it made on the thermals this morning."

"And?"

"And it's registered to a Sgt. Zane Ezekiel Storch, US Army Special Forces Fifth Group, retired. You may or may not've seen the report. He burned down his store and shot two of the three local law in Furnace Creek."

"Ah, yes." From what little of Storch's tale of woe and misdirected wrath had trickled down to him, Greenaway saw a prime candidate for a cutout in the China Lake heist. Perhaps he participated, then flipped out. Or was following orders, creating a public spectacle to hamper the covert search operation. Probably, this Storch had outlived his usefulness. "Storch's body in the truck?"

"No, it's clean, except for—well, somebody took a piss in there, but we saw no signs of foul play. We're gonna tow it out and run the wreck to LA for labwork."

"Move nothing. I'll be right there," Greenaway snapped, and cut off Hunt, switched over to the pilot's channel and gave him the orders. Even if this came to nothing, Greenaway didn't trust any eyes but his own to see what there was to see. The FBI was good, but they were investigators, trained to solve crimes. This was no crime, Greenaway knew, though he alone seemed to recognize it for what it was. This was war. And, God willing, it would be *his* war.

The two Salvadoran laborers watched the helicopter dust off and claw its way back over the northwestern horizon, retreated back into the yard and shackled the gate, and tore up their green cards. "Can you believe that motherfucker? One fucking green card each."

The other chuckled. "You gave in too cheap, Medina. He would've let us send for our whole village if you could've come up with a better story."

"D'you get all that?" Medina said into his shirt pocket. "I think we'll be secure through the terminal phase, but we're gonna have to stay at condition yellow up here for the duration. That Delta asshole smelled rats."

~ 21 ~

He lay on the bed of the room in the Rambler's Rest only after stripping off the covers, which were saturated with some sort of stainguard and the residue of a fabric softener that gave him a rash. The rust-red carpet was matted with dust, and the beige curtains were mottled with vague M-shaped patterns that might've been either images of seagulls or greasy lip-prints.

The TV blurped and blathered in the corner, showing an entertainment program with celebrities he'd never seen before, all of them either inviting the camera into the most intimate corners of their lives or fleeing like gunshy game animals. He supposed people watched such shows to jump into another's skin, to live for a while inside someone beautiful and refreshingly shallow, someone who had the world's admiration, and the world's shoulder to cry on when they didn't get their way. Storch tried to feel like a normal person watching TV, tried desperately not to identify with the hunted ones. Finally, he switched it off. The knob came off in his hand.

He paced the room, too chafed by the sick city-heat to wear clothes, unable to turn on the air conditioner or relax on any of the chemically treated furniture. Whose shoulder could *he* cry on? Calling his father was a dubious prospect on normal days. Even in his lucid periods, when he knew who his son was and could speak in his own words and not just quotes from Revelations, he offered little solace. As the only surviving relative of a fugitive cop-killer, his father would be under surveillance, and any calls to the Norwalk asylum would probably be traced. Who could he call in his time of crisis?

Suddenly his mind clicked, and a plug was pulled in the floor of his skull, and all the molten confusion drained away to reveal a plan. Not a plan, actually, but a course of action. He got the phonebook out from under the Gideon Bible and the *Dianetics* in the end table and looked through the San Jose white pages business listings. There it was: Radiant Dawn Terminal Crisis Intervention Line.

His hands shaking, he punched the number, listened intently to the string of warbling rings. Four, five—perhaps it was an old phone book, perhaps they'd shut down—six rings, then: "You have reached the Radiant Dawn Terminal Crisis Intervention Line. All calls are recorded." Storch's bad hand hovered over the cutoff button.

"This is Heather. How may I help you?"

Any act he might've tried to put on to draw the lady out fell out of his mind when he heard her voice. So warm, so hypersensitive, so attuned to suffering, that he didn't want to lie to her, because if he told her the truth, she would understand, would help him see how to make it better. "I—I never called one of these things before…"

"That's okay. I'm here to listen, and help you understand what you're going through. Why don't you start by telling me your name?"

"I don't want to tell you my name right now," he snapped, and bit it back too late. Why didn't he come up with a name? Why couldn't he lie to her?

"Okay then, just tell me what you feel."

"I'm feeling real angry and kind of sick, and I've had a lot of things go…really, really wrong, and I just wish I could figure out what's real and what isn't, and who's doing this to me, if it's somebody, and get them to stop. D'you understand what that's like?"

"Indeed I do. A lot of people feel that way when they're facing a terminal illness. When there's no other hope left, we try to find a scapegoat to focus our anger, something tangible we can grasp for to try to make it stop. The sad truth is that it can't be beaten or bargained with or begged off. But there's a happy truth too, sir. Do you want to know what that is?"

Storch's voice surprised him when he heard it say, "Tell me the happy truth." He could feel a strange choking sensation deep in his throat that told him he was about to sob.

"The happy truth is that when you learn to embrace your fate, what you see as an ending can be a new beginning. Now, sir, I can tell from the sound of your voice that you've gone about as far as you can with the way things are right now. If you want to take a positive step towards embracing change, you've got to come to someone who truly understands. Do you know where our center is located?"

He replied sleepily, "It—I think it's in the book—"

"Yes, that's right. When you feel the time is right, I'd like to see you. My name is Heather, and I'll be here when you're ready. Now, if you're ready to tell me your name…"

The door shook in its frame with a furious pounding, and it was like a fist on a windshield rousing a man sleeping in an idling car full of carbon monoxide. The phone dropped from his ear and Storch was behind the door with the sentry's gun clutched in his hands.

"Who's there?"

"Zane Ezekiel Storch. Open the door, please," a deep, humorless basso voice, a cop's voice, shouted. Storch peered through a crack in the blinds, saw no flashing lights, no SWAT commandos braced by the window. Looking through the peephole, he saw only a dim pink mass that might've been chewing gum.

"Okay," he called back, opening the door and throwing it wide, lunged forward and snatched the visitor by the collar, yanked him into the room and threw him to the ground at Storch's feet. His gun jabbed into the pale, sweaty face of Ely Buggs.

"Shit, Zane, what are you doing still in the States? You got something against Mexicans?"

"Buggs, what are you doing here?"

"I mean, Jesus, man, you're headed in the wrong direction, you know? Canada's nicer, but they'll turn your ass in. They only get to pretend to be a sovereign nation at all because we don't want the *Quebecois* problem."

Storch's grip on Buggs's neck tightened, but it was no use. He needed information, and threatening Buggs with death was like menacing a spider monkey with a restraining order. He only started to make less sense.

How Buggs had found him was obvious. He made fake driver's licenses and social security cards for everybody in Thermopylae, including three sets for Storch. He'd run some kind of name-search program that scooped credit inquiries, and flagged "Dan Gundersen," the name he'd used to book the room.

"Why are you here, Buggs?" I thought you were going back east, to your computer job."

"Shit, man, I couldn't go back there, Americans are hardly even the same species, anymore. East and west coasters hate each other, can scarcely communicate, and you can tell one from another on sight. They even secrete conflicting pheromones, man. A few more generations, they won't even be able to interbreed if they want to…"

"What are you doing here, Buggs? If you wanted to talk, you could have called. Who sent you?"

Buggs laughed that maddeningly disarming patented Ely Buggs laugh. "Shit, commando, ease up. You owe me a week's pay. And besides, I don't think you're trying to leave the country at all."

"Which concerns you not at all, Buggs."

"You're working for those guys, aren't you? Those militia guys with the arsenal under your store. You're doing some dastardly shit for them, aren't you?"

Ely Buggs was an amoral freak who visited corporal punishment on fools, but he was good people, and Storch believed he was nothing if not a good judge of character. Besides, everyone else he knew was dead, insane, or somehow involved in a conspiracy to frame him for murder, if not all of the above. Storch let him go. Buggs flopped into one of the folding chairs beside the door and rubbed at his neck. Storch got a good look at him. His skin was still peeling from months of sunburn, but he'd put on weight. He wore a heinous Hawaiian shirt with lurid scenes of tiki gods and volcano virgin sacrifices, equally obnoxious plaid flannel pajama bottoms and bulky black orthopedic wrist braces on his bony pink arms. Storch remembered how Ely'd bitched about having carpal tunnel syndrome, some candy-ass injury computer geeks had invented. "Are you with them, or what?" he finally asked.

"I'm not working for anybody. I'm just looking for a man."

"Let me help you."

Buggs steered a big silver Ford Econoline van up the northbound 101. The flat brown grid of San Jose gave way to the standoffish suburban enclave of Los Altos, then to wild rolling hills. Suddenly, the unending ranks of commuter traffic looked ridiculous and unreal, and it became difficult to imagine that there was a city at either end of the road. Storch watched Buggs's bracered hands, watched the faces in the other cars, tried to nod in time to his manic spiel.

When he explained it, it all made a perfect Ely Buggs brand of sense. Cut loose from his job in Thermopylae and fresh out of his medication, Buggs's obsessive-compulsive mannerisms had begun to fester. One of these, it seemed, was an overwhelming urge to send postcards. He'd buy batches of them whenever he moved to a new place, address them to everyone he could think of, making sure they knew where he was now, that he was alive and safe, and anything else that was bothering him at the time. The rest he sent to total strangers, to people and businesses from whom he'd gotten cards months or years before. They'd simply say "Sorry to bother you," or "In the event of my death please forward this to the Federal Bureau of Investigation" or something like that. When he got his new job, he'd had to send one to Storch, and commenced to tracing him. He handed the postcard to Storch now. On the front was a picture of a mortician's workroom, where a dour clinician was embalming a famous movie cowboy's dead horse. "Greetings From Sunny Colma, California."

After Thermopylae, Buggs hitched his way to the Bay Area and Palo Alto, where he hit a bank to pick up some cash. Storch knew enough about Buggs to know what kind of bank he meant. Either through computer chicanery or some freak genetic misfire, Ely Buggs was a most eagerly sought after donor of blood and sperm, and could probably make a living off that alone.

"You won't believe the place where I'm working now. This is their van. They're—"

"A funeral home."

"Better. You know, man, if I've learned one thing about the world it's this: intelligence is a finite pool of energy, unevenly distributed among individuals of every sapient species on the planet. Every population expansion stretches it a little thinner. I think we first began to exhaust the pool in 1914. It's dangerously close to a backlash now, I think. I mean, when you look at the signs, I mean, acephalic babies being born in Texas, you know what that means? No fucking brains at all, Zane, they stop at the eyebrows."

"I'm not in the mood, right now, Buggs."

"And you'd think the government would be doing something about it, right? Well, sure they are. They've got a crash program to eugenically engineer supergeniuses, so they can stockpile intelligence, even as they're accelerating the meltdown. Wait and see if I'm wrong, in about five years, we're all going to go feral and live in the trees."

"Are you done?"

"See if I'm wrong, that's all."

They rolled through the hills, past clusters of housing developments that seemed to have been assembled by robots or lowered out of the sky or assembled by giant hornets; past vague hints of towns hiding behind mountains or stands of evergreens, hermit towns where time flowed at an agreed-upon rate, if at all, like Thermopylae for ultimate insiders. The builders of these interim towns must have felt real fear of the land they'd been forced to occupy, to have built so timidly. With the high western hills eating up the sun and the dusk drawing over the highway with an air of final abandonment, Storch, who was hitching a ride into a necropolis with a sociopath, began to see fear. He did not feel it eating him, but he sensed it skulking inside his mind, yet outside his heart.

Storch was roused out of his half-sleep by a flash-glimpse of a figure in the road directly before them: an adult doe, stiff and still as a plaster yard decoration, impaled on the van's hi-beams. What did his father call it, his father who served three tours in Vietnam but, in his saner days, had prayed only while deer hunting? Jacklighting, a mortal sin, a betrayal of the rapport between hunter and hunted.

Buggs jogged right and grazed the deer's flank against the driver's side. Storch saw the top of its head whip around confusedly as the giant steel box hurtled past, the vacuum of its passage sucking it off its feet. It did what instinct told it must be done. It leapt into the air, straight up, its legs cocked at an angle as if to fend off the Buick Le Sabre following too closely behind them. The driver of the next car lacked Ely's reflexes and sailed into the deer at seventy-eight miles per hour. The deer plunged through the windshield as if diving into a pool covered in a sheet of frost. The Le Sabre nosed into the guardrail and whipped perpendicular to the fast lane and the Weber's bread truck behind it. Buggs's van turned a snaky S-bend in the road, and the hills enveloped the scene just as a second sun seemed to rise above it.

"When are those dumb animals going to learn?" Buggs asked.

The sign at the Colma city limit claimed the population was seven hundred fourteen, but Storch never saw one above ground. Rolling green hills girded the freeway on both sides, studded with row upon row of headstones, plaques, monuments and mausoleums. The graves to the east commanded a majestic view of the gray San Francisco Bay. Storch was hard pressed to decide what was weirder, the city itself, or the creeping feeling of relief and the sense that he could learn to live here.

Buggs turned off the 280 at Route 82. They rolled past a deserted mall: florists, chapels, stonemasons, banquet halls and liquor stores. They turned south on El Camino Real, the main drag in California's grand necropolis. They passed more cemeteries than Storch had seen in his entire life. As expected, Buggs took upon himself the role of tour guide.

"Like no other city in America," Buggs said. "Over half a million residents, the real silent majority. Look at all this fucking real estate. In the future, archaeologists digging this up will conclude one of two ways: either we worshipped our dead or we were heavily into worm farming.

"About a hundred years ago, San Francisco took a good look at its zoning laws and realized all its cemeteries were illegal. Besides which, they needed the space. So they dug up every last one of them and carted them down here—except for the Presidio and the Old Mission. See that?

That's Cypress Lawn, where the rich ones go. William Randolph Hearst, Spreckels, Coit, Gertrude Atherton…"

Storch closed his eyes and pulled his ears into his skull, let himself squeeze in one last five-minute catnap. He felt himself slipping away just as the van came to a stop and the engine died. Buggs opened his door and hopped out, feet crunching on gravel as he came around and opened Storch's door. He fought not to stumble as he climbed out and surveyed Buggs's new job.

"It sure as hell looks like a funeral home."

"Used to be. The people I work for meditate a lot. They say they can't have the psychic vibrations of the living around, or something."

The building was a two-story gambrel-roofed farmhouse in the New England style, impeccably maintained, with fresh pearl-gray paint and black trim. A gravel driveway wound up to a six-car garage. Towering weeping willows framed the converted funeral home on three sides, and iron fences separated it from the crowded, neglected Greek Orthodox cemetery that encircled the property.

"Come on. Check it out."

They crossed the lawn and ascended the portico steps. A porch glider swung silently in the evening breeze, and scores of wind chimes hung from the eaves. Storch could feel an electric tingling in the lobes of his ears, but couldn't quite hear them.

Buggs slipped off his shoes and motioned for Storch to do the same.

"You've got to be really, really quiet until we get back into my workroom, man." Storch nodded and stooped to unlace his boots. Buggs unlocked the door and peeked inside, scanning the place for something. Deciding the coast was clear, he slipped inside and waved Storch in after him.

Candles and incense burned in sconces around the foyer, marking the walls rather than illuminating anything. The walls themselves were cushioned with the deep packing foam used in recording studios. The faint shuffling of their stockinged feet on the lush carpet sounded as if it was coming from down a tunnel. The pungent opiate smoke from the incense, the stifling stillness, made Storch feel sleepy.

"Where's your room?" he asked, rubbing his eyes.

Buggs shushed him, led him deeper into the house. They passed through what probably used to be the chapel. Storch could dimly make out posts hung with headphones and goggles and racks of electrical components set evenly around the room, and surrounded by piles of pillows. They turned down a narrow corridor lined with narrow doors. Some stood open, and Storch saw someone sleeping inside, goggled and headphoned. Hints of pulsating black static leaked out of them. Faint as it was, it resonated in all the cavities of Storch's skull and made the darkness come alive with impossible, predatory colors. A hand reached out of the wall and took him by the arm, pulled him into one of the rooms. The door closed behind him, and the hungry colors dissolved into black again. Silent lightning flashed, once twice, and became the cold glow of a fluorescent light. Buggs was staring into his eyes, pinning his arms at his sides.

"Are you alright, man? You're not gonna freak out and have a Desert Storm flashback, or something, are you?"

"I'm fucking fine," Storch growled, breaking loose and stepping back. "Don't touch my fucking body."

Buggs shrugged and went to a bank of light switches. The room had once been used for embalming, and still had a checkerboard-pattern tile floor and a row of steel beds with gutters in them. Computer shit was stacked to the ceiling on all five of these, and spilled over onto the floor, crowded the counter that ran along the wall, and even hung suspended from the ceiling. The floor was a carpet of cables and trash: potato chip bags, Twinkie wrappers, empty Jolt Cola cans, Ephidrene packets, cigarette butts.

"Alright, alright. Pretty weird, huh?"

"What the hell are these people on, Buggs?"

"A mystical mission," Buggs answered in a fruity, New Age voice. "They alone understand the true nature of the universe, and are destined to preserve it from destruction."

"What are you talking about?"

"All that we see or seem is but a dream within a dream of a god they call—" Buggs looked around melodramatically, then cupped his hand and whispered, "Mana Yood Sushai." He looked around again, then smiled and nodded knowingly at Storch, having confided the cult's innermost secret.

"What do they do?"

"Mostly, they just sleep, I guess, building up the energy to meditate, which is pretty much what they do the rest of the time. They use all that VR shit in the chapel to entrain their brainwaves to the same frequency, and they dream together. They think that as long as they keep dreaming and meditating and shit, Mana Yood Sushai will keep dreaming the universe. But if they stop—" again looking around for cult assassins, "He'll wake up."

Buggs went over to a tower of CPUs and started flicking switches, Things started humming and clattering and Storch could feel ions proliferating in the air around him. He wanted to go back out, find an empty cell and go to sleep in the hungry dark. To keep himself awake, he kept talking.

"How can they afford all this?"

"They're all really brilliant programmers, actually. Every so often, one of them comes out and bats out some code or does some contract database design work, makes them a few hundred grand, and goes back to sleep. They've got some people who come in to clean up and do the landscaping, but they know better than to come in here."

"What do they need you for?"

"I do a lot of different things. Network administration—they've got a couple of nodes just for decryption, websites with all kinds of ciphers and encrypted messages floating around—"

"Anything about cancer?"

"No. Why'd you ask?"

"No reason."

"But it's funny you should mention it, because what I think they really wanted me for was to screen their TV."

"What?"

"I tape all their favorite TV shows. Trekkie crap, mostly, and lots of airy-fairy New Age lectures on Public Access channels, but some CNN and Discovery Channel stuff, too, anything on genetics or paleontology— and anyway, what I do is, I edit out the commercials. It's kind of like being a poison-taster for a paranoid royal family."

When he got tired of babbling, Buggs hacked Water & Power records for *Sperling, Donald*. "Nobody else keeps better track of where you've lived," Buggs boasted as he pried their firewall open and typed in bogus passwords. The screen blew up a catalogue of numbers and addresses, going back to Sperling's college days at UC Davis.

"Look at this. Donald and Marie Sperling's power bill accounts, from the day they set up housekeeping in Davis in 1976 until the present. Notice anything weird?"

"This isn't complete," Storch muttered. "There's two and a half years missing." Then he remembered how long the commune had lasted. "Shit. He was one of them. Him and his wife were members." After July of 1979, there was no service record. Then, in December of 1981, with service charges, switch-on fee and a fifty dollar deposit for the house in Sunnyvale.

"There's where he was. Now let's find out where he is," Buggs said.

Buggs fiddled for five minutes, opening windows within windows of security, slipping through each layer with a different skeleton key. Storch tuned out his rambling explanations of the significance of each. Computers bothered him. More than anything else since he'd gone into the desert eight years before, computers had changed the world, and not for the better. It was as if a crazy new religion had burned new tongues, new prayers, new commandments, into the rest of the world. It baffled him, the way they talked about Y2K, and poured money into businesses that existed nowhere and made nothing. Everyone worshipped false gods of pure data, and trembled before an Apocalypse when the world might threaten to become real again.

"Here you go. Credit card purchases for Donald NMI Sperling for July, 1999. Hmmm, eats out a lot—alone. Not much else...Monthly Metrotram pass...oh, look at this. You came at a bad time, boss." Buggs tapped the entry at the bottom of the screen: $695 / AMERICAN AIRLINES FLIGHT 997 / SAN JOSE TO MEXICO CITY VIA LAX / ONE-WAY / 7-8-99. "He's gone on vacation."

He was gone. *How many people have to disappear before you get wise and vanish yourself?* If there really was a secret war, let it be fought by people with their heads screwed on right. Mexico—and not to find Donald Sperling, either.

"I can get into airline booking, see if his seat was filled."

"No, Buggs. Let it go."

"Well, shit, I'm real sorry I couldn't be of more help. You want me to call some of your righteous militia friends to come pick you up?"

"I don't have any righteous friends. Take me back."

Buggs dropped Storch off at a Target around the block from his motel just before ten. As he was climbing out, Buggs said, "Hey, boss. Take this."

Storch turned around and saw a roll of bills held under his nose, the two on the outside were twenties. "I can't take your money, Buggs. Thanks, anyway."

"Dude, you need money to get out of here, and you need a new look. Right now you look like a freaked-out commando in a bad disguise. You won't even stay out long enough to make it on America's Most Wanted." Buggs grinned sheepishly. "Besides, you paid me way too much. I would've done it for free. Go on, man. Take it and get the hell out of here."

Feeling like a proud farmer accepting his first welfare check, Storch took the money. "Thanks. I'll send you a postcard."

"Adios, dude," Buggs said and pulled out of the parking lot. Storch watched his last friend go until his van disappeared onto the freeway onramp. Suddenly feeling naked, he turned and walked into the Target.

He came back around the block in a new suit of clothing; ugly and uncomfortable but decidedly less paramilitary looking. He stopped dead in his tracks on the edge of the motel parking lot, crippled by a rush of foreboding about going back in there. The parking lot still had most of the same cars he'd noticed when he left, and no new arrivals. The buttery yellow lights at the front desk were on, but he saw no sign of the clerk. He'd left nothing important inside, indeed, probably not enough for a police forensics team to tell he was even there.

He looked around again, trying to seem lost, and not as if he were casing the place. Infrequent cars flew past at freeway speeds. A police car went by without taking notice of him. He went back to the intersection and crossed the street, checked into a Motel 6 that could have been stamped from the same mold as the first, checked into the room under another fake ID, and went inside.

The picture window commanded a pretty good view of his old room, and had blinds instead of curtains. He left the lights off and opened the blinds just wide enough to see across the street through a slit. He sat down in a scuffed-up naugahyde lounge chair, unlaced his boots, fitted the silencer onto the gun, laid it on the table beside him, and watched.

A few guests came and went. After about an hour, the desk clerk came out for a cigarette, his nose in a paperback.

Storch rubbed his eyes, willing adrenaline into his nervous system. He fished a bottle of pineapple juice out of his coat pocket, sipped at the too-sweet, lukewarm nectar and felt his blood thicken up, his movements become less jittery, less desperate to stay awake. He checked the clip in the automatic. An argument in one of the upstairs rooms spilled out onto the balcony, two biker-looking guys with no shirts on pushing at each other and shouting. The desk clerk went up and told them to go back inside. Storch worried that they would bring the cops, willed them to shut up and cut it out. Miraculously, they did.

Storch watched. Nothing happened. And somewhere around two-thirty, he leaned forward to check the gun again, and just kept leaning until he collapsed on the floor.

~ 22 ~

There actually wasn't that much space in the underground base, but it was so twisted upon itself that Stella, when she was allowed out of Mrachek's sight, constantly found herself rounding a corner to come face to face with one or more soldiers standing duty outside a door she was clearly not meant to enter. The soldiers always stood, impassive and silent, not even batting an eye as she asked them questions, or lambasted them with insults. They would've done the Queen's Grenadier Guards proud, but Stella quickly discovered it was largely a show for her benefit, or intimidation. One morning, at least according to the digital chronometer on the climate control in the sickbay, she stopped just short of a corner around which she knew a soldier regularly stood all night, outside what she guessed was the motor pool, until his morning relief came. She listened.

Instantly, she recognized the voices. They regularly pulled this duty, and just as regularly bitched about it. The night-guard was a Latino named Medina, a very senior noncommissioned officer whose talk was peppered with Army jargon. The relief was named Betancourt, and he talked less, perhaps because of a mild stutter and a lazy Alabama drawl that made him sound like a halfwit, even when, as now, he was talking about things Stella couldn't begin to understand.

"News?" Medina offered.

"It's b-bad, Maceo," Betancourt muttered. "Going on worse. School Of Night's gone black."

"What the fuck? What do the eggheads know?"

"Can't be sure, but they f-fear the worst. It's like the ordnance cache raid all over again."

"So *now* we're gonna have to steal a telemetry lab," Medina's voice was acidic. Stella guessed whatever this mysterious new development meant, it was widening a rift between the soldiers and the eggheads. "They scrubbing?"

Silence. Betancourt must've shaken his head, because Medina hawked and spat and composed an impromptu haiku entirely out of Spanish and Army-coined obscenities.

Betancourt reminded Stella of Eeyore the depressive donkey when he added, "Wittrock's de-de-cided to d-do it himself...on-site."

"Fucking egghead queen-bee motherfucker," Medina hissed. "Just putting more weight on an op that's already grinding on the rims. He wants a complete saturation, and we're supposed to wait to pick his ass out of the fire while he's fucking with their computer."

"That part—th-th-that still doesn't sit well with me, man," Betancourt mumbled. "They ain't luh-like us, I know, buh-b-but they ain't soldiers, man. They're fuh-folks..."

"You didn't see what homeboy did to Gene in the sickbay, man. That raid in Lone Pine, when we picked up Mrachek's guinea pigs? I've never seen anyfuckingthing take that much killing and keep on going."

"Well, wh-whatever they are, I hope the d-d-docs find a cure for 'em, so we duh-don't have to b-burn 'em out again, I tuh-t-tuh-tell you what."

Stella's ears burned as she backed away. *Guinea pigs?* Stella walked back to sick bay, and only got lost once.

On her way, as if her anger had cauterized blocked synapses in her brain, she found herself thinking clearly again. Perhaps she'd been drugged all this time, not to have wondered before.

Mrachek said they were fighting a war, and after the whirlwind of events that'd showed her what became of Seth Napier, she'd been bludgeoned into accepting Radiant Dawn as the enemy. But what had they done, besides try to survive? Whatever Stephen had become, he'd survived cancer and multiple dismemberment. What happened to Napier was an accident, a freak byproduct of whatever kept him alive. The Radiant Dawn community hadn't tried to spread beyond its own enclave. They wanted what all people want, but they had enemies. These people.

And me. When I wanted them dead, was it because I was afraid of them, or because they turned me away?

Mrachek sat with her big back to the door, hunched over a binocular microscope. Her arms were poised akimbo, her hands manipulating a syringe and an eyedropper over the petri dish under the scope. "Where've you been?" she asked, but didn't turn around. Stella crossed the sickbay a little faster than she intended. If any part of her intended harm, it wasn't keeping her forebrain informed, but it slammed on the brakes when Mrachek turned around. Her curare dartgun was in her rosy pink fist, like an extra finger. "I think it'd be best if you stuck around closer to sickbay. I can't vouch for your safety elsewhere."

"What're you going to do to Radiant Dawn?" Stella asked.

"I thought I made myself clear before. We're at war, dear heart."

"You called them a disease. I thought that meant you were trying to cure them."

"They are a disease. But there's no cure. They have to be destroyed."

"They're human beings!"

"Oh no," Mrachek clucked her tongue at Stella as if she were a potty-mouthed child. "They were human beings once; poor, dying souls who came to Radiant Dawn as their last hope for survival. Like you did. But they've been reengineered into something else, and they're an unstable population. It's either them, or us."

After the Indians, the slaves and the Jews, you'd think white people would back off that argument. *For once, don't let race cloud your thinking, don't let this become a fight, because there's nowhere to storm off to when you lose.* "They seem to want to keep to themselves. Why can't they be contained?"

"Could the first egg-stealing mammals be contained? Could primates be kept in the trees? Could we be kept from using tools to make the world we've made? Whether it's in their nature or not, they're going to spread, and they're going to replace us. Unless it's finished here." Mrachek rubbed the bridge of her nose wearily.

"But if they're what's next, who are we to stop them? Who are you to kill them off?"

"Come look at this," she said, and beckoned Stella closer to the microscope. She approached, eyes on the dartgun resting in Mrachek's palm on the countertop. She peered through the lenses, adjusting the focus until she could make out an undifferentiated sea of particulates. She dialed up the magnification by a hundred and the sea became a wall of cells, amorphous sacs, mortared together by neoplasmic streamers. Stella recognized the formless blobs immediately. Cancer cells. Organic anarchy incarnate, they had no function other than to proliferate and murder their host. Stella saw these cells in her dreams.

"They're not yours. They've been cultured from Mr. Napier, although cultured isn't the right word, because they don't even require a growth medium. They keep multiplying until they've expended all available resources, weeks after separation from the parent organism. These aren't taken from Napier's cancer. They are Napier. A small enough sample breaks down into this, the dormant state." Feeling Mrachek hovering over her, Stella backed away from the scope, stepping on the medic's toes.

She didn't seem to notice. More to herself than for Stella's benefit, she began to lecture. "Did you know, there's a theory, I didn't used to have any use for it, but some homeopathic researchers point to the origin of cancer as the result of the dead end of evolution. We've made everything for ourselves, so we can't genetically improve, and our genes are striking back the only way they know how; cancer as frustrated evolutionary force expressing itself as death. If it can't change us, it'll kill us all off and start again. But someone signed a peace treaty, and sold us out."

Was she talking about Keogh? Even before she came to Radiant Dawn, he knew what was wrong with her, had offered her words of comfort that she'd foolishly interpreted as an invitation.

"Stella dear, we're not meant to be replaced by cancer. This isn't the natural order, it's the work of a—" she faltered, busied herself with the syringe, drizzling a minuscule amount of a bluish fluid into the dish. "Look at it now," she said.

Stella had watched crystals grow as a child. It was fascinating, and she'd badgered those of her foster parents who responded at all to her desires to buy her the kits, and she'd stay up all night, watching the lowly, particolored rocks remake themselves into delicate spires and fairy-palaces before her eyes. All that wonder rushed back into her heart and turned to ashes as she realized what she was seeing.

The blue fluid coursed through the intercellular crevices and elicited an almost electrical response from the cancer cells. They bloomed. The walls of each tiny cell erupted in questing vines that sped out and intertwined with their neighbors' shoots, tangling and twisting and reaching out of the tissue sample, reaching greedy boring shoots towards the lens. Stella jerked back and her hands went to her eyes. It'd been like watching fire.

"What do you see?"

"They're becoming…nerve cells?"

"Not nerve cells. They're still cancer cells, but they take on all the traits of functional nerve cells when they're introduced to liquefied dendrite cells, or any neurotransmitters. In the last hour, this particular sample has been adipose tissue, skeletal muscle fiber, and glial brain tissue. Is that nature?"

Stella clenched her fists at her temples. A cure for what was killing her. But was it worse than death, or better than mortal life? She couldn't stand much more of this argument, unless she could drive it into personal territory. "How would you know what's natural?"

"Stella dear, I was a Major in the US Army Medical Research of Infectious Diseases—USAMRID. I treated emerging viruses in seventeen countries, and I was never afraid. I'm afraid now. Come on."

She stood and led Stella back down the back corridor, where the quarantine cells were. To the last cell, behind two doors. Where they kept Napier.

She stopped just short of the double-paned viewing slot. Seeing him—it—would be too much. When she'd seen it the last time, it'd been burned, and shot full of more bullets than she could've carried in a duffel bag, and yet it walked, and regarded her with those gray eyes that weren't Seth Napier's, or Stephen's, but something wiser than a disease. Mrachek's chubby little hand pressed at the small of her back, gently shoving her towards it. She planted her feet, but the medic's lower center of gravity and deceptive strength rocked her off her heels and she stumbled against the door.

It wasn't what she'd call a disappointment, but it wasn't anything she'd have expected, either. The thing that mauled Mrachek and the soldier was gone. Faced with inescapable containment, Napier lay in a fetal curl, naked, on his cot. In the dim reddish light, he appeared to be shivering, and Stella turned to give Mrachek hell for letting him freeze, when Mrachek switched on a bright white light in the cell.

It was like turning sunlight on a tub of nightcrawlers. Napier wasn't moving, but his skin wriggled and shifted as the vital tissues underneath waged war over the proper way to build a human body. Its head rolled back and eyes opened and fixed on Stella. Those eyes. The face around them twitched in and out of Napier's and Stephen's features, but the eyes knew her. The thing that'd been Seth Napier grinned at her and splayed out his arms, to display its new body, or to offer her a hug.

"Look at him, dear heart. Is this the next dominant species? Is this what you'd give the world to?"

Right away, she noticed that Napier's new body was younger and more powerfully muscled than either he or Stephen had been. Then she noticed the buboes. She'd never seen the symptoms of bubonic plague outside of textbooks, but that was the word that came to mind. Pendulous, purple-black sacs sprouted from his armpits and groin, a collar of them round his neck; even, she noticed, in a sort of turkey crest on his scalp.

"What's wrong with him?" Stella whispered.

"Absolutely nothing, dear. He started swelling up like that about twenty-four hours after we brought him in. They're sort of like plague buboes, but they're also like testes. They contain a virus, similar to Rouss' sarcoma virus, only much more aggressive, and infinitely more precise."

Stella knew only a little about RSV, or any of the other mutagenic viruses which caused cancer in some animals as a by-product of infection. But Stephen hadn't given Seth Napier cancer. "How do you mean?"

"They're almost more like airborne gametes, only they spawn cancer. They infect their host and immediately set about playing havoc with tumor suppressors and oncogenes in any and all tissue they encounter, and the result is swift, terminal cancer. But in subjects like Mr. Napier, who already had cancer, the effects are much more pronounced. It's somatic-cell cloning. We think he's gone into this phase because his body thinks he's the last one left. He could infect an entire city."

"Why is he...twitching like that?"

"We think they do it whenever they're under stress, or it could be because he was an accident, not properly altered. We just don't know enough, yet. Everything we learn, we're going to learn from *that*."

Stella felt sick. Mrachek stood between her and anyplace to sit, so she slumped against the wall. "How long have they been here?"

"Less than a week. They were altered shortly after midnight on the Fourth of July. But we knew they were coming. This was the result of a generational human-breeding program, among other things. We had to wait until we knew, because we couldn't kill innocent human beings. We tried to stop it, but now we have a narrow window of opportunity to stop them before they spread. And they will." Mrachek then did something Stella had suffered almost no one to do to her, let alone a captor. She wrapped her arms around Stella and Stella sagged against the woman's compact bulk. At least she wouldn't let herself cry.

"Do you see now why they have to be destroyed?" Mrachek asked.

"What do you care what I think? I'm just another guinea pig, aren't I?"

"Who told you that?"

"I've got ears. If I didn't have cancer myself, what good would I be to you? I'm going to be part of some experiment..." And she was crying now, the hell with it.

"I—I didn't want to tell you, before, but truth to tell, I didn't care for you all that much. But—yes, I would like you to participate in an experiment, when it's time."

Stella ripped free and shoved past Mrachek, bolted for the door. She was being handled, like the social workers who placed her with the hitters and the neglecters, because this was the best they could do, and if she'd just try to get along...

"Fuck you, fat white bitch," Stella hissed over her shoulder.

"I think you may want to participate," Mrachek cooed, undeterred by Stella's hostility. The dartgun was nowhere in sight, but Stella didn't want to touch the doctor long enough to hit her, anyway. She kept walking away, but she stopped dead in her tracks when the import of Mrachek's last, soft remark hit home.

"With what I can learn from the unfortunate Mr. Napier, I'll be able to cure your cancer, Stella. Without altering you. You'll be human. And alive."

"Keep your Nazi Frankenstein claws off me, fat white dyke." Stella went out the door and directly into her own cubicle across the corridor. She collapsed onto her cot and cried, and hammered her fists against the wall until they were numb and bloody. When she finally slipped into sleep, she dreamed of swimming in a sea of cancer that ignited into a fire of nerves when she dove in, a fire of fleshy wires that ate her up and made her new.

~ 23 ~

Storch's first clear thought upon waking this time was not of fear or despair or the loneliness he'd tried to bury when Buggs left. It was almost worse. He felt a vast and exhausting sense of disappointment, that the one person in this tired old world that he could count on had let him down yet again. He'd been captured. For the fourth time in as many days, Sgt. Zane Ezekiel Storch, Special Forces commando and unsung hero of the Gulf War, had been knocked down and hogtied like a second-rate Sam Spade knockoff in a hack detective yarn.

This time, they weren't taking any chances. His arms were cuffed behind his back and his feet shackled, and the two were bound by a chain sheathed in a steel bar that kept him from reaching the tools in his bootheels. He lay on his side on a cold metal bench. The metal vibrated against his cheek, telling him he was in another truck, but the steadiness and the higher pitch of the engine told him this time he was in the back of a van, or a delivery truck.

Or a paddy wagon. Don't forget the police. You're still a wanted cop-killing felon, for all they know. But somehow, Storch didn't think he was lucky enough merely to have been arrested. He knew he hadn't just fallen asleep at his post in the Motel 6, and his pants were still unsoiled, so the EMP weapon the militia used on him was out. His stomach felt like a pilotless ship on a stormy sea, and his mouth was as dry as cotton batting, so he'd probably been gassed, this time. Or drugged. Whatever the cause, whoever had him, he wasn't planning on being there when they arrived. He blinked his eyes rapidly, trying to discern some form to the darkness around him, but he may as well have been blindfolded.

"Don't try to move," a voice, a man's voice, said close to his ear.

"Are you fucking kidding?" he asked, and a clammy palm clapped over his mouth.

He could feel breath against his ear now, could feel a fine mist of spittle as the speaker leaned in closer still and said, "Keep quiet. Don't make them come back here. Don't make them—" As Storch's senses started to sharpen up to his normal capacity, he noticed a mushiness to the voice, as if it issued from a mouthful of broken teeth. *No wonder you don't want them back here. So why aren't you tied up?*

Storch nodded vehemently to indicate that he understood, and wanted the stranger's hand off his face. It was all he could do not to bite that hand. "Who's they?" he whispered. "And who the hell are you?"

"You don't know? Aren't you one of them? If you crossed them, they wouldn't keep you alive. You must be awfully important to them, for them to take you alive. We—he—he never wanted to hurt anybody before, you know? He was—he changed, I guess…"

"For the last fucking time," Storch said, sounding as unlike a helpless prisoner in shackles as he possibly could, "who are they?"

"They're the Radiant Dawn. Or, like, they're the new Radiant Dawn. They're different, but more like themselves than they ever were," a mirthless chuckle of pain and irony. "I was—I'm—"

And it clicked in Storch's head. "You're Sperling."

"Yes. Yes, that's—How do you know me?"

"I've been looking for you. I'm the one who found your daughter."

"You're the one who called me?" Sperling spat, ignoring his own warning. "Then this is all your fault. If you wouldn't have called me, they would've left me alone—" hyperventilating, face purpling, "was almost free—got me at the airport…" The weakness, the shrinking, self-pitying tone of Sperling's voice made Storch want to break him in half. Then he settled back on a bench across from Storch and drew his knees up, wrapped them in his skinny arms, caught his breath. "Oh, bullshit. I knew someday they'd come for me. Quesada never wastes anything."

"Who's Quesada?"

"He's probably using another name, now. But that's who he was when I—when my wife and I—" his words broke up into hitching sobs. Storch tried to maintain his own self-control long enough to get answers out of the man.

"This Quesada, he ran Radiant Dawn, the cult in the Seventies?"

"He—yes, he was the leader. Our father, we called him. Our radiant father."

"And he took Sidra from you nine years ago."

"Yes, but—"

"And you let him keep her. You didn't tell the police."

"It wasn't like that. You don't—please try to understand, it wasn't how it looked. We couldn't—" Sperling reached down into himself and pulled out a cloak of eerie calm. If Storch had been a policeman instead of a soldier, he would have recognized the sublime, almost blissful state that overcomes a fugitive when at last the time has come to confess.

"He was able to keep it all submerged—out of the news, and so far down in our heads, that we'd never remember. He had this way of looking into you that just blew everything you thought you wanted for yourself right out of your head, everything you thought you were. After Sidra was taken, we started to remember. He preached Tantric sex, and made us have orgies in front of x-ray machines, microwave ovens, and do shit I couldn't begin to describe. He wanted us to be bathed in the radiance when we procreated, so that while our spirits intertwined with the infinite and came unhinged from our bodies, the radiation would reshape our bodies, moving them up the ladder towards perfection, until we would no longer need bodies. Then one day, he told us he was finished, and threw us out. Don't look at me like that, you have no idea what it's like until you've been inside it, until he's been inside you."

Because Storch was a soldier, and a soldier hogtied in the back of a truck, he couldn't find the velvet glove he needed to stroke Sperling. He wanted to kill him more than ever. "You're a piece of shit. How could you let somebody else degrade you like that, and then give him your only child? What did you think you were going to get out of it?"

"*My* child? Why didn't we go to the press after he threw us out? Why didn't we sue him or have him arrested when most of us were diagnosed with terminal cancer within a few years of leaving? Wouldn't you? Well, we didn't. We did everything we did for the good of the species. We believed we were changing ourselves for our children's sake. And when the time came, those of us who survived were glad to give up our kids, because they were his, too." He sat back and let the words rattle around the space between them, as if it should've made sense to Storch, should've silenced all his accusations, cut his judgment down to size.

"We were all sterile," he went on at last. "He was their father. Our wives were the mothers, and radiation was the midwife. Not a single birth defect, you know. Picture of health, every one of them. We never contacted each other after he threw us out, but I think everybody kept track of everybody else. When he came for them nine years ago, we each handled it our own way. Marie and I told as much of the truth as we had to, that our daughter was gone. She was his child, they were all his kids, and he was welcome to them."

"I don't want to hear any more," Storch cut in. "Help me get free, and I'll get you out of here."

Sperling's laughter was louder, if not cheerier, than before. "There's no escaping. The children—the children of the Dawn—the Moon-Ladder…"

"Shut up and open the heel on my right boot. I'll get us out of here, and you can go to Mexico, or lay down and die, whatever the hell you want." Storch didn't like the way his own voice sounded, now. Wheedling. He felt like one of those desperate animatronic pirate convicts on the Pirates Of The Caribbean ride at Disneyland, trying to coax the little dog with the keyring in its mouth to come closer before the burning stockade collapsed. It wasn't a position Storch had ever thought he'd be in.

"Lay down and die," Sperling repeated, as if he was saying, he'd like to go to Hawaii and spend the rest of his life drinking coconut milk and shagging hula girls. "What I wouldn't give to be dead right now."

"That can be arranged, too," Storch said. "If you open the heel on my right boot, I'll give you the quickest, cleanest death you could ever ask for." What the hell was he saying?

Sperling sat there, balled up and hating himself for an unguessable time. Storch didn't like himself a whole lot either, at the moment, and couldn't bring himself to sweeten the offer anymore. He almost thought Sperling had gone to sleep for awhile and set to trying to wriggle free of the cuffs. If he dislocated the wrist of his bad hand—

A hand touched his ankle. Storch kicked out at it, an impotent gesture that served to do nothing more than rattle his shackles a little. The hands returned, fumbling at the heel of his right boot. "I can't figure it out—it's useless…"

"Goddamit, feel along the back, there's a catch. Push it in and pull out the wire."

"What good's wire going to be?"

"Do it."

The hands clumsily fiddled around with his foot for what felt like hours. Storch suffered the hands touching him for as long as he was able, then hissed, "Let go, asshole, if you can't—"

"There. Is this what you wanted?" The clammy hands touched his, and the spool of cutting wire was pressed into his palm. He could feel Sperling hovering over him, feel his sour breath on his face and smell the rank flop-sweat oozing from his yellow pores. "Get the fuck away from me, will you? Can't concentrate."

"Sorry," Sperling mumbled, and backed away.

Cursing his numb fingers, he pulled one end of it out and wrapped it around the linking chain between the cuffs. It was considerably blunter since he'd used it on the cargo container, but in about five minutes, the chains jingled and fell away. Instantly, liquid fire poured into his arms. Storch suppressed a shriek as his circulation resumed, wiggling the arms, like floppy dead things that had been stapled to his torso by an inept meatball surgeon. After a time, when the pain subsided, he sat up and started to work on his leg shackles, but the tool was almost useless after cutting through the chain that bound them to the handcuffs. Now his legs sang grand opera for awhile and he used the time to slide the steel bar off the chains and pull the little stabbing knife out of his left boot. The T-shaped handle fit into his fist so that the three inch blade stood out between his index and middle fingers. It was hardly lethal in and of itself, but with Storch's training it was more than adequate for cutting vital plumbing.

Storch stood, getting his sea-legs, breathing deep and slow until the last agonizing tingle of sleep flowed out of his limbs. In the darkness, he could barely make out the hunched ball of Donald Sperling, now regarding him with a black spot in the bottom of his face that had to be his slack, open mouth.

"How many of them are there?" he asked Sperling, and the man's mouth clamped shut. "Two," he said after a moment. *Just two? Who did these stupid assholes think they were dealing with, here?* Storch had never been overly proud of his killing skills, and he'd always abhorred bragging: There's those that do it, and those that talk about it. But sending two people for him, to knock him out with gas and truss him up in his sleep? *And it worked!* This new outrage pushed him over the top. These people's faces would not haunt him, and if they did it would be a sweet dream indeed.

"What're you going to try to do?" Sperling asked. Storch didn't like that one bit; not *do*, but *try to do*. Don Sperling was one hell of a cheerleader.

Without answering, Storch turned and moved to the front of the cell. A sliding pass-through port was in the middle of the front wall. Storch noticed it was unlocked. Evidently, his captors didn't think any more of Sperling's will to survive than he did. Crouching beside the door, Storch braced himself. The knife in one fist and the bar clenched in the other, he took one more deep breath, held it, and threw the door wide open.

The light, as dim as it was, hurt his eyes. A wash of black tarmac and indigo sky, and the dots and dashes of dashboard panel lights blurred together, but Storch lunged into the midst of it, swinging the bar like a caveman defending his woman from sabertooth tigers. He swung left first, felt the bar connect with something hard that yielded to the force of steel and became soft as a trashbag full of mashed potatoes.

There was no scream, only a twinned intake of breath, as of some mild surprise along the road, a realization, perhaps that they were lower on gas than they thought they'd be. He swung the bar to the right now, got stuck as the bar seemed to be mired in something where the driver was supposed to be. He let the bar go and stabbed out at the passenger with his knife, right about where a throat should be. Something received the knife, alright, but it didn't feel like a neck. It gave like butter, but beneath it Storch could feel something unyielding pressing back through the knife—something that moved, and took his knife away.

Storch blinked, his retinas finally contracted to where he could make out more than blobs of light and shadow. And he saw what was happening.

The driver was a teenaged boy, couldn't be more than fifteen or sixteen, lean and lanky, but still too short to be more than a pair of knuckles and some buzzcut hair to anyone driving past. He was looking at Storch with what passed for mild irritation, but Storch couldn't get that far. He was still staring at the bar he'd swung at the boy, the bar that was still embedded in the side of his skull. Even as he bit his upper lip clean through, squinted and looked again, he still saw the skull knitting itself back up around the bar. Saw black, bladdery masses surge up out of the fissure like clotted oil and pull the sides together. The bar popped back out with an audible *ptui*, and Storch saw something that looked all too much like a black and pink tongue loll out of the boy's smashed cranium and pull the edges of skin together, like some monstrous cartoon oyster tucking itself into bed.

Only then did it occur to him to look back at the passenger, who could have merrily shot and stabbed him ten times over while he was ogling the freakshow in the driver's seat.

A heavy-set middle-aged woman with tightly curled brown hair, she looked like a secretary, except that she, like the boy, wore a black tracksuit. She was also looking at him, paying no mind whatsoever to the ragged hole Storch had punched in her jugular vein. A fan of blood had sluiced down her track suit, but now the hole was closed over, although her neck was marred by an unsightly, shiny bulge; those cartoon tumors again, already hard at work.

"Please go back to your seat," the woman said in a scolding, shushing voice, like a typing teacher at an all-school assembly.

"You're going to cause an accident," the boy added.

The voices made Storch shiver, and he was halfway to getting up to obey when he realized what was so weird about them. They spoke with the same voice, and it didn't sound right coming out of either of their mouths.

He threw himself into the cab and snatched the keys out of the ignition. He backed away, but he didn't get to his bench. He hopped drunkenly in the leg shackles and slammed into the back wall. The van was still running, and speeding up.

They were somewhere on the interstate, probably on the 5, from the flat brown featureless country he'd glimpsed between eyefuls of the insane fucking shit in the cab.

"That was stupid," Sperling offered. He was still sitting there on the bench with his skinny little arms around his legs, looking like the unacknowledged fourth monkey that followed SEE NO EVIL, HEAR NO EVIL and SPEAK NO EVIL: HAVE NO FUN.

"Shut up, maggot. I didn't—" Storch left off getting defensive with Sperling, but he couldn't get his head on straight. His fingers fumbled through the odd assortment of keys on the ring, but he wasn't seeing them, wasn't hearing the woman climbing out of the cab.

He'd expected something unpredictable, but probably bad, to happen, but what he'd seen whipped his internal probability curve clear out of sight, sent all predictive outcomes, based as they were on a lifetime of make-believe warfighting, right off the board. He was standing there, leaning against the rear doors, trying to replay what he'd seen in his mind so it didn't make him want to go screaming into catatonia. He thought of a stupid quote some hack British writer had written of Saddam Hussein during Desert Shield, one that had made the whole squad laugh until their prostates burst: "Who he kills dies," the hack said of the ol' Saddamizer, and the self-evidence of it was hysterical at the time. But suddenly it seemed like a logical thing to say. Because suddenly there were people in Storch's world who didn't die when you killed them.

"See? I told you," Sperling whined. "Now are you happy?"

The fat lady was climbing through the pass-through door, and it was a very tight squeeze indeed, but somehow, Storch didn't doubt she'd get through. People who could seal up a punctured throat could do lots of weird stuff.

Storch found the key to the shackles and twisted it in the lock. His feet swelled with liquid fire. He rolled over and tried to find the lock for the cargo door, but of course there was no such thing on the inside of the van.

He did not look back. He did not panic. He ticked off the state capitals in his head as he turned and retrieved the cutting wire from his boot, dropped it between the door until he saw it slip behind the bolt that held them shut. He caught the bottom end and yanked hard, then started frantically sawing through it. The wire was way too blunt now. He looked over his shoulder and saw the passenger climbing ponderously to her feet, swaying like a tourist at her first hula lesson as she stalked toward the back of the van.

"You really mustn't leave yet, Zane. Donald's told you a few things, but we have things to teach you, as well. We know you, Zane. You have in you the potential to be among the very best of us…" The woman opened her arms and reached out to him, as if she were expecting him to break down and hug her. Storch almost did. Any other course of action made his head throb, as if he were trying to kill himself by disobeying. He pushed back against the doors, the lock only half cut through, and pressed his shoulder feebly against it.

"God, I think even I could've done better than that," Sperling said to himself. It wasn't enough to make the throbbing stop, but it kept him from noticing it long enough.

He stepped into the hug and pivoted even as the arms closed around his shoulders. At the same time, his left leg swept both the fat woman's legs out from under her and she was tumbling, dragging them both toward the floor. Storch heaved her up on his hip as he completed the pivot, so that they were both falling at the rear doors. With a heave and two steps, he hurled them both into the door so hard it knocked the wind out of them both. The bolt cracked with a dull ping and both doors flew open. Icy wind sucked the dank air out of the truck, ripped at clothing, ears, eyes. Storch braced himself for what was to come next. Gripping two fistfuls of the fat woman's track suit and the great, flaccid teats underneath, he brought his right knee up and drove it into her belly, forcing his weight against her to throw her over the edge. He screamed in her face, a high, wordless ululation of pure killing joy.

She didn't budge.

She smiled at him, her blue-gray eyes uncannily like those of someone he'd seen before… "Come with us, Zane," she said, and he was letting her go when Donald Sperling loomed over his shoulder and shoved him as hard as he could, and they were both falling out of the truck onto Interstate 5 at upwards of eighty miles per hour. Storch exulted in the momentary glimpse of surprise that leaked through that leaden grin. He planted his knees against her body and prepared to slam into the tarmac. If he timed it right, he could soak up about half of their speed on the woman's body on the first impact, then roll to the side in a judo fall that would distribute the rest of the impact across his ass and arms.

The first impact reminded him how little he really knew about physics. The woman hit the road with a sickening *splat*, and her torso settled under him with a chorus of crunching. He bore out most of the initial shock in his taut arms and legs, but his left knee slid off her and touched the road. His jeans vaporized against the concrete, and the flesh over his patella slid off like a greased sock. Then the road really bit into the woman's back and yanked out from under like a world-sized carpet. She bucked upright and knocked heads with him so hard he saw stars and heard a bell toll amidst the rest of it. Veering away from the burning of his knee, Storch was tossed off the woman and over the broken white line into the passing lane. He managed at least to keep tightly rolled up, but at each contact, the road took a bite out of him: his ass, his back, his knees, his scalp.

He rolled to a stop finally, two hundred feet from where he'd hit the road. Getting up was currently out of the question, so he tried to triage himself. He was pretty sure he'd hairline fractured his left arm and had multiple semi-critical roadrashes, but remarkably well-preserved for a first-time highway body-surfer. He was laughing at that when two pieces of information bore themselves in on him in rapid succession.

The van screeched to a stop in the lane to his right, not a hundred feet from where he'd come to rest, and the driver was getting out. He was holding the bar.

A Peterbilt with an open trailer full of sand bore down on the whole scene, its horn blasting monolithic indignance at what was happening in its lane. Swerving out of the right-hand lane to avoid the parked van, the truck jerked into the passing lane, but not before it clipped the woman, who was—no shit—sitting up. For numerous obvious reasons, the woman hadn't taken the fall as gracefully as Storch. In fact she appeared to have tumbled end over end, because her face was a casserole and her lower half was turned 180 degrees from its previous orientation. Even over the air horn and the wind and the oceanic roaring of shock in his ears, he heard her shriek in that voice that wasn't hers: "YOU WILL SEE THE RADIANT—" and then the truck cut her off, quite literally. She snapped back face-down on the road and vanished beneath the onrushing chrome grille and the blinding headlights that were headed for him next.

Storch tried to get to his feet, but they weren't obeying. Oh God, was he paralyzed? *Maybe it's God's will, killer.* He whipped himself over on his stomach and jerked his body so it lay straight and parallel with the path of the truck, and the horns and the lights came and swallowed him up in darkness—

—and he took his hands off his head and saw the truck passing over him like a spent tornado, heard the squealing of its brakes as the trucker, probably insane with panic, fought to bring the truck to a halt without jackknifing.

It passed over him and he struggled to lift his head. The truck came up wheel-to-wheel with the van, and the driver hopped out and ran towards him with a weird, stilted gait, screaming, "What the motherpusnutsfucking shit is going on out here? I didn't see a goddamned thing." And he was looking off in the direction of the woman he'd hit, who was now on her feet again, two hundred plus pounds of roadkill on the march. He backed up again, reaching for the step-up, to climb back into his cab.

"Wait!" The young Radiant Dawn driver called mildly, "we have to exchange insurance."

Storch belly-crawled up the length of the truck, watching the driver's left foot climb up onto the step. He reached out, screamed "Wait!" and grabbed hold of one booted foot, tugged for all he was worth. The driver jerked free with a girlish scream, but in his awkward position, he stumbled and fell on his ass beside Storch. Storch shivered and dropped the trucker's leg, which clanged on the tarmac between his legs. "What the fuck are you?"

"Help me," Storch gasped. "They're gonna kill me…"

"What—" the driver sputtered again, but he seemed to be getting farther and farther from grasping the situation. As he reached for his prosthetic leg, Storch saw his arms, where his flannel shirt was rolled up. Alongside a tattoo of a harem girl wearing only a veil, was a written legend that had once sent Storch and his squadmates into hysterics for days. DESSERT RAT, it said. But it was supposed to be DESERT RAT. Only the Ranger Battalion that worked with the SAS in the Gulf were ever that stupid. "Ranger," Storch gulped. "I was a Ranger…"

"Which battalion?" This question, in this context, should've seemed like a sure sign the truck driver had lost it. But it wouldn't have seemed absurd to someone who'd been a soldier.

"Ninth, '85 to '88, under Colonel Anfanger, only guy on the base, didn't know his wife was a raging dyke. Get me outta here, they're…kill us both…"

"Shit, whyn't you say so?" the ex-Ranger trucker yelled and hauled Storch up by one arm. The van driver was coming around the front of the truck now, tapping the bar across his palm as if he'd just confiscated it from an errant child, but intended to return it. Storch fought to pull his legs into the truck, gave way gratefully as the trucker shoved him across into the passenger seat, climbed in behind him, and put the truck in gear.

~ 24 ~

Special Agent Martin Cundieffe stepped out of his rental car and crossed the lawn towards the School Of Night in the middle of Colma. The sun was already high in the morning sky, but the mist from the miles of overwatered cemetery lawns all around them wrapped the necropolis in a pall of silvery gray. As he looked over the line of ambulances, coroner's wagons, police cars and newsvans arrayed all around the house as if preparing to lay in a siege, he was reminded once again, of ants. All the uniformed functionaries streaming in and out of the big, elegant mansion, packing up bagged evidence, taking photographs, shuttling gurneys laden with shrouded forms out to the wagons. He noted with interest that the local authorities had come up short on ambulances, and had pressed a dozen hearses into service.

Cundieffe wasn't overly bothered by cemeteries or mass suicides. His office in LA overlooked the Veteran's Cemetery across Wilshire Boulevard, and he had studied the files on the Branch Davidian and Heaven's Gate incidents extensively to prepare himself psychologically. Other agents scoffed, said you'd never be ready the first time you experience something like that. He wasn't quite surprised to find that it didn't faze him at all.

Agents Dorsey and Chen spotted him and met him halfway across the swampy, overgrown grass. The two were from the San Francisco office, and looked as if they'd rather be in church. Unless the investigation took a dramatic turn, their job would amount to crowd control and technical support.

"I'm Martin Cundieffe. I believe I spoke to Agent Dorsey?"

"That's me." Dorsey offered his hand. It was cold and water trickled up Cundieffe's wrist. "Sprinklers came on a few minutes ago. Whole mickeymouse operation the cops're making out of this, they better pray it's a clean suicide."

Cundieffe felt water seeping into his socks. He hustled across the lawn to the front porch steps, lingered along the rail while two Colma sheriff's deputies dragged a loaded gurney out and two paramedics wheeled an empty one in. "So how many are there?"

"Twenty-seven bodies, all adults, no visible cause of death. And one—" Dorsey looked up at his partner, a much taller Asian agent with spiky hair and a mangled plastic coffee stir clamped in his teeth. "You think they're done photographing it, Theo? I'll go check."

Chen adjusted his stirstick and nodded, and Dorsey disappeared into the house. Cundieffe smiled at him. He could already tell they didn't like him. Disapproved of his surprise intrusion onto their crime scene, didn't like Division agents in general, didn't like his looks. For his part, Cundieffe wasn't too keen on Chen, either, though less for his obvious ill will than for his weak character. The agent was riding the dregs of a coffee binge. Hoover never let his agents drink coffee, not in the office, and never, ever, in public. Martin Cundieffe, Sr. never touched the stuff. These days, coffee was the fuel of choice at the Bureau, and everyone thought Cundieffe was a Mormon, except the Mormons, of course, of whom he disapproved even more strongly because excessive religious fervor was every bit as much a vice in his eyes as drug use.

Chen finally cleared his throat. "What exactly brings you up from LA? Dorsey said a related case, but he didn't get told much."

"Well, it's a counterterrorism case. Suspect in a murder-arson down in Death Valley was sighted in the area. We—" We? The Royal We, surely not the Federal We "—we think he might be a part of a larger militia group."

"We've got our own counterterrorism task force."

"You don't want to catch him. Heck, I don't want to catch him. I'm only hoping to find out where he's going. That's why I'm here. You see, a local called in the sighting anonymously last night, a little after midnight. Your office followed up on it right away, but no soap. Then this. Has the coroner established a time of death yet?"

"Sometime early this morning, eight to ten hours ago. All of them went about the same time."

Chen waded into the flood and Cundieffe followed. He leaned across a gurney, felt a stiff claw brush his crotch as he lurched sideways through the door. A line-up of deputies and policemen crowded both sides of the entry hall. Twenty-seven people died here last night, so now every cop in town was here, standing guard over the one place where something was bound not to happen. Cundieffe considered flashing his badge to make a hole. Chen had no trouble plowing through, and would spread the word about his high-handedness if he started making a nuisance of himself. So he squeezed through the front doorway and veered into the front sitting room. There was a policemen's ball going on here, too, but it was more spread out. They had room to drink coffee. There was nothing to sit on, though, and the walls were padded with black velvet. It looks like a recording studio, Cundieffe thought. He spotted Dorsey across the room, talking to a sixtyish hippie college professor in a chocolate brown three-piece suit. The man's hands grabbed at the air as he held forth, as if protesting his innocence. No, lecturing, trying to prove a point. Dorsey looked bored.

Cundieffe made his way for the pair. "Sorry," he said to Chen. "Gotta mingle."

Cundieffe elbowed his way through to Dorsey and beamed at the stranger, but said nothing. Dorsey didn't introduce him. The stranger's eyes crawled around on Cundieffe for a moment, then he started talking again, and Cundieffe put together who and what he was.

"So, the question you're asking is impossible to answer to any degree of certainty. Who is this man?" He pointed at Cundieffe.

"He's an agent on an unrelated case."

"Agent Martin Cundieffe. And you are?"

Still looking at Cundieffe, the man said, "I don't think I want to say anything else without my lawyer here."

"Sir, the case I'm working may well be related to this one. I'm looking for a man I have reason to believe was in this area last night at the time that this unfortunate event occurred. If there's any corroborating evidence that he was here, and foul play is indicated, he may be our prime suspect, and anything you can tell us that will expedite the satisfactory resolution of this tragedy will stand in your good stead. Now what is it you were trying to tell my colleague Agent Dorsey that he either won't believe or doesn't understand?"

Dorsey snorted and spilled coffee. The man seemed to go for his approach in a big way. "Linus Ullman. I teach over at Stanford, and I design biofeedback equipment—it's based on the principle of—"

"I'm aware of biofeedback. Please continue."

"Yes, well, Charles Angell—the founder of this group is—was—an old friend of mine. I put together the system in use at this place. I think—it may have had something to do with their deaths."

"How do you mean?" Cundieffe listened intently, nodding vigorously to keep Ullman talking.

"To put it as simply as possible, the School Of Night were into deep meditation, conscious Delta state trances. Only enlightened gurus in the East have mastered this capability even infrequently. But they meditated as a group. They wanted a system that would link up all of their brainwaves into a sort of symphony of harmonics, and they would work towards syncing up. I'd never seen anything like it, not even in Nepal."

"So you're suggesting that they could have used your system to drive their brainwaves below a level at which even autonomic life functions can be sustained?"

"Yes. That's it exactly. This other agent seems to believe they've been poisoned."

"Preliminary tox screens show they were on something," Dorsey added.

"Did you know them to consume narcotics?" Cundieffe asked.

"Herbal stimulants and copious amounts of hashish, but nothing else. For something like what I'm suggesting, they would've had to ingest several grams of hashish each, just to slow their heartrates to the threshold where this could even, uh, conceivably occur. I'm sorry. This is just such a shock…" Ullman looked around the room, as if he expected to see a familiar face. Behind him, the corridor was strung with klieg lights, illuminating open cells running down both sides. They'd only just gotten the last of the bodies out of them. "I want it to go on record that I never anticipated something like this happening. This was not possible using the device as it was originally designed."

"Then what makes you so sure it was the cause of death?"

"Have you seen the back room? Where all the computers are?"

Dorsey put a hand on his arm, but Cundieffe slipped out from under it. "No. Show me."

Ullman led him down the hall. Flashes popped in several of the cells, the whine of recharging batteries, and the litany of forensic details being recorded. It was incredible how the acoustic padding drank the sounds out of the room. He saw people talking across the room, but couldn't hear a word.

Ullman reached the end of the hall and stopped beside a closed door. A yellow CAUTION ribbon was draped across the doorway. Cundieffe pulled down the tape and opened the door. Ullman pushed past him and rushed into the room. Dorsey grabbed at Cundieffe's arm again, but again he got free.

He stepped into the room and immediately slipped. The floor was slimy with something. His hands shot out and grabbed the doorframe, and he steadied himself, flicked on the light.

Ullman was gingerly padding across the floor with his hands out like a tightrope walker. Plastic tarp crinkled under his feet. "Look at what they did!" he shouted. His voice was achingly loud here, because this room was all bare floor and mainframes. All the computers were shut down, not even flashing backup lights were evident. And the floor was awash in tacky blood.

Ullman made his way over to the far wall, and when he did, he moved out of the way so that Cundieffe could see what Dorsey'd mentioned earlier. "Look at what they did!" Ullman shouted.

A big black leather office chair sat before the main computer console. A man sat in it with his hands splayed out on a keyboard resting in his lap. His throat was slashed down to the bone. His head was thrown back, all his vital plumbing laid open for the world to see. It was indecent, like a skin magazine photograph. What's more, someone had taken every sharp tool out of a toolbox and a kitchen knifeblock to the victim's head. They were all still there, rammed to the hilt into his eyesockets, his nostrils, ears, cheeks, even through the dome of his skull. The butt ends of these last were scuffed, so a mallet had been employed to drive them in. The raw, primal hatred of the act made Cundieffe's head swim. The head had been totally ravaged, as if the killer had wished to erase every detail of the victim's features. It was the explosion of a catastrophic mania. Cundieffe closed his eyes and reviewed the shots of Sheriff Twombley and his deputy, filled with so much lead the killer must've reloaded at least a second banana clip. Overkill.

"Has this man been identified yet?" Cundieffe asked.

"He's Kaman-Thah," Ullman said in a wistful, lost voice. "The Teacher and the Keeper of the Gate of Deeper Slumber."

"He's Charles Walter Angell, the leader," Dorsey said from outside. "There's no fingerprints on him."

"Have all the residents been accounted for?"

"Yes," Dorsey answered too quick, too loud, eyes boring into Cundieffe's, beaming *Who died and made you Agent-In-Charge, Four Eyes?*

"What about hired help?"

"Enough of this." Chen pushed Dorsey aside and stepped into the room. "Agent Cundieffe, why don't you get with the Colma Sheriff's to find out if the man you're looking for was even here while we take care of this?"

Cundieffe leaned round the looming local agent to fix on Ullman. "Professor, what did they do to your computer?"

"Well, look at this. There's a CPU hardwired into my system that wasn't there before. The soldering on it's still soft. Aside from the rest of it—"

"Agent Chen, respectfully submitted, were the computers already shut off when the police arrived?"

Chen scowled at him. "Nothing has been changed, except for the footprints everywhere."

"That's what I'm talking about!" Ullman said. "The whole system is shorted out. All the motherboards are fused. Something hit this network like a lightning bolt and destroyed every piece of hardware."

"So it won't be possible to retrieve any of their files."

"No, there's nothing left to retrieve. The current turned the chips to slag."

"Maybe they did it on purpose, to ditch something else," Chen thought out loud.

"Or whoever did this to them destroyed the computer to keep his or her identity a secret," Dorsey added.

"Or whoever did this ruined the network in the process of trying to get something out of it. Is that possible, professor?"

"Oh, certainly, for people this computer-literate, and as obsessed with secrecy as they were—" Ullman was looking at Angell's corpse now, and he ran out of words.

"Gentlemen," Cundieffe said, "I think this is now a counterterrorism case."

~ 25 ~

Storch pulled into the parking lot of the Mojave Outpost truckstop just as dusk fell on the central valley. The car, a late model Taurus station wagon, ate up its last ghosts of fuel fumes dragging itself onto the vast plain of the lot. The engine sputtered and died, and the power steering went out, the lumbering family battlewagon suddenly as hard to steer as a runaway locomotive in mud, and Storch with only one hand to manage it. He was afraid to step on the brakes and lose momentum in the middle of the lot. He'd risked calling enough attention to himself just getting here.

The trucker, Nathaniel Stumbo, had picked him up two miles north of a tiny, spooky burg called Atwater, and they'd continued south. Storch helped himself to Stumbo's first aid kit, used all the gauze and antiseptic and most of the surgical tape to shore up his calf, and borrowed a musty black and orange flannel shirt he found in the sleeping cabin to make a sling for his left arm. He even found a lockpick set in a ceiling compartment, and after breaking one pick off in the lock of his left ankle shackle, got the others off and tossed them out the window.

Stumbo talked a lot, and Storch wagered he'd have picked him up regardless of the circumstances or his military background, just to have an ear to bend. Stumbo'd lost all of his right leg and half of his left in an accident of some kind just two months out of the service. Storch watched the man talking, the monotonous low growl lulling him into sleep. He dug his ragged fingernails into the meat of his palms to keep alert. He watched Stumbo and kept catching himself trying to figure out which side the trucker was on, if he'd have to kill him at the end of the ride to insure his silence.

This became a nonissue when they approached Fresno, and Storch spotted the unmarked Chrysler sedans parked in the lot at the weigh station. FBI, looking at trucks. He ordered Stumbo to merge into the slowest lane, backed up a quarter mile longer than the others and standing still. The trucker looked askance at him, but did as he was told. Storch leaned out the window and surveyed the end of the line in a quick glance, then ducked back out of sight. The line was backed up because of a convoy of flatbeds carrying prefabricated houses. The highway patrol and two men in blue windbreakers were walking through each house. Up and down the line, horns honked, and Storch saw the other lanes getting the same treatment. There was a massive search on, but he doubted it was for him. It was like a smuggling inspection. They would recognize him, though. People who were just doing their jobs would end up getting killed.

"You got a gun?" Storch asked Stumbo, who looked at him as if he'd just materialized in his cab.

"What? Shit, man, I thought you did. Well, I got a little police special under my seat—"

He started to go for it, but Storch was faster, and had it out of its plastic snapcase. He popped out the barrel, scooped up one of the three speedloaders packed with it and notched one in. Stumbo watched him and then looked over at the checkpoint, and whatever rapport he'd built up with Storch drained right out of his face. "Whatcha gonna do, man? Those're cops."

Storch dropped out of the cab and limped down the line, almost hopping to keep weight off his ravaged left leg. When he reached the last truck, a BP tanker, he jogged left and ran down the shoulder to the cover of a stand of eucalyptus trees. As soon as he felt secure under their canopy, he turned to see if he'd been spotted. The lines inched on, and Storch wondered if he hadn't made a big mistake not killing Stumbo. It could've been done neatly enough that murder wouldn't be suspected until an autopsy was performed, and by then, he'd be gone. Stumbo's big mouth would give him fifteen minutes, at best, to get away. On foot.

Then, for the first time since the Fourth of July, Storch had cause to feel lucky. Just beyond the stand of trees and a partially collapsed chainlink fence, lay a commuter train station. Storch took note of the stop, for the suburb of Madera, and paced the line of cars at the edge of the lot. He picked the station wagon, because it would be least likely to get pulled over on looks alone, and had tinted windows, and a green ticket on the dash, which meant the driver was paying by the day, so he'd have the four hours he'd need to get back to the truckstop. He'd sat in the driver's seat for longer than was healthy, thinking about which way to go. An impulse he couldn't name or put completely down told him to go southwest to Norwalk, and see his father. If only to have a mirror in which to see the extent of his own damage. They'd be waiting for him there. He doubted he'd have much chance to turn himself in, if it came to that. He would go straight to the truck stop, and repair himself by getting answers, instead.

It hadn't been that easy.

Traffic backed up in Oildale, six miles north of Bakersfield, and Storch panicked. What if this was a full checkpoint? There'd be nowhere to run, especially if Stumbo had given them a description. He considered bolting the car and picking up another, but he knew it wouldn't pay to tempt fate twice. The cars lurched forwards a few lengths and then stopped again, at a measured pace that Storch began to count off with questions:

Where are you coming from?

Where are you headed?

Have you seen this man?

Thank you, sir or ma'am.

He bit his lip as the traffic came around a bend and into a concrete canyon, walls rising up as offramps peeled off the main highway to feed the outlying towns of Bakersfield. A perfect boxing in. It was already too late to run. If he could hold out until he actually approached the checkpoint, there'd be a moment's chance to disarm the highway patrolman and take him as a hostage. A chance to get away, stepping over the bodies of more policemen, this time ones he'd actually killed.

The walls of the freeway flashed red and blue, scattered huge, multifaceted silhouettes of walking figures flitting up and down the walls like patrolling ghosts. All the light came from the median. Storch sank into the seat, exhaling and exhaling until he was empty of stale air and fear. It was an accident. Just a fucking freeway accident, and all these assholes slowing down to rubberneck.

When he finally did reach the accident, he looked too, having paid in time for the privilege. The ambulance was loaded and had its lights on, but seemed in no hurry to shove off into traffic, and two tow trucks, three police cars and a pair of CHP motorcycles were lined up behind the spent combatants, a minivan and an old El Camino. Storch's eyes glanced across the wreck and back to the road, then ricocheted back to the minivan just as it passed by his window. He rolled it down to get a better view, and, yes, the front driver's side of the minivan is smashed in, but the El Camino's hood is smashed in, too. They'd have to have hit head-on. In the argent glow of the roadflares, the minivan's white paint and smashed grill were flecked with dark paint. It might've been blue or green or black, but it wasn't the faded phlegm yellow of the El Camino. He fumbled at the switch closing the window and glanced around. Then up.

And he saw them.

Four men in dark raincoats stood at the rail on the overpass, spaced out so that one overlooked each lane. Each had a tripod-mounted camera with a lens like the barrel of an elephant gun. Each was closely surveying each vehicle that inched beneath him and past the fake accident.

Jesus Christ, that's for me, that's it. Suddenly, the moral question of killing cops didn't hold much water. They thought he was a cop killer and would treat him accordingly, thus, making him one. He'd done things to change his appearance, but he was no master of escape and evasion in urban areas, this was stupid, he could just get out of the car now, and give himself up.

He almost did. Then a horn honking behind him became a symphony of monotone fury and he noticed that the lane in front of him was empty to the horizon. He wouldn't look up, they were looking down at him, snapping pictures, turn myself in? Fuck that. He stomped on the gas pedal and didn't stop until the gas gauge needle lay inches past the E, and luck was with him again, because with its last gasp, the Taurus had brought him right back where he started from.

Lucky.

The station wagon coasted up to the rows of cars parked in front of the truck stop's diner. Storch looked around long and hard before he got out, painfully aware of all the flavors of stupid he was already dipping in. He should've ditched the car after the surveillance stop in Bakersfield. He should've stopped Stumbo's heart. He should've gone to Mexico in the first fucking place, and then none of this would've happened. Now it was too late. If they paid this much attention to highways in Bakersfield, there'd be a federal law enforcement convention from San Ysidro to Brownsville. But it was no stupider, any of it, than what he was about to do.

Storch was born into the Army, had hardwired its rigorous discipline and chains of command into his psyche long before he enlisted. Alone, he'd made a piss-poor showing for himself. Cut off from any opportunity to go to the authorities, trapped in a situation he couldn't begin to grasp, he needed to go somewhere where things made sense, needed someone to point out the enemy and send him at them, or he might as well go into the hills and kill himself. Down to his bones, he was a soldier, and without an army behind him, he would be trampled by both sides.

He saw no immediate threat in or out of the truck stop. Semis parked in ranks like an invading army at the far end of the lot, and beside them, encircled by a barbed wire-topped hurricane fence, were the cargo containers where they'd kept him before.

He reached around into the pouch he'd sewed into the waistband of this and all his other pairs of boxers and pulled out the phone list he'd taken off the sentry in this place two days ago. He got out the station wagon's cell phone from the drivetrain storage box, flipped it open and began trying the numbers.

The first of ten got him an automated weather report. The second was a highway patrol communications center in Barstow. Storch stabbed the hang-up and tried the third. This one was disconnected. Likewise the fourth, and the fifth, and the sixth. Probably, the numbers were deactivated when the phone was lost. He skipped down to the last. No answer. So were six, seven, eight and nine. He tried the last number, and let it ring.

And ring.

And ring.

An answering machine picked up on the fourth. A bored middle-aged man's voice with a slight Hispanic inflection said, "You have reached Liberty Salvage and Storage. Our regular business hours are Monday, Thursday and Friday, ten AM to three PM. Your call is very important to us, so leave a message. For towing, call somebody else." Storch barely heard the words as he tried to frame something that would make sense without giving himself up to the wrong people if the number was a bust. To this was added the pure agony of talking to an answering machine. Storch loathed them, thought of them as one of the best things about having nobody to call, and would have gladly done just about anything else to get their attention.

A beep, then Storch was on. "This is the man you picked up by the side of the road the other day. I'm right back in the place you dropped me off, and if it's not too much trouble, I sure would appreciate another lift. Send somebody as soon as you can, because I'll be gone by dawn, one way or another."

He hit the OFF button and pocketed the phone. He looked around, half-expecting to see someone closing in on him now, rifle shouldered and trained on his head. He was out of gas, hope and destinations, but slowly, he began to feel lifted. His scalp burned and itched like it was sprouting barbed wire, he hadn't eaten anything since he got back from Colma, and he was pretty sure he'd vomited that up when he'd been gassed out in his motel room. His leg screamed for attention and his arm throbbed dire warnings of permanent damage through the painkillers he'd gobbled. But when he closed his eyes, he felt as if he was rising, being lifted out if this sorry, tattered, hunted skin and into something else.

The stench of his own body odor mingled with the heady reek of diesel filtering in from outside, making Storch's empty stomach flipflop and hinting nastily at the return of the Headache. The frigid, dusty desert wind rocked the Taurus on its suspension, and he could imagine he was on a slow river. Which he was, really, except not slow so much as a series of cataracts, sheer drops and narrow chutes down which his future flailed and struggled not to be dragged under. He'd been fighting to get out for so long that he'd just about drowned himself before any of the unseen predators below could finish him. Now he'd committed himself to swimming the falls, he could feel the world around him again, and begin to fit what he'd seen into it.

He did this for about a half an hour, and nobody came to kill or claim him. Then, *Fuck it*, he thought, *I'm gonna go eat*.

Two paces from the car, he gagged on the unfiltered olfactory roar of diesel fumes, and slumped across the hood. Blood thickened, nerves rolled up and went on strike, lungs tried to slam shut against the poisons flooding them. His legs buckled, and he clawed at the rain gutters at the base of the windshield to keep from sprawling on the ground. He felt as if his body was rebelling against him, dragging him away from the controls and deep within himself like a snail in a sandstorm. This was the sickness he'd hidden away from for eight long years. It would not take him here, not like this. Biting deep furrows in the meat of his lower lip, Storch levered himself upright with his slinged left arm and balanced himself precariously on locked knees and wobbly ankles. In another five minutes, he reached the big glass revolving door at the nearest end of the truckstop. He threw his whole weight against the door to make it swing round and deposit him inside.

His first breath of the air inside began uncoiling his wound-up system, even as the freon and canned humidity of the air conditioning began to work on his lungs. Still, it was nothing he couldn't eat through.

The diner occupied the bottom of the colossal L-shaped truckstop; the elbow was a convenience store, with phones, restrooms and showers; the upper end was a truckers-only area, with lounge, sleeping facilities and a rec room. A drowsy teenaged girl stood guard at the entrance to the truckers' lounge, checking licenses.

Storch knew it would be wiser to buy some snack foods, go back to the station wagon and eat, then see about some other form of transportation out of here if no one came. But he went into the diner and took the last booth beside the window.

Even for four in the morning in the middle of the Mojave Desert, the place was doing a slow trade. A heavyset man in flannel shirt and jeans and a Snap-On Tools baseball cap slept undisturbed beside a half-eaten bowl of chili. Two bikers at the end of the counter sipped coffee and watched the door. He might've been invisible as he passed through their glazed gazes. Through the kitchen, he could see the cook and the busboy standing out on the back loading dock, sharing a cigarette. He waited, and joined in watching the door and the still black night outside.

The busboy didn't even look at him as he slung a glass of ice water and a menu across the table. The waitress was so jacked up on something that she never looked at Storch as she took his order. A big green salad with lots of tomatoes, any fruit juice they might have, and any fresh fruit, especially pineapple. She rolled her eyes and said, "Wendy's at the next exit has a salad bar," and skated back into the kitchen. He heard a door slam.

Then Storch heard movement behind him, and turned to see the sleeping man had risen and closed the door leading to the truckstop, and was coming down the aisle towards him. Eyes flicking towards the kitchen once or twice, but not with the guilty, fearful look of one about to do evil, but only concern that no one will get hurt who shouldn't. A silencered automatic of the kind cops used to carry in ankle holsters looked like a party favor in his meaty hand. His features were Hispanic, his carriage noncom, a lifetime sergeant with a serious impulse control problem.

Storch ducked down in the seat and checked behind him. The bikers were both up and less than twenty feet away, with line of sight on him under the table. They both carried silencered MP5 assault rifles slung at their sides.

Any reaction he might've once taken instantly and instinctively completely failed him. His good hand trembled, but wouldn't go for his gun. He settled back in the booth. The room smelled like coffee, refried potatoes and overcooked chili, a not unpleasant funk that smothered the stink of his own sweat. His pains and his exhaustion faded into the background as the moment took hold of him and made him ready for what was to come. He closed his eyes and prepared himself for judgment.

"I'm kind of disappointed," Storch called out. "Last time was sort of original, but this…"

"You got a lot of nerve coming back here, homes," the Hispanic man said, leaning across his table to close the blinds, the gun leveled at a businesslike relationship with Storch's head. "You were lucky the first time, and we were stupid. We paid for that."

Storch blinked, looked round for the bikers. He could feel their breath on the back of his neck. "What are you talking about?"

"Where'd you go, homes?"

"I don't see where that concerns you, Sergeant."

"You're always ending up in the wrong place, that's why. I don't buy your Gulf War sickness bullshit, and I don't buy you. We came here to kill you, homes." He waited too long to see some glint of fear well up in Storch's eyes. Storch's bland stare gave him one of his own.

One of the bikers hauled the big man back. "Leave it, man. He's for the Major." The sergeant tucked his gun in an armpit holster, turned and stormed off. The bikers waved Storch out of the booth with the guns. Storch followed the sergeant out of the diner and into the convenience store. None of the handful of sleepy tourists or sped-up clerks took notice of them as they passed through, so Storch assumed the guns had been concealed again. The sergeant strolled over to the truckers' refuge and had a word with the stoned, pregnant girl watching the door. He held the door open for Storch and the bikers. Storch rubbed his eyes at the dimness inside.

A meeting hall-sized room with a snack bar along one side and cafeteria tables taking up one-half. The rest was taken up with heavy floor-mounted recliners with TVs built into the arms. The tables were empty, but a few truckers dozed or tweaked out in the blue glow of the screens. Through an open double door on the far side of the room, Storch heard the clack of billiard balls and the spastic burble of video games. The sergeant led the way down an adjoining corridor into the lodging area. Sizing up the accommodations, Storch fondly remembered the cargo container as more comfortable and easier on the eyes. The sergeant stopped before a door and slid a chewed-up plastic card through a slot beside an equally chewed-up door. He popped the door open and seized Storch's lame arm. Storch dug in his heels, but the sergeant yanked outwards on the arm, and Storch wobbled with the searing pain, and before the bones had stopped grinding together, he was plunged into complete darkness.

The cell couldn't be much deeper than Storch could reach from the door. He was more impressed than surprised to find someone'd lifted his gun. He stood stock-still, willing his eyes to adjust to the imperceptible glow of the thread of light from beneath the door. The stink of sweat, cleanser and stale cigarette smoke almost gave the darkness a color, then a face, No, it was a man, in here with him, no, two. Storch had been in the room at least three minutes before he could see them, and never heard them breathing. Despite himself, Storch stepped back to the door and reached behind him for the knob. There wasn't one.

"Why did you come back, Sergeant Storch?" a voice asked, ringing bells in Storch's head. The officer type in the cargo container, the major.

"I'm getting pretty sick of people asking me questions in the dark, sir," Storch said. "I don't know what I did to piss you folks off, but I—"

A brilliant white light stabbed Storch's eyes. He recoiled and clamped his eyes shut. The other soldier asked, "That better?"

"Tell us what you did in San Jose, Sergeant," the Major asked.

Storch scrubbed his face. He was beyond exhausted and his painkillers were starting to wear off, it was so hard to focus, to try to play their game. Maybe if he played along, they would help him get out of the country, or at least help him understand what the hell had happened. But how much to tell? How much did they already know? He told them where he went and what happened in San Jose, leaving out only his visit with Buggs. This thing had already burned away nearly all the meager store of friends and acquaintances he'd managed to gather. He wasn't going to sacrifice the only person who'd helped him.

The Major steepled his fingers in front of his face. Storch could see well enough now to tell that the Major was a black man in his middle fifties, close to two hundred pounds and in excellent shape. Even sitting on a bunk bed in dungarees and a plaid flannel shirt, he looked like the men who'd run Storch's life from the moment of his conception—moving his family hither and thither, committing his father, sending him into the desert. The other man, holding the flashlight in one hand and an exotic sawed-off shotgun in the other. He was younger, white, a grunt with close-set, Appalachian features and a huge jaw that didn't quite set right, a nose like a smashed ax blade, broken so many times the bridge was almost concave. A Marine, Storch would bet his broken arm on it.

He was impressed by these men, though he hadn't tested them. They were former military, and flint-hard with battle-training—the sergeant probably a Ranger, the bikers were probably either SEALS or Green Berets.

Once Storch had found Special Forces, he'd discovered his allegiance was not to the Army or to his country so much as to the ideals of his caste. If the right catalysts had been introduced at the right time in his career, if he hadn't gone on the mission in the war, who knows? He might've been among these men long ago.

"You're skipping something. That makes you look like a liar, Sergeant." The Major's voice was calm, cool, anything but condemning. Storch flashed on the first time he'd heard this voice. It'd been scrambled, but the combination of a mild, upper Southern accent—Kentucky, maybe Maryland—and carefully enunciated r's, told him the Major had been the man on the phone in his trailer. The man whose wake-up call had first set him running.

"Fucker's fucked us twice, Major. We're here to grease him, so let's." The Marine switched off the flashlight. Storch heard the shotgun pump ratchet. He tried to picture the space between him and the gun and wondered if he could fill it with fists before the Marine blew him in half. Slowly, silently, he went into a crouch, preparing to dodge at the slightest sound, opting instead to lunge for the Major and hope the jarhead liked the Major more than he hated Storch.

"Unfuck yourself, Draper. Those were civilian orders. Now, Sergeant. What else can you tell us about your visit to San Jose? It's very important."

Storch racked his brains so hard the truth came spilling out, even as he tried to bite it back. He wanted to be a truth-teller in front of these soldiers, he wasn't going to try to lie, not now. "A friend of mine from Thermopylae came down to see me."

"Did you contact this friend?"

"No, he tracked me down. He knows computers. Anyway, he took me up to his new work and tried to help me run down Sperling, and then he took me home."

"What is your friend's name?"

"I don't see where that figures in," Storch said. "He's just a guy who used to work for me, up until last week—"

"So you don't know anything about this," the Major cut him off again, and the flashlight flared again, pointed at the floor between them. The morning Los Angeles Times, still crisp and white, with its too-bright color spread showing a nighttime view of an old gambrel-roofed house on a bright green lawn, surrounded by ambulances, coroners' wagons and police cars. A bucket brigade of medical examiners passed bagged bodies out the front door and down to the ambulances on the crushed gravel drive. Storch sucked in a long, deep breath and blinked several times before he felt ready to read the headline.

SAN FRANCISCO AREA RELIGIOUS SECT WIPED OUT IN MASS SUICIDE; 28 DEAD

Death followed him. They followed him, and Buggs—

"You were there?"

Dumbfounded, Storch just nodded. "But everything was fine. They were all just asleep."

The light went out again.

"The School Of Night was our eyes and ears, Sergeant. Without them, our task is next to impossible. I had orders to kill you as a traitor, but I believed what Harley Pettigrew told me about you. He said you were unbelievably stupid and probably insane, but trustworthy. Who was this friend of yours?"

Storch started to say his name when it hit him.

Fucker's fucked us twice—

—always ending up in the wrong place, that's why.

I would've done it for free.

"Oh shit," Storch groaned, and sank to his knees. "Ely Buggs," he muttered. "He came to work for me about three months ago. He was just a clerk—"

"There were armaments under your store for four months," the Major replied. "I can't believe they used the same fucking guy twice."

"I can't believe it worked twice," Draper said. "But this fucker's still trash."

"Sir," Storch swallowed and started off, "I don't understand what the fuck's going on these last few days, but I want to get out of it. And I'm starting to see the only way out is down to the bottom and through. If you're fighting these motherfuckers that burned down my store and killed Harley and that girl and I don't know what else…I'm in."

"Sergeant, you're stupider than Pettigrew let on, and definitely insane. But now, more than ever, I need stupid, crazy grunts to fulfill my task. You can't leave here if you say no, but don't think for a minute that saying yes is going to save your life. We've all killed for this cause, and we're all going to die for it."

"I think I'd be a liar to pledge that kind of loyalty, sir. With all due respect." He drank a long drink of the close, stale trucker's-coffin air, and closed his eyes. What else could they expect him to say?

"Did Sperling tell you what Radiant Dawn did with his daughter?" the Major asked, and Storch cocked his head and thought for a moment about this tangential question.

Storch blinked, it was darker with his eyes open. "He told me some, but I don't see what—"

"We want to show you something, Sergeant."

A break in the blackness, a black box he recognized must be a TV just as it exploded into blinding snow, staring into it until tears came to adjust his eyes. A picture swam up out of the snow, squiggled as the tracking settled itself.

A plain TV studio set, grainy, public-access quality video, shot through with confetti-bursts of spastic static. A middle-aged man with silver hair and plastic wraparound shades sits in a leather chair, his lips moving and hands gesticulating absently. The man looked familiar, like something he might've skipped over while channel-surfing. Draper adjusted the volume.

"—and this striving to transform is so powerful within us, that it takes a lifetime of programming to overcome it. That frustrated energy has to go somewhere—"

The image froze in crystal clarity, not skipping like his cheap VCR. "This is Cyril Keogh," the Major said. "He transmits this program via satellite each week. It is called *Radiant Dawn*. It is not a popular program, but it is accessible to several hundred million people all over the world. As you can see, little effort is expended on the program itself, but stego decryption reveals that the program itself is only a Trojan Horse for a private transmission."

The pixels began to flicker, every atom of the New Age lecturer's freaky visage strobing, becoming snow again, until another image came out of the Technicolor blizzard.

This was not the same program.

A young girl lies on a steel examination table, naked and bound, and oh, so very pregnant. Her distended belly towers over her prone form, splaying her legs out at right angles to her torso, reminding Storch of the monstrous abdomens of termite queens. She appears to be sedated, her breath slowly, steadily fogging up an oxygen mask.

Still, he recognized her. It was Sidra Sperling.

A figure shrouded in crimson surgeon's robes circles round to the girl's pelvis, which is screened off from the rest of the patient under a red gauze tent. The surgeon selects a tiny radial saw and matter-of-factly worries away at the mons veneris, elegantly extending the vaginal canal to accommodate the monster fetus within.

Look how efficient he can afford to be, Storch realized, when he never intends to close her back up.

The surgeon lays aside the tool and selects another, much larger, like the barbecue tongs his father used to use to flip whole turkeys on the grill. His free hand plunges into the widened birth canal, disappears up to the elbow. With the other he gingerly inserts the tool. Another robed figure steps into frame to check Sidra's anesthesia, then moves out. After wrangling around inside the girl for a whole minute, the surgeon seems to latch onto something and withdraws his hands. He grasps the handles of the turkey-tongs and begins to pull, and for a moment looks as if he's going to brace one foot against the edge of the table.

All at once, something inside her gives with an audible crack and, on the crest of a small tsunami of milky fluid, out slides a child.

Storch couldn't properly call it a baby, because it was the size of a kindergartner. A caul covered its facial features, if it had any.

"Geneticists routinely use fruit flies to study mutations, because they have a new generation every week or so," said the Major. "Our enemy has achieved similar results with…higher animals."

The gigantic fetus stirs sleepily, its rubbery legs extending to reveal a horribly bloated belly. The surgeon injects the fetus with a hypodermic gun and, again, takes up the radial saw.

"Oh my God…" Storch whispered. Unborn, a prisoner of the womb, it was pregnant, too.

When the surgeon finally lays down his tools, there are seven fetuses, all laid out on the examination table like Russian nesting dolls that fit inside each other. Each is markedly less human than the last, the skeletal structure gradually withdrawing from the limbs, which become pliant, muscular tentacles. The skulls flare out like morning glories, grotesque horns of plenty from which pour luxuriant, convoluted brainsacs.

The last is scarcely larger than the surgeon's index finger, and indistinguishable from the placental nodule that it embraces with its whiplike limbs. Then he steps aside again, and the table is being cleared by a giant of a man in a flak vest and no shirt.

So tall was he that his head loomed out of frame, but Storch was staring at his forearm, at the tattoo almost obscured by the wiry tufts of hair and scars, but he could read it.

Don't Mess With Texas

And he remembered what really happened.

~ 26 ~

SA Martin Cundieffe sat in the back of the chopper carrying the twelve extra agents assigned to China Lake. No one paid him much attention, which suited him fine. His eyes pored over the opened file atop the stack of files on his lap, his lips moving mutely and so quickly he seemed to have a facial tic. The more astute of the agents took this as a sign of nerves, that Cundieffe wasn't up to the enormous task laid upon him, and they relished his apparent squirming. The rest simply saw Cundieffe's trademark overachievement in action, and resented him for it. Though he was well aware of their cynicism and hostility, he couldn't be bothered to disabuse them of their misreading, because he was practicing his speech.

In his short, exciting time in the field, Cundieffe had discovered the practical value of interpersonal communication as a skill. He'd been taken aback at first at his inability to finesse interview subjects. He was used to simply reading the aggregated data about a subject and composing a list of cardinal points for Lane Hunt to use in interrogations. He felt deeply chagrined that he'd actually had to threaten that pony-tailed Pentagon functionary, Tuttle. Though nothing had come of it, Cundieffe had taken stock of his abilities, and laid down a rigid self-improvement regimen. For a mentor, he'd looked no further than the Director. Mr. Hoover was a legendary master of rhetorical manipulation and psychological intimidation, who, one stenographer allegedly complained, could reach a peak oratory rate of four hundred words per minute. With this awesome power, the Director persuaded hostile political opponents to let him build the Bureau into an awesome force for law and order, and to operate without any meaningful oversight for nearly fifty years. Beneath the blunt, orderly plain of his thousands of statements before Congressional panels lay a jungle of circuitous logical bypasses and semantic clover-leaves in which any mind that dared to penetrate would be swallowed whole. Cundieffe had acquired several volumes of congressional transcripts, particularly from the Director's embattled early fifties, marked off the word counts in blue pen, and devoured them whole, reciting silently with a stopwatch balanced on his knee. He'd topped out at two hundred fifteen words per minute after six hours of practice, fast enough that everyone but Assistant Director Wyler blinked and nodded like zombies when he wound into a verbal attack. Cundieffe would guess that Wyler spoke at least three hundred words per minute. Maybe he should record Wyler and use his speech patterns instead. It would have to wait until after his presentation to the military arm of the China Lake investigation. The FBI had pressed for, and gotten, sole control of the case, and graciously opted to retain the Delta Force and the Navy in an advise & support capacity. Cundieffe had been given only the skeleton of a mission order, and had fleshed it out to AD Wyler's thorough satisfaction. The sell would not be any easier for having been bought and paid for in Washington. The FBI was not eager to place its elite tactical agents in the way of napalm-slinging terrorists, let alone in the potentially disastrous proximity to the media in Los Angeles. He would have to tell the Delta Force commander, Lt. Col. Greenaway, he of the short temper and the broken ballpoint, to accept the hazards of the mission, but make none of the decisions.

The other lesson he'd taken from the Director had been much easier to manage given his new association with AD Wyler. *Know Everything* was Hoover's unspoken credo—his father bragged that the Director knew Lucille Ball was pregnant before Ricky did. Beneath the outline for his presentation, he had an itemized mission order and timeline for the resolution of the China Lake investigation; DoD files on several DARPA projects, including RADIANT; separate SFPD and FBI reports on the School Of Night investigation; confidential dossiers on several of the officers he'd be meeting; and the OPR's preliminary report on Lane Hunt, whom he'd come to relieve. Cundieffe had yet to practice that speech.

The flight crew scrambled to prepare for landing. Cundieffe had never been to Death Valley before; though he'd memorized the temperature extremes tables along with everything else in the almanacs and Guinness Book of World Records before he was ten, and every year since, he was shocked to feel the heat closing around him, like the blasting wind of a kiln. The temperature was only a few degrees below the average July high of one hundred and four, but the humidity remained a freakishly high fifty percent. He mopped his forehead with a handkerchief and applied a fresh coat of prescription-strength zinc cream to his face and bare scalp. He'd already sweated great sopping racing stripes down the sides of his shirt, and putting his jacket on only aggravated the condition. The other agents, all in meshback FBI baseball caps and navy blue windbreakers, were looking to him, or looking at him, many openly laughing. He packed up his files and pulled himself to his feet, hanging from an overhead rail and swaying much more than befitted the dignity of a team leader. His eyes roved over them, pinning each on the authority of his gaze, and stopping the laughter, the conversations.

"Listen up, everyone. As of twelve hundred hours today, the FBI assumes full responsibility for the resolution of this case. I know my appointment comes as a surprise to all of you, and for most, not a pleasant one. I've never participated in a field operation, let alone led one, so your doubts are not wholly unfounded. However, I was selected to lead this investigation because the Assistant Director believes the assessment I've made of the situation is the most likely, and my proactive strategy for resolving this crisis promises to be more effective than the military solution, which has been to fly around California, knocking down doors and getting themselves killed in needless accidents. I think if you allow yourselves to wholeheartedly accept the strategic decisions I've been empowered to implement and implement them to the best of your respective abilities, the perpetrators will be neutralized without loss of life or property within seventy-two hours. I'm going to hand out assignment packets as soon as we hit the ground. I know these assignments may strike some of you as unorthodox, and may entail some subterfuge on our part in coordination with the Navy and Joint Special Forces elements of the investigation, but I assure you that we have the sanction and legal authority of the Attorney General of these United States, and I urge you to follow them with all due diligence. Are there any questions?"

There were none. They gawked at him in bemusement, and not a little awe. He'd shouted out his prepared speech over the chopper noise in just under sixty seconds. A new personal best.

Cundieffe could pick Lt. Col. Greenaway out of the crowd on the landing pad long before they touched down and the ground crew helped them out. He wore desert camo fatigues with no insignia, but stood a head taller than the other officers and the matched pair of Delta Force bookends flanking him with assault rifles at port arms. Cundieffe doubted this was an accident. It spoke volumes about Greenaway, sealed conclusions Cundieffe had reached upon his first contact with the Delta Forces commander.

Greenaway would never rise above his present rank, never ascend into the world of palace intrigues and "perfumed princes," as lower echelon officers referred to generals. He took a perverse pride in this, and probably hated everything about the military except the camaraderie of his men and the quickening thrill of battle. According to a file Wyler'd had delivered to him minutes before they left Los Angeles, Greenaway became Special Forces in 1971 and took part in Operation White Star, the CIA's covert campaign in Cambodia. He quit the Army after the end of Vietnam and disappeared into merc work in Africa—Rhodesia, Mozambique and Congo that they knew about, training guerrillas here, government troops there, before coming back to the States in 1978 to join Delta Force. The circumstances of his reinstatement were muddled by footnotes to documents which had evidently been shredded long ago; Wyler had filled in the blanks in blue pen— *"He blackmailed his way back into the service—White Star dirt."* Greenaway's first action with the new elite antiterrorist unit was Operation Desert One, the ill-fated attempt to rescue the hostages in the American Embassy in Teheran. Greenaway stayed on the ground, but saw most of his comrades killed in a helicopter accident which would officially be blamed on bad CIA intel. From that day, he'd made no secret of his ardent hatred for the intelligence services, and he'd only risen through the ranks on his unmatched tactical skill and personal charisma. Cundieffe imagined the generals he held in such contempt must worship him as much as they feared him.

Drawing on these facts, Cundieffe felt comfortable with Greenaway. He might even be able to tell him some of the truth.

The ground rushed up at Cundieffe's flailing legs as the helicopter bucked up six feet under him, and the ground crewman seized his hand and yanked him off. He hit the ground hard on the ball of his right foot and leaned on one of the crewmen so as not to collapse or drop the bulky attaché case he carried. The shooting pain incapacitated his whole right side for a moment, but Cundieffe waved with his left and forced himself to walk up to Lt. Col. Greenaway. He didn't offer his hand to be shook, nor did Greenaway offer one. Higher ranking naval officers were present, but their body language deferred to Greenaway, so Cundieffe did not look at them. He met Greenaway's stare without blinking or smiling. It took mighty effort, for Greenaway's ability to project images of extreme personal violence out of his eyes was more nakedly demonstrated here than in the briefing room. He approached Cundieffe and one hand snapped up as if he were going to backhand the FBI agent across the helipad. His huge hand spread out before Cundieffe's eyes. He bit his lower lip clean through, but he didn't flinch.

"Give it here," Greenaway said. His hand wagged impatiently at Cundieffe's blank look. "The bag, it's got your reports in it. Give it here."

"I'm afraid there's been a misunderstanding, Lieutenant Colonel. I'm surprised you weren't informed. As of twelve hundred hours PST today, the FBI assumes control over this investigation, by joint order of the Attorney General and the Director and Assistant Director of the Federal Bureau of Investigations. It's been approved by the President, though I'm sure you understand why he wouldn't want to sign it himself." He plucked out a document on thick machined parchment, which flapped like a flag in the helicopter's blade wash. "Here's a copy for your records."

Greenaway snapped the paper out of his hands and looked it over for a moment. His forehead wrinkled and turned redder than the desert sun had already made it, but when he returned to Cundieffe-bashing with his eyes, he was smiling. "Best news I've heard all year. This was a fucking goat-rope, anyway. You're welcome to it, Junior."

Cundieffe bit his lip again. "I think you need to read the document again, Lieutenant Colonel. Your services will still be required here, but under the directives of the FBI. This is now a criminal investigation, but we're going to need your help now more than ever."

The cords in Greenaway's neck snapped with an audible twang as he rounded on Cundieffe and seized him by the arms. His face filled Cundieffe's field of view; he could see just enough of the world around him to sense that no one was moving to stop the Delta Force Commander from beating him to death. "Well, please convey my sincerest and humblest apologies to the President and the Attorney General for bungling this operation," he shouted, his spit hot flying in Cundieffe's face, "and thank them for sending us the FBI to dig us out. What can we do to help?"

Cundieffe started to open his mouth, an impromptu four hundred word oratory outlining the strategic improvements in the search which he would bring to the table, but Greenaway cut him off with a wordless hiss and a slashing hand that grazed his throat. "You—know—shit." A moment to let this blunt ground-truth sink in, then, "Your SAC on this base is a pathetic, grabasstic pussyhound who couldn't draw his weapon unless it was for a photo op. You don't know what happened here, and you're not going to find them unless they want you to."

Now Cundieffe did smile, and blood ringed his white teeth, as he said, "He's not in charge anymore. I am. And I think I do know what happened here, and who did it, and why. if you'll take me to a secure place, I'll endeavor to enlighten you."

Once Greenaway overcame his natural repulsion for Cundieffe, the junior FBI agent couldn't ask for a more receptive audience. Sequestered in a basement conference room with a silent gallery of naval officers and DoD functionaries looking on, Cundieffe launched into his presentation, beginning with a heavily expurgated recital of his theories regarding the China Lake heist and its implications. A few of the DoD people were predictably skeptical at the outset, but Cundieffe played to Lt. Col. Greenaway, particularly to his mistrust of defense intelligence, and within a few minutes Greenaway told them to shut the hell up. He asked insightful, pragmatic questions and didn't tell Cundieffe to slow down when he replied with exhaustive statistics and sketchy speculation.

Greenaway was a statue all through his strategy briefing. They would fall back to passive observational positions across the southeastern quarter of the state, and bolster defenses at all of the eight military installations in the area, especially proving grounds, storage and research facilities. FBI spotters would continue to watch interstate traffic and cargo shipping, and the military would wait. On the proactive side, they would use secure military channels and DARPA encryption to try to open negotiations with the group, which surely included defected DARPA and military personnel. He dropped his last bombshell only after the assembled officers had reluctantly assented to its role in the FBI plan.

"That's the plan, gentlemen—oh yes, one final thing. We feel the time is right to release an expurgated account of the theft to the media." Reaching into the stack of files spilling out of his opened attaché case, he produced half a dozen single-sheet copies and handed one to Greenaway, and the rest to a DoD official, who passed the rest on. "I'm a bit short on copies, so look on with your neighbors, some of you."

They read for a full minute, many, Cundieffe noticed with a suppressed smirk, moving their lips as they digested the short statement.

Essentially, it had the Navy admitting that they'd been burglarized by a small group of disgruntled ex-sailors; that some outmoded and relatively harmless ordnance and/or intel (the Navy was free to fill in this blank with whatever it deemed least damaging to its own credibility) had been stolen, most likely for potential sale to a foreign power; and that SEALS and Operational Detachment Delta had been deployed to root out the idiots who'd done the deed in a half-maneuver, half-demonstration of military overkill to deter further pointless and petty thefts.

The base commander was the first to be heard above the rising din of complaints. "This makes us out to be complete idiots. There's no way we'll go along with it. The Admiral will shit kittens when this gets out."

"The Admiral signed off on it last night, and I think if you stop and think about it, the Navy looks far less ridiculous if it admits to having been robbed of some obsolete junk, than if napalm were stolen from them by a handful of men with magic sleep rays. It won't be long before someone tells the real story to the press, and a reporter follows the technology back to the DoD. The sooner a cover story is laid out, the easier it'll be to discredit everything that comes after as idle smoke blown by dysfunctional military peons. This can still be resolved without any real skeletons tottering out of the closet."

They calmed down as a herd under his further persuasions, and the briefing adjourned with a grim but businesslike air that emboldened Cundieffe to brace Greenaway in the hall. The commander stopped and stared at the bald spot on top of Cundieffe's head.

"There's more," Cundieffe started, "I couldn't talk about it in front of them, but you're the field commander. There's things you should know. We may have hostile elements on our side of the fence, if you take my meaning."

Greenaway made a sour face, but looked around, and led Cundieffe to an empty office. He circled around a blank desk, but didn't sit. He leaned across it and waited. Cundieffe wiped his brow and began.

"I told you that the suspected leaders of the terrorist group were involved with SDI research. I neglected to mention that there are connections to the School Of Night mass-suicide in Colma. The group's leader, a Professor Angell, was a longtime associate of Dr. Armitage—they taught together at MIT and worked on several missile guidance and directed energy projects for DARPA. In 1980, Angell had a nervous breakdown, and took a lecturer's post at Stanford."

"This is fascinating," Greenaway said. "Keep talking, I'm leaving."

"Wait, wait, it ties in." Cundieffe drank in a deep breath and began talking faster than he ever had in his life. "All of the School Of Night's computers were flash-fried at the time of their deaths, but a hard T1 line was traced to a University server which handles only large, sensitive downloads for faculty and researchers. Professor Angell's accounts for the last year consisted almost entirely of downloads from Jet Propulsion Laboratories, Lick and Palomar observatories. He put in several hundred requests for radar and photographic imagery of the orbital paths around the earth. He was looking for a satellite."

Greenaway shook his head like a bear with tinnitus. "I don't follow. What has that got to do with the napalm theft?"

"It's SDI, Lieutenant Colonel. Armitage and the rest did work on an SDI project called RADIANT, that ended in some kind of disaster, then he and several of his colleagues dropped out and, we suspect, went underground. They've come out now because there's a satellite up there that's modeled on—or is—RADIANT, about which they presumably had very strong feelings."

"So they're going to drop napalm on it. From where? The moon?"

"We don't believe RADIANT was a defensive weapon. We think it was a First Strike project, capable of effecting targets in the atmosphere— maybe even on the ground. We think they're going to try to disrupt a test of the weapon, or destroy the command/control elements, or even a research installation where a new RADIANT may be in development."

"Bullshit," Greenaway said. "So you don't even know if it exists, yet. Nothing like that could ever be built. It's too expensive, even if they had the technology, which they don't."

"And yet they're out there, aren't they? Whether or not it exists, there's some very clever people out there with napalm—and I doubt that's all they have. But the point is, they're going to strike at the military-industrial complex, and the DoD has tipped its hand. They know who we're looking for, and they've been fighting a covert war against them on our home soil."

"You're fucking crazy."

"You know about the Special Forces Sergeant who snapped and killed the Furnace Creek sheriff? The surviving deputy was in no shape to give a statement. He took a swing at an FBI agent who approached him shortly after the incident. He was restrained and drugged, and only spoke to us a day ago. He told us that a tactical squad of federal agents stormed Storch's surplus store in a squatter community in Death Valley, and removed an arsenal of weapons and chemicals. They made no arrests, and gagged the sheriff for twenty-four hours, but then Storch allegedly shot him and the other deputy. But there were no federal agents anywhere in Death Valley, and certainly no seizures like he described. Now, suppose that Storch was an agent of this terrorist group, and sitting on a stockpile of chemical weapons and explosives for them. Who raided him? They posed as federal agents, but never identified their bureau of origin, let alone produced a search or arrest warrant."

"Fuck me. Covert ops. That's how they work in-country. But I've never heard of anything like that actually being put together, and SpecWar's a small fucking world."

"It doesn't include the CIA's tactical commando unit," Cundieffe said, "or the FBI's. But the group simply turned around and stole napalm from the weapons station. Now they're waiting for the ideal time to use it."

"Maybe it's not going to happen at all, then," Greenaway said. "If their arsenal was swept up so efficiently, maybe they've all been taken out."

"No, the DoD is still frightened, or they wouldn't have agreed to the leak. No, it's going to happen soon, and we're in the right area."

"What makes you so sure?"

Cundieffe allowed himself to smile as he handed Greenaway an eight by ten glossy photograph, highly pixelated from digital transmission, but crystal clear from arm's length, because it was taken with a high-speed digital camera through a starlight lens. The picture showed a bird's eye view of a late-model Taurus station wagon on a five lane highway. A tall, tense-looking man with a San Jose State Spartans baseball cap tugged down over the tops of his ears sat behind the wheel, his upturned face flattened by the light, his mouth beginning to open in shock as he locked eyes on the camera lens.

"That's Sergeant Storch, photographed just outside of Bakersfield, at the intersection of state highways 99 and 58. We don't think he's an isolated nut. After Furnace Creek, he was sighted in Colma the day of the School Of Night mass suicide. He was shot here headed south, in our direction. An aerial tail was placed on him, but called off over Tehachapi, and the ground tail he was turned over to failed to catch up to him. The station wagon was discovered parked at a truckstop in the Mojave desert two hours later, and a thorough search of the place failed to turn up any trace of him. He's gone to ground here. He's with them."

"But if he had something to do with what happened in Colma, he could very likely be a double agent."

"Exactly," Cundieffe replied. "Whether he knows it or not."

"Fucking DI," Greenaway sighed. "This shit is them all over."

"I sincerely hope so," Cundieffe said, wrinkling his nose in distaste. "You understand now why we felt you could be trusted, where they couldn't."

"I'll work with you, G-boy," Greenaway said. "They'll be taken alive, if it'll ratfuck the Pentagon. But any of my men gets hurt because of your book smarts fucking up my operations, nobody'll ever find your bones."

"I wouldn't want it any other way," Cundieffe said.

If Cundieffe hoped for an equally rosy reception from Lane Hunt, he saw pretty quickly that he would be disappointed. When Hunt hadn't shown up for the briefing, Cundieffe had assumed the team SAC was preparing to leave on the sly, and he was willing to let him get away with it. He needed no briefing from Hunt, having thoroughly digested his reports to AD Wyler, and he knew Hunt to have an almost Japanese obsession with preserving face in personal affairs. He expected that Hunt would not ride out the suspension, let alone the OPR review. Cundieffe knew Hunt's preliminary OPR review file by heart, was instrumental in collecting much of the background data himself, as per AD Wyler's request. It was a painful, shameful duty, but one he carried out with the understanding that Hunt had brought this on himself, and the timing, though fortuitous for himself, could only serve to save the Bureau from grave embarrassment, should they become a matter of public record.

As he strode into the FBI's temporary HQ in a bungalow on the same remote edge of the China Lake Weapons Station where the purloined napalm had been kept, he felt a glow of pride. The agents he'd brought worked at their new tasks with a feverish pace undiminished by the brutal heat—the Navy had pled to a shortage of air conditioners, though Cundieffe had observed condensation on the windows of many vacant office bungalows closer to the heart of the base. Another item to add to the agenda—secure his team's comfort, and their trust would follow. He greeted each of the agents by name, receiving half-smiles and absent nods as he passed. His shirt and his jacket were plastered to his slight torso, and his shorts were riding up fearsomely. He looked forward to an opportunity to change, and was about to inquire about their quarters, when he stopped in mid-stride and looked around.

His nose wrinkled and the saliva on his palate curdled as a sickening vapor reached his nose. "Do I smell…alcohol?"

Heads swiveled and shook for several uncomfortable moments, and some offered weak, mumbled excuses, but a bright young female agent named Eugenie Hanchett pointed to the cubicle in the far corner of the sweltering bungalow. "He said he was waiting for you," she whispered.

Cundieffe set down his attaché case and assigned Hanchett to watch over it, then made a beeline for the cubicle. The odor of hard alcohol was a roiling cloud spilling out the narrow doorway, which was blocked by a back-tilted office chair. Lane Hunt sat in it with his back to Cundieffe. A bottle of tequila sat on the desk beside a phone and a blotter with a bramble of notes and doodles scribbled on it. "Step into my office," Hunt said.

"Lane, I want to express my outrage at this complete breakdown of professionalism, and request that you leave forthwith to minimize the already considerable damage you've done to the morale of this investigation."

"Why now?" Hunt asked. "Why you?"

"Lane, this is not the time or the place—"

"Why now, Martin? I told the field office SAC about it two years ago, and it was no big deal. If somebody wanted to make something of it, they could have done it then, or any time since."

Cundieffe bit back a retort that would, in Hunt's condition, probably have provoked a physical confrontation. Three years ago, swinging bachelor Special Agent Lane Hunt met a young lady, Rachel Lieberman, aged twenty-four, at a Pasadena night club, took her home and, beating all the requisite odds and countermeasures, impregnated her. When Ms. Lieberman sought Hunt out with the news, he pressured her to have an abortion, and—Cundieffe's ears burned up just thinking about it—invoked his status as a federal agent to coerce her. He had friends in the IRS who could make her life interesting, not to mention what he and the Bureau could do to her and her friends and family. It'd been a bluff, conceived in a paranoid, and probably drunken, rage, but it worked. Ms. Lieberman never contacted him again, and moved to Oregon shortly thereafter. Hunt was apparently in the clear, having spilled the story to a sympathetic SAC over drinks at an official function. It'd been a dead issue, until AD Wyler had asked SA Cundieffe if there was anything the OPR should know about SA Lane Willard Hunt.

He let Hunt rant on, in the hope that he'd simmer down and recover a shred of dignity, and leave. He peeled his shirt away from his chest with a sucking sound, but made no reply until the drunk got personal. "And why you, of all the fucking guys in the division, real counterterrorist guys who break down doors and aren't afraid of guns, why you?"

"I didn't ask for this case, Lane, and I didn't hope for anything to damage your career. But you have no one to blame for your troubles but yourself. An FBI agent must hold himself to a higher standard, because one never knows when one will be tested. I was chosen to relieve you because I'm most familiar with your methods, and have done the lion's share of the research on the case. I know how to close it." He came around Hunt's chair and seized the tequila bottle, batted Hunt's hands away as he dropped it in a wastebasket. "And I resent your insinuation that I fear guns. The Director himself presided over this Bureau for forty-eight years, indeed built it out of an illegitimate and corrupt office into the finest investigative agency the world has ever known, and he never once had to resort to firing a gun in anger."

Hunt leaned in close and sneered. If his intent was to knock Cundieffe unconscious with his breath, he half succeeded. "J. Edgar Hoover was a slimy, psychopathic cocksucker who would have been just as happy working for Hitler..." His train of thought petered out, presumably because Cundieffe was supposed to have hit him by now. But Cundieffe stood fast, delicate fists clenching nails into sweaty skin, stinging, pain clearing his burning, swirling head.

"I'll assume that you are drunk and irrational with remorse at the discovery of your past indiscretions, but I won't hear you badmouth the Director. Leave now, Lane, or I will be forced to have you carried out."

"At least Hoover was a man," Hunt said in a louder tone, "and not some sad fucking court eunuch like you, Martin. J. Edgar got his rocks off with Clyde in the DoJ inner sanctum, but at least he had rocks. You're not even a man, Cundieffe."

Cundieffe's hands came up and Hunt flinched in a drunken attempt to evade the junior agent's fists, but they never came close, cupping over his purpling ears. He looked like a puny kindergartner on the schoolyard, seconds away from bursting into raw, hot tears. Hunt had a moment to relish the moment he punctured Cundieffe's composure, but it was over before his bleary eyes could fully imprint the sight in his memory, for Cundieffe's mask resurfaced and his hands came down in a defensive pose as he leaned into Hunt's face. "I never asked to replace you, Lane," Cundieffe whispered, "but make no mistake: I'm *the man* who burned you, and I'm *the man* who's going to see that you never hold a position of responsibility ever again. You're finished, Lane. Go home and do the honorable thing before I'm forced to burn you again."

Hunt staggered backwards into a desk with such force that many in the office believed the junior agent had indeed struck him. "Backstabbing faggot, I'll fucking kill you!" Hunt's invective stream devolved into growls as he charged Cundieffe, who easily sidestepped him and summoned four of the more physically adept agents to carry him out.

Once all the commotion had died down, Cundieffe ordered the agents back to work, and moved Hunt's files to a less pungent cubicle in which to sit and update them.

~ 27 ~

It was after the gas and before the helicopters.

Storch was crawling away from the holes, inching forward just ahead of the creeping gas tide, retching and vomiting fluid out of every orifice in his body. The faceplate of his MOPP suit became a Jackson Pollock splatterscape. His arms heeded only every fourth or fifth command to move to hold him up. He was falling down, and he was going to sink under the tide of gas when a hand seized him and lifted him up out of the wave of green death. His hood was snatched off and he found himself dangling in front of the face of the biggest, meanest-looking motherfucker he'd ever seen in his entire life.

"Well, hello, little camper," said the commando in a voice so impossibly deep that it seemed to come from within Storch's own bowels. He heard the others gasping for breath, heard bubbling sounds of lungs trying to work through foam, heard death-rattles and prayers and pleas. But he wasn't dying. Cold, pure night air flooded his lungs, the breath kept coming until he thought he might burst. He felt something else. Deep, deep inside himself, he felt something *other,* from outside, reaching into him and actively transporting the poisons out of his bloodstream. Gradually, his nerveless limbs returned to him, his fingers and toes tingling with pins and needles, as if he'd slept on them for weeks. He jerked and wriggled with the pain of it, but the soldier's hooklike hands held him fast. And Storch knew that it was the soldier's hands inside him, growing through his suit and his fatigues and his skin and his muscles, into his veins and arteries, into his blood.

"What is…this shit?" Storch managed.

"Just a favor for a brother Beret," the commando answered. "You'd do the same for us, if you could."

Storch looked around now, saw the other two phantom soldiers holding two men each by the throats, but he knew they weren't choking them. They were sucking the poison out of them.

The men who saved them were giants, plain and simple, and not like the fragile, acromegalic freaks in the Guinness Book, either. The one who held Storch stood seven feet and change, every inch of it rawboned angles and knobby muscle, with a weatherbeaten, scar-torn hide stretched so taut over it that it creaked like the rigging of a ship when he moved. He smiled broadly, his jaw was a beartrap, each of his teeth the size of a big toe, and set down his load, a Barrett sniping rifle and a cylindrical steel case that looked like something you'd carry bubonic plague in, if you had to. Storch studied the forearm that held him. In the dim starlight, he could barely make out the tattoo on that corded, knurly limb: *Don't Mess With Texas.*

The man next to him could be charitably described as morbidly obese, but he looked like he ate morbidly obese people for breakfast. No military in the world would have such a man; indeed, Storch had never seen such a fat man standing up. Yet this man was standing, and not even breathing hard while holding Preston and Wachowiak over his head. His belly lolled halfway to his knees like a gigantic tongue, greasy and gray in the stark moonlight. He carried a weird-looking flamethrower with corrugated metal hoses running back to a humming sprayer on his back. His face, too, split in a monstrous grin that made Tue's look like a fawning puppy's.

The third man was as slim as the last was fat, but whipcord muscles rippled in his arms like elevator cables as he held Chappelle and Gagliardo. Slung over his shoulders were some kind of pressurized oildrum and a battered old M-16 with a mounted grenade launcher. Every muscle in his body gave off an almost audible hum of galvanic tension. Veins like gardenhoses pulsated and writhed in his temples and throat as he surveyed his two…rescuees? Captives? Victims? He did not smile.

All three wore ancient flak jackets that were black with old stains and scrawled obscenities, ragged fatigue pants and steel-toed boots. Storch was reminded of the gear his father had brought home from Vietnam and kept in his closet, forever damp and pungent with jungle-rot—even ten years later, wherever they lay for more than a week, black mold began to grow. The men they held in their grips—Storch's men, now—twisted on the commandos' arms like hanged suicides who could not die, their eyes half-lidded and streaming foamy tears, their mouths gobbling and bubbling discolored drool. How conscious they were remained a mystery.

"You don't know how glad we are to see you boys still here," the soldier said, sounding so warm and boisterous Storch could close his eyes and imagine he was at a GI bar back home. "Sorry 'bout the natives. Got some snacks from a little Shiite village a few klicks back. They were none too anxious to part with 'em, I'll tell you that."

"Who—what the fuck are you?" Storch gasped.

"Pardon me all to hell, Sergeant. Lieutenant Dyson, Spike Team Texas. This unstoppable sex machine here is Sergeant Holroyd," nodding towards the stupendously fat man, "but we just call him 'Royd. And this here is Sergeant Avery, but you can't call him anything."

"Nobody else was supposed to be here. What's your mission?"

"Why, that's funny, we knew y'all'd be here, didn't we, 'Royd?"

"First to go, last to know," 'Royd gurgled.

"Fuckin' reg'lar Army bullshit," Avery grated, the words striking bloody sparks.

"Are we in the same Army, Dyson? I don't know who the fuck you are or how you got here—" With a start, Storch realized suddenly that he could breathe easily again. Now it was his mind that was choking up.

"That should tell you all you need to know, right there. Let's mount up, boys. Our ride's comin' fast." The three dropped the survivors like infants and picked up their gear, tromped back to the rocky peak. Storch dimly heard rotor blades chopping the air, ripping away the last threads of green death that swirled around them. A chopper—Storch tried to get to his feet, tried to find his voice again to order the men—his men—to get ready to exfil out of this place, but a gentle, firm hand pressed against his chest, forced him back to the ground.

"This isn't your ride, little Sergeant," Dyson said. "You just forget about everything you saw tonight, you'll be one happy prick. Have patience. This, too, will pass." And Storch settled back down on the ground as the wind whipped sand and stinging gravel over him and carried the three commandos away. And the silence closed over them, broken only by the sounds of his fellow soldiers' steady breathing, like the distant sound of a sleepy ocean. Storch sank into that sound, into the tidal rush of his own breathing, let it wash him away, let himself forget.

And finally, the chopper came for them, the chopper that had been grounded in Bedrock for one hundred and ten minutes because of sand in its rotors.

~ 28 ~

Stella was sound asleep and wrapped in nourishing, shapeless dreams that she would not remember when she awakened, but which were the glue without which her mind would have choked on its own bile months ago. Cold, dry hands reached into her dreams and dragged her out into fluorescent lights and the round, cheerless Mrs. Claus mask of Mrachek. "I need your help. There's a wounded man." Mrachek scurried out of her cell, into the thick of the commotion across the corridor, leaving Stella to pull herself together.

It was yet another strange awakening in a string of them that was fast making her incapable of imagining waking up to a normal day. She had no desire to make Mrachek's life any easier, but curiosity got the better of her. She'd never heard so many people in one place in the complex before, let alone heard them shouting as they were now. She slipped on one of the one-piece surgical scrub suits she'd been issued, slipped a net over her hair, and went to sickbay.

Stella stopped at the door, unable to get any further into the room and unwilling to make her self noticed just yet. If she'd been hoping for trouble, she wasn't disappointed. No less than eight soldiers crowded the main room, squared off against five nerdish types who radiated civilian harmlessness and braininess though they wore the same unmarked military fatigues. Between them, strapped onto a gurney and under deep sedation, lay the apparent bone of contention. It was the soldier they'd caught at the truck stop, the one they'd made such a fuss about grabbing, the one who'd escaped. And he was much the worse for wear since she'd seen him last. One arm lay across his chest in a makeshift sling, and one of his legs looked as if it'd been dragged here from Las Vegas. His stubbled skull was dinged up, but not critically, and the brutally economical bone structure of his face was marred by bruises across one cheek and around one eye. Stella recognized road rash, having seen more than her share of superbike crash injuries, and wondered that the soldier wasn't much more badly beaten up. He must've had something soft to land on. She wondered for a moment if he hadn't suffered these injuries at the hands of his captors. No one had tried to harm her, but he'd gotten away from them once, and they seemed pretty inflamed about what to do with him. Stella knew she'd probably begin to hate him the moment he woke up and opened his mouth, but for the moment, she began to like him very much.

One of the soldiers, the older black man the others called the Major, shouted in the face of the senior egghead. "It's my operation, my men to risk. I have too damned few of them as it is."

The scientist looked to be in his early sixties, with skin so pale and unlined it looked as if he'd never used his face for anything but reading. His oiled black hair was clipped short like the others', but still managed to look untidy, as if he'd done it himself. A profound detachment informed all his gestures; his gaze focused on the wounded soldier as the officer raged at him, his head shaking in minute arcs that totally negated the officer's argument.

"It's no good, Bangs, for a number of reasons I thought we were clear on already. Even discounting the unresolved issue of his loyalties, he's unstable. He's unmotivated. He's probably incapable of grasping the significance of the Mission even if there was sufficient time, and, in case you haven't noticed, he's critically injured. If you'd simply followed your instructions—"

Major Bangs leaned across the body and into the scientist's face, as if he fully intended to bite off the smaller man's nose. "To execute him? Fuck you! He's right here, he's strapped down, and your stand on the value of human life is legendary around here, so why don't you do it?" The officer unholstered a huge automatic pistol and handed it grip-first to the scientist. His men went crazy at the exposed weapon, grabbing at his arms and shouting at him to stand down. When he made no move to take the gun, Bangs waved at Mrachek. "Maybe that's too messy for you. Delores, get a hypo full of air for Dr. Wittrock to execute Sergeant Storch, here."

Wittrock shook his head and managed a wooden grimace. His voice became increasingly strident as he spoke over the angry soldiers, but it never betrayed a mote of anger. "Major Bangs, your instability is tolerated because of your leadership skills and your dedication to the Mission, but I must caution you that no one is so valuable as to jeopardize it. That holds true for all of us. I urge you to dispose of this...questionable man forthwith, and prepare for the terminal phase."

"I believe Harley Pettigrew," Bangs said, jamming his gun back in its holster. "He gave everything for the Mission, and he said this man was gold."

"I believe he also said that this man was unfit for duty," Wittrock retorted, "which is why he was never brought in, in the first place. What you're asking is beyond the pale of acceptable risk, and, frankly, leaves me with serious doubts as to your sanity."

Bangs made a visible effort to regain control of himself as he explained, "There. Are. Not. Enough. Men. We were spread too thin in the original plan. We can not execute our part of the operation and secure an area for you to work. You, and I, and all of my men, will die. For nothing."

"And one broken-down, sociopathic Gulf veteran will tip the balance."

"We'd need at least ten, but I only have the one." He did something then that took Stella's breath away, and would've melted any dissent away in a normal opponent. "Please," he said, "let me use him." He seemed to break open, his schooled battlefield exterior giving way to a deeply wounded, frightened man with too many dead soldiers on his conscience. Stella thought she understood Major Bangs, then.

"Forty-eight hours, Major," Wittrock said. "Don't get too attached to him." The other scientists followed him out.

Stella cracked her knuckles, said, "Okay, now how about the rest of you get the hell out of here? This man is beat up." They left anyway, but it felt good to pretend she was in control of something.

~ 29 ~

Storch hunkered down behind a rusted-out row of file cabinets, willing his eyes and ears to open as wide as they could, and tried to stay calm. Sludge and stagnant water pooled around his ankles, the stink rising up and making his vision double. The rusty copper light from the shielded bulb in the center of the room's buckling concrete ceiling only gave jagged edges to the darkness. His left arm throbbed in its fiberglass cast where the stout, stubby barrel of his assault weapon rested on it, a pain so bright he felt sure they'd see it in the dark.

They were coming for him.

He could hear them in the corridor outside, perhaps three doors down. The smash of a door being kicked in, the whumph and sizzle of a flash grenade, stuttering assault-rifle fire, faint splashing, a single shout. The black rectangle of his doorway flared dimly for a moment in the grenade's glow, and he could see into the corridor, the algae-flecked brown river churned to a froth of bubbles as men ran up and down just out of sight. They'd run one of the others to ground, and regrouped to take him out. If he was going to move, it would have to be now.

Slowly, planting each foot toe-first into the slime to avoid the slightest sound, he edged around the file cabinets and crossed the room to press himself flat just inside the doorway. Another flash grenade went off, this time in the hall, and the bitter tang of teargas billowed out. Sneaking a quick peek round the corner, a staggering form surrounded by three hunters, all of whom trained their rifles on the blinded fugitive and shot him.

Storch leapt across the corridor in two bounds, fire on his tail chasing him through the opposite doorway. He whirled and stuck his gun out into the hall, blind-firing half the clip. "Shit! Shit! I'm hit! I'm hit! Goddamit, get that motherfucker!" Splashing growing louder, it was all he could do to focus on the new room. Little better than the other, but the file cabinets here were stacked against the wall. He backed up beside them and leaned against the outermost cabinet with his broken arm. It squealed in protest, but wrenched free of the scum on the floor and toppled over, crumbled into clods of reddish dust. A flurry of movement outside, Storch's gun bucked in his hand and they fell back. He shoved another file cabinet, which went over easier than the first, slumping against the skeleton of its neighbor. Behind them, what he'd hoped to find, a door, opening on the next room. It'd been painted over, so he had to brace himself against the cabinets and deliver a forceful kick to the door to get it open. The door split neatly in half, but neither half fell out of the frame. Outside, someone passed before the door, firing wild over his head. He responded in kind, but the force of the fire overbalanced him and he toppled into the sludge.

A flash grenade erupted into the room, turning the darkness inside out before he could cover his eyes. He aimed at where he remembered the corridor doorway having been and emptied his clip at it even as he burrowed behind the toppled cabinets and huddled against the broken, jammed door. Silence, punctuated by dripping water and mud sucking at shuffling boots. Out in the corridor, he could hear the rasp of their gasmasks.

Swapping out the unfamiliar clip one-handed would've been difficult, but with his eyes out of commission, it was next to impossible. He'd taped them together head to tail, so, in theory, it was a simple matter of yanking it out, turning it round, and popping it back in. He visualized the mechanism of the small weapon, but he'd had too little time with the gun before he'd had to use it. He jammed the clip again into the slot, but the gun slipped out of its cradle on his broken arm and splashed into the water.

He heard shots in the corridor and in the next room. There was only one other man left out there, so this was his last chance before they'd concentrate entirely on him. He took out his handkerchief and dipped it in the foul water on the floor, took a quick whiff, found it stank of organic, not chemical rot and, sucking in a last great breath, wrapped it tightly around his mouth and nose. He lunged for the jammed door, digging his heels in against the pile of file cabinets and pivoting so his left shoulder struck the heavy wooden door squarely in the center of the crack he'd made with his foot. The door flew apart under his weight, and he stumbled through it into a poison, glowing fog.

His eyes, already feeding him only a purple void after the flash grenade, instantly seemed to melt. He barreled across the small room and came up hard against the far wall, then went limp, ducking as low as he could without laying in the slime. Even with his eyes clamped shut, they burned. Shots popped off in the small room, echoes and rounds rebounding around the cell above Storch's head, but incredibly, none hit him. He must still be invisible because of the gas, or the hunters had blinded themselves with their flash grenades. Instinct screamed at him to cover his head and lie low until the shooting stopped, but he stretched out, feeling for the body he knew he'd find here, the last other fugitive. He was there, only inches from his feet, prone on its back with a rifle still slung loosely across its chest. Storch splashed some of the water into his eyes and blinked it away. Now the room was like a starfield, past and present muzzle flashes dotting the purple emptiness, and before him, the guttering red sun of a dying flare. Everything else was murk and rumors of form, though because of the gas or his temporary blindness, he couldn't tell.

Storch went on his right leg and hauled the limp fugitive up onto his knee. Scooping him up under the armpits, he grunted as he lifted the body up before him and charged the corridor.

"Bravo One-two, one-four, he's coming out." A hunter backed down the corridor, peppering his human shield as Storch bore down on him at a dead run. Storch slid into the hunter and dumped the body on him at as high an angle as he could manage, and the two went down in a tangle of limbs. Storch fell on them both and wrenched the hunter's gun from his hand, shot him in the head. Before he could press the advantage, he saw the other two hunters coming up the corridor firing. Storch pivoted to his left and ducked for the door back into his hiding place when three shots stitched up his right side. The air whoofed out of his lungs and his legs went limp under him, and he slumped against the doorframe, his eyes only vaguely perceiving the silhouettes of the masked hunters as they closed around him.

"Nailed 'im!" one of them shouted. "Time?"

"Eighty-five seconds, a new personal best," the other answered. "And only two casualties," he added, looking down at the bodies before them.

"Fucker cheated," complained the third hunter from under the fugitive's body. "If Lonnie was really cold meat, he wouldn't have been jerking around like that, and he wouldn't have got my gun."

"I wouldn't have been jerking, you wouldn't keep shooting, fuckwit," Lonnie answered. "You got done with your own gun, Draper."

The hunters disentangled the pair and propped them up against the wall, then checked on Storch.

He felt as if his whole body, everything below his arms, had simply gone to sleep, as if he'd passed out with a small passenger sedan resting on his chest. He slapped at his legs, but it was like slapping a side of beef. He ripped the shit-stinking handkerchief off his face and dropped it into the slime, then held out his arms to get lifted up.

"Goes away in a few minutes," the first hunter, a mulatto ex-SEAL named Seawood, told him. "We tried using paint, but all these fuckers cheat." They lifted him to his feet and propped him in the doorway, and Storch found he could stand if he locked his knees, which was the extent of his control over his lower body.

The second hunter offered him a flask of something that burned going down, but warmed him from the inside out. If there was alcohol in it, his body clearly wasn't going to fight it. Diebenkorn, the second hunter, took off his gasmask and unplugged the nightvision scope built into the eyepieces. He favored Storch with a half-smile, said, "I think you're ready to hunt us, next time, Sarge."

About a day after he woke up, they let him out to walk around, just up and down the corridor, still manacled, followed by two armed guards. In his time in the hole, Storch had gotten to know a little about each of them. They were brothers in the shadow services. Rich Diebenkorn was a Ranger. Major Bangs and he had worked together, and arranged for him to become Missing, Presumed Dead during Operation Just Cause in Panama. Otis Seawood was a SEAL for nine years, and retired from service in 1984, after the botched insertion of SEALS off the coast of Grenada drowned two of his closest friends. He signed on for private security work with a front company run by the Mission, and was gradually brought inside. Both were hardcore loyalists to Bangs and to the Mission, which seemed to be what they called themselves as well as what they were doing. They respected him enough to talk to him, but they spoke over his head, in frustrating vagaries that assumed he knew, or would know, soon enough. Or that he wasn't worth explaining to. Then, as if they'd been waiting for clearance, they took him down to the Kill-House.

The bottom level of the complex was sealed off from the rest, because the added weight of the refurbishments the Mission had installed further aggravated the cheaply built concrete structure and caused a sewage line to break through and slowly flood it. The soldiers had made it into an improvised kill-house, a training area for house-to-house combat. They trained hard, two sessions each day in rotating three-man teams, hunting two of their own, and Storch. After six hours of stalking him through darksome puddles of fetid sewage, they seemed ready to accept him.

"You ready to go again?" Diebenkorn asked him, after Draper and Lonnie had been rehabilitated.

"Not yet," Storch lied. "I still can't feel my legs. How long have you guys been here?" They'd refused to tell him where *here* was time and again.

"'Bout a year," Seawood said, his eyes flicking over the others' faces. Storch already had him pegged as the unit's resident mouth, and was relieved to see none of the others cared if he talked.

"Seems like a big place," he said. "Black budget money?"

"Shit no," said Seawood, hissing through his teeth in something like laughter. "This shit is all obtainium." An obscure military euphemism for stolen gear.

"Seems like you could make enough napalm down here in a year, you wouldn't have to steal it from the Navy," Storch fished. They'd filled him in on China Lake by way of idle gossip, but let him see none of the larger picture.

Storch could feel them looking at each other behind his back. "We had another plan," Diebenkorn answered, "but it fell through. We had to improvise." Storch's mind snapped him a shot; of Arabic canisters beneath the floor of his store.

"But don't you think it'll be hard to launch a tactical mission with the FBI and the Navy looking for you? They'll find you in a matter of days. You can't hide a place like this. I could've found it by myself."

"Nobody knows," Seawood said. "Those that know, don't ever want to tell."

Diebenkorn filled in. "On paper it's a junkyard. They set up a dummy company and sent a lobbyist over to the State Assembly to pay off the representative and the EPA. They think it's a toxic waste dump, and we've got them on tape taking money not to blow the whistle."

"Somebody's bound to blow it, anyway; you'll be found out."

"In a week, maybe. But four days is all we need. Then this place won't be here, anymore."

He knew better than to ask them about the Mission. They trusted him enough not to shoot real bullets at him just now, but they weren't training for pride or practice. They were training for their lives, against something that was coming in four days.

An intercom buzzed. Seawood answered it, watching Storch. He hung up and went over to the heavy blast door leading upstairs into the complex. "You're going to see the eggheads," Seawood said.

They led him to the elevator, and blindfolded him. He was turned around and around and mixed up by men who knew how well he'd been trained to maintain his sense of direction. He couldn't tell if the elevator they were in left from the kill house, or if they'd traveled up a ramp while they were disorienting him. He took it in good humor. They'd had plenty of chances to kill him that were at least as clean as this. They wanted him for something.

He could feel this entire place, with its small crew of zealots—no more than a dozen soldiers, eight or nine scientists, five or six technicians and two pilots—tensing like a muscle, straining not to burst under so many strains before they could deliver their climactic blow. The Mission, the capital tall and reverent in their voices when they whispered of it. He had a part in it, now. Once they'd discovered that he wasn't a spy, that he was just a dumb grunt, he'd begun to become one of them. He still had little to no idea what that meant, but he felt nigh invulnerable just belonging to an army, again.

They stopped him at a door; he waited while they worked whatever complicated ritual was required to open it. He listened to the air; it was louder here, moving more forcefully, so he knew he stood in a corridor, and the air was extremely damp, so he was still deep within the complex. A series of bolts slammed open and hot, bone-dry air gushed in his face. The desert? No, the air felt cooked, charged with positive ions. Storch felt the stubble on the back of his neck stiffen, and fight-or-flight scenarios flashed through the violet darkness behind the blindfold. The air sizzled with artificial anxiety, and knowing it did nothing to reduce its work on his nerves, which still hadn't settled down from the kill-house. He planted his feet, and again they had to shove him over the threshold. Someone whispered in his ear, "Remember. Wittrock's an egghead, and you're a stupid grunt. And maybe they won't kill you."

Someone else, Storch thought he recognized the voice of Medina, added, "Like they ever killed anybody themselves."

Storch made himself walk into the new room, felt the door close behind him. Neither of the soldiers followed him in. The air continued to blast over him, Storch recognizing the breath of machines, but no oil, no tang of metallic friction. Computers. They wouldn't be able to just vent the heat from a big computer set-up without drawing the state police or the DEA, at least not at night. Against the hushed roar of the air, Storch could make out subtle clattering noises that hinted at people typing at keyboards, but he couldn't guess how many. He knew it was the ions, but he felt testy, felt the Headache coming back hard, and he barely kept in check the urge to just yell until somebody did something. But more pressing business kept him waiting in silence for long minutes that stretched into an hour before he felt he'd earned the right to make a sound.

He opened his mouth to speak, when a nimble hand undid his blindfold and snatched it away. He blinked a few times, but he was struck speechless by what he saw.

The room was not much larger than a bank vault. The thick concrete walls were reinforced with steel I-beams and draped with foam insulation, forming niches in which stood stacked computer towers. Six workstations—four against the walls, and two in the center of the vault. Four people of indeterminate sex and race sat at the outer workstations, swaddled from head to foot in white cleansuits and particle masks.

The floor was carpeted in plastic tarps, but under it Storch could feel a dense weave of cables crisscrossing the room. This system was easily the rival of the unorthodox mainframe he'd seen at the School Of Night. He suspected the same people might've had a hand in the design of this system, as well. The generators for it must be enormous, and there must be a satellite uplink around here, as well, because tapping into the local power grid would cause brownouts, and a telephonic connection would be easily traceable to its source.

"How are you feeling, Sergeant Storch?" a reedy voice demanded from behind him. Storch stepped forward, pivoted and brought his head down, but the man was no immediate threat, at least not physically. He was old, but Storch couldn't guess how old, because he had no wrinkles, and unnaturally black hair. His face looked aged, but somehow unused. His hand lay upon a small plastic gun that looked like it shot darts or pepper spray, but he looked completely unfazed by Storch's potential for violence. He was a civilian, and a scientist on top of it. This was the one they'd warned him about—Wittrock.

"I'm as comfortable as can be expected. I was led to believe somebody here was going to tell me what the hell is going on."

"How many people have you killed, Sergeant?"

"What? That's—I have four confirmed kills on my Army record, but the truth is probably closer to twenty-five. Men." *Well, and one woman, but she had it coming, even in cold blood. Yep. I don't want to think about her.* "What has that got to do with anything?"

"How do you sleep at night?"

"Fu—What is this?"

"Answer the question."

"They don't keep me awake at night, *Doctor.* I know what people say about me, and I say fuck 'em. There's—something..." *something, oh yeah* "...something wrong with my immune system, but it doesn't get in my way, if anybody fucks with me."

"That's why you're here, is it? To get even? Sergeant, in the course of my career with the Department of Defense, I have been directly responsible for nearly twenty-five thousand deaths, nearly all of them civilians. I see every one of them every time I close my eyes. We came to be here because we share a common disgust with killing, but still, we have need of killers. Major Bangs seems to think he needs you, and Bangs must be indulged, to a point. We are not mercenaries, nor are we terrorists. But we have committed acts of high treason and acts of war against the government of the United States. We are feared and hated in Washington, as much for what we did for them as for our current task. We'd like to use you, but not simply to get even. It is imperative that you understand. Are you capable of understanding?"

Finally. "Jesus, God, yes. Try me."

Wittrock made a still sourer face, as if he'd been hoping for another answer. "You'll be an enemy of the state. Even if you survive the Mission, you'll be forced to flee the country. No retiring to the vegetative existence you lived before. Frankly, I find it hard to believe that anyone who comprehends the situation would cast his lot in with us. You could still leave."

Sure. Major Bangs had made it abundantly clear that there was no going home, as if there were a home to go back to. "Doctor, I have nowhere else to go."

"Is that the new recruit? Send him in, Witt." The voice was too faint, too feeble, to have a bodily source. Storch looked around for a speaker, but Wittrock turned and went to a niche and reached for one of the computer panels, took hold of it just so, and the wall opened and a low, short corridor lit by dim red bulbs yawned in the opening.

"He's not stable, Darwin. I—have misgivings." Wittrock stood before it with one hand still fluttering over his gun, studying Storch with a dubious expression.

Even cuffed, Storch could easily have bulled past him and broken his nose in the bargain, but he balked as the voice inside the tunnel crumbled into deathbed laughter. "I'm sure there's nothing he could do to me that I wouldn't welcome, Witt. Let him come. If he's so intent on dying with us, he should at least have the benefit of knowing just what sort of lunatic asylum he's signed up with."

Wittrock bit back a further protest, then stepped aside. "In there…he'll tell you what you need to know. Don't talk. Listen."

Storch watched Wittrock as he walked into the tunnel. He had to duck his head—this was never meant for human traffic, was probably some sort of conduit for pipes when it was supposed to be a toxic waste dump. As it was, the tunnel provided marvelous defense. He stumbled twice, both times rearing up and bashing his head against the ceiling. The second time, he struck the steel lintel of a doorway, and ducked through it, cursing. He stopped short in a small cell lit only by a computer screen spewing waterfalls of digits. The walls were draped in huge sheets of drafting paper, stained with umber streaks by leakage through the concrete walls— schematics of circuitry boards, or maybe blueprints of a housing development.

A man sat in a chair beside the computer, his face etched rather than illuminated by the glow of the screen. No, not a chair, a wheelchair. And no, not quite a man. Not anymore.

He was completely hairless, and wore a loose robe that looked distressingly like a funeral shroud. He looked to be about four sizes too small for his skin. It shifted and slipped around him, masking tremors that bespoke grievous neural damage. His face, neck and hands were mottled with splashes of dead white, the colorless color of moonstone. He coughed chronically, an explosive sound like bags of wet sand bursting on concrete from a very great height. In a voice like callused, flaking hands rubbing together, he spoke.

"My name is Armitage, and all of this is as much my fault as anyone's. We—Calvin and I, some others here—used to design weapon systems for the Defense Advanced Research Projects Agency. Never heard of it?"

"No, sir. I was in Fifth Special Forces, Rangers before that."

"I'm well aware of your service record, Sergeant, and I'm not surprised you never heard of us. We worked out of bases with no names, on projects the public wouldn't know about for decades. We were the heirs of the Manhattan Project, but we were insulated from the ethical pitfalls of our work by the lessons of Los Alamos. We were not after cumbersome doomsday weapons, but precise solutions to the problem of force. Besides, most of what we thought up, we knew they'd never build. Too expensive, too risky, too frivolous, too awful. Anything we drew up that looked feasible was peddled to a private contractor. So we played with toys, and never thought we'd have to turn them on a living being. That's how you make doomsday weapons, Sergeant. You let scientists play with toys.

"In 1983, when Reagan introduced the Strategic Defense Initiative, he got together over fifteen billion dollars for research to build a utopian system that would render nuclear weapons obsolete. Within a year, it was a big joke; they weren't even hoping to have the technology until the mid-1990s, and the President's own science advisor admitted to the press that the whole SDI package was a hypothetical bargaining chip, that just the threat of the U.S. someday developing such a system might deter the Soviets from building more missiles. The truth was, they didn't blow fifteen billion on pipe-dream missile defense projects, any more than they spent seven grand on a coffee maker. There were countless smaller projects in the offing that were very real possibilities, weapons that would bring the Russians to the bargaining table in a cold sweat.

"The worst of them was dropped in our laps in the summer of '83, right after Reagan broke open the piggy bank. The most conservative cost estimates for building a space-based laser even today, run over two billion. *He* brought us plans for an affordable orbital weapon platform, but not for missile defense, oh no, not for defense at all. All the preliminary research was already done, all the R&D was neatly wrapped up. All we had to do was build the thing, and the weapon itself was cheaper than a single M1A1 Abrams tank. He called it RADIANT."

"Who?" Storch didn't want to interrupt the old man, but he was straying into territory he must assume Storch understood.

With a start, he realized Wittrock had slipped up behind him. "He doesn't need to know all of it," he said, but Armitage dismissed him with a wave of one palsied claw.

"It was Keogh," he went on. "He called himself Keitel, then, and he wore a different face, but it was the same...man, for want of a better word. We didn't know who he was, and the government told us not to ask. He handed us all his research from the seventies. At first, we thought he'd only tested it on animals. By the time he'd wormed his way in and we knew the truth, nobody in charge cared. They did a background check, but there was nothing, at least nothing they cared about. If he would have gone to the Pentagon, or the Department of Defense, or Lockheed, or even the CIA, he would've been arrested, discredited, all his research buried deeper than Tesla's. Keitel walked into the right office at the exact right time—it was a meeting of DARPA, a very goal-oriented division that cut across all of those groups. He showed us plans for something that, if all it did was what he promised, it still would've been damned unthinkable, and the DoD was flush with cash and power and paranoia, so they told us to build it. I'd heard that our government took in Japanese and German concentration camp doctors in return for their research on human subjects, but I never believed it. Keitel changed all that for me."

"What the fuck was it?"

"The absolute apex of anti-personnel weapons technology, and so elegantly simple it could've been built in the Renaissance. Basically, it was nothing more than an array of lenses in a satellite. It collected the sun's energy and fed it through the lenses, so it could pour it with pinpoint accuracy on any spot on the globe."

"It was a laser?"

"A laser is just an ultra-high frequency wave of light, generated with solid fuel and a large mirror. Lasers are to the emission from this thing what the sound of white noise is to Stravinsky's Firebird. It didn't just intensify the light. It perverted it, mutated it. The waves did some damnably odd things—Keitel said he was tuning the harmonics, called it a scalar wave. It didn't burn, it didn't even get hot, but it scrambled animal cells, disrupted DNA at a molecular level. The waves were embedded with packets of information, he said. It sounded like New Age, cold-fusion-style rhetoric, but Keitel's results showed subjects dying of multisystemic cancer within one week of exposure. He'd tuned it up a lot since his first field tests. His working model turned chimps inside out, but he kept insisting it'd have to be fired from outside the atmosphere to achieve the full effect.

"It wasn't hard to convince the brass; they were excited about the very idea of a magic wand that could give the Politburo cancer in their beds. We built the whole thing in less than two months, the lens array was the hardest part, and Keitel kept that whole part to himself. They sent it up on the Enterprise shuttle launch in February of '84; one of the many secret military payloads that nobody ever wonders about. They brought it online without a hitch. The first test from orbit was also the first government-sanctioned test on human subjects.

"Not that they were undeserving, we were told. Along with the cows and the pigs and the chickens and the chimps, they staked out twelve military prisoners, including some men from Vietnam who'd been caged up in the States. Men who defected, and radioed our boys into ambushes in the jungle. They were still listed as MIA, and the Pentagon just never had the stones to execute them. They were Special Forces boys like yourself. They managed never to find their way back from Vietnam, and were only picked up in 1978. The things they supposedly did over there made the Khmer Rouge look like the Salvation Army. They actually told us that we were to look at it as a military execution, nothing more."

Storch's teeth clicked together on the end of his tongue. Spike Team Texas. What was wrong with him, he'd gotten from them. And what they were, they'd become because of RADIANT.

"In March of 1984, they set up the prisoners and the barnyard exhibit on one of the few atolls in the South Pacific that the Army didn't nuke in the forties, and they fired it up. Even in broad daylight, it was some show. White light poured down from the sky like the hand of God, but I never saw anything look so wrong as it did. And it worked. All twelve subjects bloomed into glorious terminal cancer inside of a day. They congratulated us, that day. Told us we would go down in history as the men who stuffed the nuclear genie back in the bottle.

"Then things went wrong. They lost contact with the satellite. And three of the subjects' cancers just kept on growing—but they never died.

"What happened next is one of those classic examples of government oversight. Any one person would probably have seen through the whole thing right then, but no one person was looking. I didn't see it myself, even though I was sick to death of myself for going along with it."

"What happened?"

"The satellite reported a critical failure in its heat exchangers and burned up. That Keitel had written the on-board computer's software and designed the lens array himself only convinced them of his incompetence. So they chalked it up to experience, fired Keitel, reassigned us, buried the budget expenses in toilet seats and coffee makers, and had Keitel's private plane shot down over the South Pacific that evening. That was when we walked."

"You quit the defense service."

"We couldn't walk away entirely, of course. If you run, you make it easier for them to get you. No, we all went into the private sector, and very visibly, very quietly, worked on very boring research for a year. Then, one by one, we died. On the side, we began to pool our resources; initially, for our own defense, but we saw that we couldn't just hide our heads. We'd helped to perpetrate a great evil, and we owed it to our children, and to the people in whose name we'd created the damned thing, to make sure it never happened again.

"We kept in touch with a few people who stayed inside, both military and scientists. They were budgeted to build a thirty megawatt chemical laser for space-based missile defense, but they were all really working on a new prototype of Keitel's satellite. They couldn't duplicate whatever he'd done to the lens, though, and it melted down or exploded every time they tested it. They finally built one that worked, or at least our friends said it would, and they tried to deploy it in January of 1986. They didn't take our threats seriously. They left us no choice."

"Go fuck yourself. You say you blew up the Challenger?" When neither of them answered, Storch figured they were waiting for him to get over it. Clearly, every man in the Mission was insane. So be it. "So that was the end of it, then."

"We thought so. We parted ways with the government, went underground to monitor them should they try to build another one, or anything like it, ever again. We left the United States. We sold noncritical weapons secrets to the Soviets up until they collapsed, and to the Israelis and France afterwards. We financed the development of the softkill arsenal we'd proposed to the DoD ten years before, and we made it work. For thirteen long years, we thought we'd won, with our flush of grim triumph and harmless war toys that would end senseless killing forever. Then, about six months ago, we intercepted a signal from earth to a location in space where no satellites were supposed to be. It was a stream of numbers, preceded by the password activating RADIANT's CPU."

"It was still up there all this time, and nobody saw it?"

"Who knows? A lot of detritus floating around up there. We'd coated the outer hull with the polymer they used on the F117 with, and if it wasn't transmitting, it wouldn't show up unless somebody bumped into it. Perhaps it really did burn up, and he launched a new one. God knows it's cheap enough to do, now. Whatever, RADIANT went active again, and Keitel, or Keogh, as he calls himself now, was reprogramming it."

"To do what?" Clearly, Storch was supposed to ask questions, but Armitage wouldn't be rushed to answer them. He felt as if he were listening to a man confess in his sleep, and wondered if Armitage even knew to whom he was speaking anymore.

"The transmission went almost continuously for two weeks, but trying to trace the signal got us nowhere. The uplink changed every couple of hours; they were hacking dishes all around the world, whenever it stopped transmitting for its owners, it would pick up Keogh's signal and pass it on. We tried to splice in a virus to get it to self-destruct or at least reveal its position, but we couldn't do that, either. The School Of Night worked on cracking intercepted bits of the stream, and narrowed it down to a four variable system of base pairs—a genetic sequence.

"We followed the signal upstream through dozens of bounces throughout the national phone system, and, just ten days ago, we traced it to the Radiant Dawn Hospice Village in Inyo County. But we were too late. The thing went off just eight days ago over the village."

"That's stupid as hell! Why would they zap themselves?"

Wittrock broke in. "Haven't you been listening? As Quesada, he rounded up a group of human guinea pigs and bred them while exposing them to radiation. As Keitel, he refined the process to offer it to the government, the only people rich enough and bloody-minded enough to build it for him. Then he arranged for it to lose itself, and let them think they'd killed him. He resurfaced as Keogh and set up a hospice for terminal cancer patients, because the radiation reacts with pre-existing cancerous cells. They don't kill the host; they become the host, rebuild it, replace it. He's taken the children from Radiant Dawn's first incarnation and continued to breed them under heavy radiation all these years, searching for some kind of beneficial mutation, and he found it six months ago. He fed the results of his eugenics experiments into the satellite and used it to irradiate the hospice. It's not a destructive weapon, anymore. It's far more dangerous than that. It's a way to change humans into cancer."

Storch's mind reeled. The last piece of the puzzle—the one they apparently didn't have, because they never spoke to Sperling—floated just out of his grasp. Quesada didn't just breed his followers, he bred with them, so any result of the experiment would be his own offspring, the DNA sequence would be, at least in part, his DNA. None of it added up, so the piece drifted away on a wave of incredulity.

"That's who you're fighting," Storch said, hoping he'd come to some ground of understanding. "These...new people."

"We always joked," Armitage said, "that if we did blow up the world, we'd only be clearing the way for something better to make a go of it. All this fuss between races over who were the chosen people, when it was clear the cockroaches were really God's favorites. But this...this isn't evolution. This isn't God's plan."

"So these—mutants?—have to go." *That's what the napalm is for, and the drilling, that's why everyone here looks sick to his stomach.* They were preparing to wage a campaign of genocide.

"The government won't help us—can't help us—for fear of exposure, even if they could accept it. We're all alone against them."

Storch thought about what Spike Team Texas had done to his life. He thought about what he'd hoped to achieve in the Army, and what he'd tried to forget in Death Valley. He thought about his father, who, being a career soldier and insane, would've instantly understood. "I want to go," he said.

Major Bangs was waiting at the door when Storch came out. Even the low light of the corridors outside the computer vault was blinding, but he stared into a bulb for a minute until he could see clearly again. He was so tired that if he ate, he'd fall asleep sitting up, but he wasn't hungry, and his mind wouldn't settle down. He wanted to go sit and think, to try to sort everything everyone had told him into something that jibed with what he'd seen. As he threaded his way back to his cell, he felt Bangs's eyes on him.

"You believe any of that shit?" Bangs asked out of the side of his mouth, lower than a whisper, as if someone were eavesdropping. In this place, someone probably was.

"What shit? About the Challenger?"

"No, about the satellite. About the government not knowing about it."

In the last week, Storch had quickly learned to believe whatever he was told, no matter how ridiculous it seemed. He had become a soldier again. But it was fast becoming clear that every officer in this little army was crazier than his dad. "I've seen a lot of people killed for something so important nobody seems to know what it is, Major. Tell me what you want me to believe."

"The government spent time and money on a weapons project with that kind of promise and let it slip out of their hands? For one man to use? They're not *quite* that stupid, and they're sure as hell aren't that quick to give up."

He noticed Bangs's eyes, the whites completely visible around his dark-dilated pupils, and it occurred to him that he had yet to see or hear about anyone here actually going to sleep. "What are you really saying, Major Bangs?"

"I was in charge of a JSOC detail that was sent to Guyana under the CIA in '78, Storch. Wargame maneuvers, they told the Pentagon, but we were supposed to surround the People's Temple compound and 'contain' it. They say it was mass suicide, and everybody beat their breasts and wailed that it could've been stopped. It couldn't, and it wasn't mass suicide. People's Temple was a CIA-sponsored concentration camp. They tested germs, drugs, mind-control, torture techniques, every sick fucking thing you can imagine, and we were the camp guards, us, the fucking Green Berets, Storch. And when it was all over, when it was time to clean house, most of the cultists still had enough of their minds left to try to flee. And we mowed them down. We were so clean that the handful of survivors never even knew we were there."

"So you think Radiant Dawn is another People's Temple."

"I think it goes beyond anything humans have ever tried before on this earth, but, as God is my witness, the CIA, the Pentagon and the President are behind it. They never lost touch with that fucking satellite, or if it did burn up, they launched another one, and they helped Keitel fake his death and come back as Keogh. Blowing up Challenger didn't mean a fucking thing. They helped him rebuild Radiant Dawn into a new kind of concentration camp so they could recreate the South Pacific experiment on a larger scale, with the kids he spawned in the cult back in the seventies. He's gathering them there because only people with cancer can survive the radiation, and change. It's gone beyond a Star Wars offensive weapon, but the powers that be are the ones sitting on the button. Armitage won't accept it, but you have to."

"Why should I believe you, and not them? Did you serve with my father?" *Or maybe share a padded cell with him?*

"You know what I'm talking about. I've read your file. When you came back from Iraq, did they admit they knew what was wrong with you, or even try to find out? Why should they, if they already knew? They inserted a strike team into that chemical weapons plant to steal what the Iraqis were working on, which was a chemical weapon that might neutralize the controlled mutations our side's trying to produce at Radiant Dawn. You know they hung your squad out to dry. You know they exposed you to something that makes you different than you were. Why else would you be so important to them now? You said yourself everybody else in your squad is either dead or still in the service, under their thumbs. Who else but the government could do what they've done to you?"

Storch didn't want to be seen in this much pain, knew they'd mistake it for weakness. All of them so hard up to get inside his head and squeeze his brains; their paranoia as poisonous as the palpable miasma of machine oil from the motor pool. "So what you're afraid of, is that we're going to have to fight the real Army?"

"I'm afraid we won't," the Major said without shame, his eyes so wide and glassy they seemed to be throwing off a light of their own. "Do you know what I'm saying? I'm afraid there is *no* right side of this conflict."

"I need to go lie down," Storch said. "Respectfully submitted, sir, I suggest you do the same." His cell was drawing nearer, and Bangs stopped, still staring at him.

~ 30 ~

Dr. Delores Mrachek hadn't gotten out of her chair at the computer in twenty-four hours. Stella sat on the examination table, her legs drawn up under her, and watched the stout little doctor plug away, and she knew that things, as strange as they'd become, were about to change again. Mrachek hadn't responded to any of her attempts to draw attention to herself, ignoring bribes, taunts and sincere begging for an explanation. She paused from her work only to inject herself with a stimulant from an unlabeled bottle she kept in a minifridge on the counter beside her terminal every couple of hours.

That they were about to relocate was clear, for Mrachek had assembled the irreplaceable components of the lab—mostly tissue samples in ice chests and cardboard boxes of printouts, and a few pieces of inscrutably complex equipment—in an hour, and then set to downloading the entire contents of her medical computer onto several bulky portable hard drives in bulletproof cases. Stella thought this must be what the black boxes of airliners look like.

Outside, the soldiers sprinted up and down the corridor carrying gear. In stark contrast to the monastic silence of the previous week, the shouting and cursing for no reason at all reminded her of Mexican immigrants in the moments before *la emigra* broke down the door. Stella felt an odd flutter of nervous excitement and dread deep down, in the deadly nether-heart beating in her liver. There would be flight, and if there was a chance to escape, it would be today. But she thought of the Stephen/Napier-thing in the ice chests, and what it'd taken to get it in there. They would be more likely to kill her and can her parts for their experiments than let her run loose.

Mrachek seemed to be lost in contemplation of a molecular diagram endlessly unraveling in three dimensions, then zipping back up. Every so often, she'd freeze the transformation and tweak a carbon chain or alter the ambient pH or temperature levels, then lose herself again in the new permutation. Stella climbed off the table and went to Mrachek and covered her eyes with both hands. Immediately, she regretted it. Mrachek's skin was cold and dry as marble. Her eyebrows were drawn on. And she was shivering so fast she felt like a precision motor racing at top rpm's with the clutch engaged. In her frustration, Stella had put her in gear.

Mrachek's arm snaked around Stella's arm and yanked her off-balance. Her other dry little hand poked Stella's windpipe with three ramrod stiff fingers, gave it a little jab to emphasize how quickly she'd come upon death.

"Don't—ever—touch—me," she hissed in Stella's face.

"Can somebody get me some aspirin?" a tired man's voice split the moment before things could get any uglier.

Mrachek froze, giving Stella room to disentangle herself. She turned to face the interloper, and she, too, froze. It was the killer they couldn't keep in a cage, the one they'd been fighting over. Her breath stung in her throat, and she couldn't bring herself to speak. Unconscious, bound and sedated, he'd intrigued her, because he frightened her captors. Awake and advancing on her, with a fiberglass brace on his left arm like a battering ram, he scared her half to death for just a moment before she could wrap herself in the blanket of her native anger. "See to him, and get him out of here," Mrachek muttered, then returned to her screen-gazing.

"What're you doing out of your cage?" Stella asked, trying to sound bolder than she felt.

"I've got a powerful bad headache, and I need to get some sleep," Storch said. "I'd be much obliged if you could make it happen, ma'am."

Stella nodded and crossed the room to the first aid dispensary, but she watched Storch like a rabid dog on a weak leash. His eyes flicked around the sickbay, taking in the luggage and Mrachek at her computer. He showed no reaction other than a mute, quizzical expression that quickly melted back into the default of incredibly tense neutrality. *He doesn't know what's happening, either. He's not one of them, not quite, not yet.* But he wasn't in the same boat as her. They were going to use him, and for something far harder than their plans for her. She opened the case and found several packets of ibuprofen, then stiffened as she felt his breath on her neck. She turned and saw that he was still standing across the room. What was he doing to her? It made her angrier, as it made her more afraid.

"So," he said, visibly uncomfortable, "looks like moving day. Where're you headed?"

"Nobody tells me anything, soldier. I'm not one of them." She came over and pressed the packets into his broad, knobby hand. "I'm a dual-purpose hostage-guinea pig, right, Doctor?" Mrachek was lost in contemplation.

He looked at the packets and dropped them on the examination table. "I can't take these, ma'am. Just plain old aspirin'll do fine." He rubbed his temples, and his jaw muscles bulged as he bit back a new surge of pain. She could almost see the blood vessels in his temples and in his eyes dilate and writhe. "And please don't stand so close, no offense. It's just—your perfume—it makes me…sick."

"I'm not wearing perfume, asshole," she said. "I didn't think anyone who'd killed so many people would whine about a little headache."

"I've had this headache off and on for going on nine years," he said.

"Gulf War syndrome?"

"You could call it that."

"You're an even bigger whiner than I thought, then."

The braced left arm came up, and Stella flinched, but it only grazed his forehead, hovering before her long enough to see he had no thumb, and his palm was shot through with a starburst of scars where the hand was messily sewn up. He backed away from her and rooted around in the dispensary case until he found what he was looking for. He unscrewed the lid off the aspirin bottle and tipped it back into his mouth, gobbling down at least a dozen. "Mind if I keep the bottle?" he asked.

"I told you, it's not mine. What about you? You're one of them, now?"

"What do you know about it, ma'am?"

"I know they were going to kill you before, and now you're one of the merry men."

"I don't see where I have much choice in the matter," he answered, keeping hold of a cool he evidently was far from feeling. "I don't much care for the way they do things, but we have a common enemy."

"So you're going to help them murder Radiant Dawn."

"It's war, ma'am. I didn't fire the first shot. They've got it coming."

"That's what the Nazis said. Do you have a hard-on for killing them, or just killing in general?"

"I'm not a machine, ma'am. They hurt me and mine, they're going to pay. And you talk an awful lot for a guinea pig." He turned and made to walk out of the sickbay, and she was about to call him another name, just for the all-important sake of having the last word in, when he staggered and flopped against the examination table. His shoulders shook, and she heard something that might've been a choked sob escape from his audibly chattering teeth.

Before better judgment reminded her of her all-too recent brush with death at the hands of Mrachek, she raced to him. Her hands stopped short of touching his back, but she felt her resentment of him falling apart under the piteous weight of his obvious suffering. Everyone in this tomb was damaged goods, and she'd been prepared for him to be the worst of them all. But in the last few minutes, he'd talked to her more than anyone had since her capture. He lacked either the sense or the insecurity to rise to her barbs, and she was starting to see why she couldn't stop being mean to him. It was a strange and scary feeling, one she'd never had to endure for more than a few minutes before she scared the object of it away.

"What's wrong with you? Can't hold your aspirin?"

"This…place…makes me…sick." Words struggled to escape his lungs, which sounded as if they were filling up with phlegm, or collapsing. She knew enough about Gulf War sickness to recognize that it had a myriad of symptoms, but that many took the form of environmental sensitivity. Exposure to fossil fuels, certain drugs, in fact just about any inorganic compound which released fumes, aggravated the condition. But most Gulf War sufferers that she'd seen—on TV, never in the flesh—looked ravaged, devoured and weakened. This man looked hale, tanned and healthy, trembling fits notwithstanding. Built more like a marathon runner or a swimmer than the hulking brutes who comprised the Mission militia, he might've been faking it if he looked like the kind of man who could stand to seem weak in front of a woman. This guy didn't look as if he could stand to be weak in front of himself. "Get along…You can't…help me."

Stella grabbed his arms and maneuvered him onto the examination table. He didn't resist, she doubted he could've. "Here," she said, reaching under the table and fumbling around on the utility shelf. She found what she was looking for and handed it to him. His hands were shaking too badly, so she tied it over his face.

With a sterile gauze mask over his mouth and nose, he immediately began to breathe easier, and his eyes stopped tearing. They focused on her, weighing her, but not judging her. She looked away, but he filled the room for her, and there was nowhere in or out of it that she could go and get away. She had to make him hate her, or this would only get worse.

"You Mexican?" he asked, his voice softer and clear, but sleepy.

"My parents were from Mexico, but I'm an American citizen. The white doctor won't have anything to do with you."

"I was just gonna say…you're a real pretty…" the next word was a sustained snore.

Stella wouldn't remember how long she watched him sleep. She was too busy trying to figure out how to make him hate her.

~ 31 ~

The tenth of July set records in Death Valley and the surrounding regions, but not for heat. The second cloudburst in as many weeks visited upon the hottest place on the globe spasms of flashflooding that resculpted the terrain like hatchets in clay. As the afternoon guttered out into early evening and the shadows began to bubble up out of fissures in the cracked desert floor, the air felt almost humid on Special Agent Cundieffe's face.

"Have you ever had to fire your weapon?" the Delta Force lieutenant asked Martin Cundieffe.

"Never in the line of duty," Cundieffe answered. "Force has never been my strong suit. That's why the Lieutenant Colonel had the good sense to send you gentlemen along." He smiled at the lieutenant and the other three commandos, but the smile was growing tired. They'd been having a lot of fun at his and the Bureau's expense for the last couple of days, and despite his resolve to represent his agency in the best possible light, they were getting to him. He turned to Special Agent Hanchett and whispered in her ear, "See that next time we get an FBI tactical squad to accompany us. I don't care what the Colonel says, this is disruptive to the search. His people are contributing nothing but static." Hanchett nodded and made a note on her laptop.

They were over the Ubehebe Crater, about sixty-five miles north of Furnace Creek, sweeping the bottom of a grid at the outer edge of the search pattern. An FBI helicopter, an FBI pilot, and a cargo of totally useless, foulmouthed, insolent counterterrorism specialists. Cundieffe regretted the deal he'd struck with Lt. Col. Greenaway for the thousandth time, but there was no helping it for the present. He had prepared a new report for Deputy Assistant Director Wyler this morning, in which he posited that the search had become a secondary layer of obfuscation to deflect the Bureau from the objective. Greenaway had concentrated his own searches in the southeast quadrant, going back over twice-examined territory and flatly refusing to allow FBI agents onboard. In speculations he dared not forward to Wyler just yet, he'd alleged that Greenaway already knew where the enemy was, and was circling to either contain or contact them. Perhaps he'd tipped his hand too soon, misreading Greenaway as more than just another assassin. But it would still come down to a race, as it would have, anyway.

The hole beneath them was half a mile wide and six hundred feet deep, the result of a seismic convulsion a few thousand years ago which had created a starburst-shaped corona of cinders six miles wide. A gravel parking lot was dotted with a few campers and pickups, and a ranger's truck beside public restrooms. Two of the commandos spotted land features and vehicles with binoculars. Suspicious groupings of vehicles were tagged and the numbers fed to Hanchett, who ran checks on NCIC and the California DMV database. They had found twelve stolen cars and two felons with outstanding warrants, but no terrorist militia, and no stockpiles of napalm. Cundieffe spent four hours in the air each day, then eight in the Bureau's HQ at China Lake, reviewing reports from agents up and down the state, as well as DEA and INS data from the border region. Then he went back up in the air for another four hours until just before dawn, scanning the desert floor through infrared goggles, looking for telltale heat signatures of underground activity. The night searches had yielded only a few drug smugglers and off-road enthusiasts on state parkland. He slept for four hours, and spent his first four hours each morning drafting reports and requisitioning more men.

The Bureau was talking to the Mexican Federal Police, who had pledged their support but taken serious issue with the United States Navy crossing their borders in gunships. Lt. Col. Greenaway had successfully pushed all Navy personnel onto the ground search, and placed his own officers in all the choppers, and was probably crossing the border out of the sanctioned search grid. It was enough to make one seriously wonder what side they were really on.

"—for Special Agent Cundieffe?" a tinny voice crackled in his ear. He pressed the earphone deeper into his ear and swung the microphone up under his nose.

"This is Cundieffe. Say again?"

"SA Tufts here, sir, in Tango Rainbow Seven. We're at mappoint seventy-two, thirty-eight, returning from completed sweep of grid twenty-nine. We're almost out of fuel, so we're turning back. But I saw a wrecked truck off a dirt side road in Titus Canyon. It matches the description of the Storch vehicle posted in the ready room."

"Tufts, that notice also made note of the date the vehicle was recovered, at mappoint thirty-two, nineteen, nearly a week ago."

"I know that, sir, but it's the same make and model, with the back window shot full of shotgun blasts. Someone dumped it here."

Cundieffe cut Tufts off and hailed the pilot.

Titus Canyon cut a narrow, winding twenty-six mile rain gutter through the eroded ramparts of the Grapevine Mountains, between Death Valley and Beatty, Nevada. The trail that wound through it was closed through the heart of the summer, sand-blasted signs hanging from chains snaked across either end proclaimed that flashflooding had washed the roads out. For a fugitive who knew the terrain, it was a perfect route for fleeing the state, because the sheer walls of limestone, sand and crystalline concrete shadowed the rutted trail, affording excellent coverage, even from an air search. Today, the trail stood out as a ribbon of livid green through the blinding bone-colored mountains. The local flora had made the most of the previous week's rainstorm, and with the further encouragement of this morning's downpour, had run riot in the alkaline sand: spiky, unforgiving balls of rocknettle already choked the trail in spots, with here and there a splash of orange poppies and globemallow, shoots of sacred datura and wispy veils of white gravel ghost, like standing shrouds of mist. Where there was an inch of space, or a day of rain, nature went berserk in its variety and hostile generosity.

Cundieffe studied the canyon as it unfurled beneath them through binoculars, poring over the bleached remains of the ghost town of Leadfield; the picked-over bones of a bighorn sheep scattered at the foot of a cliff; the sparkling decay of crystalline fields and scummy brown pondlets in the crooks and spreading hollows of the canyon.

They were hovering over the map point, but Cundieffe could see nothing. Through the telescoping lenses, the furrowed waves of undulating earth became an angry, ancient abstract painting, or an image of capillary tissue seen through a stereo microscope. Paradoxically, this let him focus and let loose his insecurities about the size of the search. He was searching a section of tissue removed from a body called the earth, for a foreign object—and like *that*, a brilliant flare of sunlight off chrome filled his vision and burned a violet phosphene nova onto his sight. "Come around this point ninety degrees," he shouted to the pilot, and looked again. Ignoring the chuckling whispers of the Delta Force contingent, he ordered the pilot to set down.

The pilot fretted and hemmed and hawed, but finally negotiated a stable landing place of sorts on a plain of brittle, dried mud at the floor of a bowl beside the trail. The canyon walls recorded a war between gods, strata burrowing into each other, lines of accreted geologic time plunging under invading rock of radically variant composition, as if the land itself here sometimes turned to water. Perhaps when the rainstorms had been more generous here, this had been a cauldron-lake, for at least part of the year, but for nature, this would have been more than enough. Cundieffe had heard of aquatic plants, frogs, and even "primitive" fish which could seal themselves in a membrane of water and sleep for decades, perhaps even centuries, until water came again. Cundieffe imagined the ground beneath him churning with forgotten species resurrected by the fleeting rainstorm, and plotted the shortest path to solid rock.

The skids settled a good couple of inches into the crust, and Cundieffe leapt out, splaying his hands out before him as a rough hand shoved at the small of his back. He hit the ground running and awkwardly caught up with his own forward momentum, the ground beneath his feet crumbling like petrified ash, turned and shielded his eyes from the portable sandstorm from the prop wash, watched the Delta Force commandos fan out to form a secure perimeter around the chopper. Unassisted, Hanchett climbed down and, steadying herself against the chopper deck, reached back in and dragged out an evidence kit. A few of the commandos joked about her bringing too much makeup, another answering back too loud that they didn't make enough makeup for a face like that, but she didn't give them the satisfaction of a blush as she crossed the mud flat towards him. She was a credit to her gender and to the Bureau, Cundieffe thought. He felt very warmly towards her.

"Too hot for this shit," one of the commandos groaned.

"Actually," Cundieffe broke in on their griping, "today's temperature is far below the average for this time of year. The high record was set on this day in 1913, and it was one hundred thirty-four Fahrenheit at two-thirty in the afternoon. Right now, it's six-thirty PM, and the temperature is only a little above ninety-four. The focus of our search is up that box canyon there, less than a quarter mile to the northwest of our present position. If you gentlemen can maintain your unparalleled professionalism and expedite rather than hinder our collection of evidence on this site, we can be in the air again before sunset. Agreed?"

They looked at each other, equal parts bewilderment and relief. "We'll sit tight," the lieutenant said finally. "You call out, if you need help."

Cundieffe hadn't even had to ask. He was afraid of agreeing too quickly, because then he was sure the lieutenant would feel obligated to send along his two least-disciplined men as an "escort." He made a tight, lipless smile to indicate his resignation, and led Hanchett up into the narrow box canyon.

Hanchett insisted on carrying the evidence kit herself. The canyon was scarcely wide enough for them to walk abreast, and Cundieffe took the lead, though he had a harder time keeping his smooth-soled leather shoes under him than Hanchett, who had thought to wear boots.

The rutted trail up the canyon was more of a gutter, not quite flat, and choked in a thick carpet of eroded sand, packed to the consistency of asphalt by the rain that had pried it loose from the canyon walls. The walls themselves loomed forty feet above them on both sides, the jagged, interlocking facets of the opposing faces testifying to a bygone cataclysm that had split this mountain neatly into halves. They were walking up into a jaw of earthbone, that would take far less of a seismic upheaval to close it again. Cundieffe picked up his pace, though Hanchett dogged him by less than a full stride, and almost caught him several times when the sand gave way under him.

"Sir?" Agent Hanchett called. "May I ask what might be deemed an impertinent question?"

To his mild chagrin, he had a harder time than she did finding his breath, but he managed, "Go ahead, Hanchett. And—" huff "—don't call me sir. We're both garden-variety field agents."

"Yes, Agent Cundieffe, but—well, perhaps you're unaware of it, but the entire task force holds you in the highest esteem, and has expressed nothing but admiration for your handling of the case since you stepped in, but…"

"That's untrue in my experience, but thank you, Agent Hanchett. Was that your impertinent question?"

"No sir, I was going to ask—are you absolutely positive this is the best disposition of our resources at this time?" She stopped, and Cundieffe gratefully settled back against a rock wall and caught his breath, looked at her quizzically. "I didn't mean it like that, I apologize. I had no intention of second-guessing you, sir, but, Agent Tufts' report sounded a bit speculative, and I—well, many of us on the task force have had occasion to question his observations in the line of duty. And, well, if you saw something, then that settles it, but we've come close to a half-mile from the landing point, and we haven't seen anything."

"Look at the ground, Hanchett," Cundieffe said. This canyon could not possibly accommodate a vehicle of the description of Storch's truck, and in the other direction, according to the survey map, is a sheer wall fifty feet high. That was where I saw the wreck of a vehicle, which would indicate that the vehicle in question was driven into the canyon off the cliff, with intent to dispose of it. The vehicle I observed, though partially obscured by a fan of eroded soil, was not corroded, and the chrome reflected light back. It's been there after the first rainstorm, but probably before last night's. So, if you've no more doubts—"

"I'm sorry, si—Agent Cundieffe. I never meant to question your—"

"Forget it, Agent Hanchett. We have some ground to cover, so let's get a move on."

Three turns of the canyon later, they found it.

The truck lay nose down in the basin of the dead end of the canyon, the walls like termite-gnawed wood spilling petrifying sand over its matte black hood and one exposed wall of the truckbed. A chuckwalla, a fearsome-looking lizard nearly a foot long, scurried out the shattered windshield and sought cover as they picked a careful path to the truck.

The truck had not been here long. Cundieffe's guess from the air had been spot-on. It had been exposed by last night's storm. It was an uncomfortable revelation, to say the least. The Highway Patrol and Death Valley Junction sheriff's deputies who pursued Storch out of Furnace Creek had claimed to have fired several dozen shotgun rounds at the truck, yet the vehicle they'd recovered had shown no damage from gunfire. Cundieffe had not taken the discrepancy seriously because, well, there was the damnable truck, with the plates and matching VIN numbers on the engine block and doorframes, everything tallied up with Storch's DMV records, and Storch was the one who'd left Sheriff Twombley's office, according to several witnesses in town, and the surviving deputy himself, when he recovered his senses.

But that had not been the truck. This was the truck that had fled the Furnace Creek massacre, Cundieffe was sure of it. The license plates might match, the VIN numbers might even match, but unless there were two Zane Ezekiel Storches walking the earth, the man who'd killed Sheriff Twombley and his deputy was, it now appeared, someone else entirely.

Hanchett sank to her knees behind the vehicle, methodically turning the sand piled up over the back bumper until she paused, brushed at something before her and called out, "The plates match those of the other truck, sir."

Cundieffe peered into the cabin through the shot-up rear windscreen. The entire back wall of the cabin was like a screen door, or the top of a salt-shaker, the headrests virtually atomized, but there was no blood. His understanding of forensics in extreme climes such as this were woefully deficient, but he knew enough to expect that no one operating this truck could have survived such an onslaught without shedding a single drop of blood. The tumulus of soil on the seats and in the footwells was still damp from the rains, but he could see the instrument panels inside. They were covered in dirt, but unbroken. Cundieffe closed his eyes and calculated, variables shunting into orderly columns, wild cards shuffled to the side for later consideration. He was left with very little to go on. Something had soaked up the hail of deadly lead that had penetrated this truck, but had not bled. Someone had taken this truck, which matched Storch's in every respect, and committed mass murder in his name. And that's when he'd begun running. The apocryphal raid had only sent him into hiding. It hadn't been enough, though, so this had been arranged. What did Storch know, that he merited such an elaborate ruse? What was Storch, that someone was using him so? And for what?

Out here, Cundieffe held his eyes closed and discovered what a disquieting sensation true silence was. All the background sounds that Cundieffe had always taken for granted as the humming of the world simply existing, were stilled here. The numbing music of air conditioners, appliances, traffic, power lines, the oceanic hush of millions of humans breathing, was painfully absent. The noise of a man's mind could run amok here, spreading to fill the silence like the frantically proliferating plant life, exploding in a riot of impossible color before drying out and dying, and going the way of the shadows at noon in this godforsaken place.

His cell phone trilled in his breast pocket. He took it out and flipped it open, still gazing into the dank cabin of the wreck.

"Special Agent Cundieffe here. Talk to me."

"Agent Simpson, sir, in Tango Delta. Sir, there's been a report—a sighting!"

"What? Of what?"

"The choppers! They're in the air again! They just crossed highway 190 on a northbound bearing—" clattering, hot sounds burning out the signal, Simpson's voice, muted, shouting, "Give that back!" a long, low whistle, and dead air.

"Good lord! Hanchett, we've got to get back to the chopper, now!"

She stood and looked at him. "What is it?"

"They're in the air! Whatever's going to happen, is going to happen now!" They both scrambled around the shifting wall of the basin, and were halfway around when Cundieffe heard it.

He looked up and his hand went for his sidearm. He almost expected to see them passing directly overhead—the two black sharks of the sky that had bedeviled the combined brains and might of the United States government for a week. That they were within earshot at all was astounding but—no it was only one chopper. It did pass overhead, though, and as it banked, he felt sure he could see the Delta Force lieutenant inside his chopper, waving to him before they passed out of sight over the far wall.

Then the silence came roaring back in.

~ 32 ~

The rain had stopped as quickly as it had begun, but the cloud cover would be stalled over the eastern half of the state until the high evening winds of twilight caused by the desert's massive convection cells swept them away.

They flew at dusk.

Clinging to the open ground, ducking under powerlines and snaking into canyons and the shadows of mountains at over one hundred miles per hour, they left no ripple on radar screens, left only pictures of clouds for the satellites, and if their shadows happened to fall across the hood of a semi or a station wagon on highway 190 as they skulked out of the Argus Mountains and into the Inyos, they were five miles of trackless wilderness away by the time the driver shaded his eyes to look. Like sharks on a blood trail, they traced the path of least habitation over one hundred and fifty miles of California, from Baker to the Owens Valley.

Only a little boy saw them. Riding a two-stroke dirtbike outside of Independence without a helmet or his parents' permission, he'd managed to total the bike and break his leg in three places in a dried-up tributary of the Owens River. As he lay screaming in the fine powdered sediment of the dead riverbed, he'd fallen silent as the sound of the cicadas in the trees on the unreachable bank thickened and became the susurrant roar of a helicopter. He was going to be rescued, just like in the Vietnam movies, he was going to be evacced to an aid station, and his parents would be so frightened and awestruck by his ordeal that they'd forget all about his reckless adventure and buy him a new bike.

Then they'd burst out of the trees and flashed overhead as they came to an almost complete stop, banked on the angle of the Owens riverbed, and vanished. There were two of them, and there was no mistaking them for Life Flight.

He'd seen these choppers in the movies, too, in *Rambo*, and *Apocalypse Now*. One was Russian, the other American, but both were black and unmarked, their matte hulls reflecting none of the dying golden light of the sunset. Big silver cables were wrapped around the bodies of both helicopters, like they were held together with duct tape. But what he would remember most vividly, though it was long gone before its image was a ghost on his retina, was the man sitting in the open doorway of the American chopper, wearing a tricked-out Army-green spacesuit and holding some kind of space helmet on his knee and a badass rifle between his legs. He was bent over as if in intense concentration, but as they passed overhead, he heaved violently and threw up.

Sgt. Storch wiped his mouth and leaned back out of the punishing rush of balmy evening air flowing along the body of the Black Hawk. The crewman observing the terrain below resumed his position and gave Storch a hand finding his bench.

In his old unit, losing your lunch before a mission would've provoked a storm of jeers and contempt and a score of derisive nicknames, but everyone onboard was otherwise preoccupied—checking weapons and suit seals, pecking at laptop computers, praying. There was none of the boisterous bullpen chatter that solid soldiers used to keep nerves at bay, but the silence in the cabin was a sign of the web of tension that radiated out from the two commanders on the front benches, just behind the flight deck. The freefall inertia of the helicopter was only half of the reason Storch had to put a racing stripe on the chopper's hull. He had only to look around to see how far he was from the real Army.

Major Bangs worked furiously to secure extra fuel pods to the barrel of some kind of flamethrower, then wrapped them in fireproof tape before handing it off to one of his men and starting another. He did not spare a second to look at his men, hadn't spoken a word since they boarded. His concern for the safety of his men was scary in its fierce intensity, and Storch hadn't yet decided whether it was genuine, or just a symptom of his insanity. He looked sure enough that Storch would follow him, but only if the alternative was jumping off the helicopter in mid-flight. The pep talk he'd given Storch yesterday came up unbidden in his mind. *I'm afraid—*

The other commander was a surprise, and not a pleasant one. Dr. Wittrock tapped at a laptop, its blue-white screen making his face a cadaverous white island in the murky red sea of the cabin lights. Periodically, he fiddled with the cable connecting his computer with one of the drives in the pizza-rack of nav and radar deflection systems beside the co-pilot's station. He wore an olive drab flight suit, a gashelmet and black jumpboots, but they only accentuated his frail, stooped physique. A mission with two commanders is a doomed mission, Storch thought, and with a civilian in charge—no, a scientist...

Although everyone around him worked as if they'd been drilling the Mission for years, he'd felt a reek of mickeymouse desperation penetrating to the core of its execution from the moment they'd awakened him this morning. That, at least, had been like the real Army.

Fingers clamping both his earlobes, jolting him with pain and the rush of blood goosed into his brain. Diebenkorn's face in his, eyes intent, like he'd been watching him sleep.

"Would you be ready if it was now?"

"What—where—" His head swam up out of dream-logic, tried to roll back over, saying, *this is just another dream*, but Diebenkorn's eyes said, *no*. "I'm awake," he mumbled. "I'm good."

"Good. Because it's now. Get your shit together." And he'd left the room, the door standing open to the flurry of running soldiers. As he disappeared, he holstered a pistol that Storch hadn't noticed hovering beside his temple. Were they being raided? No alarms, no gunfire. *It's now.*

What the fuck? He'd had only the vaguest idea of what the Mission was, knew only that the operation was imminent and that he had a part in it. There'd been no briefing, no review of plans like in Desert Storm, when they'd holed up in a remote tent at the edge of Bedrock for twenty-four hours before setting foot on the chopper. He supposed he understood the reasons for it: this operation would be contingent on any number of factors, from meteorology to the military, and probably had to be thrown together at a moment's notice. Also, Bangs had to know how Storch was trained. He'd know that Storch would meticulously plot and internalize his part of the Mission, so that the execution would be like another episode of a recurring dream. He'd need to shake every detail for oversights that could jeopardize his life in the field, and reject elements that didn't fit. He'd want to walk away from a plan that would mean certain death. Thus, the wake-up stunt.

He'd dressed and fallen into the flow of men towards the motor pool, where he'd stopped short and marveled at what he saw. The choppers were untarped and dressed out for take-off, only their rotor-blades furled in the massive space. Two crewmen unfolded out the rotor assembly of the Hind; presumably, they'd open up the Black Hawk after the Hind had taken off. Which would be easy, because the ceiling was gone; a brown mesh tarpaulin stretched over the yawning space above, but Storch could make out flecks of gray, cloudy sky through it.

Every outward inch of both helicopters was covered in a dull black surface that looked like foam rubber, inlaid with networks of heavy silver cable. Storch guessed it was Stealth technology, something the Mission scientists had helped the government develop and then stolen back.

Then he'd noticed the bomb racks under both choppers, and wondered if they'd get off the ground at all. The Black Hawk had over a dozen fat, barrel-shaped bombs and as many short-range missiles in a jungle-gym of a multitiered rig stretching out from the landing gear, and the Hind carried half again as large a payload, with missiles even hanging from secondary stabilizer wings above the loading doors. Surely they didn't intend to carry troops, too?

Finally, he'd noticed Medina standing beside the door, waiting patiently to be noticed. He handed Storch a bundle of heavy vinyl and a helmet. It looked like a GI spacesuit, and came with a Kevlar flak-vest and thigh-pads. It was the kind of fantasy protective gear the Pentagon might've issued in Desert Storm if they'd been intelligent and responsible fiscal planners and genuinely concerned for the welfare of their men. "Put this on," Medina said, "and get on the Black Hawk."

Storch pointed at the Hind. "That's a Russian chopper."

"No shit," Medina replied. "Bought it off the Cubans. Carries more freight and firepower than anything we make."

"What about the briefing?" Storch asked without much hope.

Medina chuckled. "You missed it. It was a month ago. We'll fill you in, in the air."

"This is bullshit," Storch growled.

"Yeah, so? Just stay close to somebody who has the evac plan and the safehouse list memorized, and you'll be good."

Storch joined the milling group of eleven soldiers in their MOPP suits, checking out weapons from the armory adjacent to the motor pool. Another cause for slack-jawed staring. Their arsenal was as far past the Army's standard issue as the Army was above Turkish bandits. The infantry standard was a modified Pancor jackhammer, an automatic shotgun. About half were fitted with a beltfeed option, but Storch gave this up after inspecting the triple beltfeed and the curiously color-coded shells in each. He took a jackhammer, but slung an MP5 over his shoulder for the security of the familiar. There were flamethrowers with wide-gauge nozzles that seemed rigged to throw incendiary gel instead of liquid fuel, maybe even napalm. He reminded himself to stay the hell away from anyone with one of those.

Major Bangs had come in with Dr. Wittrock, and the men fell into formation without prompting. Storch noticed that they stood in two groups of four and a threesome. Storch drifted towards the three and stood with Medina, Draper and a wiry Texan named Tarnell, who favored him with a crooked smile before turning away. Against his natural and justifiable caution, Storch had immediately come to like Tarnell and supposed everybody else did the same. He was the kind of open, naturally charming soldier a unit needed to be more than just a gang of goons with guns. Whatever they were going to do, whoever they were going to do it to, if Tarnell was in his team, it couldn't be as bad as everybody feared. Of course, everybody else here was crazy…

Bangs signaled wordlessly for the floor. "It's now," he said, and the gravity of the words made every soldier stand a little taller under the crushing weight of their gear, as if the enemy were right outside. "Remember the briefings and follow the Mission protocols, but don't be robots. Expect extremely unconventional resistance, and be prepared for every contingency we discussed. This is our Mission. For whatever reason each of you has that says so, this has to be done. And we will do it. Now." He turned and started to get onboard, but Wittrock clamped his wrist and whispered agitatedly in his ear. Bangs turned and hissed something back that made Wittrock wince, then look in Storch's direction. "I want to take this up with Armitage," Wittrock announced loudly. "Now."

Bangs grabbed him more roughly than he needed to and waved Storch over. "Sergeant Storch. Apologies for cutting you out of the final briefings, but you looked like you needed the sleep, and somebody thought you were a security risk. You're on the D Team, with me. Your mission objective is twofold, thus the extra man, but your primary task is to protect this man," he said, pointing his finger in Wittrock's face. "If I think you're a risk, I'll take you out myself. Same goes for the other three, and you'll never see it coming. Will I have to put you down?"

Storch looked Wittrock over. The man clearly disliked and mistrusted him, but if he was going, he was important. Storch was going to free up a man for the other teams, which would probably comprise some sort of assault force. "You won't have any trouble from me, sir."

"Do you want to spend the night in storytime with Dr. Armitage, or do you want to do this thing?" Bangs asked, and Wittrock seemed to deflate. They got on the chopper.

They'd waited only five minutes after the tarp was rolled back and the Hind took off. The crew worked frantically on their rotors, then climbed down and in even as the pilot fired up the stack of computers behind his chair. Then the motor pool and the underground complex dropped away, and the desert horizon unfurled around them, a featureless brown plane sandwiched against a gray one, the buffer of setting sun melting away to the west. Storch recognized the place immediately. It was a junkyard that used to be a drive-in, just outside of Baker. He'd been here several times— with Harley Pettigrew, poking around amongst the totaled auto skeletons while Harley haggled with the "manager." He wondered how much else in the last eight years had been nothing like it seemed, passing unnoticed by his dulled, hermit's eyes.

In the hour-long flight, Medina had taken it upon himself to fill Storch in on the rough outlines of the mission, and it'd been then, with the sickening dip and sway of the helicopter, the enervating red dimness of the cabin, the stink of gun oil, sweat, fuel and napalm, and the clear understanding of what they were about to do laid out before him, that he'd felt the urge to vomit.

He sat back now and tried to break the Mission down into a piece he could swallow. He was going to protect a man, a package of vital strategic value, nothing more. That was his job, and he could do it, the rest of it was somebody else's job, he just had to guard the scientist.

Draper nudged him, leaned in close to whisper in his ear. "Sorry about before," he said. "At the truckstop."

"'Salright," Storch said, wanting to be left alone.

"I didn't want to grease you, buddy," Draper went on. "I was just following orders. From that asshole." and he pointed at Wittrock. The physicist never looked up from his computer.

Outside, the rolling Inyo Mountains dropped away and the drained dust-plain of the Owens Valley opened out beneath them. On the northern horizon, about five miles off, Storch glimpsed the feeble glow of a town, maybe Big Pine, maybe Independence. The helicopter bore due west as it came out of the mountains; the side-door spotter shouted into his headset that he had a visual mark on Highway 395, and Major Bangs called five minutes to target. The soldiers stood and secured their gear, bunched together into their three-man teams.

Storch stood between Medina and Draper with his eyes closed, and tried to find a quiet place. In all the violence and panic and confusion of the last week, the only bright, silent center he could grasp was yesterday, when he'd lain in the sickbay, and the pretty nurse, who looked more like an Indian than a Mexican, and had a mean mouth but soft eyes, had watched him. Probably, she thought he was asleep, and Storch wasn't about to disabuse her of it, if it meant she'd start up talking again, or worse, go away. Where any other person in the world might've creeped him out by lurking over him in a position of weakness, it had made him feel warm and safe, like he could go to sleep for real and not have the Hostage Show dream, or wake up to the Headache. It wasn't that Storch was some kind of lonely bedwetter who yearned for human contact but couldn't deal with it while conscious—rather, he'd felt he could stand her looking at him for so long because he could see through his slitted eyes that she was really trying to *see* him. He wondered if he could get her to shut up and look at him like that when he was really awake, after all this. *After. That's funny, Storch.*

"Arms up and helmets on, we're one minute to target," Bangs shouted. Storch clamped his helmet down on his head and held his breath. The worse-than-puke stench of new plastic flooded his nostrils, seemed to solidify into slime on his tongue. Medina reached over and connected his airfeed to the canister sewed into the small of his back, dogged the seals on his helmet and gave him a thumbs-up. The canned air was better than nothing, but not by much. Storch made himself take several deep gulps, holding each for several seconds to try to get his panic in check. *Nobody else is freaking out.* He began to calm down, and took in the genius of the helmet without hating it much less. A gasmask built into a full enclosure steel and high-impact plastic helmet, the visor allowed a full field view, and seals could be opened to breathe filtered ambient air when the canister ran out.

A headset built into the helmet fed him the sound of every soldier's labored breathing, and via Bangs's frequency, the muted rapid-fire chatter of the pilots and crews of both choppers. The Mission moved forward like a live thing, and they were its muscles, and its claws.

Bangs bulled his way down the crowded catwalk and stood in the open loading door. His big broad face was stretched tighter than a drum, but there was no shake to it. Putting troops on the ground, Storch decided, the Major was anything but afraid. "The world is not going to understand what we are about to do. They are going to brand us terrorists and extremists, and it is very doubtful that any of us will live to see them, in the fullness of time, come to recognize the importance of our sacrifice. I want to thank each and every one of you for participating in this Mission, for turning your back on country and the order of law to do what's right. And it is: if you never hear it again, I want you to fix this in your brains and take it to your graves. This is right. This is just. *This is the natural order.* It's been a privilege to serve with you all. Twenty seconds to target. Ivan, advance on target and commence strategic bombing."

Storch craned his neck to see around Bangs and the spotter, but there was only textured darkness and the sawtooth wave of mountains on the

Radiant Dawn

horizon. The cloud cover was starting to tear itself apart in the upper atmosphere. There was no moon, but he could make out glistering beds of naked stars in the darkening sky. In minutes, they would be laid bare to satellite imagery, which would be a damn sight harder to fool than radar. He wondered about the escape plan, and then, looking at the faces of the men around him, wondered if there was any such thing.

Then they crested a hill and pivoted, frozen over a bowl of light.

Storch struggled with the others to get a view of the objective. He saw a circular community of tract homes with a blocky, fortress-like four-story tower in the center. Arc-sodium streetlamps cast golden circles on street corners and an open field with tennis courts and a swimming pool. *This is right.*

The Hind appeared over the far ridge and dove into the bowl like a greedy fly, overripe with inflammable eggs. As the Black Hawk closed up the last quarter mile to the edge of the community, Storch averted his eyes from a flash of light like a hole in the material world. Missiles stabbed the ground in a widening arc as the Hind traversed the diameter of the community, picking and annihilating targets according to a program too fast for a human co-pilot to follow. The first strike knocked out the lights: the grid went out in one big wave on the heels of the deafening boom of the impact. The second took out a garage complex. The others hit targets invisible to Storch's eyes, but probably no less important: phone switchers, satellite dishes, back-up generators.

"They're cut off. You've got about thirty minutes before we can expect formal resistance."

"Damn fine shooting, Ivan. Back up for insertion. Troops, get ready to jump."

The Hind ceased fire and hovered in place over the tennis courts, resplendent in the glow of the burning village. The soldiers aboard the Black Hawk seized handholds as the helicopter banked and took a straight course for the tower, just like Medina had said they would.

"This isn't right," Storch said to himself. There was no antiaircraft fire, not even small weapons resistance, and the Mission didn't seem to expect any. If not for the precision with which the Hind had cut off the community from the outside world, Storch would've concluded that they'd come to the wrong place. He shouldered past Bangs and hung out the door. The wind was already foul with burning. Then he saw the people running out of their houses and looking up at the sky with wide black mouths, the way people would in any suburb in America in the event of a bombing raid. Some of them were children. *This is just.*

266

"We're over the target, Ivan," Bangs said into his headset. Commence perimeter saturation bombing."

"Major, what the hell are we doing?" Storch shouted, forgetting the headset, and banging his visor against the Major's for emphasis. "Those are normal fucking people down there. There're kids down there! What is this, really?"

Bangs grabbed the sides of his helmet and wrenched him off balance before he could steady himself on a handhold, and dangled him out the doorway. "Look again, Sergeant. Is that normal?"

Below him, Storch could see the roof of the tower, a featureless deck with a pillbox-shaped staircase and a hatch that might admit an elevator car, if it had the telescoping lift shaft design. Beyond and below, he could see people running down the street from the far edge of Radiant Dawn, where the Hind was starting to drop napalm. They ran in an orderly single-file line like participants in a fire drill, seemingly oblivious to the fact that each and every one of them was on fire. Like cartoon candles, their little legs carried them on when the very air around them was burning hot enough to crack most tempered metals.

"IS THAT NORMAL?"

A blob of flames rolled out of the maelstrom in pursuit of the flaming refugees, like a runaway bouncing betty. As the flames lost their intensity, Storch could make out that it was a mob of people clinging to a golfcart. The burning cart collapsed a block away from the tower, and the burning people leapt off and joined the rest on foot. They were converging on the tower. He didn't know whether to be relieved or horrified further when they began, finally, one by one and with agonizing slowness for people who were mostly ash, to lie down and die.

This is the natural order.

Bangs dragged Storch back in and leaned back outside himself. "Take us down, Joe. Team chiefs sound off!"

"A-Team, good to go."

"B-Team, good to go."

"C-Team, good to go."

"D-Team, good to go," Medina called out.

The Black Hawk settled on the rooftop and the soldiers poured out and scattered like army ants on a dinner plate, fanning out to the corners and surveying the street below, securing the stairs and ripping the hatch off the elevator shaft. The Black Hawk sprang back up into the air and almost immediately vanished into the ceiling of smoke that covered Radiant Dawn.

Storch followed Medina to the staircase and covered him as he ran down to the bottom and back, reported all clear. Several men at the edges took potshots at the refugees below, but their chiefs told them to save it. They dropped charges down the shaft and ran back to the edge. Two seconds later, a plume of white fire shot out of the hole. Bangs waved A, B and C down the stairs and turned to face Wittrock and his team. "Let's go in. Tarnell, Draper, maintain this position and cover the exterior entrances. Maintain contact on my channel. Be prepared to get downstairs in a hurry."

They barked yessirs and ran to the edges with grenade launchers at port arms. Bangs strode off to the stairs. Medina sprinted ahead of him and took up point, Wittrock followed, looking like a prisoner of martial astronauts, with Storch bringing up the rear. The stairway was dark, but the assault teams had dropped lo-glow flares on the landings as they swept the building. Storch followed Wittrock's stooped shoulders down the stairs and into a corridor with white tiles on the walls and ceiling, as well as the floor. It looked like a hospital, or another computer clean room. Medina signed all clear again, and they advanced to a heavy steel door with red and green lights above it, like a TV studio, or a radiology lab. The green light was on.

Wittrock set to unlocking the door with his laptop, while Medina and Storch circled the floor without finding a soul. He saw more than a few bullet holes in doors, and a shattered water cooler which had spilled water and icy glass shards out into the corridor.

"These guys spook easy," Storch whispered.

"Have you ever fought room-to-room against people who don't curl up and die when you pour nape on them, Storch?" Medina asked. Storch shut up.

When they came back around, they found the door open and Wittrock and Bangs inside. He walked into the room and looked around at the banks of computers and the console in the center at which Wittrock sat, connecting his laptop to a bank of sockets in a recess in the desk. All the computers were still aglow and humming, presumably fed on a separate emergency generator somewhere in the tower.

Bangs sat on the edge of the desk with his arms crossed. From the haunted look in his eyes, Storch could tell he was starting to think about what he'd done. *I'm afraid there is no right side—*

"There's nobody," Storch reported. "No resistance at all." his last was not a report, but an accusation.

Bangs rolled his eyes. "I pray you're right, Sergeant."

Storch thought of Spike Team Texas. Would he be here, doing this, up to his neck in cold-blooded death, if he hadn't thought they'd be here? They had to be here. "They had a SWAT team last week."

"Ordinary citizens. They were asleep in their beds. Their imitation of humans is their defense, but it is also their weakness, Sergeant. They're not like you or me. They become what their environment demands to survive, and to reproduce."

"Why are you on the ground, Major?" Storch asked. "If the Mission's gonna have a prayer of getting out of here, shouldn't you be running things from the air?"

"Don't ask stupid questions, Sergeant."

"Major! A-1 in the lobby! We have a situation! Please advise!" the voice crackled from a speaker built into the desk, into which Bangs had connected his headset. The reception sounded bad, but the distortion was the muffled barking of gunfire.

Bangs stood up and began pacing. "Go ahead, A-1."

"We got the motherfucker! The primary! The goddamn primary!"

"Repeat that," Bangs and Wittrock both said. They looked like expectant fathers.

"It's Keitel! He came running in with his ass on fire and we pinned him down!"

Wittrock looked cautiously elated as he looked up from his work. "Is this confirmable?" At the same time, Bangs blurted, "Is he dead?"

"Not yet, not yet, but he's all fucked up. Burn him again, Jack! Burn him—"

Wittrock rocked back in his chair and let out a breath that he'd been holding for over a decade. "Then it's done," he said.

"B-2, Major, on level two, with an urgent situation! Goddamit, goddam—"

"Where's B-1, Bobby? Where's El Rey? El Rey, speak!"

"El Rey's gone, Major! The primary got him!"

"What? What primary?"

"Keitel, or Keogh, whatever his fucking name is! He's pinned down in a corner office. He's—he's got El Rey, and he's—he was eating him alive, sir, and I didn't, I wasn't gonna—Oh, god, man, I'm sorry…But he won't fucking die!"

"He's wrong, Major," A-1 broke in. "No disrespect to El Rey, man, but you're wrong. We nailed his ass down here."

"Shut up, Dicky," Bangs barked, then his voice went all cool to take the panic out of the new chief of B-Team. "Bobby, listen to me. Have you been listening to the all channels frequency?"

"Shit, Major, I wasn't listening to shit on the radio, I had—"

"OK, OK, where did you first encounter the primary?"

"We cleared the floor, and then we caught the motherfucker climbing in a window. He was burned so bad we didn't think he'd—put up much of a fight—shit—but his face was—I've seen the primary's picture enough times to know it was him."

"He's wrong, major," A-1 shot back. "I'm looking at the motherfucker right now. I was there, Bobby. I was a green SF warrant officer on the goddamned boat when they tested RADIANT. He borrowed my binoculars! This is him. Major, he said my goddamned name!"

"Clearly, this is another defense mechanism," Wittrock said calmly. "We will have to assume that none of them is the primary."

Bangs nodded, asked, "Bobby, Dicky, assume none of them is the primary. It's some kind of camouflage. You look outside, you'll probably see more of them."

They're all his children, Storch thought. *And now, maybe all of them are him.*

"Bobby, lay claymores and barricades at all the windows, then fall back to the staircase. Dicky, hold those fucking doors until I call you back up. You still awake, Storch?" Bangs shouted. He snapped to attention.

"Sir, yes, sir."

"Good, you and Medina do the perimeter again. Check the windows. These fuckers can probably jump pretty high, to get out of a fire."

"Yes sir." He turned to leave, when a new voice squelched out of the speaker. Storch kept running, but switched his headset link to all-channels, and steadied his rifle on his armbrace. The seemingly airtight security they'd established in the tower had been punctured and they'd begun to take casualties. As impossible as it seemed, Storch now began to function as he hadn't a few minutes before, indeed, as he hadn't in nearly ten years. He was in a war, again.

"Major, I'm dodging SAMs out here!" The pilot sounded almost giddy. "They finally started fighting back!"

Medina met Storch in the corridor and flanked him as they walked the halls.

"Are you in imminent peril, Ivan?" Bangs's voice rasped in their ears.

"No, Major, we're too close for the dumb shits to lock on, and they're firing blind through smoke. I think I put one of them out, but there's another one out there. They're just shoulder-held shit, I don't think— Jesus, what was that?"

Storch turned a corner and brought his rifle up. A man-shaped silhouette approached him down the corridor. He steadied himself and saw it was just his own shadow, cast by a flashlight Medina had attached to his rifle barrel. His foot slipped out from under him in a puddle of water and he skidded a few feet, his unwieldy Jackhammer slipped down on his brace and went off with a brutal stutter that carved a jagged S into the opposite wall. Medina came up alongside him and crouched, pointing his flashlight down the hall. "Spook easy?" he asked.

Storch went to a window and looked out. The outer eighty percent of Radiant Dawn was an Old Testament lake of fire. The inner island around the tower was merely burning and overrun by little dancing points of light that one had to work real hard to reconcile as people. He settled down and listened to the channel chatter, listened to the mission come apart at the seams.

"Major, D-3 on the roof, something just ran up the side of the goddamned buildin', and it's up here and it's burning, but it won't die, and it's really fuckin' pissed—"

"Fall back, Tarnell, fall back—"

"Shit no, Major, this bitch is toast. Draper, get him—holy shit, didja see that?"

"See what?" Bangs demanded. "Tarnell? Answer me!"

"Major, Ivan here, you won't believe this, somebody just jumped off the roof of the tower, and they're—shit, Timbob, heel off, he's—Jesus Christ, fall down! He's fucking flying! Oh shit—He's on the outside—"

Screaming over the pilot, Tarnell reporting on the same event from the roof. "Major, the shitbird jumped off the roof, like a goddamn rocket, he's on the Hind, I repeat, there's a burnin' fucker on the Hind, and he's inside it, now—"

"Timbob, where's he at? Take the sidearm, go back and—where's Edgeworth? What? Major, we're pretty sure he's still on the outside of the chopper, we're trying to maneuver so Joe can pick him off—"

"Joe, do not re-enter the target area until we're ready to extract, do you hear? You're our ride home!"

"Joe here, Ivan, I do not see anybody on your hull, I repeat, no visual on a—"

"Ivan, he's in your cargo space—"

"Timbob! Timbob? Edgeworth? Oh my God, don't—"

"Fuck me! What was that, Ivan? Ivan?"

"Ivan's not here, boy."

"Who said that? Who the fuck is this?"

"Shit! Shit! Shit! Oh my God! They're going down—"

Storch and Medina ran back to the windows and looked out. By pure luck, they had an excellent view. The Hind was spinning out of control over the less-cremated portion of Radiant Dawn. It's bomb racks were all empty, and the dangling assembly made the Russian chopper look more than ever like a vicious tropical insect. He stared in awe as he realized that the flashing flames he saw in the windshield were not reflections. The cabin was burning, and the chopper was going down like an anvil.

"Holy shit," Medina, Tarnell, Draper and the Black Hawk pilot all said as one.

The Hind hit a burning three-bedroom split-level tract home just across the wide avenue from the tower, knifed squarely through the center of its roof. The walls buckled and collapsed outwards under the terrific force of the impact even as the hurricane of rotors hacked them to splinters. The house and its neighbors were engulfed in a sphere of fire that quickly swallowed itself, leaving only a pillar of deeper black against the burning night sky.

"Major, this is Joe. I still have a signal from Ivan's black box. Do you want me to arm it?"

"Do that, Joe."

"What's the black box?" Storch asked. Medina shrugged.

"A-1, give me a sitrep on the ground."

"Like the surface of the sun out here, Major. Ain't nothing walking away from this. What happened to Ivan?"

"Tell you later. B-2—Bobby, what's it like down there?"

"Secure, Major. I think it's dead."

"Good man. Stay put. D-3, what do you see?"

"All quiet, now, Major. I don't see any—wait. Oh shit, you've got to be fucking kidding me. Major, he's walking away from it—"

"Major, A-1 here, we got fire in the lobby!"

"Somebody's shooting at you?"

"No, fire, real fire, he's—breathing fire—"

"Say again, A-1, your signal's breaking up—"

"There's two of 'em—AAAAAHHHHH!!!"

"A-1, come back! Speak, goddamit! B-2 what is your position?"

"We're in the stairwell on our way to support A-Team, but I don't hear any shooting. There's fire everywhere, shit, falling back into the stairwell, the lobby's torched. A-1's not talking back, Major, they—oh, no—"

"B-Team, come back! Bobby, come back...oh, Goddamit...D-Team, rally on the fourth floor at my position."

"Even us, Major?"

"Yes, all of you get here now. This is the primary objective, and something's moving up the tower in force. Assume A and B Teams are

KIA, say again, A and B Teams are gone, there's just us. This gets done, we get to go home. How close, Witt?"

Storch and Medina, rounding the corner to come back to the computer room, almost shot Tarnell and Draper as they loped out of the stairwell. Both were blackened from head to toe, with their helmets off, and coughing like terminal lungers. Their eyes were like eggs, and their teeth were chattering. Nobody said a word, they just took up positions outside the door.

"I can fix its position in orbit," Wittrock answered after a long, deliberate pause, "but its interface is remaining aloof for the time being. None of the original RADIANT codestrings work, anymore. I'm uploading its tracking signature so that if we can't neutralize it tonight—"

"It gets done tonight, Witt, or so help me God I'll leave you here." Bangs walked out into the hall and looked over the surviving team. He clenched his fists like a man trying to hurt himself so he won't cry.

"See, Brutus? I tole ya. Some dumbass nigger's trynta make off wit our teevee." The voice echoed up from the bowels of the stairwell leading down from the roof. They'd been watching the down stairwell, and were caught by surprise, some more than others. Because the voice was the one they'd heard over Ivan's frequency in the moments before the Hind crashed.

Bangs, Medina, Storch, Tarnell and Draper turned to face a big man wearing nothing but ashes and carbonized scabs like the exoskeleton of a lobster, and a chopper pilot's helmet—Ivan's. Storch saw he was unarmed and was turning back to warn Wittrock when he made out the dog tags dangling from his corded neck. He looked harder. More from the posture than from what was left of his face, Storch recognized Avery Tucker.

Draper stitched bullets up Tucker's torso with his MP5, walking backwards and shooting as coolly as a man watering his lawn. The stream of lead washed up Tucker's neck and across his head, two shots going right through and blowing out a fluorescent in the corridor. It was a textbook kill—twenty-four shots, sixteen hits, every vital area a weeping crater. He shouldn't have been just dead; he should've been a wall mural. Avery Tucker stood there, looking down at the light coming through the holes in his body, and when he looked up, he looked to be well past pissed.

"You stupid fuckin hillbilly, ya crushed mah cigarettes!" Draper emptied his clip into the vet, who might've rocked back on his heels a little. "Yore mama's gonna hafta pay fer those, boy."

If Draper said something in response, it was lost in the whoomp of his shotgun. The exploding depleted uranium shells caught Tucker in the throat, but where they should've taken his head off, they simply sank out of sight. Veins stood out on his temples for a moment, and he bowed his head as if to gather patience, murmured, "Boy, I ain't gonna tell you again—" Then his head became a red cloud, and all the glass panels on the relays shattered and Storch's ears rang like amps at a Who concert. Draper was getting up off the floor and looking over Storch's shoulder and pointing and shouting something.

Storch started to turn when he saw something rise up behind Draper. He pointed, and yelled, "Behind you!" but couldn't hear his own words. Avery Tucker, very much alive from the shoulders down, clambered across the desk and fell on Draper. Oblivious to Storch, Medina and Bangs shooting him, Tucker's headless body pinned Draper's shoulders with his knees and fumbled around until he found Draper's neck. To his credit, Draper writhed and kicked and even bit into the tendons of Tucker's wrist as the vet took hold of his victim's head and wrenched it off. Storch and Bangs paused to reload, Medina remove his helmet and vomit on his boots.

Tucker held Draper's head high for a few seconds, steadying himself atop the bucking corpse. Then he set the head atop his own shoulders. A moment passed as the thing that wore Draper's head hooked itself up. When the eyes opened, they were not Draper's eyes anymore.

Bangs clapped a fresh clip into his rifle, spat, "Fuck this shit. Fall back. Witt, we're blowing this place up and getting the fuck out of Dodge."

Storch remembered Draper's warning and wheeled on the door and saw it was blocked by something like a weather balloon, or a parade float made out of liver, trying to force its way through the door. He turned back to Bangs, shouting, "What is that?" Bangs stepped back, tripped over a wheeled office chair and sat down hard.

Medina scrambled backwards and took cover behind a copier, loaded the grenade-launcher on his rifle. Tucker was still standing there, getting the feel of his new head. Wittrock continued to scroll through menu screens, Tarnell to reload his Jackhammer, as if none of this was happening, as if this was still a winnable battle, and not the most awful debacle any of them had ever witnessed. "I need three more minutes, Bangs," Wittrock said. "Three minutes, or we might as well stay here forever."

Storch approached the mass that protruded a good foot and a half into the room, a taut sac of flesh that filled their exit from floor to ceiling. Tiny cracks began to appear on the wall around the door. "Bangs, we've got another big fucking problem here—"

"Fix it, Storch. We got a plateful of shit to eat, already."

Storch looked back just as a giant he instantly recognized as Brutus Dyson loomed up behind Bangs with a length of chain stretched taut between his knurly fists. He seemed to grow two feet taller, and before Storch could make a sound, looped it three times around the Major's throat and yanked so hard that Bangs's head popped right off his body, rocketing across the room like a champagne cork. A gory fountain gushed out of the stump and Dyson's mouth closed over it. With an audible string of pops, his jaw unhinged and his mouth grew to the size of a manhole, engulfed Bang's corpse up to the waist.

Storch was not idle in this time, nor was he stunned to inaction. He emptied a full magazine of shotgun shells into Dyson, switched to the MP5 and stitched him up and down with hollow-point rounds, but none of it mattered. He might've been spitting at him for all the results he got.

Dyson's features flushed livid purple with the strain of eating another man whole, crumpled and ran like a waxwork in a microwave, twisted into suckered tentacles that flailed at Bangs's body, shredding it into digestible portions. One of them drew Bangs's Walther PPK from his belt holster and waved it around awkwardly, then blew itself off at the root.

Hunched over the dead man, Dyson's impossibly broad back seemed to sizzle and pop, and he let out a pained roar that gave Storch momentary hope that he'd tried to go too far, and was about to die. Bubbles formed and burst in the liquefying skin and opened up, like the thousand pockets in the back of a mother Surinam toad, brimming with squirming larvae. Tiny, half-formed tumor-tadpoles reached out of Dyson's back and mewed like drowning kittens. And Storch, perversely, understood. Dyson was digesting Bangs's body already. His flesh had to do something, anything with the extra mass immediately, and it was going insane with the effort, as only a walking, talking cancer can go insane.

Nobody noticed Tucker was moving again until he tapped Medina on the shoulder. The enormous muscles and tendons in Tucker's neck surged out like a frilled lizard's, and Draper's stolen face contorted and cried boiling blood. His limbs froze up inches from Medina's face. Medina turned to look at Storch, shouted, "He's having a fucking coronary—" and the veins in Tucker's neck ripped themselves free, whipping through the air like runaway firehoses. Medina went into a crouch with his arm up to catch the shower of blood, but the veins latched onto his throat like crazed lampreys, bore into his own circulatory system and pumped Tucker's blood into it. Medina's eyes and tongue bugged out further with each thundering pulse of Tucker's heart. Storch could feel the throbbing tocsin of that muscle in the soles of his feet as if they were going to sleep. Tucker poured an ocean of blood into Medina before he burst. Then the flow from the monster veins seemed to reverse, and hoovered up every last drop of blood, his own and that of his victim.

Storch was on his last clip. He slotted it and turned once again to the blocked doorway just as the frame gave way and the third vet spilled into the room.

Gibby Holroyd looked and smelled like an avalanche of day-old castoffs from a slaughterhouse—a turgid mountain of diseased innards bound together in coils of intestinal rope, a mammoth digestive tract on legs. Noisome anuses blew out noxious gases from every fold in the gargantuan carcass, and thousands of fleshy cilia waved from patches on his body like some unspeakable new hybrid of sea anemones and jungle rot, presumably gleaning microscopic life from the air and eating it. Storch shot eighteen rounds into Holroyd before he could force the rest of himself through the door. Bilious yellow fluids erupted from the holes, burning craters in the concrete floor wherever they splattered.

Before Storch's horrified eyes, the offspring of Brutus Dyson matured, sprouted black membranous wings, and took flight. They orbited their sire like angry killer bees, though each was the size of a crow. Something like a frog, like a hornet, a maggot or a human fetus, they moved too fast to make out details.

Tarnell backed up until he was shoulder-to-shoulder with Storch. Behind them, Wittrock worked furiously at the computer, seemingly oblivious to the massacre. "If you can do it, do it now," Storch told him. "We're all about to die."

"Make more time, Sergeant. This is more complicated than I'd anticipated." By the strain in his voice, Storch knew that the scientist understood very well what was happening in the room. It also told him that the Mission, with all its awful surprises and sacrifices, was going to fail.

"That dog won't hunt, Sergeant," Dyson growled over the buzzing of his spawn. "Tell the geek there he can leave off."

"Wittrock?" Storch hissed over his shoulder.

"He's right, you know," Wittrock said, and Storch heard him spinning in the office chair, dropping his trembling hands like dying birds in his lap. "None of the primary command functions can be accessed from here, now. None of the viruses will upload. The system won't crash. The satellite is over Siberia right now, but it'll be overhead in about two hours."

"Then we're fucked," Tarnell shouted, his nerve finally going. "The whole thing—everybody dyin', was for shit!"

"Fuckin' A," Holroyd gobbled.

"Naw," Dyson said, and everyone turned to look at him, and most were sorry they did. The thing that'd been Dyson had doubled in size. Where his head had been, a cluster of muscular tentacles thrashed and coiled, glistening with the gore of Major Bangs. From somewhere inside that mass came a voice more or less like Dyson's. "You let us walk in Iraq, and took the heat for what we done to the natives. We owe you for that, and we hate owin' anybody. You can go, Storch. You an your pal."

"But there's three of us," Storch said, and immediately, painfully, understood.

"You got to pick one."

Dyson was letting him go only to headfuck him with officer's choices, to make him sacrifice either Tarnell or Wittrock. Storch hated the little fucker inside out, but the Major had charged Storch with protecting him, and if there would ever be a chance of knocking the satellite down, Wittrock would probably be the one to do it.

To his credit, Tarnell caught on pretty quickly how things would have to go before Storch could muster some kind of apology. "This is bullshit, you motherfucker! Die!" He shouldered his rifle, but even as he twitched the trigger for his grenade launcher, Dyson's offspring were swarming him. Storch had time to grab Wittrock and dive behind the computer console before the grenade went off inside Brutus Dyson.

Incredibly, the explosion had been little louder than a belch, and now the sounds of Holroyd's suet-choked laughter and Tarnell's muffled screams became deafening. Under it all, the pilot of Joe howling for somebody, anybody to tell him what had happened. A hail of shrapnel, glass and Dyson pelted the walls and floor around them. Incredibly, Wittrock had managed to hold on to the laptop, and Storch wondered idly if it wasn't worth more than the scientist, now. It'd certainly be easier to carry out of here.

"Get up," he shouted in Wittrock's ear. The scientist looked stunned for once, and it was a goose in the glands to see him realize this wasn't going according to plan, anymore. Storch dragged him to his feet by his airhose. "Get up and go," he said. "When Tarnell's dead, they'll probably change their minds."

Wittrock snapped to and regained his bland composure, as if he'd been mentally recalculating the breakdown of the Mission and now had the formula for extricating his own ass from it. "Of course. Lead the way."

Storch turned and peeked over the top of the desk. Dyson was calling home the winged larva and trying to make himself a new torso with them. Holroyd was eating Tarnell alive, his distended head like a giant anaconda's as he gulped down the big Texan's pelvis and wrapped multiple barbed tongues around his abdomen. Tarnell flailed at Holroyd, but his arms were so badly broken that they pinwheeled and flopped uselessly, adding to his agony. Tucker sat watching. His new head was already starting to look like his old one, as the grinding pressure of his inborn rage wrenched all the facial muscles into bulging, trembling straps of leather.

"Remarkable," Wittrock observed. "The others were limited to autonomic reactions to their environment. *Their* bodies respond to volition. Do you know what this means, Sergeant?"

"Means we lost," Storch said. He wanted to vomit, wanted to spend his last few bullets on himself for letting this happen *again*, for letting everyone who trusted him die AGAIN. For failing to kill them AGAIN. He wanted to rail at them until they killed him, and the worthless scientist who'd brought them here. But Wittrock sprinted past him, and he thought, if that little shit's gonna get away, there's no reason for me to die here.

He backed out of the room, but he might have already left for all the attention they paid him. Then he looked at Tarnell again, still alive, but only to pain. Storch shot him in the head. Holroyd went on eating, oblivious. *At last, a confirmed kill on this shitty mission.* He turned and started down the hall at a dead run, but froze as Dyson called after him.

"See you at the movies, little Sergeant."

Oh fuck.

He ran as fast as he could, overtook Wittrock at the foot of the staircase.

"Wittrock, they know where your base is."

"No matter," he answered. "Everyone should already be evacuated. We'll proceed with the evasion protocol Bangs briefed you on."

Storch only stared blankly. If he'd been a healthier, better-humored man, he might've laughed in Wittrock's face.

"You are familiar with the evasion protocols, aren't you?" The convex lens of his facemask made Wittrock's eyes look like fried eggs.

"You better hope the pilot is."

"Yes, um, well, I notified him, and he'll be picking us up in a minute." Wittrock looked down at his computer. For him, Storch thought with a fresh thrill of disgust, this was probably at least a partial victory. "Sergeant, I realize it may be a little late for this, but I want you to know that I no longer have any substantive doubts about your loyalty."

Storch hit him as hard as he could with his casted arm. He cried out at the pain of grating bones, but Wittrock's head pinged off the walls of his helmet and he dropped like a poleaxed ostrich. Storch scooped him and the laptop up and ascended to the roof to wait for the Black Hawk.

~ 33 ~

On days like this, it didn't bother Mort Greenaway that he would never rise above the rank of Lieutenant Colonel. Let the perfumed princes have their plush bunkers and their armored limousines and the ears of politicians. Greenaway had been promoted high enough above his God-given vocation, and it was a rare enough occasion, like tonight, that he could return to it.

Tonight, Greenaway could hunt.

The call reached him just after sunset, trickling though layers of filtration, through handlers and operators, so he'd cut through them all to get the truth himself: a Highway Patrolman on the 190 had overheard CB chatter about a pair of black helicopters traveling north, going hell-for-leather through the mountains like a war sortie, less than a hundred feet above the road. They had passed out of the Argus Mountains about a half-hour ago. Greenaway bit his tongue through thinking of the wasted opportunity, the lost time. By now they were over Visalia, headed for the Bay Area, or backing off their northbound feint over Death Valley Junction on the way to Vegas, or dropping bombs on Bakersfield. Greenaway had noted the point on a map and alerted all the search choppers with ordnance onboard to move into an intercept course, but he'd started to look south on the map, and he'd smiled at what he saw.

Most of the likely targets were already under discreet guard; FBI spotters overlooked all the major thoroughfares of every major city in southern and central California, as well as Las Vegas. The federal centers in most cities even had camouflaged SAM batteries, on the closed rooftops of nearby parking structures, or atop the buildings themselves.

Heightened security was enacted at potential targets throughout the country, on the remotest chance that the terrorists had slipped the Navy's dragnet and yet not fled the country. National Guard units were on alert from here to San Francisco, and every law enforcement aircraft in the state was aloft and looking. Looking for two stealth-equipped choppers with softkill weaponry, at night in the largest mountain chain west of the Rockies. There were little or no new developments, and the fed funnel through which all his intel spewed ran so slow and so ineptly he began to wonder whose side they were on. Shit, it wouldn't be the first time.

They play their games. I play mine.

He radioed the crewman to get him a secured phone line and called the National Weather Service. It was a matter of minutes before he had a technician capable of accessing the most immediate satellite imagery of California, and another few minutes before he could impress upon him the importance of his task.

"You can see brush fires with those things?"

"Of course, we can shoot thermographic gradient images, but the interpretation people have all gone home for the day."

"Do *you* know what fire looks like? Digitally, don't bother printing anything."

"Yes, but—"

"There's a really big fire somewhere in California, or there's going to be, very shortly. I want your satellite to keep shooting and I want you to look at every image and call me at the number my lieutenant is going to give you the instant you see an image."

"Is this an official request, sir? because I'm going to have to get at least a verbal authorization from—ah, Jeez, I don't even know where to begin."

"This is a military state of emergency, son. Do you know what that means?"

Silence: paper shuffling and flop-sweat dripping.

"It means I'm sending someone to help you unfuck yourself and do what I've asked, and maybe execute you as a traitor by negligence, in the bargain. Do you follow me?"

"Nobody—nobody has to come here—"

And within minutes, Lt. Col. Greenaway was looking at richly detailed thermographic images of the whole lower half of California and the western wastelands of Nevada. Blowing them up and strolling up and down them was a maddeningly slow and aggravating process, as the modem speed fluttered and intermittently froze. But he learned much. The whole eastern portion of the state was only now throwing off a blanket of rain clouds that'd provided excellent cover for the assault. He'd thought of it himself only this morning, but rationally, what did it come to? He hadn't actually expected anything to come of the napalm theft, had honestly believed that if they were still in the country, they were lying low, and ruing the day they'd provoked the US military into the kind of war it fought best: a secret one. Now they were loose on the land, and he could only hope to find them by the destruction they'd wreak.

Five pointless minutes later, cruising over Bishop, he'd gotten a call from someone he'd hoped not to have to deal with: Special Agent Cundieffe, calling from his HQ back at China Lake. He'd shown either rare ingenuity or astonishing dumb luck in getting back from where he'd been dumped only a little over an hour ago. Greenaway reluctantly admitted the little ratfucker was loaded with both.

"Colonel, you have been less than cooperative in the course of this investigation."

"You've been less than baggage, Cundieffe."

"I expect it was under such an opinion that your goon squad left us in Titus Canyon a little while ago. Your conduct has been criminal if they were under your orders, and incompetent if it was not. All of this is being recorded and transmitted to my superior's offices in Washington, by the by."

"Then I have nothing to say."

"I do. I thought you'd like to know where they are."

A scheme to throw him off. *Over my dead body will this ever be a criminal investigation.* Best to play along. It would be too late to keep this from becoming a media event or push the Pentagon's buttons, but he could still insure there would be no embarrassing jailcell interviews. "Where are they?"

"Near Convict Lake, south of Big Pine. Local volunteer fire department responded to a cell phone call from a passing motorist who said he saw a fireball one mile east of the 395, about sixty miles north of my present position. I've only just gotten off the phone with the chief. Nice man, he's not afraid to admit it's way out of his league. It's a full napalm strike, Colonel."

This time, his interest wasn't feigned. "On what? What the hell's out there?"

"Only a hospice community for terminal cancer patients. The chief says two helicopters cremated it. I can't get there, but maybe you or some of your thugs could take the initiative and force them to land."

Force them to land. All the while looking at the map, their present location lay over Devil's Postpile National Monument, ruling out a remote speculation by some genius at Naval Intelligence that the choppers were radical environmentalists bound for the logging operations bordering Yosemite. Convict Lake was less than fifty miles south of here. He hung up on Cundieffe and told the pilot to turn around and proceed to Convict Lake, and relay the order to all other armed aircraft.

A minute later, the tech from the National Weather Service called back, excited and out of breath. Greenaway had his lieutenant answer the phone as the head night orderly at the Mendocino County Mental Institution, and apologize for the harassment.

They reached the northern tip of the Owens River valley in ten minutes. After they passed over the smallish city of Bishop, the pilot didn't need to navigate by radar. The fire stood out on the lip of the barren valley wall fifteen miles away, the monstrous column of black smoke like a divine arrow pointing at the biggest, strangest terrorist operation in American history.

The pilot called back, "I don't see anything in the air, and I'm looking down to the ground. I think the bastards scrambled."

"Maybe, maybe not," Greenaway answered, already drawing up a containment maneuver around the valley on his map. "They're stealthed up the ass. How long 'til the first reinforcements arrive?"

"Nearest one is five minutes off, at landmark Olancha."

Greenaway handed the map to his LT, who started calling the support choppers. "Go weapons hot and approach. Watch your thermals, if you see them at all, it'll be by heat."

The fire grew on the horizon, and Greenaway held his breath in awed appreciation of the destruction unfolding before him. They had certainly gotten their money's worth out of every ounce of napalm. Radiant Dawn had been a village of forty or so single-story tract homes and an incongruously large four-story tower nestled in a one hundred-square-acre circular valley at the foot of the Sierra Nevadas. Now it was a cauldron of fire; only the skeleton of the tower reached out of the flames, a ruined castle in hell, still collapsing upon itself from a recent missile strike. There was a skirt of flashing red lights atop a ridge overlooking the crater from the east, but they only provided scale for the vast field of fire. There was no hope of containing this, no looking for survivors. Lt. Col. Greenaway got a chill. With Operation White Star in Cambodia, he'd seen more than his share of carpet-bombing: villages reduced to ash and slag, children running torches lighting the hidden Cong trails for machine-gunners to mop up the survivors. But he'd never seen any place so thoroughly *destroyed*. Cancer patients. What the hell did it mean? Either it was some kind of fanaticism, a grotesque mistake, or Radiant Dawn was something more.

Radiant Dawn. RADIANT. Fucking DI Spooks.

The helicopter nosed up and just as abruptly plunged, like a boat slamming into breakers. Even a mile away, the thermals rising up from the fire played hell with the pilot's best efforts to keep them level. They circled around Radiant Dawn along the high ground on the western side, staring into the fire and smoke until their eyes bled tears, but afraid to blink.

"Holy shit, sir, I have one chopper at nine o'clock, heading away at speed!"

"Pursue!" Greenaway barked, and only then looked out the window. Nine o'clock was a curtain of smoke over the center of the crater, and Greenaway grabbed the nightgoggles off the doorman's head and slipped them on, cranking up the infrared reception and narrowing the focus to screen out the blinding napalm glow.

There. It was like seeing the Invisible Man revealed by a splash of paint. Only the reflected heat of the fire gave it away. A streamlined blob of heat dwindled in his sights even as he focused on it, heading southeast on an intercept course with the river. A single Black Hawk with stripped bomb racks, passing even now over the emergency vehicles on the ridge. Only one. Was the other one down there, somewhere, or was it somewhere else in the state, hitting the real target? Were these people sick enough to do something like this as a diversion?

The pilot took them up two hundred feet and raced around the southern edge of Radiant Dawn. "We can overtake them just past Owens River, sir," the pilot said. "We can stay on them until support arrives, then force them down."

"No. They're armed with unconventional weaponry. They're capable of disabling troops at range, and there's only one accounted for. Another one's out there. We'll force *this one* down." He moved into the flight deck, crowded into the narrow space between the co-pilot and the comm officer, so his breath fell on the back of the pilot's neck, and his alpha male pheromones would make it viscerally clear that his authority went way deeper than Army rank. "Knock them out of the sky, Captain. Now."

The pilot started to look around for support, but he couldn't see around Greenaway. He shrugged, flipped up the safety guard on the firing system and vocally prepped it, "Fox One to Target One, locking…" He pressed a button with one thumb, held it for a second, and a nova burst into furious, screaming life under their left wing. "And away," he finished lamely. "That was a *direct* order, right, sir?"

Greenaway didn't answer. They were passing over the emergency scrimmage line themselves, now, and time slowed to a crawl and space scaled down to the tube between the missile and its target, the burn of its thruster a thermal period to the runaway sentence of the helicopter.

Then the missile fell out of the sky. A blip of flame registered on the ground, and swiftly passed under them. "What the fuck was that?" Greenaway demanded. His head flicked around the flight deck, the co-pilot and comm officer staring at him with hands upraised in surrender.

"It went dead-stick just short of the target. They've got a jamming countermeasure—"

"Bring us in Vulcan range, and shoot their rotors off," Greenaway ordered. His hands balled up into fists, and he knew in a moment they would start shaking. These motherfuckers were like black magicians. They made warfighting into a fucking parlor game with their tricks.

"Sir, we're being hailed," the comm officer said in a passionately scared tone.

"Let's hear it," Greenaway answered. Maybe they'd explain themselves before he shot them down.

A thin, but totally unshakable voice cut in. "Pursuing helicopter, wish to advise we are not armed, and have no hostile intent. You must land immediately and power down—"

Greenaway shouted, "Set down or be shot down, goddamit. I've had enough of this shit!"

"—Unless you are insulated against EMP radiation bursts in excess of—" the rest was washed away in static.

"What is he talking about?" Greenaway blustered. Then it hit him. The bastards could zap them and knock out every onboard circuit. They'd be dead in the air, a stone. "Shoot them down now!"

"We apologize. This is necessary."

The lieutenant saw it first. He was looking northwest at the crater, keeping an eye out for the unaccounted-for Hind, and he screamed that he was blind. Greenaway took off his goggles before he turned around, but even so, he would see the violet ghost image of the sight on the back wall of his eyeballs for days afterwards.

A sphere of white light rose up out of Radiant Dawn valley, filling it with a miniature sun that made the previous conflagration look like a brushfire. Greenaway watched, stunned as it fell in on itself and rose again into a columnar, roiling mushroom cloud.

He was still watching it when he realized everybody else on the chopper was screaming, and all the lights were out.

The flight deck erupted into a fireworks show. The crew struggled get out of their harnesses, their flight suits burning. The helicopter dipp again, and the forward wall became the floor, the lieutenant flew p st Greenaway and smashed into the windscreen, and the other four soldiers rained down on him in a dogpile. The doorman undid his tether and leapt out the open door into the night. Greenaway tried to untangle himself from his men when the chopper slammed into the ground, no, into the river, and green water rushed into the cabin, lifted his men off him and flooded the flight deck. As the waters closed over his head, Greenaway could see only the phosphene echo of the mushroom cloud against the blackness. He reached out, kicking off the flight deck's firewall and fumbling for the rungs that framed the loading door, fighting against the current flooding the chopper until he felt it fall away behind him, and only the sluggish tug of the river's current dragged at his sodden fatigues. Kick, claw, hold your breath a second more, you're almost to the surface, or the bottom, almost…

Floundering onto the muddy shore, Greenaway found only three of his men waiting for him. They raised a ragged cheer as he staggered across the mud flats and snapped them a salute. They looked like death, one of them only semi-conscious, with skull fragments sticking out of his hair. None of them had salvaged a rifle, they had only his sidearm between them. The tail of the chopper stood at a forty-five degree angle to the lazy river. No one else was coming out of it.

The fuckers nuked us. There was no sane explanation for it, no angle that made it any less nightmarish than the stark reality. He now had to admit to himself that he never knew what the fuck was happening here, and now probably never would. *Goddamned electromagnetic pulse knocked us out of the air. Fucking budget cuts, fucking uninsulated circuits in a fucking old, cheap chopper killed my men and cost us a war.*

"I don't suppose anybody has a radio that works?" Greenaway said.

One of the soldiers took out his belt kit and opened a Zip-Loc bag with a PRC emergency beacon in it. "This ought to work, sir," he mumbled, "but what're you going to tell them? Those fuckers are gone."

Greenaway's smile reassured the shivering soldier. "I know where they're going."

~ 34 ~

Stella knew when Delores Mrachek apologized to her for the way she'd been treated this last week that they weren't going to be leaving with the others. She watched as the last load of medical specimens was shuttled out of sickbay and down to the motorpool, and she'd looked at Mrachek to find her looking uncomfortable, so Stella knew she needed a favor. It was something she couldn't just make her do, which made her wonder. What was so damned important that it couldn't wait, when everyone else had taken off in separate cars exactly sixty minutes after the helicopters left?

"What do you want me to do?" Stella asked.

Mrachek blinked, but said impassively, "I'd appreciate your help moving a very sick man."

Stella thought of Napier and grimaced, but he was dead, wasn't he? She'd seen nobody else that merited special attention. She shrugged and followed Mrachek down the hall, back into the empty warren of tunnels to a vault door which Mrachek had to enter a code to open. Hot, ionized air blasted her, and she thought of a walk-in microwave, but Mrachek walked into it, merging into red shadows and looking back at her as if to make her feel foolish. It worked, and she walked into the room.

Until recently, this must have been the hub of the Mission's operations, but now it was deserted, but for one technician in a white paper cleansuit, seated at a computer terminal. Stella looked around at the walls of the octagonal room, at the walls that were skyscrapers of computer chips, from the spotless bare concrete floor to the ceiling, lost in the dark above the red bulbs. She wondered that anyone would want to work in darkroom light, then supposed that geeks liked to feel that their work was dangerous and important.

She was beginning to feel like ants were crawling all over her. Mrachek stood by the lone computer technician, patiently waiting to get his attention. Stella walked up on her faster than she'd intended, came dangerously close once again to violating the no-touching rule. "He looks like he got better. Why don't we go? The light is giving me a headache."

"White light makes his corneas bleed," the technician said in a thick Hindi accent. "He will be ready in a moment, if you will please wait here."

"Dr. Armitage is a great man," Mrachek said. "A giant in the field of applied physics, he has suffered grievous neurological damage, and requires special handling."

"Then why wasn't he moved first?"

"He wouldn't go until the birds were in the air," Mrachek said, "and there's lots of computer records to be dumped, or changed, in places that're hard to get at. I need your help."

"She doesn't trust me to do it," the tech said.

"Shut up, Vijay. Go up topside and get the van ready."

"Madame Dr. Mrachek, I designed the final release version of the guidance system software of the Phobos antisatellite system before my twenty-fourth birthday, and I am now thirty-eight. I am not a soldier, and I am no one's porter."

"Do you see anyone else here? Just get the godblessed van, already."

Vijay stood and turned on Dr. Mrachek. He yanked off his surgical mask and polished his thick glasses with it. His dark face was traced with worry lines, and his bushy eyebrows were shot through with gray. He smirked in anticipation of something to be savored before he said it, but a frail voice from an intercom at his workstation cut him short.

"Vijay, I'm just about finished in here. Is my ride here, yet?"

"Make yourself decent, Cornelius," Mrachek said. "We don't have time to mess around."

Vijay entered a code at his workstation and a false wall opened up on a tunnel, and he waved them in. It was even darker in here, and she stumbled into the doctor when she stopped just short of a dull green glow around a corner. "He is still a very brilliant man, in full possession of his faculties. What you see is not who he is."

"I'm a nurse," Stella said. "I won't make fun of your boyfriend."

Mrachek went around the corner and Stella followed her. The man on the bed wasn't the worst-off specimen of humanity she'd ever seen, but he could've given Seth Napier a run for his money in the swimsuit competition. His skin was so mottled Stella couldn't tell if he was black or white, he twitched so badly she couldn't see his face at all, and patches on his skull and neck were so silvery-shiny she could almost see her own reflection in them. He wore only a robe, but looked as if he were wearing wrinkled leopard-print pajamas underneath. This, she realized with chagrin as Mrachek laid open the robe to take his pulse, was his bare skin. A splatter of melanomas covered him from shoulders to belly. His hands roamed the bedsheets like starving rodents and, upon discovering each other in his lap, seemed to devour each other. Mrachek shot her a silencing glance, then returned to Armitage, whispering in his ear.

Stella busied herself looking elsewhere, at the sick man's computer terminal, at the pharmacopoeia neatly arranged in a wheeled caddy beside the bed, at the stained blueprints on the walls. She recognized them immediately, though she'd never seen it from the air. Radiant Dawn. They'd held out the promise of surviving her cancer, and she'd turned her back on them in rashness, joined the people who were going to exterminate them. Had Dr. Keogh seemed so insane, or so sick, as this? *I belong here*, she thought. *With these sick, cast-off killers.*

Mrachek showed Stella how to inject Armitage in the tender part of his scaly, shivering spine, just below his occipital ridges, while she monitored his heart rate. They had to do it seven times, as his dosage fluctuated wildly, and, she explained, his excitability made him resistant. Stella didn't ask what was wrong with him besides the obvious, or what the drugs were supposed to do.

"Dr. Mrachek tells me you're interested in our pilot study," Armitage said. Stella drove home the last needle and injected him with something that looked like antifreeze.

"I have six months to live, is what they told me in Bishop."

"Stick by Delores. She's an unlovable sociopath with an unhealthy codependency fixation on yours truly, but if anyone can find a cure, it'll be her."

The intercom on Armitage's workstation bleeped a long string of meaningful-sounding bleeps. Mrachek entered a code into the computer, and a command window came up with "Descrambling" in it, and an avalanche of digits. The bleeps abruptly transformed into the unflappable voice of Dr. Wittrock.

"You're supposed to be gone," Wittrock said.

"But we're here," Armitage snapped back. What news?"

"There were setbacks. The previous Mission parameters will have to be adjusted, in light of the new developments."

"Such as?" Armitage started shaking worse, Mrachek's restraining hands on his shoulders, he was trying to get up, but his feet seemed content to dance around each other and ignore him.

"The Radiant Dawn compound was destroyed, with a probable one hundred percent casualty rate. Unfortunately, RADIANT was not approachable from the site, and is still up. I have vital telemetry data that will allow us to fix its position at a later date, after regrouping with Aranda's cell. We have no confirmation on Keitel's death, for reasons I'll have to explain at length later. We're proceeding with our original evasion plan, but that's going to present a few snags as well."

"Quit talking in circles, dammit! What's the problem?"

"There's only four of us left, including the pilots. And I exercised my option to activate the package."

"Jesus, what didn't you bungle?"

"They know where the base is. Sergeant Storch seems convinced there'll be a retaliatory strike within the next hour. He thinks they'll try to use RADIANT on you."

"We won't be here," Mrachek said curtly. "Lie down, Cornelius." She pressed down on his shoulders and arranged him on his bed, drawing the sheets up to his neck and reaching around the bed and bringing up straps to hold him in place at his chest, waist and knees. Then she raised the bed up to its full height, and wheeled it towards the door.

Vijay stood in her way. His paper suit was torn in several places, revealing maroon chinos, a plaid shirt, and nasty but shallow abrasions on his knees and elbows. "We have nowhere to go," he said. "I went outside, and imagine my surprise to find we are surrounded by military and civilian federal law enforcement authorities? They did not seem concerned for my continued wellbeing, but I convinced them to refrain from attacking for the present."

"How'd you do that?" Stella asked.

Vijay smiled apologetically. "I told them we have a hostage."

Storch lay on his side on the empty bench of the helicopter's troop compartment. They were well away from Radiant Dawn, but he found he preferred to keep the gas mask on. Everything smelled burnt. He barely noticed the pilot's terse dialogue with the pursuing chopper, and merely nodded absently at the detonation of the tactical nuke onboard the ruined Hind. Well, there's the end of it, he thought. Tough Spike Team Texas might've been, but the big A was something else again. Wasn't it? He couldn't make himself believe it. They'd be back, only now they'd glow.

They moved a lot faster with no napalm or soldiers onboard. Wittrock sat up front with the crew, occasionally looking over his shoulder at Storch. *He didn't even breathe hard at Radiant Dawn, but he's scared shitless of me.*

As near as Storch could tell, their plan was to land at a small general aviation airport just over the Nevada border. There, they'd destroy the chopper and split up (ha!) in small cars and head separately for the border. There was a rendezvous point somewhere in Central Mexico, but Storch didn't give a shit. There was nowhere to go that would make him forget. But he'd done it before, blocked out the part of the incident in Iraq that defied all reason, even as it explained his condition. His body wasn't sick—it was trying too hard to be healthy, trying to adapt to environmental stressors without the full arsenal of genetic tools for true evolution. All these years, his body had been trying to be like Brutus Dyson's. How would he live with that? It was an island of comfort, the idea that he could fall asleep and awaken with no memory of the last twelve hours. When his hair started to fall out from radiation poisoning, or he had flashbacks of burning children and men eating men whole, he could tell himself it was the Gulf War Syndrome again. That wouldn't be so bad.

Wittrock was shouting into the radio, his thin voice cutting through the droning harmonics of the helicopter to drive Storch out of his approaching sleep. He thought about beating the physicist up again, but his body wasn't up to the task; he barely wrangled his legs into a sort of locomotion, loping up to the flight deck on the bobbing, terrain-hugging motion of the chopper.

"Why didn't you get out when you had the chance, goddammit? This is exactly the scenario we least wanted to even consider!"

"What's wrong?" Storch asked, thinking it would be about the airport, or the Mexican rendezvous point.

Wittrock flinched and looked at Storch, still wearing his body armor and gashelmet and holding his MP5 out from his side and pointed at the windshield. "Some of our personnel are still in the base. They're surrounded by Navy and FBI tactical forces."

"So we're going to have to get them out?"

"I'm afraid it's impossible," Wittrock said, and thumbed the microphone's send button. "Cornelius, we never seriously anticipated this happening, but we did plan for it."

Armitage's deathly rasp cut him off. "I'm well aware of that, Witt. I'm in good hands. You don't have to worry about me."

"Godspeed, Witt." Storch recognized the deep feminine voice of the dykey doctor. "Vijay and I will see to it. The charges are already set, and we'll administer the final evasion kits ourselves, then take care of each other."

"What?" Storch said.

"We can't take the chance of their being caught," Wittrock calmly explained. "None of us is legally alive in the United States, so at the level we'd be held and questioned, torture is a very real possibility, and we still have so much to lose. Other units, other projects, and then there's the possibility that Radiant Dawn operated under government sanction. Cornelius could never bring himself to seriously consider it. He could still feel loyal to a stupid government, but not an evil one." Wittrock bowed his head in the most profound display of emotion Storch had ever seen from him. Here, at last, was someone for whom he would cry, someday. Maybe it was only because of the strategic setback to the Mission, but it would bring him pain. Good. "Do what you have to do, and good luck to you. It's been an honor to serve with you."

Another voice broke in over whatever final farewell Mrachek was about to deliver, and Storch blinked and bit his lip as he heard it. "You want me to kill myself? Fuck you, you crazy bitch! You're gonna have to kill me!"

It was the nurse. *Stella...*

Storch kicked Wittrock in the back and stepped over him, nocked the barrel of the MP5 in the pilot's neck. "Turn back south, buddy. That lady doesn't want to die with your people."

Wittrock took the co-pilot's sidearm and pressed it against Storch's helmet, then, reconsidering, looked for a soft spot in the armor on his back. He gave Storch more than enough time to elbow him in the throat and knock him back into the troop cabin, where he spilled onto his back and lay still, trying to focus on getting a whole breath of air in.

The pilot looked Storch over and made the course correction. "It's suicide for all of us," he said. "They're probably already dead."

"I hope not, buddy, and so do you. Just get on the phone and tell them we're coming."

"It's not that simple," the co-pilot put in desperately. "There's set scrambler channels, but the feds probably have them monitored by now. They'll know we're coming. We're still twenty minutes out."

"How'd you do that magic trick at China Lake? Just do that again."

"We're not rigged with the infrasonic generator. It's on its way to Mexico right now. We had to make weight to carry the troops."

"Then we'll all have to think of something, real quick. You got them on the horn, yet?"

The pilot handed Storch the mic. He thumbed the button. "You still there, Stella?"

Armitage coughed. "They're gone. Who is this?"

Storch swallowed hard. "Sergeant Storch, Doctor. Had a crazy idea we could try to get you out, but—"

"Nothing doing, Sergeant. Mrachek's off chasing that damned Orozco woman, but when she comes back, we're all going to our greater rewards, right, Vijay?"

"Sir, I must urge you to take the pill."

"No, none of that, can't swallow it, anyway. Gimme your gun."

"Then—she's still alive?"

"Who? Delores? Far as I know. That nurse she brought in is leading her a merry chase, but there's no way out of here. Nobody can be taken alive, Sergeant. It's the nature of the Mission. Everyone who takes up the cause understands that. No, Vijay, get your hands off it, I can do this, would you kindly let me for Chrissakes do this one last thing with my own goddamned hands."

"Sir, I'm only worried that you might—"

BANG

He waited a moment, but heard nothing. The line might've gone dead, but for a faint beeping that might've been a smoke alarm. "Guess he did it right," Storch said, and let the connection go dead.

The pilot seemed to float up in his seat with relief. "So we can return to course, now, right?"

"Did I say that? Stay southbound and step on it, or I'll take my chances your friend here can fly the fucking chopper."

It felt good to have somewhere to go, and someone to go to. He only hoped he wasn't too late.

~ 35 ~

"It doesn't have to end like this," Mrachek called out as she stalked the corridors of the Mission's abandoned base. Her echoes ran amok through the honeycomb of bare concrete chambers, but even when she stopped and tuned into the silence, she couldn't pick out the sounds of her quarry over the ambient dripping and crumbling of the structure. The runaway nurse wouldn't be found easily, but Mrachek thought she could count on her seeming inability to leave an argument unanswered. "There's no other alternative, Stella. The base is rigged with plastique in all the load-bearing struts. It's going to implode. And there's no way out. Even if you get outside, what then? The feds will shoot you, or if they take you alive, you'll spend the rest of your short life in federal custody, trying to clear your name. You'll die in jail, or in a safehouse, which amounts to the same thing, eaten up by your cancer. This way, at least, it'll be quick and peaceful, and no one'll ever associate you with this place, or what we've done. Stella?"

It was indeed hard not to rise to the bait. Stella watched the stocky doctor pass by her hiding place twice, belting out her twisted case for euthanasia with her queer little dartgun extended out in front of her in the strangest gesture of peace she'd ever seen. In the end, it was not self-control, but futility, that held Stella's tongue. She was right. Stella'd run and run around the base, easily outpacing Mrachek, but quickly becoming lost. She'd found the big corrugated steel doors opening on the motor pool, but they were locked and spot-welded shut.

Fumbling around them, looking over her shoulder at each of the four corridors that fed into this antechamber, she'd thought she was saved when she heard whispered voices on the other side. Risking all, she'd screamed, "I'm a hostage! Get me out of here, they're trying to kill me!" Whoever was on the other side probably couldn't make out her words, or just didn't care, because they'd strafed the doors, punching a zigzagging line of holes across both doors. Stella ducked behind a concrete pillar and clamped her hands over her ears. Then they'd started in with a battering ram; the doors rippled with each deafening crash, but refused to buckle. They'd have to blow their way in, and friendly or not, they'd probably kill her in the process, so she'd started running again, with Mrachek's voice before and behind her, growing louder on all sides as the doctor's patience began to falter.

Fearing she'd come around a corner and catch up to Mrachek from behind, she'd followed the stairways down and away from the motor pool, and backed into a shadowy stairway leading into a mold-stinking cellar, and sat down on the top step and tried not to cry.

It was hard enough just catching her breath from one to the next. She thought of all the mass-suicides which had dotted the last twenty years. She'd never understood the hysterical sense of tragedy the media and general public attached to such events, as she'd always assumed the people involved had wanted to die. If they were so weak or deluded, so be it, the world was better off without them. Now she understood that such a rash decision was never a unanimous one, and she found a new kind of fear she'd never imagined possible, for how could one defend oneself against those who had already decided to die, and wanted only to take her with them? If she wanted to get out of this, being quicker or craftier would amount to nothing. She would have to kill. It was a far cry from simply wanting to survive, but she found she'd be willing to kill someone far dearer to her heart than Delores Mrachek to get out of this. To live and die in federal custody, eaten by cancer, would be heaven compared to dying like this, for a fanatic's vision she couldn't even say she understood. *The soldier wouldn't let them do this,* she thought. Zane Ezekiel Storch, that was his name. He would get out of this hole, and go through anybody who deigned to stand in his way, even if there was no *out* to get to. Maybe if she got out, she could see him again.

Get it together, you're not getting any closer to the exit. Think. She closed her eyes and tried to visualize the base and thread a path from her current bolthole to the motor pool. It was two levels above her, but Mrachek would hear her long before she got to them, if she wasn't camping out there now. Vijay was out there too, but she doubted he'd leave Armitage. A fanatic's fanatic, Vijay was probably dead beside his leader with a smile on his face.

"It has to be this way, Stella." Mrachek's voice, distorted and faint, snaked through the base to her ears: "None of us wanted it to end like this, but being taken by the feds is not an option." The voice was far off, yet near; Stella looked around, darting her head into the corridor and jumping back before she realized she'd seen nothing. No. Looking again, she saw where the voice was coming from.

A grated ventilation shaft in the wall, just above eye level. Regularly spaced holes in the concrete beneath it hinted at iron rungs ripped out of the wall, but she took heart at the sight of them. The shafts were intended for men to travel them, probably to access the lower levels once they were jam-packed with the barrels of toxic waste that were supposed to be here. She rushed to the shaft and hauled herself up onto the narrow lip below the grate, and yanked with all her weight. The latch groaned, but didn't give; globs of unrusted metal covered it, someone had welded it shut, but the hinges themselves were still rusted. *Come on*, she hissed to herself, ignoring the squeal and scrape of the protesting grate that must be reverberating throughout the base. She braced her legs against the wall to either side of the grate and leaned back, pumping rhythmically until the hinges gave way all at once and she was falling backwards into space, the grate a lodestone on her chest that smashed her flat when she hit the floor. Her back wrenched and all the air whooshed out of her lungs; her hands, still entangled in the grate, wouldn't come free in time to soften the blow. She gasped and rolled the heavy grate off her chest, sobbing with pain. Mrachek would hear this, and come running. She had to get up and move. Without breath, without energy, without anywhere to go, she had to get up and move.

It was far harder to climb up to the ventilation shaft the second time. Her lungs were raw and her ribs badly bruised, and her fingers refused to completely unclench from the claws she'd made of them to get the grate off. Her scrubs were drenched in sweat, the oversized boots chafing her feet, which slipped around inside them when she tried to get traction to lever her body up into the hole. When she finally flopped onto her side in the shaft, she'd heard Mrachek's heavy footsteps thudding down the corridor below her, and knew this time she couldn't hide. Fighting panic, she reached up the crumbling wall, praying that whoever ripped out the rungs in the corridor hadn't stripped the whole shaft. Her knuckles grazed one, and flakes of rust rained down into her eyes and mouth. She pulled on it, felt it wobble in her grip, but its anchorage held—just barely.

"There's something else, Stella," Mrachek's voice found her, she was at the mouth, not ten feet below her, and out of sight only by the elbow of the shaft. "Wittrock couldn't knock down their satellite. That's how they did it, you know. He says it's still active, and they know where we are. Keogh's going to retaliate any minute now. There's no hiding from it, Stella. It's like an X-ray, but it penetrates a good hundred feet below the surface. No bunkers can protect you from it, Stella. We'd all die horribly, but you—you'd *change*, Stella. Is that what you want? To be like Mr. Napier, a thing made of cancer?"

Stella had fought her way up to the midpoint of the shaft, and dangled over open space with both arms locked at the elbows around a loose rung. She watched the badly eroded mortar sifting out of the crack around the block that held the rung in place, like an hourglass measuring out the span of the rest of her life. "I want to live," she growled. "Let me go, please—"

"You want to be one of them? I'm afraid I can't let that happen, Stella. Let it go, it's not worth all this."

From the resigned, pleading tone of her voice, Stella guessed Mrachek was giving up, or maybe she just couldn't get her chunky ass up the shaft. This thought helped her find a last pocket of adrenaline and injected it into her sputtering system. She found the strength to drag herself up to the next rung, and the next.

Blinding white light filled the tunnel from below. Mrachek shining a flashlight up the shaft with one hand, aiming the dartgun with the other. "You brought this on yourself," Mrachek said, and fired twice. The gun gave two sharp, short whistles as it let fly.

Stella kicked out with both feet, half a reflexive defense, and half slipping out of pure panic, as her animal midbrain told her the only way to dodge the darts was to drop off the ladder, even though falling down the shaft, Mrachek or no Mrachek, would break both her legs. She felt something strike her left heel, and something else hit her right toe. Her feet flailed at the ladder, kicking the loose rung again and again, but refusing to grab hold of it. She felt the rung give way under her left foot and the whole concrete block in which it was moored came crumbling out of the wall and toppled down, down, and there was a scream and a resonant crunch, and Mrachek's light went out.

She clung to the next to last rung until she could breathe regularly again, and her eyes stopped tearing up. She'd earned the right to live, now. She had to get out, now it'd been paid for.

When she felt able to move, she climbed the next rung and pressed her hand against the ceiling. *Let this be easy, I've earned that much, haven't I?*

Evidently not, because it was as hard as everything else. She managed to get one shoulder against the shaft's cap, which was a trapdoor. After much griping, it gave a little, and oily clumps of sand spilled through the crack and into her face. Sand. She was on the surface. With renewed vigor, she threw herself at the trapdoor, but no matter how much she beat herself up on it, she couldn't get it more than nine inches wide. It banged against something directly overhead; by jamming her head into the gap, Stella could see she was under a parked car. Rays of starlight sprinkled through the yawning cavity of the car's engine compartment. Starlight. Night sky. Freedom.

She knew she was meant to live through this, everything had brought her to this place. She knew now why she'd been born small, as she wriggled through the gap and lay in a crusted pool of motor oil under the gutted '72 Duster, and examined her boots. One dart was broken off in the rubber heel of the left boot, another still protruded through the toe of her right, having missed her diminutive foot by a scant inch. There was a reason for everything. She was destined to live, and to learn something from this.

She was in a junkyard. The ground lay in low ridges, like the staggered ground of a drive-in, littered with piles of stripped car skeletons. A corrugated metal movie screen loomed at the far end of the junkyard, its whitewashed face awash in strobing red and blue lights from the mass of vehicles outside. She heard helicopters circling overhead, and saw the probing beams of searchlights. Peering out through the hood of the Duster, she saw military choppers, not newscrews, with snipers hanging out of the doors, watching the ground through comically oversized starlight scopes. This was not a criminal situation like any she'd seen on TV. There were no TV helicopters in the sky, and no police shouting for a peaceful outcome over bullhorns. This was the Army, or the Navy, or whoever, but they weren't fucking around. Surrendering to them might not be possible.

What about the other thing?

Had Mrachek been making it up to break her down? The satellite—

The Moon-Ladder

You'd change—

Was it better to die than change? What she'd seen had been horrific, but it was new and strange, not inherently evil. Napier's transformation had been an aberration, he was infected by Stephen's tissue, it wouldn't be the same for her. She would live through this, and through the cancer, too, and whatever else was different, she could learn to accept, just as she'd come to accept her own mortality when it'd seemed there was no way out.

Yes, she'd stay right here, and pray that it would come before the feds found her. It was what was meant to be.

The Black Hawk cleared a ridge and swept down into the hollow over the highway like a bird made of smoke, only to find the road was clogged with troop carriers, the sky alive with helicopters. The junkyard was aglow with searchlights, like a lighted beacon on the black face of the desert, and like a moth, they headed for it.

Storch hadn't moved since he'd settled in behind the pilot, except to stare down Wittrock every so often. Though there were still plenty of weapons still stowed in the racks on the walls of the cabin, Wittrock only sat on the deck with his arms wrapped defensively around his legs, frowning peevishly but daring to do or say nothing that would provoke another beating.

"What can we do?" Storch asked.

"I've got a wideband jam going. Their comm channels, their phones, headsets, they're all deaf, but all we've got left is the Vulcans."

"Jesus, I've got missile locks incoming."

"Jamming countermeasures online, but we're within shooting range, we'll get cut down."

"Get us to the yard and put down for two seconds, I don't give a damn what you do after that," Storch told the pilot, and backed out of the flight deck. "I can still see you," he added.

He went to the loading door and hung out of it long enough to see the yard rushing up on the horizon, and the convention of APCs and government-issue sedans all around it, and the pair of Apache assault helicopters in position directly above it, and the older choppers with snipers and machine gun pods swiveling to take them in, and the blooms of disabled missiles detonating impotently on the ground. One erupted in the midst of the troops, who were already scrambling like disturbed ants without any network of command buzzing in their ears. The hull of the Black Hawk vibrated and pinged with ricocheting machine gunfire from the ground and the loose sortie of choppers hemming them in on all sides. It looked like they'd be able to crash-land in the yard, if they were lucky.

Maybe he'd see her again before he died. It was stupid to think about, now, stupider still to hope for, but he'd found himself looking back on that hour he'd lain in the sickbay with her watching him, telling him something she couldn't see herself when he was awake. Too late, he realized he was meant for something more than battlefield-fodder, and he wanted to make a gesture of his last moments. Like his father's insane crusade to exorcise the 1992 Presidential election, it was something he'd learned. How you die can be more important than how you lived, if there's something to believe in.

The Black Hawk swooped so low so fast Storch thought they were falling, but leaning out the door, he saw the wisdom of this. The three choppers nearest them shied away from going so low, and with the armada of ground vehicles beneath them, they daren't fire. Small arms fire from below still pinged off the underhull, a rain so steady, it sounded as if they were sledding across a field of pinballs. They ducked under power lines, less than thirty feet above the ground, and the pilot called out, "Dust-off countermeasures away, watch your eyes," and the ground vanished under a shower of phosphorus flash cluster-bombs that burst from pods mounted on the inside curves of the landing skids. The gunfire didn't stop, but it stopped hitting them.

"You're going to get us all killed—for nothing," Wittrock said. Storch looked over at him still lying on the deck with his laptop clutched to his sunken chest.

"That's what tonight's been all about, hasn't it, Wittrock? That's what the Mission's really all about; everybody laying down their lives for something you eggheads did years ago. Well, Mission accomplished, motherfucker."

The razor-wired perimeter fence of the yard was coming up fast, and their altitude now couldn't be higher than twenty feet. One flash-blinded sharpshooter kneeling on top of a troop truck passed by so close, Storch could've reached out and slapped him.

"You're wrong!" Wittrock shouted. "We were sworn to lay down our lives to protect the human species from its unelected successors! We can still win!"

"It's over," Storch shouted back, and leapt from the chopper.

For a split-second he floated over the junked cars and the startled counterterrorist squads standing around the gaping pit of the motor pool. He hadn't quite hit yet when the Black Hawk dumped another fusillade of flash bombs across the length of the yard and slipped out of sight over the far fence, both Apaches in full, shooting pursuit.

Storch kept his head down as the ground rushed up, landing in a poised squat on the roof of a '83 Cadillac with a yucca tree growing out of its trunk. The massive white leather-topped roof dipped with a thunderous crump, but soaked up most of the force of impact. He rolled off and into the crawlspace between the Cadillac and the next wreck. Bullets banged off cars and smashed safety glass all around him, but he couldn't be sure if there was anyone actually aiming at him. He took a deep breath through his nose, held it, and thought. He would not kill US soldiers or police officers in the course of doing their jobs, but he would not allow them to kill or take him before he got the lady out. Alive or dead, she deserved better than what the Mission had served her.

Abruptly, his bottled air ran out and shut off, and he was sucking empty plastic. Something must've been wrong with the gauge, because the first he became aware of this was when black spots pooled on the yard and began eating up the scenery. He switched it over to filtered, then figured, fuck it. He undogged the seals on the helmet and tore it off. It wouldn't save him from the kind of whup-ass the soldiers would open up on him if he exposed himself, and if he found her—when he found her—he wanted her to know it was him, and not another Mission goon or a fed. It offered him only slim reassurance that she wouldn't shoot him anyway if she was armed, but he didn't want to die with his head in a fishbowl. Maybe, when he found her, she might kiss him—

Footsteps outside his hiding place, soldiers running through the yard, firing wild into every crevice and shouting at each other like they were playing blind man's bluff. Storch hugged the dirt and rolled under the Cadillac as a spray of bullets pelted the neighboring car. He thought about breaking out of cover and running for the motor pool, but it was a stupid idea. The Mission would've sealed the doors when they left, and if the feds had broken in, that would be their staging area. There were other ways in, he was sure of it, but he didn't have time to find them. Hiding like this was stupid, running in was stupid. He crawled out from under the Cadillac and raised his arms in the air. "I surrender! I'm not shooting! Hey, goddamit, over here, I'm a hostage, there's more of us inside!"

The soldiers turned and started firing. Storch hit the dirt again, and crawled back between the cars, screaming over the shooting, but only leading them closer to where he was hiding. "Stop shooting at me! I'm not gonna fight with you, you stupid fuckers! I'm trying to get a hostage out of the fucking hole!"

"Sergeant Storch? Where are you?"

Storch heard her clearly through a momentary break in the shooting, but he thought he was hallucinating. It was her! He stood up and threw down his weapon. "I'm unarmed! Don't you fucking shoot me, you bastards!"

"Get down! Get down on the fucking ground right now! Hot shit! We got a live one!"

Storch lay down on the ground, trying to make them hear him, that they all had to get out of here immediately, that something very bad was going to happen, from above or from below, but soon.

One of them squatted on his back and was securing his hands when the starlight curdled and turned to luminous smoke. The soldier rolled off him and started screaming, they were all screaming, and as soon as the soldier got off him, Storch started screaming, too.

It was like turning inside out at a cellular level, like every fundamental building block of Zane Storch was the flashpoint of a revolution, locked with its sister cells in a battle to fling off the yoke of multicellular tyranny and become a microscopic free agent. He clenched every muscle of his body as if to relax would let them all fly away into the sky, into the starscraping cone of unholy quicksilver unlight that bathed the junkyard. It passed through everything, living and inanimate alike, and suffused the entire scene with a lambent glow of sublime wrongness. He could see the marrow of his bones before his eyes, could feel his heart stuttering and oxygen-depleted blood backflushing into his veins, and his arteries tugging on a vacuum; could feel his bowels writhing as if there was some refuge inside his abdominal cavity from the awful invasion; could feel his brain bubbling and sparking flashes of intracranial light like incandescent gas in an overcharged streetlamp. He willed himself to force his perceptions back outside the turmoil inside his skin, and opened his eyes and saw again.

The strongest of the soldiers were crawling towards the gate, while the rest lay twitching in the sand, emitting choked, gobbling screams and crying for help into radios that still didn't work. Willing his mind to retake the reins of his body, he gathered his legs and hauled himself to his feet against a school bus that lay on its side amid a mountain of sun-bleached aluminum cans. "Ms. Orozco?" Ms.? Shit, for all he knew, she was happily married, or gay, or—

"Storch! Do you see it? It's beautiful!" Stella Orozco clambered out of the hollowed-out engine compartment of a Duster and crossed the open center of the junkyard towards him. She looked like an angel in the light, somehow her face and the way she gleamed in it turned it all back on itself, this was no end, it was a new beginning, nothing that she could welcome this way could be deadly. His body was lying to him. There she is. He ran to her.

When Stella Orozco saw Sgt. Storch lumbering out of the maze of wrecked cars and into the open field beside the motor pool pit, her heart leaped. First the light had come, in spite of all, and she knew in her bones that she was cured, though she felt as if the cure might kill her dead in the first seconds, and now here was the man the Mission and Radiant Dawn together couldn't kill, come to take her away. It was like the next rung of fate bodying forth out of the dark, and all the troubles and terrors of the last week bound themselves up in a lesson, for what was this, if not deliverance and the chance to remake herself, reinvent her life?

With a step that was half a dance, Stella ran to Zane Storch. The light swirled between them like a curtain of plumed serpents changing them, freeing them, uniting them. When the ground beneath her feet rose up like the skin of a bubble and burst, she thought it was her own step that threw her so high into the air, for didn't she feel as if she could fly? When he was only inches from her fingertips, the earth cracked like a bullwhip, hurling Storch high into the air and back among the maze of cars, and opened up beneath her earthbound feet in a ravening fissure and commenced to suck the whole junkyard into itself. For a second, she floated in the air, looking into the empty space where Storch had just been a moment ago, when it had looked as if she'd broken through some invisible barrier and into someone else's life. Then she fell, into the black, fiery hole of her destiny.

~ 36 ~

Cundieffe had been on the phone from the moment the chopper dusted off, leaving him and Agent Hanchett standing beside the wrecked, partially buried pickup truck. While Hanchett arranged for a Bureau-flown chopper to come pick them up, he'd been in touch with his team at China Lake, who were fielding reports from spotter teams and satellite interpreters across the state. As closely as he could, he'd followed the flurry of pursuit as the helicopters switched from fishing to actively hunting the two aircraft, piecing the third-hand stream of information into a model in his head. On his laminated pocket road atlas of California, he'd drawn dots for the patrol choppers, and speculated with dotted lines on the most likely destination for the two rogues. By shading out the zones negatively proven by searchers, he still found himself looking at a corridor half the width of the state. They were headed north at the one brief visual sighting, but he knew that meant nothing. Even if the eyewitness were to be believed, the choppers were following the Inyo mountains, and might change course at any time to strike anywhere between Reno or Nellis Air Force Base and Fresno or Bakersfield. Worst case scenario, they had more than expected fuel capacity, and were already well on their way to Los Angeles. There were too many possibilities hovering around the one sighting, which might be a false alarm. Most telling, however, was the way the Delta Force soldiers had reacted. There would be legal repercussions that would be felt at the Joint Chiefs level, if Cundieffe knew Assistant Director Wyler. Somehow, they'd felt it was worth it to get to them first, and unobserved by the DOJ. All Wyler's spooky talk about space-age softkill weapons technology and a Pentagon conspiracy now seemed less far-fetched than it had a few days ago.

Not long after the chopper arrived and took them out of the canyon, Cundieffe received the first of the reports about the fire in the Owens Valley. A hospice community was on fire, the flames clearly visible to anyone on the street in the town of Big Pine, seven miles to the north. Big Pine's volunteer Fire Chief called for reinforcements from Bishop and Independence, then reported that the village was being bombed.

He'd made a critical error then, he now realized, mistaking authority for power in trying to rein in Greenaway even as he turned him loose on the terrorists. He'd assumed that Greenaway could, and would, handle the situation responsibly. That was the last he'd heard of Greenaway.

All the news after that had concerned the Bomb.

The awfulness of it dug icy claws into his brain. Only by massaging blood into his temples had he been able to keep from fainting. The pain was like his father's voice.

On your watch.

A handful of terrorists in Army surplus helicopters crossed California and dropped napalm on a *for the love of God!* hospice village. *Knowing they were coming, you let it happen A hospice village called Radiant Dawn. RADIANT.*

Then they nuked it. They cremated God only knew how many sick, innocent human beings, and then they dropped an atom bomb on their ashes. And then they got away.

On your watch, Martin.

It was all over, the flurries of apocryphal sightings tailing away from the explosion, like the Doppler waves from a passing siren, dwindling down to nothing. Out of opaque blackness both physical and political, they had materialized, and just as swiftly vanished. Cundieffe had been sitting down to dash off a memo, head in hands, stricken mute as all the vast, jagged implications of the case's unspeakably disastrous outcome came tumbling down onto the blank screen before him. He'd been sitting there still when SA Hanchett had come in, her eager little hands clutching sheaves of printouts.

"Sir? Lieutenant Colonel Greenaway just issued an order to all the military search parties and Delta Force squads onbase."

That's news," he answered in as neutral a tone as he could muster. "Where is he?"

"At a payphone at a gas station outside Big Pine. Apparently, he crashed. He scrambled them to a location near Baker. He then rattled off a bunch of code-phrases, and got confirmations back from ten choppers in the field and three squads onbase. They're on the move as we speak, sir."

Baker was less than ten miles from the eastern perimeter fence of Ft. Irwin Military Reservation, China Lake's next door neighbor. Eight choppers in the air with FBI agents onboard were in the sortie, but the agents had not called in, and presumably were not allowed to. It was as if the lieutenant colonel knew where they were—or where they were going.

Cundieffe clapped his hands excitedly. Something could still be snatched out of this debacle; the perpetrators of this act, their technology, or at the very least, a military scapegoat. He couldn't simply contact Greenaway again and let him know he was under scrutiny. "Put together every available agent with some tactical gear and let's get out there."

"An excellent idea, but I'm afraid I'll be needing your talents right here, Special Agent Cundieffe."

A long shadow fell across his desk. He looked up and saw Assistant Director Wyler himself standing in the doorway of his office. He waved Hanchett away and folded his arms across his chest, his head cocked at a tired angle. He sighed and seemed to shrink six inches. "This situation appears to have spiraled out of our collective control."

On your watch. He almost fainted again.

"What—I'm—Sir! This is a surprise. I was working to prepare a preliminary report, when—the—new developments—"

"Put nothing down on record for the time being, Martin. This is going to get much worse before it gets any better." His face was grave and deeply lined. His toupee sat a few degrees off the beam. Had he ever noticed the Assistant Director wore a toupee? Did anyone else know?

"Worse, sir?"

"Oh, yes. What happened tonight was a declaration of war. A second civil war, the consequences of which could be far more devastating than the first." He turned and walked away, his hand absently gesturing for Cundieffe to follow. "But in every war, Martin, the most pivotal victories often pass beneath history's notice. Such a victory will soon fall to us, Martin."

Cundieffe stood up and started to follow, but balked when he saw where the Assistant Director was going. Wyler stopped with his hand on the door of the Men's restroom, his brow furrowed.

Cundieffe took another step, then froze again. What the devil was the Assistant Director playing at? President Johnson dragged many of his policy briefings with White House staffers into the lavatory in a crude but effective demonstration of alpha male dominance. According to a tale he'd overheard a retired Secret Service agent tell his father at a barbecue, when then Attorney General Ramsey Clark had encouraged Johnson to force the Director into retirement, the President had pronounced his fiat by "accideliberately micturating" on the AG's sensible black brogans. If that was the Assistant Director's strategy, what could he expect in compensation for allowing an atomic bomb to be dropped on American soil?

Then again, there was that oily, uninvited sensation he'd gotten in the limousine at the airport. That fleeting twinge at the physical intimacy of the Assistant Director's presence. Surely it was his own insecurity projecting itself on his superior. AD Wyler wasn't the first bureaucrat to be tarred with that brush, first and foremost among them the Director himself, for choosing duty over family. Dear Lord, what if it was him?

Get a hold of yourself, Martin! If you're going to panic, at least concentrate on the real situation, there's plenty to keep you wetting your pants, there, too.

This is some sort of briefing, that's all it is. Damage control. Mustn't allow anything to embarrass the Bureau. He realized with relief that his feet were carrying him towards the Assistant Director. They were alone in the office, but Wyler waved impatiently. "God's sake, Cundieffe," he stage-whispered, "get inside. It's imperative that we speak privately, and immediately, but I desperately need to micturate."

Cundieffe edged past the Assistant Director into the restroom, glancing around as he crossed the painfully white tiled room to stand beside the last sink, pointedly not looking into the mirror. Assistant Director fumbled out a set of jingling keys and locked the door.

Cundieffe turned and started to protest, but Assistant Director Wyler was climbing onto the first sink and, steadying himself against the fluorescent light fixture, he pried an adhesive air freshener off the wall, just inches below the assiduously scrubbed ceiling. Cundieffe helped him climb down and followed him as he went to a toilet stall and tossed the air freshener into the basin, flushed. To Cundieffe's blank stare, he asked, "You didn't know that was in here?"

"We—was that a surveillance device?"

"Yes, audio-video, installed by Naval Intelligence. Didn't your people sweep for bugs?"

"We never thought we had anything to hide from the Navy, sir. I mean, really—"

Wyler brushed past him and went to a urinal, unzipped his fly and looked over his shoulder at Cundieffe, who retreated again to the sink. "You have no idea what this is about, do you?"

"What this would that be, sir? If you're referring to the terrorist situation—"

"—Is only the beginning, Martin. We stand at the cusp of a watershed moment in human history. The future has never been closer, but we have never been closed to complete and utter chaos. Order is going to be tested, and the enemies, many of them, are already among us."

Cundieffe looked around blearily, resumed scrubbing his hands. The soap was the good old abrasive powder variety, not that glutinous syrup most public restrooms offered. He ground the pumice-based soap into the meat of his palms, one after the other long after both were pink as boiled lab rats. "I don't know what to say, sir. I've always felt a calling to serve the Bureau."

"That's right. It's in your blood, isn't it? Your father and your mother both, sixty-five years of service between them. You're trustworthy, utterly selfless, the model of a Bureau agent. It's hard, not being not like most other people, isn't it, Martin?"

"I don't follow you, sir."

"Your perceptive and cognitive faculties have always made you a keen observer of human behavior, but it only isolated you from your peers. You never excelled in physical, manly pursuits, and others resented you, treated you as if your intellect made you less of a man. The Bureau was your instinctual niche, it's where you could excel by using your natural talents, and serve the public good by preserving order. Am I right so far?"

"Sir, are you—can I turn around now?" He stole a glance at the mirror before him. AD Wyler still stood before the urinal, one hand planted against the wall. His head turned, his eyes met Cundieffe's and glittered.

"Have you ever wondered why you felt this way, Martin? Why you felt compelled to give over your life to protect a populace that never made a place for you? Have you ever felt a deeper cause for the—stirrings that drive you?"

Cundieffe braced himself against the sink, focusing on a relatively fresh wad of chewing gum affixed to the spotless chrome neck of the faucet. Wrigley's Spearmint, he observed, noting its uncanny resemblance to brain matter after a thorough chewing. Probably left there by Special Agent Normand, he must make a note and remind Normand about careless hygiene—

"You're not alone, Martin." He heard a hushed clink of metal on tile. It was the sound of a belt buckle.

He sucked wind for a long, long moment before he let himself talk. "Sir, I'm not a judgmental person in the least, and my—I'm extremely discreet, but—I think you should know that I'm not a—"

"Neither am I, Martin. Look at me."

"What? Sir, are you—done?"

"Turn around, Martin. There's no other way, son. I need you to see, before we can trust you."

"What? Sir, with all due respect, what is this?"

"Turn around, Goddammit!"

Cundieffe whirled around now, his face flushing with anger. "There's no need to swear—Oh my God, sir!"

From the moment he first met AD Wyler at a special dinner at the Academy, Cundieffe had felt a strange vibration from AD Wyler that he couldn't admit to himself was something sexual, and so he'd buried it as something unworthy of himself. It was a unique experience, never repeated, even when he came into contact with real homosexuals. Now he understood why.

AD Wyler stood before Cundieffe with his pants around his ankles, and his spindly, hairless legs planted akimbo to afford Cundieffe an unobstructed view of the featureless join of flesh where every other member of the human species, it was fairly certain, had some sort of reproductive organs. At first he thought the Assistant Director was tucking, but there was nowhere to hide anything; nor was he wounded, for there were no scars, no pubic hair, no vestigial traces of either sex; only a tiny urethra on the forward edge of the pelvic bone, a purely neutral means of passing waste.

An atomic bomb was a horrible event to be sure, but it was as of yet an abstract notion, and a real one, with precedent. This was Cundieffe's atomic bomb. "What happened to—What—What are you?"

"I'm a human being, Martin, just like you. Just like six and a half billion human beings on this planet. We're no different from them, except for the niggling detail that we do not reproduce."

"'We?' How many of you are there?"

Wyler stooped and hoisted his pants, fastidiously tucking in his shirt. "Only a few thousand accounted for, but we expect that's going to change. There's been a lot of speculation among us about how we came to be— viruses, radiation, even controlled experiments—but most of us believe we're a natural product of evolution. We're the answer to the world's overpopulation problem, Martin, and it's wars, and famines, and depleted environment.

"Look at ants, Martin. One of nature's oldest living creations, and largely unchanged. Because they have mastered specialization. Workers and soldiers give up their reproductive duties to their queen, and specialize in their respective talents for the survival of the nest. In the last few hundred years, homo sapiens has forced an evolutionary crisis and become its own agent of extinction. We are born without the costly investment in reproduction which burdens other human beings, and instead have those energies expressed themselves in higher intellects, greater stamina, and an instinctual public ethic. All of us hold positions of some influence in government, academia and business, and all of us work for the continued survival of the species, and to keep our secret. We are nature's plan for keeping the human race alive." Wyler washed his hands, watching Cundieffe. "So, now you know whose side you're on."

Cundieffe backed away from Wyler in the general direction of the toilet stalls. "Sir, I don't think you understand—"

"Martin, there's nothing to be upset about. It's what you are, it's what we are."

Cundieffe turned and raced for the first stall, slammed the door and bolted it. His face was hot and slick with sweat and tears. Why was AD Wyler doing this to him? All he'd ever wanted was to serve the Bureau, to be accepted, and now these head games, this mutant bullshit.

By God, Martin, you are a BOY! And you will ACT LIKE ONE!

He was a man. Compared to AD Wyler, he was a man.

His mother explained to him when he was nine, and going off to summer camp. How other boys had different parts from his, and might tease him, but not to take it personally, it wasn't his fault, it was just the way God had made him, and God had His reasons.

"Martin, come out of there at once."

Cundieffe undid his belt and tore open his slacks, yanked down his shorts and there it was.

He was a man.

Martin had indeed taken some ribbing at summer camp that year, and at high school, he'd refused to bathe with the other boys. No one but his mother had laid eyes on it since that summer camp, excepting his regular physician, who was a very kind man and an old friend of the family, and so had never stared or made him feel uncomfortable.

Martin's penis was less than half the length of his pinky, and incapable of becoming erect. His mother had told him that due to a birth defect affecting his glands—not her words, oh no, she called it a "heavenly test"—his male organ had simply stopped growing in infancy. Despite the painful hormone shots that'd made him sick and furious by turns throughout his later childhood, puberty had simply never arrived. He had no testicles whatsoever, and no hair had ever grown to hide the minuscule thing he micturated with, but would never entertain the quixotic notion of showing it to a human being.

Until now.

"Assistant Director Wyler? I don't understand the full implications of this incident, but I want to state in the clearest, yet most respectful terms, that a grave error has been made. I—I need you to see this, I guess—"

Before he could think better of it, he shoved open the stall door and shambled out with his slacks down. For a moment he dreaded that Wyler would be gone, or worse, that someone else would be here. At least no one in the Navy knew, because he always used the stalls, for fear that someone would peek at him. It didn't make him any less of a man, if his mother had told him once, she'd told him a thousand times.

Wyler was there, and he didn't laugh. Instead, he only shook his head sadly and clucked his tongue. "My God, what did they do to you?"

"What? Sir, I didn't judge you—You were born—as you were, and I—well, I'm a man."

"No, Martin, no, you're not."

"Look at me! I have a penis! I'm a man!"

"That is a surgical construct, and not a very good one. Your parents, like many who have borne one of us, couldn't face up to the ambiguity. They had your sex assigned with a knife, Martin. A penis was built for you while you were still a baby, but by the looks of it, they abandoned the procedure midway through. You had hormone shots, but they didn't help. Because the receptors for those hormones simply didn't exist in you."

Cundieffe sat back down on the restroom floor, the chill tile leaching the warmth out of his bony, naked ass. He stared blankly ahead while Wyler circled around him and stooped to speak into his ear. "You've lived all your life trying to play a role that doesn't suit you, Martin. You're one of us, Martin. You can help us, and we can help you."

When Cundieffe fainted, he swooned into the Assistant Director's waiting arms.

~ 37 ~

There were snapshots from the moments after the irradiation, unstuck in time and shuffling themselves into view only when there was nothing else to see or hear. Like now.

Soldiers clawing at their bowels and eyes, tearing themselves open to let something out; screaming their vocal cords to shreds as their healthier comrades restrain them.

A fountain of sand and pulverized concrete where Stella Orozco was standing, the greedy hole pulling the whole junkyard in after it.

His feet hanging in space, his fingers snarled in a toppled stand of chainlink fence.

A young, homely woman in a smart blazer and skirt shouting nose to nose with a hulking officer in unmarked black fatigues. His hand shoves at her shoulder one too many times, and she jabs him with a taser. Everyone pointing guns, they're fighting over him.

Guns and medics surrounding him, shuddering with the vibrations of the truck beneath them. One of the medics sedates him, then carefully pries open his left eye, then his right, clears his throat and spits into them.

He felt crippling nausea sloshing through him in slowly subsiding waves. His skin felt two sizes smaller, and his insides felt as if they'd been stirred with a stick and mixed with a generous portion of army ants. His ears still rang from the explosion. He snapped his fingers beside each ear, and could barely hear clicking, as on a dead long distance line.

He was not restrained, but he lay still. If he moved, he knew, his skin would break open wherever he put weight on it and blood like clotted ketchup would dribble out of him, and his hair and teeth would fall away, but he wouldn't have to look, because his eyes would have scabbed over. He'd been cooked by that fucking light, and he would die soon, and die horribly. It was something to hope for, given the alternative. Maybe he was in a lighted room now, with officers and feds and the press watching him in eager anticipation of the months of interrogation, the years of trials, and the inevitable execution. Because that was what the United States government did with terrorists.

And a terrorist he was. He'd participated in a monumental act of butchery, an insane campaign of genocide he could never hope to explain.

Your Honor, they weren't human, they were—things.

I didn't know the full extent of the plan.

I was only following orders.

He hoped to God they would catch Wittrock, but knew they wouldn't. Men like that never got caught or killed, not when they could persuade others to do it for them.

Presently, because he could suddenly feel them burning, he knew his eyes were open. He blinked furiously, sloughing off crust and dust until planes of gray lesser darkness took shape around him and resolved into the cinderblock walls of his cell. Letting his head droop to one side, he peered through slitted lids at the faint nimbus of fluorescent light visible through the bars. A tiny square of window in a door let it into the cell block—or *brig*, wasn't that what squids called their jails, even on land? The meager stream of light haloed a minimalist steel head beside his bunk and a steel washbasin and scuffed steel mirror set into the wall above it. The floor was ever so slightly concave, with a drain in the center of the poured concrete floor, and a horizontal slot at waist level was set into the door. A man could live and die in this cell with no excuse to leave, Storch thought, but he doubted he'd be here for long. This was probably the brig at China Lake, or possibly Twenty-Nine Palms. In the morning, he'd be transferred with much fanfare to a federal holding facility, where the interrogations would begin. He wondered how well his counterinterrogation training would hold up against the people who thought it up.

He could see no one in the neighboring cells, but he caught his breath and held it when he spotted the outline of a sentry in a chair beside the outer door. The chair was tipped back against the wall, and the guard's hands lay folded in his lap, his feet propped on another chair. His features were wreathed in shadow, but Storch believed he was asleep.

He jerked and went rigid when he heard the voice. "You awake."

Storch kept playing possum, though the voice made him itch all over, like the light again. The acoustics in the cell refracted the interrogator's voice at him from a thousand angles, as if he were lying in a tuning fork. The voice cut through the oscillating wail in his eardrums, rode it like a carrier signal into the fillings in his teeth and the reptilian basement of his brain.

"Feel the dust of one billion years crumble away from your eyes," the voice whispered. "Hear the voices of the cells of your body singing of the unspeakable wonder of the outside world with new voices. Feel them changing to meet that world as flower, or as fist.

"Breathe in the air and feel the tide of myriad invaders absorbed and turned into antibodies, to devour their own kind. Reach for the barrier between your body and your mind; that wall is gone, never to return. Listen to the harmony of your bodysong, Zane Storch. Gone is the strident clash of the mind and body. You are not a ghost anchored in flesh. You are sentient flesh."

He felt battered and sunburned and sick to his stomach, and if the interrogator's words had proven true, he would have willed his own heart to stop. It was *him!* The motherfucker who made RADIANT, who destroyed his life and set him on his blind dive into this awful present. He'd infiltrated the base, him or one of his clones, or perhaps he or it had been here all along. *How many of them are there, really?* If there was one, then the Mission's failure was total. His might not be. Keogh, or Quesada, or whatever he really was, had come to gloat and gibber. Storch willed himself to lie still, to invite him closer by his passivity. But he was too weak not to listen.

"You have evolved.

"Only hours ago, you killed me. In their hate and fear, your friends have killed so many of me this night that I have reached out to you, that my message will not be snuffed out. I have come to show you the whole truth, of which the Mission only taught you a tiny shred. For it is the way of education, which must needs be a series of ever more complicated lies. Forgive me if I must lie a little to you now, but the path to the close of this stage is a long one, and you are not yet ready for the whole truth.

"It is hard for the individual to face even a ray of that truth, for it is so vast. To perceive that we are not the finished product of a perfected creation, but one rung on a ladder that time and nature are climbing, that is unacceptable to most. As an individual, you are but one iteration of one species that is itself a fleeting expression of the Life Force on the earth. What can we do? For all that we try to learn, to improve ourselves, we are hardwired from conception; even the degree to which we may improve is etched in protein. The human animal is a big, stupid ape, but his cells are smart, each smart enough to believe *it* is the ape. It is not so. Not yet.

"You have climbed further up the ladder in this night than the human species has in nine million years, as an individual. Natural selection chooses traits, species, not individuals. You, my beautiful mutant, have broken the rules. Why have I given you this gift, my self-proclaimed enemy, who would destroy my work and stop the climbing of the ladder?

"We are all becoming one sentient flesh, one body. The internecine warfare of life, the malignancies of death-fear and selfism, will stop. I would have you understand.

"Once, all the earth was a proving ground. Life reached out to conquer new environments, reproduced like mad and passed their superior genes on to their children. Animal DNA was far more elastic, then; life changed as the earth changed, and it was changing so fast in those days... When the earth turned cold, some became smaller and warmer, and they took to stealing their dinosaur neighbors' eggs for food when everything else dried up. And they became mammals, and they became us. And to move to the next stage, all we have to do is want to bad enough.

"Now look at the mess we've made of evolution. One fine day out on the alluvial plain, we became self-aware, and we figured out how to cheat natural selection before sundown. We learned how to make tools, and suddenly we could effortlessly vanquish any predator, tame fire so we could stay up all night brooding. We shaped animals into tools and food supplies and wiped out everything else. And we built a wall against death, against the tide of natural selection. And we will colonize other worlds someday, spreading through the universe like a metastasizing cancer.

"We've become the gods of our world, and what has it cost us? Every day, the gulf between what humans are and what they have grows larger and larger. For every tool we invent that makes life easier, we grow weaker. We're feeding our life force into a lie, Zane. We've run so far so long into the dead end that we think we can't turn back. Our cells want to evolve, though we're trying to freeze them. We thwart our bodies' struggles to adapt to our artificial environments, and that frustrated energy expresses itself as organic entropy, as cellular madness. As cancer.

"Radiation can cause cancer, but it can also mutate an organism, cause changes that pass on to future generations. It's like a jump-start, but most radiation doesn't do much but stir things up, entropy wreaking havoc in the system. But there are thousands of seemingly random amino acid sequences between each gene in our DNA. Scientists have dismissed them as mere buffers, but they are the keys to evolution. Encode that radiation, and it'll impose a new order on cancer cells, where the adaptive 'buffers' are rendered naked to activation. Neoplasm is the blank slate on which the light writes. With it, you can cause the system to become entropy, and death becomes life without end."

The shadowy interrogator rose and approached the bars. Storch could barely make out his lips moving, barely hear his hands rapping against the bars, over the din of his whispering voice.

"Imagine the flow of life through species, the accretion of traits over millions of years, as the passage of a lifetime. Imagine you are that animal. The wind blows, and you grow a pelt. The water table sinks, and you grow claws to follow it, and a hump to store it. A virus invades you, and you build up an immunity, and make your own viruses to defend yourself against predators. The world changes, and you adapt. This is the gift I have given you. Your flesh is alive to the changes evolution takes millions of years and billions of lives to recognize. This is the gift I would give the world. I would wreak the greatest single evolutionary step in the history of humankind without taking a single human life. The Mission would call me a monster and kill me and all my children, and steal my gift from the world. Has nature ever been so generous, or so merciful, as I?"

In the echoing split-second after he fell silent, Storch sprang out of the bunk and hurled himself at the bars. His left leg gave out under him almost immediately, and he fell, Keogh starting to back away even as Storch's hands coiled round his tie and one lapel of his blazer. Storch barreled full-bore and unprotected into the bars, head splitting in stars and all the blood seemed to drop out his brain at once, and the impact turned it to a whirling cloud of ash. Still his hands clamped Keogh's clothes, the man-thing's struggles banging his head against the bars several times more before Storch came alive and pulled back, bracing one foot against the bars.

Keogh was screaming, and whispering at the same time. "Please! God! Don't! Guard! Guard! *You can't kill me.*"

"Motherfucker, I can kill you for the rest of your life," Storch growled, the words mangled by an upper lip split to the bone. He threw all of his weight backwards, hands coiled up in the flailing Keogh. He smashed into the bars like a piñata and his screams cut off abruptly in a sibilant gurgle, his skull settling like the wrapped shards of a shattered vase. His head poked halfway into the cell, drizzling bright arterial blood and pale, pureed brain into the pool of fluorescent light on the floor. His collarbones smashed, arms stuck out at odd backward angles, as if they were trying to become wings. He hung there without moving, without healing or fighting back despite his sudden and total dissolution. Storch stepped back from the body and marveled at the meaning of this.

Perhaps Keogh himself was human. Perhaps this was only a human dupe of some kind, like Buggs. Storch saw now that the man he'd killed was black, and younger than himself. Dressed in a conservative suit, with an empty shoulder holster under his jacket. An FBI agent. Had Keogh been speaking though this man? Had he dreamt the whole thing? Not this. The dead man, at least, was real.

As if on a television in an adjacent cellblock, he heard the frantic scrabbling of keys against the outer door, saw the light blocked by close-shaven heads and Shore Patrol helmets and black berets.

But what about himself? The awful damage he'd wrought on the body was out of all proportion to the worst violence he ever could have dealt out with his hands—or a car, for that matter. The whisperer had been right about one thing. He was changing. The thought of it was scarier than knowing he was going to die a hated terrorist.

"You've only begun to change," the whispered voice told him. He jumped away from the dead thing jammed into the bars, but it hung still, silhouetted by blinding light as the outer door opened. Guards recoiled from the transfixed corpse, tried in vain to pull it down, had to settle for reaching around it to get at the lock. Screaming, "Get down! Lie down on the fucking ground, now!" But he could scarcely hear them.

The whispering voice was the tube of a tsunami, folding over him with crushing, godlike force. It was a voice from within his own head.

Storch whirled and faced himself in the cloudy steel mirror on the wall. He splashed water on it and clawed at it with his hands, but no matter how hard he tried, he couldn't see himself past the strange, wizened face with blue-gray eyes. "Let me be your guide," the face said, with his voice.

He was already screaming when the guards set in beating him with truncheons, surrounding him and pounding his back like a chain gang digging a trench. The pounding mirrored his own heartbeat, which in turn marched in lock-step with the pulse of Keogh in his veins.

Long after his body stopped reacting even reflexively to the pounding, the guards hoisted him up by both arms and dragged him into the corridor. They turned away from the light and bore him down into the darksome core of the brig. One guard opened a heavy steel door set into a blank concrete door, like the entrance to a kiln. They threw him into it and slammed the door shut behind him. For a long time, he heard locks slamming home, and shouting voices, bits of flotsam on the ocean of sound roaring inside him.

"NOW WE CAN BE ALONE, the Keogh in his brain proclaimed. "NOW YOUR EVOLUTION CAN BEGIN."

Coming in 2001 - Radiant Dawn II